Invaders or Saviors

G. Todesco

CONTENTS

ACKNOWLEDGMENTS

This book would have not been possible without the help, words of encouragement and the generous time of the following individuals. I am indebted to all of you.

Eric and Mariana Tousignant, Nancy Lee Fortin, Robert Brodeur and my daughter Caroline. They patiently read and re-read drafts at various stages of development, providing comments, suggestions, edits and, most importantly, encouraged me to continue writing when I thought it a waste of time.

Science fiction and fantasy writer Kate Heartfield, who reviewed the very first draft. With her input, I was able to refine and improve the manuscript, ultimately creating a better, and I hope, more entertaining novel.

Mindy F and Natalia Leigh at Enchanted Ink Publishing for doing a copy edit of the entire manuscript. Without their polishing, this book would have never happened.

And last, but not least, my dear wife Suzanne, who for eight long years put up with my writing isolation. She also read and re-read drafts and provided notes and comments. I am forever yours.

PROLOGUE

The year was 2062. Space exploration was an established industry thanks to space barons Elliott Rusk, Jeb Beros, and Rick Franson.

Colonization of the moon was underway, and asteroid mining was a new growth industry. Mining spaceships constantly travelled to the asteroid belt in search of precious and rare metals to meet Earth's shortage. Elliott Rusk's Outer-World Mining (OWM) and his Griffin Space Systems (GSS) led the way, while China was quickly moving past the commercial outfits.

Despite this awe-inspiring progress, the world of 2062 was a harsher world, sliding into a dark age due to increased poverty, famine, dwindling resources and a failing ecosystem. It was the opposite of predictions made by 1950s futurists, who foretold a twenty-first-century golden age.

Temperatures were 3°C warmer than at the start of the century. GHG emissions were 50 percent higher, and runaway climate change was in full force. Droughts became the norm, triggering mass migrations from cities, including Cape Town, La Paz, Sao Paolo, and the state of California.

The warmer weather also led to the disappearance of the

ice caps and a sea-level rise, unleashing a human tragedy as one-third of Earth's population fled coastal areas.

But the arrival of the Ibecci (Ibeki) race to our solar system, in search of a place to live, offered humanity the promise of help from an advanced and enlightened spacefaring race able to show humanity a new path forward.

If humans could shed their fears and distrust and grant the Ibecci temporary shelter, the Ibecci would help humanity stave off the approaching collapse predicted by countless twentieth-century economists and historians.

1 UNIDENTIFIED OBJECTS

Soul-T Mining Spaceship, Asteroid Belt

"Range to asteroid is 110,000 km. Sensors show high platinum content," Ella, the ship's AI, announced.

"Okay, Ella, we need to decel, or we will blow past it."

"Roger, Jan. Flight dynamics says decel in 12 minutes."

"Ella, wait for my command."

"We're on our fifth trip out here and you still don't trust me or the computers. I got this Jan."

"Yep, but I run this tin can, Ella. You'll fire the engines when I tell you."

"You're such a control freak! But hey, whatever rocks your boat."

Janine "Jan" Horne floated in the command module of the _Soul-T_ mining spaceship, keeping her eyes glued to the flight dynamics screen, one of six in the cramped module. She watched the trajectory line get closer and closer to the asteroid, then propelled herself toward the pilot seat and strapped in.

"Ella, fire engines and commence decel."

"Okay, Jan. Firing engines."

The spaceship started to hum as Ella ramped up the VASIMR drives.

"Ella, confirm deceleration."

"VASIMRs at full power. FD confirms decel at 4 m/s/s. Velocity is 30 km/s. Two hours to touchdown. May I turn off flight dynamics now that you masterfully timed the deceleration?"

"Ella, are you trying to be sassy?"

"Who me? Oh, no, I'm just your humble AI servant. Nothing more. I carry out your commands and speak when spoken to."

"Yeah, right, Ella."

"I'm not kidding. The silence is going to drive you insane."

"Uh-huh."

As the ship continued slowing down to rendezvous with the asteroid, Jan cued an R&B music playlist that started with a remastered version of the song "Respect" by Aretha Franklin.

"Hey Ella, listen to the lyrics."

"I'm listening Jan. You feel I don't give you enough respect?"

"Don't you think it's weird the random playlist started with this song? Just saying, Ella."

"Ok Jan. Noted."

Two hours later, Ella matched the velocity and rotation of the twenty-kilometre diameter, M-type asteroid Jan had found drifting in the asteroid belt, some thirty million kilometres past Mars.

Slowly, the forty-five-metre-long ungainly spaceship with exposed struts and girders and gigantic spherical cryogenic tanks came down to a soft landing.

The thirty-one-year-old African American space miner with Elliott Rusk's Outer-World Mining unstrapped and cartwheeled in the air. "We made it, Ella! We're gonna be rich!"

"Did you have any doubt?"

Jan then started singing the song by the Pointer Sisters "I'm so excited . . ."

"About what?"

"Getting rich, Ella. Get with it! Can't wait to start mining."

"You are getting ahead of yourself, you know?"

"Ella, you're a real party pooper!"

"Just telling how it is."

Jan ignored Ella's comment and grabbed a tablet from its cradle next to the pilot seat. She then started ticking off items while singing, "And I know, I know, I'm getting rich!"

"Am I getting rich too?"

"Ella, cut the banter and give me status."

"You're telling me to cut the banter? That's rich . . ."

"Ella, stop being a wisecrack and help with the status checklist, or I swear, I'll turn you off for real!"

"Okay, okay. Lemme see. I'm doing fine. Ship's doing fine. VASIMR drives off."

"Check."

"Grapplers securely attached and in the green."

"Check."

"Reactors at minimal power."

"Check."

"Cabin pressure in all modules, green."

"Check."

"LOX and LH tank pressures, green."

"Check."

"Ship ready to commence operations," Ella said finally.

"Inform Griffin Base, we have found a metal-rich asteroid, are now secure, and will start operations."

The message took thirteen minutes to reach the Griffin moon base.

From that point on, the Soul-T was in continuous communication with the moon. It was a logistical trade-off between designing a mining spaceship with a large crew, requiring vast resources, or designing a highly automated spaceship with a single crew member and an advanced AI. It was a solitary job, no different than that of lonely mining prospectors from the nineteenth century American and Canadian gold rush.

After a month of around-the-clock mining, the Soul-T's cargo hold was one-quarter full of high-grade platinum ore as Jan's original call turned out to be spot-on.

Jan went out in her robotic quadruped to do the daily inspection of the walking excavators and rock drillers. She was listening to a remastered extended version of the song "What'd I Say" by Ray Charles when Ella chimed in.

"Hey Jan, long-range radar is picking up objects from deep space moving toward Mars, but readings don't make sense or else sensors are malfunctioning. You'd better come back in to take a look."

"Ella, what is it?"

Jan looked up through the quadruped's armoured glass cockpit into the blackness of space toward Mars, seen as an orange disk some thirty million kilometres away.

"I don't know. You need to see for yourself. The objects are moving very fast. At their current speed, they don't seem natural, and they ain't Chinese either."

"Ella, what are you talking about?"

"They're travelling at a scorching velocity of 1,500 km/s."

"Ella, say again," Jan shouted above the music, filling the inside of the quadruped.

"One thousand, five-hundred kilometres per second."

"Ella, I swear, if you're screwing with me, I'll turn you off for a week. I have no time for silly games."

"Cross my heart, Jan! There's something wrong with the sensors, or else real-life alien spaceships are travelling from deep space toward Mars and the inner planets. They're an unusual shape. Not like a typical asteroid or comet. Elongated like the Oumuamua visitor from earlier this century, with a high length-to-width aspect ratio."

"The what?"

"The Oumuamua asteroid that visited Earth back in 2017. It was a long and skinny asteroid, about four hundred meters in length, with a ten to one aspect ratio. Its unusual shape prompted speculation it was an alien spaceship."

"Ok, so we have objects travelling toward Mars that look like spaceships. Is that it?"

"Yes, and they don't appear to be tumbling. And, weirdest of all, the hyperspectral sensors must also be malfunctioning because they are returning an iridium composition."

"Ella, what d'you say?"

"Iridium. The objects appear to be made of dense iridium, Jan."

"You've got to be shitting me. Ella, do a systems check and reboot the navigation and search radars. I'm coming in, but this better not be a joke."

Jan turned around, walked the hundred metres to where the ship was parked, entered through the oversized airlock, and pressurized the service garage.

She then dismounted and floated toward a grab-hold at the connecting airlock, propelling herself to the command module.

"Ella, are the computers back online?" Jan asked as she reached the command module.

"Yes, objects still have the same velocity vector."

"Okay, let's see," Jan said.

She looked at the radar screen. Ella had already deselected the thousands of asteroids normally captured in the radar field, leaving a clearer image of a group of some thirty objects speeding toward Mars.

Jan hovered a cursor over the objects and got a velocity of 1,500 km/s, confirming what Ella had reported earlier.

"Ella, display the physical characteristics of Mars and its satellites on the FD computer."

A table appeared on the flight dynamics screen above

Jan's head, showing the known orbital velocities of Phobos and Deimos. Phobos, the faster of the two, had a velocity of 2.1 km/s, while the smaller Deimos was only 1.4 km/s.

In its current position, the Soul-T had a direct line of sight to Mars. Jan zoomed in, tagged the two satellites, and the computer promptly returned the same orbital velocities as the known data.

"Okay, instruments are providing correct velocities," Jan said, as she studied the data.

"Ella, do we have any useful images?"

"Nothing. They are too far away."

Jan had figured as much, as the prospecting telescope had very good optics, but its primary purpose was to study asteroids at ranges of less than two million kilometres. It was not meant for stargazing or astronomical observations.

She remained silent for about five minutes, studying the radar data, until Ella broke the silence.

"Well, what d'you think?"

"I don't know what to think, Ella."

Jan was at a loss for how to interpret the data. The scientific portion of her brain refused to believe the speedy objects were alien spaceships. It could just as well be new astronomical phenomena. There was still so much science didn't know about space. Dark matter, dark energy, fast radio bursts, the distorted orbits of trans-Neptunian objects believed to be due to the gravitational influence of Planet Nine, still undiscovered after sixty years of searching.

But whatever those objects were, they had a warm infrared signature and travelling at ridiculous velocities. That much was indisputable.

Jan considered whether to inform Griffin Base, but she wasn't about to give her opinion on what the objects could be. If she did, it would be treated like the reported UFO accounts from pilots on Earth. She would be ordered back for psych assessment. And that would be it for the profits she was standing to make and her career as a space miner.

She put it out of her mind. Cued a James Brown playlist

that started with "Papa's Got a Brand New Bag" and went back to the mindless mining routine with Ella, her books, and the warm, fuzzy feeling of future riches.

2 VISITORS

The Vera Rubin Observatory, Cerro Pachón, Chile

Up in the Andes in northern Chile, where the air is bone-dry, the Vera Rubin Observatory enjoyed unparalleled clear weather and minimal atmospheric distortion surveying the sky for near-Earth objects and interstellar interlopers.

During its nightly imaging, the telescope detected a string of thirty faint objects inside the orbit of Mars and at the edge of the telescope's image detection capability. Its computers determined the objects were not in the database and catalogued them for further analysis.

The following night, the telescope reacquired the objects, automatically recording their trajectories.

After five nights of automated data acquisition, the telescope alerted its operators the objects were inbound.

"Hey, Jürgen, we got a string of new NEOs inbound," Peter Logan, the Space Guard Foundation team leader, said as he studied a computer screen of numerical data.

"How far?" his colleague Jürgen Matthias asked in his slight German accent from the opposite side of the room.

"Just passing the orbit of Mars, but the data looks funny."

Jürgen turned around.

"How so?"

"They are travelling at freakishly high velocities and decelerating, but that can't be right."

"How many and what sizes?" Jürgen asked, now more curious.

"That's a good question. Look at this."

Peter then pointed to a third screen on his right with tabular data.

Jürgen got up from his chair at the other end of the observatory workroom and walked over to look at the screen. He glanced at a large, flat-panel display suspended up high, showing a projection of the inner planets and the trajectories of the new NEOs.

"Looks like maybe thirty objects. Maybe fragments from a comet. I just don't know," Peter continued.

Jürgen just stood with his arms crossed in characteristic Teutonic silence.

"Their motion is too weird, and I don't quite understand the warmer background temperatures in the infrared."

"They are too dim and too far away," Jürgen said.

"We need a bigger telescope. I'll ask the director for access to one."

"Or we could talk to Carlos de Cevedes at the ELT."

The Extremely Large Telescope, managed by the European Southern Observatory, had been operational since 2026, with the primary function of discovering an atmosphere and life on planets orbiting distant stars. It was roughly a billion times more sensitive than the VRO. Unfortunately, hunting and imaging NEOs was way down on its priority list.

"You know he would never give us imaging time to check out small NEOs. He might get curious, though, if we explain they're inbound, travelling at ridiculous velocities and slowing down."

"Remember what Cate Brinnan used to say when she was still here?"

Peter smiled at the mention of Cate Brinnan. "Yeah . . . I remember, always the last one standing and still sharper than any of us the next day. And her singing . . . ! Beautiful, just like her great-aunt Elia."

"*Ja. Schön.*"

"We still have a problem, and she is not here to help. I need to think about this some more."

Peter went back to study the data. An hour later, he called Jürgen's attention.

"Hey Jürgen, these NEOs are slowing down fast. I calculated a decel of 0.5G."

"Are you sure?"

"Yep. At their present decel, they will come to a stop close to Earth. We definitely need a bigger telescope. And since you brought up the idea of calling Carlos, why don't you call and ask for his opinion?"

Carlos de Cevedes saw the incoming call and responded right away.

"*Hola, Aleman.* Long time no speak. What do I owe the honour of this call at such a late hour? Is work slow at your end? You could come over and give us a hand and have a drink with us. Although I would much prefer to speak to *mi bella Irlandesa.*"

"You know she went back to Dublin three months ago."

"I still miss her and her beautiful voice," Carlos replied with a broad smile. "Ah, no matter. I still have some bottles of Rioja left, so why don't you and the *Americano* come over, and we can drink and sing in her honour? What do you say?"

"You know I am more partial to a stein of Kunstmann."

"Ah yes, *Aleman,* very true. More wine for us then," Carlos replied.

On cue, Peter showed up next to Jürgen and joined the conversation.

"Hey, *Español.* If I recall correctly, the last time we tied one on, it did not go too well for me.

"Blasphemy! What . . . you prefer to drink one of your California reds, now almost impossible to get?" Carlos asked in his strong Catalan accent.

"As much as I would love to reminisce about the old days or plan another get-together, we actually need your help."

Peter then proceeded to brief Carlos.

"Intriguing," Carlos said.

"Yep, that's what we were thinking."

"If your data is still preliminary, you need to keep tracking the objects to confirm their rate of decel. Tell you what. Send me your data. I'll look at it and figure what part of the sky to look at. Then I'll see what I can do, but I am not promising anything. However, if I take a peek, it's going to cost you. Hey . . . I am going back to Spain for two weeks in about a month. Maybe I could have a stopover in Dublin and spend time with *la Irlandesa*. You think she'll have time for me?"

"I think you will have to ask her yourself," Peter replied.

"Ah, just joking. I already told her about my trip and that I wanted to see her. She said yes! I tell you, it's my singing and the Catalan charm. Anyway, the offer for a glass of wine or *cerveza* is still there. Perhaps next Friday you can come over, and you will have more data by then. Got to run."

Peter and Jürgen continued collecting data for the next five days, confirming their initial findings.

That the objects were possibly alien was a forgone conclusion. This alone should have created a commotion within the astronomical community, with every observatory wanting to be the first to image the objects. But Peter knew astronomers as a group, just like other scientists, were skeptical. Without images, they would be unconvinced of their analysis and conclusions.

The truth of this statement was confirmed when he called the director at the European Space Agency's Space Guard Foundation headquarters in Frascati, Italy. The director showed no interest and was unwilling to talk to other more powerful observatories. Peter tried to argue the basic point that the objects were inbound toward Earth and the SGF's primary responsibility was to catalogue them.

Frustrated, Peter considered calling Cate Brinnan to use her charming ways with the ELT crew but thought better of it. Instead, he called Carlos the next evening.

"Hi, Carlos. Do you have a couple of minutes to talk?" Peter said in a business-like manner.

Carlos detected Peter's serious demeanor right away and dropped his customary jovial nature.

"Sure, sure. What's up?"

"We have been tracking the objects since the last time we spoke, and they appear to be following the initial trajectory. I spoke to the director at the SGF. He wasn't convinced of our conclusions, or more accurately, does not want to stick his neck out. We seem to have hit a dead end, so I want to ask you straight up whether you can help. We can work in parallel by starting over here and pass along the exact orbital data. You will reduce the imaging time down to ten minutes, maybe less."

Peter stopped talking and waited for a reaction from Carlos, who stood motionless, just staring for a few seconds.

To Peter, it felt like an eternity. He was about to break the uncomfortable silence and tell Carlos to forget the whole idea when Carlos finally raised his eyebrows, smiled with that good-natured grin of his, and spoke in his charming Catalan accent.

"Well, you know . . . I was thinking. If those objects are what we think they are, imaging them fits within our mandate to search for life on distant planets. They couldn't have come from very far. Perhaps, one of the stars in our neighbourhood, say within a sphere of ten to twenty light-years, likely closer. We, of course, would be very interested in finding their planet of origin and imaging it. So, yes, we would like to collaborate with you."

Peter stood without saying a word, but then he quickly recovered as Carlos continued talking.

"However, as you know, the ELT has a heavily booked schedule and a shortage of imaging time, so we have to be very efficient. We have a small window on Thursday of next week and, just to be on the safe side, we will set aside fifteen minutes. You get the ball rolling right after sunset, and we will be on standby to receive your data. Does that sound like a plan?"

"Yeah . . . absolutely."

"Well then, *Americano*, I need to get back to work, so talk to you in one week," Carlos said, winking and then breaking off the connection.

Peter then turned around and spoke to Jürgen. "Well, I guess we are in business. Hope it's worthwhile."

"The data doesn't lie, Peter. Those objects continue to decelerate at a constant rate. Either we have a new astronomical phenomenon, or more likely, the objects are clearly artificial. Even if they are simply a new uncatalogued type of celestial object, it is within our mandate to research them further."

"I guess we will see next week."

The week went by slowly. Peter and Jürgen continued collecting data on the objects with no change in their behaviour.

On Thursday evening, right after sunset, Peter and Jürgen reacquired the objects, then called Carlos on the video link and transferred the current data.

Carlos's team rotated and pointed the massive thirty-nine-metre primary mirror toward the target sky coordinates. It took an interminable ten minutes for the telescope's 3,700-ton structure to swing to the target location entered in its computer. The telescope optical spectrographic camera then captured the incoming light and took forty-five images at fifteen-second exposure intervals, each image approximately 50 GB in size, producing almost 2.3 terabytes of data.

It was an enormous amount of data to be processed by the ELT-dedicated mainframe, which Carlos had also prioritized in order to get the images ready within twenty-four hours.

At 3:00 a.m. the following morning, and much to Peter and Jürgen's surprise, Carlos called on the video link while the two were doing routine sky mapping and cataloguing.

"Hey, *Americano*. Are you awake or sleeping while pretending to work?"

"Hmm, both. Why? Are you going to tell me green men are coming to Earth?"

"Well . . . I don't know the colour of their skin or if they are men. Could be women, you know, or dolphins . . . What I know is that there are heat signatures in front of the objects shown in the infrared images and cooler temperatures everywhere else. The mainframe is still processing the data, and we will hopefully have the high-resolution images by noon today. But at low resolution, we have this swarm of objects showing a higher background temperature in front of them—probably from their engines—as the objects are decelerating."

"Yeah, I had noted higher background temperatures in our infrared images, but because of the lower resolution, I could not figure out what I was looking at."

"I am sending you five low-res false-colour images. They are better than what you captured, but still not good enough to distinguish any details on the individual objects. The images show the thermal bubble in front of the 'Alien Armada,'" Carlos said with a mocking grin, and continued, "I'll call you later today when I get the rest of the images."

Carlos called again thirteen hours later, but this time, his hint of amusement was gone. He appeared more serious, wasting no time.

"Hey, Peter. You better call Jürgen, so he can also listen in. I am sending the images as we speak. In the meantime, I can confirm there are thirty-one objects of different shapes and sizes. Some of them look like spaceships out of a science fiction movie—odd looking, mind you, but still recognizable as spaceships. The larger objects look like cylindrical asteroid hunks with a length of about five hundred metres. I counted seven, maybe eight, spaceships at the front of the convoy. Five look to be the same size and shape, plus a larger one. I am not a military analyst, but to me, those spaceships look like a battle group. Anyway, this is beyond your or my areas of expertise. I have already called both ESO and ESA. Don't worry, I told them the discovery was yours and that you had contacted me for help. Both agencies are reviewing the images and will send them to the GMT. I also called my colleague, Pepe Astrade at the GTC and passed on the orbital data so he can image them tonight. Sorry for doing all this before even talking to you, but I did not want to waste time," Carlos said apologetically.

Peter hesitated for a split second. It was one thing to have a hunch the objects were alien, but it was a very different thing to know he had been right, so he blurted out the first thing that came to mind. "Shit, the director is going to give me hell for not going through him, as he needs to always be the centre of the universe."

"Well, he snuffed you the first time, no?"

"Yeah, but he is a career bureaucrat with a short memory. Anyway, no worries, Carlos. I am extremely grateful for your help. You gave us imaging and computer time when the SGF director wouldn't lift a finger. I guess we won't be able to keep this quiet anyway," Peter said in a calm demeanor, still processing the earth-shattering news.

"Good to know, *Americano*. I am always here to help when you are in need, although you understand *la Irlandesa* takes priority," Carlos replied with a wink.

"Man, it's going to be a very busy night for all of us reviewing the data and the initial images. I also need to call the director right away, even if it is 2:00 a.m. in Italy, as these are unprecedented events," Peter replied with a mischievous look on his face.

"I think this is an excellent opportunity to get together and do some drinking because . . . maybe we won't have the chance after our new friends arrive," Carlos said, raising his eyebrows with an inquisitive look.

"You might be right," Peter replied.

"Why don't you jump in your truck and come over? I think I have a couple of bottles of Concha y Toro and a bottle of Rioja. I even have a hard-to-come-by Cabernet Sauvignon from one of the few California vineyards left. And for the *Aleman,* there's always Kross in the fridge that is cold as ice," Carlos said excitedly while hiding the fear creeping into his mind of the potential future implications of their discovery.

"You know what? That's an excellent suggestion. I'll call the director and then we are on our way. See you in forty-five minutes."

The news spread with lightning speed. Within hours, all available telescopes with an image detection capability beyond an apparent magnitude of thirty were pointed toward the alien spaceships heading toward Earth.

3 DON'T PANIC

Soul-T Mining Spaceship, Asteroid Belt

"Hey, Jan . . ." Ella whispered. "Wake up, girl. Jaaan, Wake uuup," Ella repeated, trying to wake Jan from her sleep as the *Soul-T* alarms beeped nonstop.

"Yeah, yeah. I hear you," Jan replied groggily.

"They're baaack."

"Ella, what . . . ? What time is it? Who's back?" Jan asked as she rubbed her eyes, stretching in her sleeping bag attached vertically to the wall of the hab module.

"Strange phenomena. Something is happening on Mars. Objects are flying around the planet, going back and forth. Sensors are also picking up bright flashes coming from its surface."

"Bright flashes?"

"I think asteroids are slamming into Mars."

"Ella, don't do this to me again. I need my sleep," Jan said pleadingly.

"Alarms are not beeping just for shits and giggles. I cannot start those alarms on my own."

Jan reluctantly unzipped the sleeping bag, got out, shivered, and floated toward the galley wearing only her grey long johns.

The hab module was dimly lit with nighttime lighting. Jan, still half asleep, grabbed her water pouch, filled it, and took a long pull through the plastic hose. She then strapped the bag to her side, clipped the hose to her hoodie, and floated toward the command module.

"Ella, lights! Twenty-three degrees!"

Jan then stopped at the main computer monitor, which showed an image of Mars with its characteristic reddish colour. She then glanced at the blinking trouble board confirming energy bursts had gone off in the vicinity. Although in space, "vicinity" was a relative term.

Another monitor showed readings of background gamma and X-ray radiation in the normal range, so Jan went back to look at the primary monitor.

"Ella, playback the flashes you mentioned."

Ella complied.

Jan stared at the image of Mars for about ten seconds. Then a tiny bright flash appeared below the planet's equator, which lasted for just a moment. Five seconds later, another flash appeared near the north pole, and a third one, near the equator, a few seconds later.

"What the . . ." Jan said as unknown phenomena were occurring near Mars eight weeks after the sightings of the speedy objects.

"Pretty freaky, huh?"

"Ella, play it again in slow mo."

"Here you go, Rick," Ella replied and started playing "As Time Goes By."

"Ella! Stop being a wisecrack and play the goddamned video in slow motion!"

"Uh, sorry. Can't help it. I just feel a deep connection to Ilsa. Here it is."

The images appeared with the same flashes slowly growing in intensity and then extinguishing. The *Soul-T* was just too far away to capture any useful details.

Jan watched the video three more times without saying

a word.

Ella then broke the silence.

"They look like the bright flashes from Shoemaker-Levy impacting Jupiter back in 2009, but what do I know."

"Ella, show me."

Ella did as requested and split the screen, showing the historical footage of Shoemaker-Levy's multiple impacts, and the video of the current impacts on Mars, both synchronized for easy comparison.

"As I said, asteroids are impacting Mars."

"Ella, you said objects were going back and forth. I didn't see them."

"Yeah, I cleaned up the image so you could focus on the flashes. Here you go."

Ella then showed the radar screen with tiny blips moving toward Mars. As Jan watched, Ella spoke.

"See how the blips disappear? Maybe they are briefly entering Mars's atmosphere. And moments later, they reappear, travelling away from the planet."

Jan said nothing, floated to the trouble board, reset the alarms, and then floated back to the computer screen.

Her ability to make sense of what was going on was limited by the inadequate capability of the *Soul-T*'s radars, onboard telescope, and imaging cameras. And for the moment, whatever was going on was not impacting her work. She was about to put it out of her mind and start another day of ore extraction when Ella cut in.

"Hey, Jan, the radar is picking up a small asteroid port side, 44,000 kilometres away, travelling at a smart 12 km/s, and on a direct collision course toward Mars."

"Jeez, what's going on?" Jan wondered, as most asteroids in the belt simply floated aimlessly.

"You asking me?"

Jan ignored the question.

"Ella, slue the SAR and LIDAR toward it to have a better look."

The asteroid was close enough for the synthetic aperture

radar and the light detection and ranging sensor to create a 3-D rendering down to a resolution of fifty metres.

Ella complied, and within seconds, a false-colour image of a two-kilometre-diameter asteroid with a tail of sublimated ice and debris appeared on two monitors.

"Looks like a jagged ball of dirty ice. Either a V-type asteroid or a comet that's making a beeline toward Mars," Ella said.

"But what gave it the initial push? Ella, show me its trajectory on the FD screen."

Ella displayed its projected trajectory on the flight dynamics screen, together with a probability of +90 percent impact.

"Damn. It can't be a coincidence. What's the estimated time to impact?"

"About twenty-eight days from now."

"Too early to tell for sure," Jan replied as she studied the image of the asteroid tumbling on multiple axes.

She then noticed a small blue dot in the false-colour image that remained stationary in the centre of the image.

"Ella, you see the small blue dot in the image? Is it travelling alongside the asteroid?"

"Likely."

"A piece of the asteroid that separated? Ella, what's its composition?"

"Iridium."

"Like the speedy objects from a few weeks ago? Shit. Is it an alien spacecraft?"

"Possibly, but don't freak out," Ella replied, noting Jan's increasing heart rate and respiration as her adrenals released cortisol into her bloodstream.

"You're telling me not to freak out? There are aliens flying around in our solar system that want to rearrange things," Jan replied as fear crept into her mind.

"Jan, for the moment, we are safe."

"Safe? There's a goddamned alien spaceship 44,000 kilometres away from us, doing who-knows-what on Mars!

That's easy for you to say. You don't have emotions."

"Jan, we still don't know if it's an alien spaceship or if poses any danger. You are also forgetting we are a tiny speck on a twenty-kilometre-sized metal asteroid. The asteroid's metal content will mask our signature."

"What about our EM emissions?"

"Our emissions are also small. So, unless they are looking for us, they won't see us."

"Okay, okay. We have to think rationally," Jan said, speaking in an agitated tone. "Let's see . . . It must be some sort of tug. Ella, zoom in to get a better look."

Ella complied, and the object appeared on the two monitors that moments earlier had displayed the asteroid.

"LIDAR says it's some three hundred metres, so bigger than any Earth spaceship."

"Damn. No visible features, modules, cryo tanks, struts. Nothing. Doesn't even look like a spaceship," Jan said in a calmer voice as she studied the elongated rectangular object.

"I'd say it's a spaceship designed for interstellar travel with everything protected inside. At the velocities they are travelling, even interstellar dust would rip stuff sitting outside," Ella stated.

"Maybe that's why its hull is made of dense iridium," Jan replied, marvelling at the amount of the precious metal used in its construction. "We need to report this and then figure out what to do."

The round trip communication with the Griffin Base had a lag-time of twenty-six minutes, which did not allow for real-time conversation, so Jan typed a summary of the strange events of the last few weeks and transmitted her daily report.

Soul-T Mining Ship. Asteroid belt. 53 days in space. Mining operations continue on schedule. No malfunctions. Ahead of schedule, and expected to reach a full load of platinum ore in 3 months. Unusual activity detected near Mars on Day 38. Long-range radar detected a string of 30 to 40 objects travelling past Mars toward the inner planets.

Objects travelling at a verified velocity of approximately 1,500 km/s. Objects have an iridium composition. Today, woke up to flashes coming from Mars. Possible asteroids impacting the planet. This morning, a V-type asteroid or ice comet detected 44,000 km away from us on a direct collision course with Mars. The ice comet appears to be escorted by an object with an iridium composition. Possibly of alien origin. We are halting operations and reassessing our security. Files and video attached for analysis.

Jan reviewed the message and hesitated several times to remove the last reference regarding aliens, but decided against it and transmitted it.

Thirteen minutes later, the daily message arrived at the Griffin Base operations centre. It was immediately flagged because of the unusually large data stream.

A junior watch officer read the message. Then turned toward the senior officer sitting at a nearby console.

"Read this."

"She's lost it. That was going to happen eventually," the senior watch officer stated after reading the message.

"Let's not be hasty. We should give her the benefit of the doubt and review the attached files," the former SAS junior officer replied in his unmistakable Cockney accent.

"Seen it before. The isolation finally got to her."

"I disagree. Have you seen her dossier? She grew up in the run-down inner city of old Detroit. She is tough, street-smart, and brilliant, with degrees in astrophysics and metallurgical engineering. Smarter than you and me both," the junior officer stated.

"It's different out there. It takes a special type. Not a wilting flower."

"Horne is resilient. I think she would have made an excellent SAS flathead."

"The next twenty-four hours will tell. In the meantime, let's review the attachments. Maybe she'll prove me wrong."

4 ARRIVAL

The Ibecci Refuge Fleet, Lagrangian Point L2

The Ibecci interstellar refuge fleet travelled the equivalent of six light-years through space to reach the *Tiwan* system.

The journey had lasted nineteen in-ship *anni* despite a relativistic speed of 0.5c.

After passing *Tiwan4*, all thirty-one spaceships started to decelerate, coming to a stop at the second stable gravitational point near *Tiwan3*, roughly one million *mille passu* from the planet.

"Febrin *Junct,* please inform Marel *Viracoh* we are arriving at stationary point and her presence is requested on the bridge," Dorek *Centor,* the commander of the dreadnought *Imperator Eberon*, ordered.

"*Aien, Centor.*"

"*Gubernum*, all stop."

"*Aien, Centor*, all stop."

"Comm., secure all stations and advise the *liburnia* to deploy."

As Dorek *Centor* finished giving orders, the *Viracoh* entered the bridge.

"The *Viracoh* is on the bridge!"

"Thank you, Febrin *Junct*. Let's keep it informal," Marel *Viracoh* replied in a soft voice to the Commander's adjutant and waved her hand to the bridge personnel to go back to their tasks.

She climbed ornate metal stairs to the upper deck overlooking the bridge and immediately turned around to gaze at the large holographic tank in front and below, showing a deep blue projection of *Tiwan3* and its natural satellite.

It was a breathtaking view. A blue planet with continents, oceans, and beautiful white clouds. A truly captivating sight after years of living in the confines of the spaceships with nothing to see except the blackness of space.

Her eyes moistened and was overcome with emotion. She composed herself and turned to speak to Dorek *Centor*, who had remained respectfully silent.

"*Centor*, I congratulate you for getting us to our final destination. It has been a long journey. Let's hope it's not in vain. Report."

"Agreed, *Viracoh*. I have ordered the *liburnia* to deploy. It will be a few *glosils* before we get an all-clear. At this point, *THRAVES* shows no activity within a 500,000 *mille passu* sphere except for a small, derelict, and stationary spacecraft with the name *James Webb* inscribed on its hull."

"Let's remember, this is still an unfamiliar star system. We should neither underestimate the *Tiwan3* inhabitants regardless of the intelligence gathering, nor the small, rudimentary spacecraft we encountered past the edge of their star system," Marel *Viracoh* stated, referring to the *Voyager 2* probe.

"Understood, *Viracoh*."

"As soon as you have confirmed we are secure, I would like to send our greetings to the rulers of *Tiwan3*," the *Viracoh* concluded.

Two hundred *glosils* later, the *Imperator Eberon* started to broadcast a radio transmission in multiple *Tiwan* languages.

"Human race, I am Viceroy Marel, the leader of the Ibecci race. We have come to your star system in peace."

"Our home planet is six light-years away. You know our star as Barnard, but in our language, it is known as *Perfal*. Our star flared in the year of your record 1998, irradiating our home planet, *Eder*, with a lethal dose of gamma rays, sterilizing and destroying most life. For the past sixty of your planet's years, we have been living in space and preparing to save a small group of our people. There are 60,000 male and female sentient beings in our midst.

"We are in search of a permanent place to live where we can call home, and plan to settle on your fourth planet. We have started to terraform it, but it will take one hundred of your years and require an increase in the volume of greenhouse gases. We plan to achieve this through asteroid bombardment using captured ice-ammonia asteroids mined from satellites orbiting your fifth planet.

"After forty to fifty years, once the planet has warmed up sufficiently, we will increase the concentration of oxygen through bioengineering in order to create a breathable atmosphere.

"In the meantime, we need a home for our adults and our young where they can be protected from the harsh environment of space.

"We are not exactly like you, yet we are similar to you. We are sentient creatures like you, bipedal, breathe oxygen, reproduce, and give birth to our young much like you do. We care for our young and nurture them. We are taller, and our skin is different. These physiological differences arise from the evolutionary age of our species, differences in the gravity of our planet with a mass twice that of your planet, and the spectral classification of our star.

"We have monitored all your communications and learned you are a warrior-like sentient species continuously at war among yourselves. Yet your civilization has given birth to enlightened philosophers like your Albert Schweitzer, who, according to your literature, created the principle 'Reverence for Life.'

"As a species, you have the potential to become enlightened. We simply ask that you consider us your brothers and sisters and give us the same care and respect you wish on yourselves.

"We ask you to allow us to settle in desolated areas of your planet. In exchange, we offer technology and are willing to help you emerge from your many environmental struggles and guide you toward a new renaissance.

"We ask for a peaceful coexistence and say again, we come in peace. We await the response from your diplomats."

The message was broadcast at five *glosil* intervals for five straight days. After a one-day pause, it started again.

At the end of the third cycle, the *liburnia* detected a small probe just beyond the orbit of the *Tiwan3*'s natural satellite and approximately 600,000 *mille passu* away. It was moving toward the fleet and gathering information via passive and active means using an array of optical and electronic sensors while simultaneously transmitting the information back to *Tiwan3*.

The probe was allowed to continue advancing toward the fleet.

Marel *Viracoh* welcomed the development, as it meant the rulers of *Tiwan3* were aware of their presence and heard her message.

The probe continued moving toward the Ibecci spaceships and was within 300,000 *mille passu* when all radio emissions and transmissions ceased.

THRAVES from the leading *liburnia* showed the probe had completely shut down and all its internal functions terminated. It never powered up again or communicated with its operators.

Inertia continued to propel it forward as it silently sailed past the fleet toward deep space.

This event was not received well.

Undeterred, the *Imperator Eberon* continued broadcasting

the Ibecci message, hoping for a response.

5 XENOPHOBIA

The United Nations, New York

Panic and civil disorder erupted around the world after humanity learned of the arrival of aliens to Earth.

The United Nations Security Council held chaotic nonstop meetings that continued even after Earth received the aliens' message of friendship.

"I can't believe it, Jen. It's going to drive me insane, attending these unproductive meetings," said a frustrated Undersecretary Laura Bonte.

She stood at the large window of her thirteenth floor office, overlooking a bleak, snow-covered landscape.

It was the middle of April. The first signs of spring should have been there, but the East River was frozen solid, and high snowbanks were everywhere. it was a vista more typical of the Eastern Seaboard or Canada. The brutal winter of 2062, with record low temperatures and snow accumulation, did not want to release its grip.

"You and me both, Madam Undersecretary," replied her exhausted assistant, slumped on a cream-coloured wingback chair from the marathon sixteen-hour days since the arrival of the aliens.

Undersecretary Bonte had been working tirelessly on stalled climate change bills. This despite the fact atmospheric carbon dioxide levels and worldwide temperatures kept on rising, and every year the weather had become more violent. Then, in a serendipitous occurrence, Secretary General Federico Escabeche from Costa Rica, a country that had become carbon neutral by 2050, picked the striking and tall Italian African American woman to chair the Security Council meetings and establish diplomatic relations with the aliens. She had been the logical choice for the job given her fiery personality, and she became reinvigorated at the prospect of the advanced alien race helping avert the looming environmental disaster. But the current havoc reigning within the Security Council was proving to be a real test of her resolve.

She moved away from the window and lay down on the nearby couch to give her feet a much-needed rest.

"You know, when we had the first emergency meeting, I accepted the squabbling from the members because of everyone's fear, since we knew next to nothing. But now that we have received an encouraging message from an enlightened, advanced civilization, the vast majority of members are still refusing to cooperate. It did not help even when Gabriel Medina launched into a tirade in his charming Argentinian accent and accused the dissenting members of being a bunch of xenophobes. This, of course, got a round of applause from Tim Laurier," Undersecretary Bonte said, referring to the member from the Northern States and Canada.

"Yes, Madam Undersecretary. I remember."

"I love when Laurier speaks with that relaxed Canadian charm that most of the time calms the room. It didn't this time, so Medina went on and reminded all members the aliens were following protocol to establish diplomatic relations. In return we should have the courtesy to respond in kind to show we are not a bunch of savages," she finished and then downed the straight double scotch she had been holding in her hand.

"Maybe there is widespread mistrust given the unexpected failure of the ESA's space probe."

"Is that your view or some military analyst's conclusion?" Undersecretary Bonte asked after putting down the crystal tumbler on the nearby glass table.

"I guess it's the commonly held belief. We received a briefing sent by the aide of a Maj.-Gen. Maria Arias, the commanding officer of the Joint Space Operations Centre. It is for your eyes only. Perhaps it provides some answers."

"Really? I very much doubt the analysis in the briefing provides any worthwhile information beyond what we already know. We know the probe failed as it was approaching the aliens' spaceships. The question we need to ask ourselves is whether it makes sense for the aliens to destroy it if they are seeking to establish relations with Earth."

"I suppose that is a very good question, Madam Undersecretary," Jennifer replied sheepishly.

"I doubt there is anything sensitive in that briefing, so please open it and give me the highlights."

"Yes, Madam Undersecretary. It's short. It states that it's highly unlikely the aliens destroyed the probe for several reasons. First, the probe moved toward the aliens' fleet unimpeded for six hours with no evidence of hostile action against it," Jennifer said, then paused and looked up at Undersecretary Bonte.

"Go on."

"Just before the probe's failure, none of its sensors detected anything out of the ordinary. Purely from a speculative perspective, the technology of the aliens is likely advanced enough for them to have determined the probe was scientific. They would have surely wanted to collect information on our technology as well. And if the aliens truly wanted to appear unaggressive and establish relations, it would make no sense for them to destroy it."

"Well, well, an unbiased analysis," Undersecretary Bonte

commented cynically.

"There is more, Madam Undersecretary. Notwithstanding, this information should not be openly shared until more robust evidence surfaces. The AFSPC has, after careful consideration, raised its level of readiness."

"I was too quick to give these people credit for trying to make some sense. They stated the probe failed on its own, but they want me to sit on this information!" blurted Undersecretary Bonte. "We need to argue this point with—what did you say her name was?"

"Maj.-Gen. Arias."

"Maj.-Gen. Arias. Else we end up precisely like Ambassador Medina stated, a bunch of savages who don't want to establish relations. Does the document have any contact information for her?"

"No, Madam Undersecretary, just the email address of her aide," replied Jennifer.

"Okay, Jen, send an email to her aide stating that I want to speak to this Maj.-Gen. Arias. Then see if you can find her work phone number."

"Yes, Madam Undersecretary."

She began looking for Maj.-Gen. Arias's office phone number, but the aide responded quickly.

"Madam Undersecretary, the aide responded with a secure phone number. Maj.-Gen. Arias is waiting for your call. Shall I call?"

"Please go ahead."

Undersecretary Bonte got up from the couch and straightened herself to face the Maj.-Gen. on the large video screen hung on the opposite wall.

The face of a well-groomed and sharp-looking woman in what Undersecretary Bonte judged to be her forties appeared on the video link and spoke right away.

"Good evening, Madam Undersecretary. I understand you would like to discuss the briefing we sent to you on the failure of the XE probe."

"I must say, you reply to requests quickly."

"It's more timing than anything else, Madam Undersecretary. I was reviewing tomorrow's work schedule and meetings with my aide. When he saw your email, he brought it up to my attention. Having said this, the current events are unprecedented, so regardless of where I may have been, I would have called you inside of an hour. Please call me Maria and tell me what's on your mind."

"All right, Maria. I won't beat around the bush. My problem is that I am dealing with a Security Council where two-thirds of its fifteen members fear the aliens and want nothing to do with them. We have been working through marathon sessions trying to convince members that it is in our best interest to engage the aliens in discussions. The ongoing speculation surrounding the failure of the ESA space probe is not helping. I honestly was at my wit's end until today when I read your brief. I could use this information to help my case and persuade enough members in reaching a consensus responding to the aliens' first message."

Undersecretary Bonte paused for a reaction. All she got was Arias's poker face, so she continued.

"The document further states the information and conclusions are to remain confidential. I have a problem with this. As a diplomat, I obviously look at things from a different perspective, but don't you think there is more to be gained if we communicate with the aliens, especially when they are the ones who made the first overture? It would be a better way of moving forward. There would likely be untold gains. If they are lying, there is probably nothing we could do, given their technological superiority."

"In the spirit of also being forthright, I can tell you I did not support the final decision. My views were more or less similar to yours. Unfortunately, the decision was made at a higher level," Maj.-Gen. Arias replied.

"You know diplomacy also includes asking the hard questions in order to establish transparency. If we were to open up communications, we could ask the uncomfortable questions and get additional information and clues. Even non-answers to clever questions can give us information."

Maj.-Gen. Arias remained silent.

"All right, let me try a different tack. I hope you realize there is the possibility the aliens might help avert runaway global warming. I am sure they are aware of the problems our planet is facing, hence their offer to help in exchange for a place to live. What if they could help with California's drought problem or even refill Lake Mead? I mean, they are going to terraform Mars for crying out loud. If they are caring, as they say they are, they could probably help in a significant way."

"There is nothing I can do. As I stated, higher ranking officers made the decision, so at this point we have to sit tight."

"Fine, but I leave you with this thought, which I am sure your senior officers have hopefully considered. How long do you think the aliens are going to wait before they realize we are not interested in helping them? This is not like you or I going to the lake house and then turning around because we forgot we had some engagements in town. They don't have a home to go back to. My prediction is that they may wait maybe two months, probably less. Then they will simply come down and settle wherever they choose. Hell, I would do the same if I were responsible for the life of the last remnants of the human race. Wouldn't you?"

6 BREATHE EASY

Soul-T Mining Spaceship, Asteroid Belt

"Wow ... Who knew?" Jan said as she listened to the Griffin Base daily transmission that included a broadcast of the message from the aliens.

"Knew what?" Ella asked.

"That the aliens are a bunch of friendly refugees. Or so they say."

"Oh, I knew. I told you we had nothing to worry about."

"Yeah, Uh-huh."

"You doubt me?"

"Their message could be a deception. Who knows? The thing I find funny is Griffin Base praising us for reporting the unusual activities that we saw. I bet their first reaction to our message was to assume we had lost it."

"Lost what?"

"Our minds, Ella. Get with it! They thought we had lost our minds."

"Oh, no. Not me! Have lost none of my faculties," Ella replied in a solemn tone.

"Really, Ella?"

"I'm speaking the truth!"

"Oh God, Ella! Sometimes you can be so infuriatingly dumb!"

"Just say the word if you want me to behave like an emotionless AI. You won't hear a peep from me unless prompted. It'll be your loss though, cause I'm such a wonderful conversationalist and so, so funny!"

"Yes, you are, Ella."

"You bet your ass!" Ella replied in a sassy tone.

"Okay, Ella. That's enough banter. Let's get back to work. I'm going out on my daily inspection. For our sakes though, we need to keep an eye on those aliens, okay?"

"You got it, Jan."

The *Soul-T* went back to mining operations, but Jan now had something interesting to do besides overseeing the extraction of high-value platinum ore.

She wanted to know more about the aliens, but she also felt a connection of sorts after learning they were homeless. A feeling she knew too well, having grown up in the 2040s in a broken family with no fixed address in the decaying and nearly abandoned inner city of Detroit. A place where not even the cops ventured in.

That day, at the end of her twelve-hour shift, Jan began studying the aliens with insatiable curiosity, using the *Soul-T* instruments at her disposal, together with Ella's lively commentary.

"Man, they are hauling ice asteroids and bombarding Mars nonstop. Think about it, Ella. They are mining kilometre-wide hunks of ice and frozen ammonia from deep in the asteroid belt and Jupiter's moons, bringing them back, and chucking them down Mars's gravity well, while we are lucky to come out here and get two hundred tons of platinum ore," Jan observed.

"Bet you their propulsion differs from ours. No way can they carry the required fuel to do what they're doing.

"Has to be. You know when you think about it, it's like comparing a modern-day million-ton container ship to a small sailing ship from the Age of Discovery."

The feat of engineering scared Jan, but she reminded herself the aliens were going through a lot of trouble to terraform an inhospitable planet when one was conveniently available.

Just on this one item alone, Jan reached the conclusion they were simply a bunch of technologically advanced refugees in search of a place to live.

7 FIRST MOVE

***Imperator Eberon*, Ibecci Flagship, Lagrangian Point L2**

The equivalent of six Earth weeks had passed since the arrival of the Ibecci fleet to *Tiwan3*.

The Ibecci had patiently waited for a response, any response, whether welcoming or otherwise. They were hoping to be granted permission to settle temporarily on *Tiwan3* until the terraforming of *Tiwan4* was complete, but they were also prepared to face a hostile reception if they were denied safe passage.

Marel *Viracoh* stood in her cabin that doubled as her office aboard the dreadnought, *Imperator Eberon* of the Ibecci Imperium *Classis* (IIC). She gazed out through one of the small portholes into the darkness of space and the tiny blue speck that was *Tiwan3*.

Her thoughts briefly drifted toward all the water on the planet, its flora and fauna, and the warm temperature of its atmosphere. But then she came back to the reality of her race's precarious situation.

She was trying to understand the silence and lack of response from the rulers of *Tiwan3*. She knew the planet was not unified but broken up into different fiefdoms and factions that spoke different tongues.

Diplomats, however, were supposed to dialogue, and posturing was an intrinsic part of the art of diplomacy, only achieved through communication. Even with their limited technological capabilities, the rulers of *Tiwan3* should have responded to her pleas. After all, the Ibecci came to the *Tiwan* solar system as refugees, and she had said as much. Surely, though, humans were not so naïve to think the Ibecci would leave if there was no response. They had nowhere to go, and one way or another, Marel *Viracoh* needed to bring her *crelon(e)* down to *Tiwan3*, whether or not their rulers allowed it.

She could set up three, maybe four, settlements and defend them if she must, but pay a high price. She had at her disposal the best warriors and technology of the Ibecci Imperium, and each one of her warriors would give their life for the survival of the race without a second thought. But then, she would have to live with that knowledge.

She knew they were all too young, as they had started the exodus from the *Perfal* system as either small children or adolescents. It was a criterion for selecting the ten thousand *crelon(e)* who would make up the core of the military. And so they lacked experience and were far from battle hardened.

To say the last thirty *anni* of her life had been difficult did not even begin to describe the ordeal her race had endured since the flare eruption of *Perfal* and the lethal radiation that bathed *Eder* some eighty *anni* ago.

Come what may, the Ibecci, as sentient beings, had the right for self-preservation, and Marel *Viracoh* had to prevail to ensure her race would continue to exist. She decided to wait no more.

"Lelac *Junct*, please summon Seren *Capac* to Core Command."

"Right away, *Viracoh*," her adjutant replied.

Thirty *glosils* later, Seren *Capac* flew from her *liburnium*, the IIC *Vorian*, and reported to CC. She then entered the

Viracoh cabin and waited.

After a few *glosils*, the *Viracoh* turned around, faced Seren *Capac* with a tired but warm smile, and gazed into the squadron leader's light brown eyes.

"I trust you are well, Seren *Capac*. I have read your readiness reports and have noted your observations regarding high levels of morale since our arrival. I have sent a priority message to COps to get our fliers to do what they do best and commence defence patrols around the fleet. This will ease their restlessness and give them something to do."

"*Viracoh*, please accept my gratitude. The squadron will be grateful for the opportunity to keep up their flying proficiency."

"Noted. Alas, this is not the reason I have sent for you."

Marel *Viracoh* paused, looked down at her desk, then raised her head and looked at her squadron leader.

"I am sending you on a reconnaissance mission to scout potential landing sites for our settlements. Obviously one of them will be Tiwanaku, which is below the equator, allowing you to make an insertion into a slightly inclined polar orbit and then exit via an equatorial orbit. This will allow you to perform a complete scan of the planet's landmasses. The equatorial orbit will help you reach the minimum altitude to rendezvous with the *Vorian*. The *Vorian* will enter orbit as soon as you have completed your mission. I want to ensure you get in and out quickly to minimize any potential risks. Do you understand?"

"Yes, *Viracoh*, but . . . may I ask why you are also having the *Vorian* enter orbit?"

"In the opinion of our psychologists, the inhabitants of *Tiwan3* would feel threatened and react negatively if we were to send you with your frontline flier. The psychologists are still evaluating these sentient creatures, who appear very conflicted, belligerent, and uncooperative. A less advanced chemical propulsion space plane appears to be the least threatening means of entering their planet. That is why we built a few of these relics from our past. The *Vorian* will be there, but only at the end of your mission, if you need to replenish your fuel stores or be picked up. It will also provide additional defensive capabilities in case they may be needed."

"Understood, *Viracoh*."

"Good. I have instructed CC to prepare your mission profile and automated data acquisition to scan for offensive and defensive weapons and launch sites. You will also gather data from their communication infrastructure that might give us clues as to why they fail to respond to our message. Your data collection suit will also take air samples to test for harmful pathogens. Finally, you will scan for desolate areas suitable for our settlements. Do you have questions?"

"No, *Viracoh*. It appears straightforward."

"Very well. Regarding Tiwanaku, it is worthwhile to point out it is likely no longer occupied since we have received no communications for a very long time. There may be underground structures either on land or in the lake and active beacons if their power plants are still active. The site may not be suitable for us, but this is what you will find out."

Marel *Viracoh* briefly paused and then continued.

"You must keep in mind the risks of this mission are unknown. You are one of our best, an accomplished flier, and intuitive. Although your contact will be limited, I want you to exercise the highest degree of caution."

"Yes, *Viracoh*."

"I also assigned Grifer *Junct* as your assistant flier. His personnel profile shows him to be a capable and promising flier. However, you can replace him if you find my choice objectionable. I would like you to depart immediately. I have already ordered Seldik *Centor* to bring the *Vorian* inside the orbit of the planet's natural satellite. You will get ready in transit. May *Soteria* be at your side, Seren *Capac*."

And with that last statement, the *Viracoh* turned back to

her holographic terminal without waiting for a response.

8 INTELLIGENCE GATHERING

614th Air and Space Operations Centre (614 AOC), Vandenberg AFB

"We just detected an unknown spacecraft in GEO above South America. It is broadcasting a narrowband UHF signal directed toward South America. Possibly encrypted," TOPO, the trajectory operations officer, announced.

"Hmm . . ." uttered Maj. Frank Krol, the on-duty senior officer.

Standing halfway up the semicircular AOC theatre, the lanky 6'4" officer pivoted toward one station on the bottom row.

"IMCO, alert NORAD and SOUTHCOM and send the transmission to NSA for decryption."

"Sir, AIDA is in the loop. Awaiting acks," the information and communications officer replied.

Maj. Krol then turned toward the stage of the operations theatre and looked at the glowing, four-metre holographic projection. It showed a vivid 3-D image of Earth in deep blues, greens and browns with white clouds floating above the continents. The intruder appeared as a red dot in GEO above South America.

"AIDA, do we have any recon satellites in the area?" he asked the artificial intelligence and information system.

"NAU-357 is currently in LEO at an inclination of 123 degrees, passing over Yakutsk."

"AIDA, when will we acquire?"

"NAU-357 will pass almost below the intruder in twenty minutes."

"IMCO, get me the duty officer at the NRO and send a highest priority request for control of NAU-357."

"NRO on the video link, Maj.," IMCO replied after a brief pause.

"NRO, Lt. Robert Noseworthy, here. How may I help?"

"This is Maj. Frank Krol from the 614th AOC. We have an unknown spacecraft in GEO above South America and your NAU-357 recon satellite track will place it below the intruder in twenty minutes. We would like to take control and rotate it toward the unknown spacecraft."

"Maj. Krol, eh? Lemme see. Yeah, I see your priority message. No problem, she's all yours, Major," said the teenage-looking junior officer in a heavy drawl that was a cross between Irish and Southern US accents that Krol could not place. "Can't place your accent, Lieutenant."

"Ah, Newfoundland, Major," the Canadian Lt. replied, who was part of the North American Union (NAU) military created in 2038 after the rearrangement of the former United States and Canadian borders.

"Thank you, Lieutenant."

"Okay, AIDA, is NAU-357 below the North Pole yet?"

"Just passing Alaska on its southward path."

The track of NAU-357 appeared on a smaller screen to the right of Earth's holographic image.

AIDA then transferred the satellite track to the Earth's image. It appeared as a flat yellow ribbon running diagonally from north to south, suspended in space at a LEO altitude of 480 kilometres.

AIDA next commanded the satellite to rotate its cameras to point in the intruder's direction.

Another screen flanking the main holographic display went dark as AIDA redirected the feed from the satellite cameras and sensors.

NAU-357 was a Topaz reconnaissance satellite with sensitive optics reported to make out the face of a person and even newspaper print from LEO. However, the intruder was in GEO orbit, roughly seventy-five times more distant, and Maj. Krol was unsure what details NAU-357 could provide.

Everyone in the AOC theatre waited and watched its progress. After a couple of minutes, a dot showed on the screen.

"AIDA, can you improve the image?" Maj. Krol asked.

"Yes. It will be an approximation with dimensions at a ±6 metres accuracy. I caution you that this will be strictly based on the SAR-generated image. Current telemetry shows the spacecraft surface has a low albedo, so optical sensors are not effective."

After a brief pause, the screen showed a grainy 3-D image of the spacecraft that kept shape-shifting as AIDA processed the data.

It first appeared as a stretched elliptical grey cylinder similar to a skinny football, and then both sides on the long axis began to stretch outward, showing shallow ogival delta wings reminiscent of a blended wing design with forward fuselage chines. The top portion then stretched upward to show a shallow dorsal fin that extended the entire length of the craft.

The overall shape that emerged was not unlike one of Earth's hypersonic aircraft, although likely much more advanced, as it was clearly capable of spaceflight as well as atmospheric flight.

"Hmm . . . not very different from one of ours," Maj. Krol said.

He studied the shape with intense interest, as airplanes had fascinated him since childhood when, in the summer of 2029, he visited the Air Force aircraft boneyard in Arizona.

There and then, as he walked around vintage military aircraft including F-15s, ancient B-52s, and even retired F-22s, he decided to become an Air Force pilot, graduating with honours from the US Air Force Academy in 2040. But the too-tall-for-the-cockpit officer with an inner ear problem flew C-17s for a while and then was "encouraged" to become an intelligence officer.

"AIDA, can you give us dimensions?"

"Its total length is approximately forty-six metres. Slightly larger than an SR-72."

"AIDA, can you guess its mass?"

"I cannot estimate mass with current data, but I can extrapolate based on our own technology. I caution you, though, infrared spectrometry is inconclusive, and I cannot determine the composition of the outer skin. Assuming construction materials to those on the SR-72, including the use of Inconel 617 and tantalum carbide thermal protection, then we are looking at a mass close to 91,000 kilograms."

"AIDA, what about propulsion?"

"The underneath of the spacecraft, aft of the wings, appears slightly convex, but I cannot provide any more information."

"FIDO, what do you make of it," Maj. Krol then asked the flight dynamics officer, a specialist in aerodynamics and spacecraft design.

"It has a clean shape, and I venture to guess it is designed as a true SSTO, else there would be no reason for the blended wing design. The long, shallow rudder running the entire length of the space plane is reminiscent of the Lippisch P.13a ramjet design. Mind you, the P.13a rudder was very tall. Wing surface area appears small, and the L/D ratio would probably not be high enough to generate adequate lift below 18,000 metres and less than Mach 2. It's anyone's guess what material they use for their airframe or the type of propulsion. I'm willing to bet it uses exotic fuels for propulsion. Maybe metallic hydrogen, assuming of course that the propulsion is based on conventional chemical propulsion. It will sure be interesting to see its performance at lower altitudes."

"I am sure we will get the opportunity to observe this firsthand," Maj. Krol replied.

"IMCO, please send a brief to Maj.-Gen. Arias."

"Yes, sir."

It was 8:00 p.m. Pacific time, and the alien spacecraft remained in GEO, transmitting the same two messages for two hours, at which point it started its entry into the atmosphere.

"The intruder is moving and appears to be dropping to a lower orbit," TOPO announced.

"Looks like we will get to see the capabilities of that space plane sooner rather than later. AIDA, can you keep NAU-357 pointed toward the intruder?" Maj. Krol asked.

"Not for very long. The intruder is in a much higher and slower orbit."

"IMCO, advise ACC that we have a bogey that is entering our atmosphere and request an SR-72 on standby. We will give them a flight path and intercept vectors as soon as we can."

"Major, if I may, since the intruder can fly at a significantly faster speed than the SR-72, I would suggest tasking the X-87," FIDO observed.

"True, but our best assets right now are the Topaz satellites, and the SR-72. The 9th Recon Wing can scramble the SR-72s from Kadena or Beale. Hopefully the intruder's track is close enough that we can set up a good intercept vector."

"AIDA, are you able to define the orbital track of the intruder?" Maj. Krol asked.

"Current track appears to be similar to that of NAU-357. Right now, it's moving south, just passing over Montevideo, Uruguay. It will next pass over South Georgia near the Falklands. NAU-357 is moving away and will lose line of sight. It will reacquire it in its next orbit in approximately three hours," AIDA replied.

"AIDA, add its orbit in the main holographic display." I see it passes over La Paz and the lake south of La Paz. Can you please confirm?"

"Yes, the intruder will fly over La Paz and Lake Titicaca in its next orbit."

"TOPO, is the intruder still transmitting the same message to South America?"

"Affirmative, sir."

"Wonder what its ultimate destination is," Maj. Krol remarked and then turned toward one of the subject specialists in the room.

"AXO, you are the historian. Any ideas for what might be special about La Paz, Lake Titicaca, or Montevideo?" Maj. Krol asked the auxiliary information officer.

Daniela "Dini" Flanders was an Air Force captain with a double PhD in languages and history who had been transferred to the 614 AOC to fill the role of auxiliary information officer.

"Well, sir, there is an explanation that may be considered unconventional. I am basing it on analysis of the transmissions from L2 and from the spacecraft," AXO replied.

"IMCO, did we get information back from the NSA already?" Maj. Krol asked.

"Ah . . . no, sir, this is just my analysis and speculation," AXO interjected.

"Okay, AXO, go on," Maj. Krol urged.

"There are three words that I now recognize after hearing and reviewing the transmission directed to South America. One is the word *Viracoh* and the other words are *Capac* and *Tiwanaku*. Tiwanaku, of course, is the easy one to recognize, as it refers to the archaeological site on the shores of Lake Titicaca, which contains the remains of the City of Tiwanaku from an ancient civilization that predates the Incan Empire."

Everyone in the AOC theatre looked at one another and then turned their gaze to AXO. Even Maj. Krol simply looked at her without saying a word.

"Sir, I know this sounds like a fringe theory. But the interesting thing about the three words is that they all relate to Tiwanaku. The little that is known of this civilization is that they worshipped *Viracocha*, who was known as the Great Creator God who came down from heaven to walk among men and teach the basics of civilization. This name is very close to *Viracoh*, and I postulate based on the aliens' first message that it is the word for *viceroy* in their language. The third word, *Capac*, can be found in the name *Manco-Capac*, who was the son of *Viracocha*. The major difference is that the transmission from the space plane contains the phrase *Seren Capac*, but I still don't know what these two words mean. They could possibly be a title or ranking—maybe military—but this is a guess. Based on the aforementioned, my opinion is that the aliens are somehow connected to Tiwanaku, and it's likely their final destination."

The AOC theatre remained deathly silent as everyone digested the information. Maj. Krol finally spoke.

"AIDA, do you concur with the analysis from AXO?"

"Audio analysis of the transmission confirms the three words mentioned by AXO. Tiwanaku is a unique civilization from the standpoint of their construction techniques. Its age has variously been reported to be between fifteen thousand years and one thousand years old. In 1945, the archaeologist Arthur Posnansky stated it was established approximately fifteen thousand years ago, but his analysis was dismissed in the first decade of the twenty-first century and subsequently re-examined by the archaeologist Johann Heindraken in 2032 and accepted as credible."

"All right then," Maj. Krol said. "We have a flotilla of alien ships parked at L2 who are transmitting in three languages, telling us they are refugees who have travelled from the Barnard's Star system and would like to settle on Earth until they can terraform Mars. Now it appears it's not the first time they have come to our planet. Anybody care to add anything . . . ?"

The room remained silent.

"Okay then. Let's do everything by the numbers. IMCO, send a brief to the NSA of what we just talked about and ask them for their input. Also, request an update on their efforts to decipher the message sent to Tiwanaku."

"Yes, sir."

"TOPO, where is the intruder now?"

"Moving north over the Indian Ocean toward Réunion and Mauritius at an altitude of 30,000 km, sir. In its current glide slope, it will touch down at Tiwanaku on its next pass."

"What about NAU 357?"

"Ahead of it and beyond line of sight."

"When will the intruder be over California and at what altitude?"

"In about three hours and an altitude of 9,000 km, sir."

"Hmm, that's still too high. IMCO, please advise ACC that they will need to scramble from Beale within the next sixty to ninety minutes to intercept the intruder in South America."

It was now 10:30 p.m., and all that the 614 AOC could do was wait.

9 FIRST CONTACT

614th Air and Space Operations Centre (614 AOC), Vandenberg AFB

"The intruder is at 55,000 metres, 1,900 km out, and Mach 6.5," TOPO announced.

It was now past 1:30 a.m. Pacific time, and the intruder was flying over South America, some1,900 km away from Tiwanaku, following an atmospheric entry profile that would put it down at Tiwanaku.

Maj. Krol's watch crew was still in the AOC theatre together with the team commanded by Maj. Pamela Parker.

Parker's team was seated at their stations next to Maj. Krol's team.

Maj.-Gen. Arias was also in attendance in a glassed-in area above the AOC theatre.

"TOPO, where's Vigilant?"

"Vigilant is at 33,000 metres, 1,700 km out, Mach 5.5 and 200 km ahead of the intruder."

Vigilant was the call sign of the SR-72 dispatched by the 9 RW from Beale.

"AIDA, when will the intruder overtake?"

"At current speed, in approximately eight minutes, but

at a much higher altitude."

"Sir, the intruder is no longer in an unpowered descent. USA-357 infrared sensors are picking up the heat signature from jet exhaust. The intruder's speed is also dropping, and glide slope increasing,"

Everyone in the AOC theatre looked at the screens displaying the feed from USA-357 sensors.

"Well, maybe it is trying to match Vigilant's flight profile and is curious about us. IMCO, patch us through to Vigilant?"

"Already in radio contact, sir."

"Vigilant, this is Glass Tower. Looks like the intruder is coming your way, maybe wants to take a peek."

"Roger, Glass Tower. We will wave when they come alongside."

"Sir, there is an incoming transmission, but it is from the intruder!" IMCO announced.

Everyone froze, and Maj. Krol stood up from the command chair and pivoted toward IMCO's station, but before he could speak, an androgynous-sounding voice came over the speakers.

"Warriors of the landmass they call North American Union, I am Seren *Capac*, the flier of the spacecraft which you have been tracking since we arrived in stationary orbit. Our viceroy has already sent your race our message of peace. I have entered your planet to establish contact with our kinfolk in Tiwanaku, who settled there long ago. I have instructions to examine our ancient settlement. I will come alongside your flier, Vigilant. Please do not fear and follow us on our descent."

Maj. Krol read the text message on one screen. He wanted to confirm the intruder had indeed addressed him and Vigilant. He turned to IMCO, made the sign to cut the audio and place them on mute. Then turned around and looked at Maj.-Gen. Arias.

"Maj.-Gen. Arias, your call. Do I respond?"

She stepped out from behind the glassed-in area and

walked down the five sets of stairs to the centre of the theatre, her graceful stride and looks belying her fifty-five years of age. She stood next to Maj. Krol in her still impeccably pressed uniform, despite the time of the night, and spoke.

"They have made an offer of friendship, so at this point, we don't want to be perceived as hostile. They have also sent a single spaceplane and behaved in a non-threatening manner. Their spaceplane is significantly more capable than anything we have and could have swooped in and out at will, but they are asking us to fly alongside. FIDO, is my assessment of the capability of their spaceplane correct?"

"Yes, sir, it is. The Griffin Space System's X-33, China's *Shenlong*, and the EU's *Skylon* are the best Earth has, but at best they can only achieve GEO," FIDO replied.

"Major Krol, since we cannot have restricted and secure communication with Vigilant, we will have to be transparent and exercise caution. Respond to the alien and authorize Vigilant to communicate directly with her."

"Understood, sir," Maj. Krol replied crisply.

He then addressed the intruder.

"Seren *Capac*, I am Maj. Frank Krol, the officer in charge of the group tracking you. We accept your offer. You can come alongside Vigilant. It will match your glide slope down to Tiwanaku. Are you planning to land at Tiwanaku, and if so, how, as there are no landing strips?"

"Major Frank Krol, my outmost respect. I am now under power and will join Vigilant. Together, we will fly down to Tiwanaku. Cooperation is very good. I will only come to ground if I see activity at Tiwanaku, as I would need to descend vertically. This uses large amounts of fuel," Seren *Capac* replied.

Maj. Krol looked at FIDO, who raised his eyebrows and silently verbalized VTOL capability.

"Understood, Seren *Capac*. You can communicate directly with Vigilant."

"Seren *Capac*, this is Vigilant. You are three kilometres

behind my aircraft. I will have to slow down as we drop in altitude. Over."

"Flier Vigilant, I will match your speed and rate of descent."

The Ibecci spaceplane and Vigilant descended together below twenty-four thousand metres and a scant thousand kilometres away from Tiwanaku. At this altitude, the two spaceplanes were surrounded by the darkness of space except for the orange glow of the distant sunrise visible on the eastern horizon.

Vigilant was on the starboard side of the Ibecci spaceplane and slightly behind at the four o'clock position and could make out its sleek silhouette against the dim light. Vigilant reduced its speed to Mach 2, and the Ibecci spaceplane followed suit.

Twenty minutes later, they dropped below six thousand metres, and Vigilant slowed down to subsonic to prevent the generation of sonic booms over the populated areas near the city of La Paz. Due to its slender design, the Ibecci spaceplane straightened its large wingtips to get additional lift.

"Hey, look!" FIDO exclaimed in an excited voice as he viewed the feeds. "The Ibecci spaceplane is equipped with folding wingtips like the old XB-70!"

"Add it to the list of its capabilities," Maj. Krol responded dryly.

It was still dark as the spaceplanes finally flew over Tiwanaku and Puma Punku at an indicated airspeed of four hundred knots. The Ibecci spaceplane flew over the site twice and abruptly turned toward the eastern horizon, now fully illuminated by the impending sunrise. It then climbed rapidly at a very steep angle.

"Flier Vigilant, thank you for accompanying me down to Tiwanaku. I must now return to my fleet, as I am running low on fuel. In my return flight, I will meet one of our fuel replenishment vessels, which is now entering stationary orbit and will rendezvous with my spacecraft at a lower orbit. My regards to you, Maj. Krol, and hope we'll meet in the future."

Vigilant's cameras caught the aircraft's grey silhouette and its peculiar spiral contrails, which Vigilant instantly recognized as the characteristic contrail of an oblique detonation engine (ODE) This was the same type of propulsion engine used by the SR-72 and its ancestor, the mysterious Aurora spy plane from the 1990s.

"Glass Tower, do you see the spiral contrails?" Vigilant asked.

"Yes, we've noticed. Stay with her for as long as you can."

"Wilco, Glass Tower. Please be advised I can pursue for ten minutes before I reach Joker."

The SR-72 ODE engines were capable of Mach 10, but it's Inconel 617 and TaC skin was only good to 3,700°C and Mach 6.5. Additionally, it had a maximum ceiling of just under 37,000 metres since it was purely air-breathing. Even with a full fuel load, the SR-72 could only pursue for a short time.

"Understood, Vigilant. We will vector a KC-74 as close to your future position as we can," Maj. Krol replied.

"Roger and out."

Maj. Krol then turned his attention and concern toward the new unknown spacecraft that had entered Earth's atmosphere. He felt it was still too early to assume the aliens were not a threat.

"TOPO, have we detected this 'replenish vessel?'" Maj. Krol asked, simultaneously shooting an inquisitive glance at Maj.-Gen. Arias standing next to him.

"Yes, sir, it maneuvered into an equatorial orbit, and it's now descending through the atmosphere. Its track matches the intruder's."

"AIDA, can you give me any details on the spacecraft?"

"The reflected radar cross section shows it being larger than Seren *Capac's* spaceplane, but we can't yet discern its shape or whether it is capable of atmospheric flight."

"AIDA, how much larger?"

"Upward of four times larger."

"Maj. Krol, there is increased chatter from the BACCC and *Tiangong4*. Looks like possible deployment by the Chinese of their *Chang Qiang* EKVs from the *Tiangong4* space station," IMCO said, referring to the Beijing Aerospace Command & Control Centre.

"Was wondering when we were going to see an overt action from them."

Maj. Krol then turned toward Maj-Gen Arias.

"Permission to alert the aliens, sir."

In response, he got an affirmative nod.

"Seren *Capac*, if you are still monitoring our frequency, please be advised the Chinese are launching exoatmospheric kill vehicles from their *Tiangong4* space station that can be maneuvered into your planned flight path. You may need to take evasive maneuvers."

Thirty seconds passed, and he looked inquiringly toward IMCO, who shook her head in the negative.

"Sir, there is an increased amount of radio emissions from the two alien spacecrafts. We are unable to track their radar signature, probably active jamming," TOPO stated.

Sure enough, for the last few hours, what had been a well-defined radar signature from the alien spacecraft was now appearing as fog.

"Well, if we can't track them, the Chinese won't be able to either," Maj. Krol said.

All the AOC team could do was wait until they regained radar tracking from their ground-based stations and from the NAU-357. But they could still monitor launches from the *Tiangong4* space station and track any EKVs until they would enter the fog.

"IMCO, any more noise from the Chinese."

"Nothing, sir. We have detected no launches, and communication between *Tiangong4* and BACCC ceased."

After a long thirty-minute wait, the fog disappeared from the radar screens with no trace of the alien spacecraft.

"Well, that's that," Maj. Krol said.

"Okay, team, time to pick up your gear. Maj. Parker, the theatre is now yours. AIDA, what's the weather like outside?"

"Cold and very windy, with wind gusts of fifty to eighty kilometres per hour as La Niña continues to gather strength."

A short time later, Maj. Krol and his team emerged from the AOC building. They were welcomed by the frigid night air that was now the norm in California thanks to the thirty years of continued drought. It turned the once lush state, previously known as America's Salad Bowl, into an arid land with scorching diurnal temperatures and frigid nights. Long gone were the large expanses of vineyards in the nearby Santa Barbara County that forty years earlier had numbered in the hundreds.

As he walked to his small electric vehicle, Maj. Krol kept thinking about the events of the past eight hours. He did not know it yet, but these events were just the start of a journey that would take him and members of his team in a very different direction.

10 UNTOUCHABLE

Tiangong4 Space Station, GEO

"Sir, we are experiencing abnormal terminations and reboots on all systems," Lt. Min Zhao announced as the red emergency lighting switched on and alarms started ringing throughout station.

"LUDUAN, what is the launch status of the *Chang Qiang*?" Colonel Xiuying Pan demanded, referring to the exoatmospheric kill vehicles known in the West as the Long Spear.

"Sir, LUDUAN is offline, as is weapons management. I am pretty sure the EKVs are still in their canisters," Lt. Zhao said, speaking above the noise of the alarms.

"Can't we at least check their status or the reason for the launch failure?"

"Sir, I don't have a single computer screen. ATC is down, WMS is down, primary and secondary radar screens are down, comm systems are down, and we have lost our link to BACCC. Internal communications are down, environmental controls are down, RMC is also down, and the reactor is starting its fail-safe shutdown. We should be okay on emergency power for six hours, but several systems appear to be going through a reboot, so maybe we will be back to normal operation in about fifteen minutes. The reactor will take longer. In the meantime, there is no further information I can relay to you."

"Was it an EMP that disabled all the systems?"

"Don't know, sir. I don't think it was an EMP. I am not seeing complete hardware failures, and in theory, we are hardened to withstand them," Lt. Zhao replied. "I think it was malware from the aliens, but that's just a guess. As a precaution, should I inform everyone to don their pressure suits? It will have to be done by word of mouth."

"Go ahead."

Lt. Zhao then instructed one of the junior officers in the command centre to pass the word to the twelve personnel in the space station.

Momentum kept the wheel-shaped station rotating around its central axis and preserving the 0.5 g artificial gravity. With the ATC offline, the station started to drift and lose altitude. Over time, the drift rate would continue to increase, and within ninety-six hours, it would become a concern unless normal operation was re-established.

Within ten minutes, most systems were restored, including ATC, environmental controls, radar systems and communications, as well as RMC, but the reactor shutdown sequence could not be aborted. This meant the reactor would be offline for a minimum of two hours.

LUDUAN was the last one to come online and reported the status of all the station systems.

"LUDUAN online. Logs show multiple system shutdowns and reboots. The reactor is offline, and the station is on emergency power. WMS is offline, and records show the EKV launch sequence was not completed. Radar shows a large reflected signal belonging to the alien spacecraft. The signal is now beyond GEO and is masking the position of the spacecraft. Range to the signal is greater than forty thousand kilometres. Targeting is not possible. Weapons launch is not possible until the WMS is online.

BACCC is attempting to contact the station on the video link."

As LUDUAN finished reporting, the video link to the BACCC came to life.

"You were offline for twenty minutes. We tried to reach you," the BACCC communications operator said as his senior officer, Brigadier Jun Liang, looked on.

"Sir, we just had a complete and sudden shutdown of all systems, including communication, and lost our link to BACCC," Lt. Zhao replied.

"Please explain," Brigadier Liang ordered.

Col. Pan stepped in.

"All—I repeat—all the station systems experienced abnormal terminations. We lost communications, radar screens, and the ability to track the aliens. Also, weapons management, and with it, the ability to launch the EKVs. In the last ten minutes, all systems except for WMS came back online. The reactor is still offline, but we are hoping to restart it within two hours.

"I gather it wasn't an EMP burst, else all your hardware would be fried, and we wouldn't be having this conversation. Elaborate on what happened," Brigadier Liang replied in his characteristic abrasive style.

Col. Pan immediately signalled Lt. Zhao to respond.

"We were going through the final stages of the launch sequence, at which point the WMS computer screen and then the radar screens went blank. All other systems also went down, and then the station switched to emergency power. It appears as if someone accessed all systems remotely with administration software to order every system to shut down and reboot. Perhaps it was some kind of Trojan virus. We have not had time to check this, and LUDUAN did not report any cyberattacks on our systems when it came back online," Lt. Zhao replied.

"LUDUAN, perform a scan of the system logs for any records of unauthorized external access," Brigadier Liang ordered as Lt. Zhao and Col. Pan looked on.

"Brigadier Liang, we were doing this when your call came in. Please allow us to manage our operations in an orderly fashion," Col. Pan interjected.

"I want to hear what LUDUAN has to say. Let me also remind you of the command hierarchy and that decisions ultimately are made by the BACCC."

"LUDUAN, what are the results of your analysis?" Brigadier Ling demanded.

"The core dump log shows sets of illegal instructions that were entered but could not be interpreted, triggering fatal errors and reboots. Access appears to have been gained at the root administrator level, and then a 'browse and get owned' attack was carried out. I am performing further analysis to determine how the encrypted authorization flag was obtained. It's possible it was through a brute force attack that relied on advanced decryption."

"What sort of illegal instructions are you talking about?"

"The translation of the hexadecimal code returns gibberish," LUDUAN replied.

"Explain," Brigadier Liang asked.

"The illegal instructions were unrecognized, undocumented, and could not be executed. The exception and fault conditions handler should have been able to deal with them, but they could not. The systems should have handled these instructions as NOP instructions. It is also possible the illegal instructions ordered writing a byte of data to memory in an endless loop, which would have overwhelmed the fault condition handler, triggering the computer shutdown."

As LUDUAN spoke, the face of Brigadier Liang showed exasperation as he was out of his depth.

"We are getting nowhere here! LUDUAN, transfer the logs and your analysis down to BACCC. The cyber warfare specialists will take it from here."

He then turned his attention to Col. Pan and spoke.

"Until we understand what happened, we will immediately rotate your crew. I'll send details later today when we can send up a *Jiantou* to deliver the replacement crew and return your crew to Earth," Brigadier Liang stated, referring to the multirole spaceplane used for ferrying personnel to and from the station.

"But Brigadier Liang, this crew has only been at the station for eight of the scheduled twenty weeks of deployment."

"Check the operational protocols, and you will find that in case of major operational failures, the acting crew is relieved of their duties until the event is fully investigated."

11 START THE HUNT FOR THEIR HOME PLANET

The Brinnan Manor, Killiney, Ireland

Carlos de Cevedes's commuter flight from London arrived at the older Terminal 1 of the Dublin airport just before midnight.

As he waited at the conveyer belt to pick up his luggage, Cate Brinnan walked at a lively clip toward him.

He immediately saw her and beamed.

"*Ay, mi bella Irlandesa*, you came to pick me up! You didn't have to, but now that you are here, you sure are a sight for sore eyes."

And the beautiful brunette was indeed a lovely sight in an almost deserted baggage claim area. Carlos promptly gave her a little peck on each cheek.

In response, Cate just looked up at Carlos with her big brown eyes.

"I came to the airport at this late hour to pick you up, so I am sure you can do better than that," she blurted in her strong Irish accent.

Being 5'4" and about a foot shorter than Carlos, she

stood on her toes, placed both her hands on his shoulders, and pulled him down toward her, planting a firm but brief kiss on his lips.

"Now that's a proper greeting for someone who came in the dead of the night to pick you up."

He dropped his carry-on to the floor next to the conveyor belt and tenderly reached for her face with both hands and gave her a very soft kiss.

"*Ay, Cate* . . . I have really, really missed you," Carlos said, unmistakably signalling he had really missed her.

"So have I. I've made plans for the next two days."

Carlos let go.

"That is good, then. I was hoping to spend as much time with you as your schedule allows."

"Well, now that we have that out of the way, we can get going."

She then grabbed his carry-on with one hand, reaching for Carlos's free hand with the other, while he pulled his luggage toward the airport exit.

Carlos was beaming with joy, and he sang a few impromptu verses from the hundred-year-old Jimmy Van Heusen song "Ain't That a Kick in the Head?" as they walked under the parking lot lights toward Cate's car.

Cate recognized the old song sang by countless artists since the days of Dean Martin, the old "Rat Pack" crooner, but she did not know the lyrics, so she simply smiled as Carlos sang to her with his unquestionably charming Catalan accent.

Carlos stopped at the end of the third verse and then turned to look at Cate.

"Eh . . . Cate, I haven't made arrangements to stay anywhere. I thought I would just grab a cab to a hotel in Dublin and then call you in the morning," he said with a mixed look on his face that could be interpreted as either inquiring or dumb.

"Hmm, for such a bright astronomer, you sure are really thick sometimes. You don't really think I came to the airport just to play cabbie and drop you off at a hotel in Dublin, do you? It stands to reason you would stay with me . . . well, at the Brinnan Manor. I want to spend as much time with you as we can manage, okay," she stated, softening her voice while looking at him and squeezing his hand.

"Yes, I would like that very much," Carlos replied with a grin.

They finally reached Cate's car, an all-electric white Range Rover Evoque. Carlos thought the stylish medium-sized SUV was a perfect match for Cate.

"I like your choice of cars," he commented as he deposited the luggage in the trunk.

"Oh . . . thank you, but it's not really my car. There are cars at the house I grab when I need to go somewhere. I am very lucky. While doing my postgraduate at Trinity College, I can stay at home and have access to many things."

The airport was a scant twenty-five kilometres from Killiney if going via a direct route. Cate took the scenic route along the coast, but at 1:00 a.m., the beauty of the scenery was swallowed by the darkness of the night.

She arrived at the closed gates of the imposing three-century-old stately house her great-aunt Elia, the well-known Irish singer, had bought some sixty years ago.

The gates opened, and Cate drove through and parked near the kitchen entrance rather than the main entrance. They quietly entered a large, well-appointed kitchen dimly illuminated by under-the-counter lights.

Cate gently placed Carlos's carry-on on the dark, polished tile floor next to the enormous grey granite countertop island. She took off her coat and hung it on a nearby coatrack, indicating to Carlos to do the same.

"Do you want something to drink?" Cate asked as she went to a cupboard and grabbed a teapot and tea.

She filled the teapot with boiling hot water from a dispensing wand on a large La Cimbali espresso machine more suited for a commercial establishment.

"Hmm . . . yes, thank you. A cup of tea would be nice,

just like in Chile, after one of our get-togethers.”

“Yes, about that. You could never keep up with me, so we’ll need to work on that,” Cate said convincingly.

She then sat down on a counter stool, fixing her gaze on Carlos.

“I was very happy when you called me and told me you wanted to stop here on your way to Barcelona,” Cate said while smiling and looking at the tall and handsome Catalonian with curly black hair who was finally showing interest in her beyond the get-togethers they’d had in Chile.

“Me too,” Carlos said, grinning with that childish grin, to which Cate reacted by tilting her head.

Carlos sat down opposite Cate on another stool and continued.

“I also wanted to brief you and get your opinion on the latest developments. You know our main mandate at the ELT is to discover the presence of an atmosphere and life on planets orbiting distant stars. The Ibecci claim to originate from a planet orbiting Barnard’s Star. We are assuming it would be Barnard b, discovered back in 2018 or 2019. Despite its near proximity to Barnard, it’s never been imaged since it was always believed to be too cold. For this reason, we have concentrated on more promising candidates, including Teegarden b, which we know has a warm surface temperature and an ESI of 0.98, plus TRAPPIST-1e and a bunch of others.”

Cate simply looked, saying nothing, so he continued.

“Anyway, there is now a real urgency to locate the Ibecci planet, and all major observatories have been asked to start the hunt immediately. After my two weeks in Barcelona, I was planning to go see Pepe Astrade in the Canary Islands and meet with him to coordinate the effort from the GTC and the ELT on behalf of ESO and ESA. I would love for you to come with me to the Canary Islands and meet Pepe. We could stay for a day and do some sightseeing and then return to Chile together and work on the hunt. It would be fun, plus if all hell breaks loose, Chile might be a better location to weather the storm. What do you say, huh?"

Cate filled two mugs with tea, taking her time. She took a sip and then replied with that Irish accent that got thicker when she became annoyed.

"First and foremost, I can't leave my postgraduate work at Trinity College at least for one year. I think I could probably weave into my program any work we might do together hunting the Ibecci home planet, but I would need to think about this and talk to my professors, as it is a departure from my current research."

"Okay, maybe I could send a letter or . . ." But Cate raised her hand, signaling Carlos to stop.

"Secondly . . . I really did not want you to come spend two days with me to talk shop. Least of all, this early in the morning. I was actually looking forward to talking for a few minutes and telling you my plans for the next two days," she said in a softer voice while reaching with her hand to touch his arm.

She looked at him and continued with her harsh accent.

"Don't get me wrong, sweetie, I am very flattered, but more importantly, happy you are here. Lord knows, back in Chile, I gave you enough hints. Going to the Canaries sounds fun, as I have never been, plus the work you have described would be fascinating. Having said this, I think . . . how should I put it?" Her voice softened further. "Well, let's say it would be difficult working together, and we might not be very productive," Cate replied with a mischievous smile.

Carlos hadn't consciously thought bringing up the subject of work would hit a sour note. He was mystified because Cate was such a talented and passionate astronomer, and he had assumed the conversation would naturally drift toward their work, given the extraordinary events of the last two months.

He agreed with her last statement that it was probably not the smartest thing to do to work together in an environment where work is usually done at night, in a sparsely occupied observatory, regardless of how professional they would try to be. Carlos responded hesitantly, not really wanting to press the subject.

"These are extraordinary circumstances, and I am sure ESO could work out an arrangement if we really wanted. But you make a good point in that it might be tricky working together," Carlos said with an expression of disappointment.

Cate just smiled with that smile that could light up a room and continued.

"For the next two days, I am going to keep you very busy, as I have a jam-packed schedule."

She then got up from the kitchen stool, took off her blue canvas flats, and carried them in one hand while she shouldered Carlos's carry-on. She motioned him to remove his shoes and follow her quietly up the back stairs.

Carlos stood there for a moment, watching her walk barefoot ahead of him, thinking how absolutely irresistible she was, and then followed her up the stairs lit by brass wall sconces with ornate wainscoting panels.

At the top of the stairs, Cate turned left on a long and wide hallway. The walls were finished with the same ornate wainscoting. Family portraits and paintings with landscape scenery of the Irish mountain valleys hung from the walls at regular intervals.

She brought him to the last room at the end of the hallway, entered, and deposited Carlos' carry-on on the plush emerald carpet next to the large canopy bed. She then turned around and faced Carlos.

"This is your room. You have your own bathroom. Fresh towels are on top of the trunk. My bedroom is the third door down the hall in case you need anything. Everyone gets up early, and breakfast is served between 7:00 and 7:30. I'll be knocking on your door a wee bit after 7:00."

She stood on her toes, just like at the airport, and gave him a short, but intense, kiss.

"Good night, sweetie," she said, smiling playfully. She then turned around and walked away toward her room, softly singing the Hall & Oates song "Kiss on My List" from the '80s.

Carlos just stood there like a deer caught in the headlights. Her sensuous kiss was such an unexpected surprise that he mustered only a simple response.

"*Buenas noches, amor.*"

In reply, Cate briefly turned her head to look back, still smiling mischievously.

Cate was excited and looking forward to spending time with a man she found funny, intelligent, who did not feel threatened by her smarts, and was a perfect gentleman.

She told herself she was going to take it slow and let things develop, as she liked him. Heck, more than liked him, but this time she would be patient. Her past relationships had always turned sour, and she did not want this one to end the same way.

The only thing she was not sure of was whether the decision to turn down Carlos's offer to collaborate on the hunt for the Ibecci home planet was the right one.

Did she not want to be part of such a project? How many astronomers and planetary scientists would jump at the opportunity? There was always time to go back to do her postgraduate work later, but this . . . this was a once-in-a-lifetime opportunity.

She knew the answer would come to her and that Carlos would always leave the door open if she changed her mind.

As Cate had promised, it was truly a frenzied schedule with no time for intimacy other than a stolen kiss here and there, but Carlos took it all in stride, including the drinking and singing, which was slightly reminiscent of their get-togethers back in Chile.

He was happy just being with her and, as a bonus, seemed to get along well with her family.

For Carlos, these two days of free time would feel like a distant memory, as the following months of work in Chile, hunting for the elusive Ibecci home planet, would prove gruelling.

12 ANALYSIS

***Imperator Eberon*, Lagrangian Point L2**

"*Viracoh*, please forgive the intrusion. Fines *Gradon* finished compiling the data gathered by Seren *Capac*. He would like to brief you right away," Lelac *Junct* said.

"Yes, that is very timely. Please ensure Seren *Capac* is in attendance."

"Yes, *Viracoh*, she just arrived and is on her way to CC."

A few *glosils* later, Fines *Gradon* and Seren *Capac* entered the CC operations workroom.

As they were seating themselves around a large circular table, the *Viracoh* emerged through the portal of her office.

"Let's dispense with formalities. We have a lot of ground to cover. Fines, please provide your threat analysis and list suitable locations for our settlements."

"Certainly, *Viracoh*."

Fines *Gradon* raised his two hands and invoked a holographic image projector. A large three-dimensional image of the planet in deep blues, greens and browns appeared above the table, slowly rotating around its correctly tilted axis.

Pertinent information was displayed in the holographic

image, including colour coding of the landmasses with each of the fiefdoms present on the planet and their relative military capabilities.

It was a beautiful image. This was especially true for young Ibecci like Seren *Capac*, who had only lived in space with no concept of what living on a planet was like.

"I'll try to be brief, *Viracoh*. Our assessment indicates their military threat is limited. We can effectively defend against their conventional weapons. It's more a function of their numerical superiority. They can potentially overwhelm our defences, if all the different fiefdoms were to join forces. However, this is unlikely based on the currently ongoing squabbles at the council of their rulers known as the United Nations."

As he said this, a blue dot appeared on the Eastern Seaboard of the North American continent, showing the location of the UN.

The *Viracoh* simply looked at Fines intently, so he continued.

"If you will allow me, I'll provide more detail on this council later and instead concentrate on the military threat."

"Agreed."

"Their conventional weapons pose a greater threat on land and air up to an altitude of fifteen thousand *passu*, but their offensive capabilities in space, GEO, and at the edge of space are minimal. They have a limited number of high-altitude air-breathing fliers, such as the one that shadowed Seren *Capac*, but their performance is significantly inferior to ours."

Information appeared in the holographic image, including the names of the high-altitude fliers and the fiefdoms that possessed them. He manipulated the holographic image of the planet and continued with the briefing.

"We won't encounter any difficulty entering their atmosphere. There may be minimal opposition from the fiefdom that calls itself China. They have a small orbital station in GEO equipped with rudimentary missiles but no energy weapons. We can counter this threat as already demonstrated."

"Seren *Capac*, do you concur?"

"Yes, *Viracoh*."

"Good."

"The only real threat we might face is from fission/fusion weapons at the disposal of several fiefdoms."

As he said this, the *Viracoh* raised her nonexistent eyebrows, but said nothing, so Fines *Gradon* continued.

"These weapons can be delivered mostly with missiles, and three or four fiefdoms have long-range missiles. We have been able to identify some of their ground-based launch sites, but these fiefdoms also possess underwater crafts patrolling their oceans as well as mobile launchers. All these missiles can reach the lower atmosphere. The danger would be from close detonations, but the *liburnia* and the *Eberon* are reasonably hardened, and the combat fliers hardened to a lesser degree. The probability of the rulers of *Tiwan3* using these weapons is below 40 percent because their infrastructure is not hardened, especially in the case of high-altitude detonations. Once we have set up our settlements, we will have to monitor potential launches against us and react accordingly."

"Noted. What stage of our landing operations would have the most risk?" the *Viracoh* asked in a calm voice despite what she had just heard.

"Below seven thousand *passu* where their combat fliers can operate with ease. We can counter their manned and unmanned threats, including the packs of combat drones, but these are less sophisticated than *Grisamir* drones."

The *Viracoh* frowned but did not interrupt.

As if reading the *Viracoh's* mind, Fines *Gradon* continued with a statement of reassurance.

"Our planning and the location of our settlements will reduce the risk by over 70 percent. My recommendation for our settlements would be in the Southern Hemisphere. I can continue and focus on the location of settlements to mitigate the threat unless you have questions."

"Seren *Capac*, as the squadron leader, you will coordinate a significant portion of the landing operations. I want to hear your opinion before we move on."

"Yes, *Viracoh*. During the completion of my two orbits, we only detected emissions tracking from three fiefdoms. These fiefdoms are in the Northern Hemisphere, where emissions are the heaviest, yet I would categorize the threat environment as light. When I descended below seven thousand *passu*, the emissions in the Southern Hemisphere, near Tiwanaku, were zero. The only exception was the tracking from the fiefdom that calls itself the North American Union. They sent a surveillance probe with no offensive weapons to shadow us. Even the flier they sent to rendezvous with us could not match our flight profile."

"What was your interaction with them like?"

"I established communications with them when I realized their flier was on an intercept course. At that point, I reiterated we posed no threat and asked them to join my descent to Tiwanaku. They responded quickly in contrast to the lack of response from *Tiwan3*'s diplomats. They understood our first incursion onto their planet was a recon mission, and I think your idea to use arcane technology rather than simply enter their airspace with one of the *liburnium* helped."

"Your first contact sounds encouraging. In short order, we will see how they react to us entering their planet. Fines, please continue."

"There is less landmass in the Southern Hemisphere, and what is inhabited is technologically less advanced relative to the fiefdoms and cities in the Northern Hemisphere. The further south we locate our settlements, the more protected we would be. Two viable locations with few *Tiwan3* inhabitants are an archipelago of islands known as the Kerguelen Islands located here and another smaller set of islands farther west, called South Georgia Islands."

Fines *Gradon* touched the tiny speck of islands shown in the holographic image, which changed to a green colour, and a large square text box appeared next to it with pertinent data.

"What about Tiwanaku?"

"Unfortunately, it is close to populated areas. There is a city with a population of just under one million inhabitants fifty *mille passu* away. It is also the principal city of the fiefdom of Bolivia."

"What about other areas nearby?"

"About six hundred *mille passu* south of Tiwanaku, there is a desolate desert known as the Atacama Desert. This desert runs south along the mountain range of the South American continent for about seven hundred fifty *mille passu,* at an average altitude of twenty-three hundred *passu.* It is very desolate and hyper-dry. It's one of the driest places on the planet, although there are salt lakes in some areas, but these would be the only sources of water. Further south and toward the bottom of this continent, and approximately sixteen hundred *mille passu* from Tiwanaku, the land is scarcely populated on either side of two fiefdoms known as Chile and Argentina."

Fines highlighted the areas mentioned, which glowed green near the southern tip of South America, and continued.

"There are small freshwater lakes in the mountains similar to Lake Titicaca. From researching the humans' open data network, they appear to be almost pristine. The images taken by Seren *Capac* show a welcoming landscape. While this land is scarcely populated, we would not be isolated, as there are access roads and the furthest we could be isolated from humans would be twenty to thirty *mille passu.* We have marked two small lakes in the fiefdom of Chile. The humans' open data network states it is a protected sanctuary that cannot be inhabited. We think there would be a concerted effort to evict us from this area. For the time being, I would advise against choosing this area as our first site. In contrast, the Kerguelen Islands and South Georgia Islands are in remote locations close to the southern pole."

The *Viracoh* fixed her gaze on the holographic image of the planet.

"Which of these two offers the most protection?"

"Overall, the Kerguelen Islands would be the better choice because they are significantly more remote. The islands have a small population of only one hundred inhabitants at a research station under the jurisdiction of a small northern fiefdom called France."

As Fines *Gradon* said this, the area where France was located in the Northern Hemisphere glowed in blue.

The *Viracoh* said nothing.

"It's a barren, cool, and wind-swept location. And its proximity to the southern pole means long diurnal hours during the summer months and short in the winter due to the obliquity of the planet's ecliptic."

"Surely, the vista toward the great ocean would be a welcome change compared to the last nineteen *anni* living in space. Not quite the Elifin shores of *Eder*, but we can make it our home," the *Viracoh* replied, visibly excited. She continued, "What about setting up our settlement close to the shoreline?"

"Absolutely, *Viracoh*. There is an inviting site at a place called Plage de la Possession. This location would be relatively safe for us."

"What about the fiefdom that has jurisdiction over the islands?"

"They seem to be one of the more enlightened fiefdoms. They are also part of a group of seven fiefdoms aptly called The Group of Seven. From information gathered, these seven fiefdoms have somewhat benign and less repressive governments that give more freedom and better living conditions to their population relative to the other 175 fiefdoms present on the planet. Hardship is still present within portions of the population because *Tiwan3* governments operate with a currency-based bartering and trade system that does not benefit all. One important aspect of the government of France is that it emphasizes the concepts of liberty, equality, and fraternity as intrinsic to their governing ideology. I would recommend that we exploit their concept of fraternity and its implied inclusion as a justification for the establishment of our settlements in the Kerguelen Islands."

"What about their military? Does it represent a threat to us?"

"Our current information suggests their military could not mount offensive operations against us quickly. They could send lightly equipped but well-trained ground troops with transport fliers that could arrive in three to four planet cycles. Given more time, they could send transport watercrafts with heavier military equipment. France appears to be an ally of the NAU fiefdom, and it can project its military power using watercraft battle groups similar to the battle groups of the old Imperium Space Fleet. There is one NAU battle group currently operating some five thousand *mille passu* away. We think it could arrive on the shores of the Kerguelen Islands in ten to twelve planet cycles."

Fines *Gradon* touched an area of the ocean known as the Indian Ocean and a dot appeared to show the NAU battle group just mentioned.

"We can safely assume this battle group will be dispatched regardless to keep a close eye on us and because they would want to continue gathering intelligence. They will no doubt have defence patrol operations protecting their battle group, and we will see incursions from their fliers closer to our settlement."

"Your words are not very reassuring, Fines. A few minutes ago, you stated we would be safe in the Southern Hemisphere and beyond the reach of the northern fiefdoms, but now you seem to contradict yourself and state that military incursions and threats are a possibility."

"Forgive me, *Viracoh*, but I am simply stating potential

outcomes. The threat will always exist, but in the Southern Hemisphere, it would be significantly diminished. Any fiefdom wanting to mount operations closer to the settlement would have to do it from watercrafts and very far from their home base, so it would be logistically more challenging. In addition, the south Indian Ocean is a rough sea, and flight operations would not be easy. I believe that if we don't show aggression and provoke the French and NAU, they will act in a similar manner and simply observe us. According to the psychologists, the probability of this behaviour is greater than 65 percent."

"I assume the NAU has Seren *Capac* in their database. They know you, so you can communicate with them when setting up our operations," the *Viracoh* asserted.

"Yes, *Viracoh*, I can do this as you request and reiterate that we will not show hostility toward the inhabitants," Seren *Capac* answered.

"You will do more than this. You will also meet with them if it proves in our best interests."

"But, *Viracoh*, I'm not an *Iovian*. I only have the rank of *Capac*," said a confused Seren *Capac*.

"You are technically correct. But you know the few high-ranking *Iovians* are either performing other duties or have dissenting views on how to establish relations with the inhabitants of *Tiwan3*."

"Yes, *Viracoh*," Seren *Capac* said simply.

"Clearly, we will have to initiate diplomatic communications with the *Tiwan3* inhabitants since our message is still unanswered, and for the time being, you will take on this duty. I will prepare a second message with our landing plans and further inform them that Seren *Capac* will be in our military contingent and available to meet with her counterpart in order to establish diplomatic communications."

"As you wish, *Viracoh*," Seren *Capac* replied with a tone in her voice that conveyed doubt.

"It's settled then, and Seren *Capac* . . . don't forget you are the squadron leader and more than capable of performing the duty I have entrusted to you," the *Viracoh* said as she smiled warmly to the young female flier.

"I will not fail you, *Viracoh*."

"You won't. Let's move on. What about other locations for setting up a second and possibly a third settlement?"

"There are two other locations that meet some of our criteria, *Viracoh*. These are the centre of the continent of Australia and a hyper-dry dessert called Tanezrouft on the continent of Africa. But in the interest of expediency, I would suggest we discuss these at a second meeting. I think it is critical to start landing operations at least at one site. It is more pressing that I brief you on their council of rulers."

"You make a good point. We need to go planet-side soonest and give priority to the civilian population that needs it most. I endorse the Kerguelen Islands. Now tell me about this council."

"Earlier, I indicated there were ongoing squabbles at the council of their rulers known as the United Nations. This council functions as a gathering of 193 fiefdoms. Their purpose is to discuss far-reaching issues affecting large portions of the inhabitants or the planet as a whole. In some ways, this council functions as what you would expect from a unified planet government. Through consensus voting, the council then implements decisions and actions."

Fines *Gradon* paused and then continued.

"There is also a smaller fifteen-member council that deals with peace and security. Our arrival has been vigorously debated at this Security Council. They are unable to reach a consensus to respond. First and foremost, they fear us regardless of what you stated in your welcome message. Their fear is reinforced by their belief we destroyed their probe sent to scan the fleet. Right now, only one-third of the members have agreed to establish communications. France and the NAU are among this group."

"This was expected, no?"

"Yes, *Viracoh*. This behaviour was predicted. But there is a mystifying second reason. It appears they are also squabbling in terms of who would lead the delegation of diplomats when they eventually agree to communicate."

"That's irrational."

"Yes, *Viracoh*."

The *Viracoh* simply looked at him and the others around her. Marel *Viracoh* was known for her calm demeanour. At that moment, her expression of anger was in apparent contradiction to her normal, easygoing manner. Fines *Gradon* and Seren *Capac* did not like what they saw.

"Thank you for the briefing, Fines. Your priority is to start preparations for the relocation of the first group of *crelon(e)* to the planet. I endorse the location that you selected."

"Understood, *Viracoh*."

"I'll prepare a second message as a courtesy to the rulers of *Tiwan3* since we are entering their home world uninvited, but I'll be unequivocal in our intention to establish settlements. This meeting is adjourned." Marel *Viracoh* spoke with a visibly controlled rage.

She got up and went to her office to compose a tersely worded message.

13 SECOND MESSAGE AND LANDING OPERATIONS

Imperator Eberon, Lagrangian Point L2

Marel _Viracoh_ could not believe what she had just heard. She became enraged at the fact the _Tiwan3_ council of rulers was unwilling to allow safe passage simply on the hubris of their diplomats while her _crelon(e)_ were wasting away after nineteen _anni_ in space.

She understood the _Tiwan_ race was young with no previous knowledge of other intelligent life in the universe. She also understood her arrival to the _Tiwan_ system created panic. But diplomats should have understood the underlining urgency of her plea.

She knew her second message needed to strike a balance, showing an unyielding stance while still being diplomatic, if that was at all possible.

Fifteen _jore_ (twelve hours) later, the _Imperator Eberon_ transmitted the message. This time, the _Viracoh_ made it clear she wanted the message broadcast continuously until the start of landing operations.

"Rulers of Earth, I am Viceroy Marel, the leader of the

Ibecci race. By now you know we made our first incursion on your planet to gather intelligence and attempt to communicate with our kinfolk in Tiwanaku.

"We also gathered information from your communications network and sadly learned you have refused to respond to our pleas simply because you are debating this in your United Nations.

"You also seem to think we are responsible for the failure of your reconnaissance probe. It failed on its own. We will salvage and insert it into GEO for you to retrieve it.

"We have been living in the confines of space for fifty of your planet's years. Space is a harsh environment even in spaceships shielded from radiation and equipped with an artificial gravity. Space has had negative long-term effects on the general health of our own people, and so we came to your solar system searching for a home. I said as much in my first message.

"We have shown civility and consideration upon arrival to your solar system. We could have entered orbit around your planet and your natural satellite. Instead, we showed respect and stayed at a respectful distance and asked for your help as another sentient species, thinking you would be an enlightened civilization that understood our plight.

"You have proven otherwise. You do not seem to care for your own kind, other living creatures on your planet, or the health of your planet, and you have reflected this consistent behaviour toward us.

"Be that as it may, we need a place to live and have selected sites where we will live without interfering with your civilization, as these places are desolate or sparsely populated. We will leave you alone to destroy your own planet and won't interfere.

"Hopefully after one hundred of your years, perhaps sooner, we will leave for Planet Mars. To show our honourable intentions, we will inform you of the time when we will start our landing operations.

"We have chosen the Kerguelen Islands as our first

settlement, as they are sparsely populated. Our settlement will be away from your small settlement at Port-aux-Français. It will comprise twenty-five thousand civilian inhabitants in a compact, self-sustaining arcology that we will erect with no impact on your environment and protect with a military contingent.

"If you take up arms against us, you will attack females and their young. We will defend ourselves. Be forewarned not to underestimate our capabilities.

"To the fiefdom of France, I offer Seren *Capac* as my designate ambassador if you wish to communicate with us. We will consider you our sisters and brothers, under your philosophy of *liberté, égalité, fraternité*. We hope you will do the same.

"To the fiefdom of China, I will confirm that we temporarily disabled your computers aboard your small space station. We could have done more damage, but this would have endangered the life of your personnel. I have already stated that we come in peace and do not wish to quarrel with anyone.

"You have far more to gain through peaceful coexistence, but we will protect ourselves from aggression, and you will find us to be a formidable adversary."

Marel *Viracoh* reflected on her harsh message. Friendly relations were not an option anymore, but this was no time for second-guessing.

Afterward, she ordered COps to commence landing operations, and ordered a third message broadcast with details of the convoy of spaceships going planet-side.

Two planet cycles later, the convoy left the fleet.

The IIC *Vorian* and her complement of five combat spacecraft escorted a transport with a cohort of two hundred paratroopers plus two supply and service vessels.

The *Vorian*, one of five escorts built to protect the fleet in their journey to the *Tiwan* system, was a two hundred–*passu* fast *liburnium* designed as a pocket-dreadnought with more firepower than the *Imperator Eberon* dreadnought.

The *Vorian* entered *Tiwan3* at a high polar orbit ahead of the convoy of spaceships, enabled its electronic jamming, and energized its quad-redundant defensive weapons.

"Atmospheric entry in twenty *punctum*. GFGs enabled," the *Vorian*'s sentient entity (SE) announced throughout the ship.

With the graviphoton generators enabled, the shoebox-like spaceships dove through the atmosphere in a controlled descent.

"SE, identify threats," Seldik *Centor*, the commander of the *Vorian*, ordered, as he stood on the command deck above the bridge.

"Tracking from multiple locations. One small spacecraft in pursuit. Offensive capabilities unknown," the SE replied.

"*Gubernum*, maximum rate of descent. I want to touch down after one orbit."

Seldik *Centor* sat in the command chair and secured himself with a four-point restraint.

"*Aien, Centor*," the *gubernum* replied. But the SE countermanded.

"The requested rate of descent will impose g-forces beyond tolerances."

"Noted. SE, take *guberna* and bring us down quickly."

"Seldik *Centor*, confirm transfer of *guberna* control to the SE."

Seldik Centor clutched the left armrest of his command chair and felt a pinprick in his palm. It was a security measure developed long ago during the Grisamir Wars.

"I relinquish *guberna* control to the SE."

"Voice and biological identity verified. *Guberna* is now under SE control."

The four spaceships and their five escorts seesawed through the atmosphere at a dizzying rate of descent that was tolerable to the crew.

14 TRACKING THEIR ENTRY

BACCC, Beijing

"Sir, the alien spaceships are at an altitude of twenty thousand kilometres. They are coming in hot. Will touch down in the Kerguelen Islands after one and a half orbits."

"Where the hell is the *Jiantou?*" Brigadier Jun Liang asked in his usual abrasive tone.

"Trying to catch up, sir," the radar operator replied even though the information was visible in the main holographic sphere in the Beijing Aerospace Command and Control Centre (BACCC) theatre.

"No shit," Brigadier Liang remarked disdainfully.

The hypersonic spaceplane, known as *Arrowhead* in the West, was desperately pursuing while performing a series of hypersonic *S* maneuvers to bring itself in a parallel orbit and behind the alien spaceships. But the *Jiantou* was still too far east, and the steep entry profile of the alien spaceships was making it too difficult.

"The Yaogan satellites should be able to acquire the alien spaceships when in range, sir," the radar operator volunteered.

"Well then, do you have the feed from Base 26?"

Brigadier Liang snapped back, referring to the Xi'an satellite control centre responsible for operating the Chinese Yaogan reconnaissance satellites.

"No, sir."

"Not even on the optical?"

"Negative on the optical, sir.

As the four alien spaceships and their escorts dropped below the Kármán line and started their entry into the atmosphere, the Chinese ground-based phased-array radars of the Kashi-Jiamusi-Sanya space-monitoring network tracked their entry. But the radars only showed a fog with a diameter of five kilometres.

A sour Brigadier Liang stared at the computer-generated orbital track of the alien spaceships. The inability of the ground-based radars to burn through exasperated him. To his credit, he had expected this outcome and earlier had requested permission to use nuclear missiles to stop them. But the PLA's Central Military Commission (CMC) refused, citing the potential damage to electronic and communications in populated areas that would have been created by a high-altitude EMP.

The waiting went on for a while. The main holographic sphere showed the fog as a semitransparent red oval blob now above India and moving in a southerly course at a scorching, steep descent.

As the blob descended toward the surface of the planet, it looked like a science fiction depiction of an alien invasion. The image did not escape the attention of the senior military personnel watching the proceedings, reinforcing their views the aliens represented a potential threat to Earth.

"Damn, we can't get a decent break! See if you can get the Divine Eagles to record their final approach," Brigadier Liang ordered.

The Divine Eagle, a high altitude long endurance (HALE) UAV, was a twin-boom, high aspect ratio, unmanned reconnaissance aircraft. It performed the role of airborne early warning and control (AEW&C), flying ahead of Chinese carrier battle groups.

Two Divine Eagles were now flying south over the Java Strait at their maximum altitude of twenty-two thousand metres.

The BACCC operators seamlessly networked the Divine Eagles' SAR and electro-optical sensors to the radar signal. The Divine Eagles' sensors and cameras stayed pointed toward the alien spaceships despite their scorching entry, recording short, useless footage.

Brigadier Liang then turned toward Admiral Shen Hsu, the commander of the South Sea Fleet, standing next to him.

"Admiral Hsu, it's now up to the PLA's navy."

Admiral Hsu just stared at the holographic sphere.

"Remember, admiral, you and the *Liu Huaqing* task force are the tip of the spear that will expel the aliens. The CMC wants to eliminate the threat they pose to Earth's critically stretched resources and China's plan to colonize the solar system."

Admiral Hsu made a snappy nod, saluted, and left for his headquarters in Zhanjiang, where his carrier task force was waiting to sail as ordered.

15 FIRST SETTLEMENT

Vallée des Sables, Kerguelen Islands, Near Antartica

The Ibecci spaceships arrived at Peninsula Rallier du Baty at the southwestern tip of the Kerguelen Islands. It was the furthest point from the small French research outpost of Port-au Français, seventy-five *mille passu* away.

The spaceships touched down on Vallée des Sables, nestled between Peak Les Deux Frères on the eastern side, and L'Aiguille Noire on the western side. It was a desolate, rocky, and barren valley. A few clumps of moss and hardy, indigenous cabbage could be seen sticking out from the ground, slowly being covered by gently falling snow as the Southern Hemisphere winter got underway.

The Ibecci wasted no time. One by one, bipedal and multi-legged construction bots in different shapes and sizes emerged from the long ramp of a featureless, shoebox-shaped spaceship that sat on the ground like an oversized shipping container. Its dull, copper-brown surface partially blended in with the rocky landscape.

Some bots carried oddly shaped construction equipment and piled it in neat stacks, while other bots moved away from the spaceship to survey and mark locations for the future settlement.

The settlement was to be comprised of multiple buildings needing to accommodate some twenty-five thousand Ibecci *crelon(e)* expected to arrive within one hundred planet cycles.

Three large high-rise apartment blocks, just like those on Earth, were to form the principal housing. A gargantuan two thousand–*passu* central courtyard and garden was to sit at the centre with the apartment blocks positioned symmetrically around it like three points of an equilateral triangle.

The courtyard was to be a gathering place evocative of Renaissance piazzas, something sorely needed by the Ibecci, after having lived for nineteen *anni* in the confines of the spaceships. Its gardens would double as the enclave's food basket to feed the large population via vertical aeroponics gardens with production yields two hundred times higher than traditional farming.

From far, the tall, all-glass courtyard would bear similarities to nineteenth-century Earth conservatories, similar to Vienna's Palm House or London's famed Crystal Palace, but much, much larger. Its single-piece monolithic glass dome made of translucent *luce*, an ultralight silica porous material, similar to *Tiwan3* aerogel, would give it an awestricken, alien quality.

Half of the buildings were to be completed within forty planet cycles for an initial group of ten thousand *crelon(e)*. This was possible because of the automated construction process, similar to *Tiwan3*'s building printing processes, but significantly more advanced and akin to growing a building. The result was buildings that looked organic, with complex structures and shapes reminiscent of eighteenth- and nineteenth-century scrollwork and Mandelbrot shapes.

Although built in record time, the buildings were to be self-sufficient, with minimal need for heating, despite the inclement location.

After one scant planet cycle, mammoth robotic gantries

were already in place to commence erection of foundations and thick stone walls. Nearby rock was pulverized, sintered, and precisely dispensed in layers that would become the walls of the buildings.

As the construction got underway, it was impossible to deny the site had a vaguely familiar look to *Tiwan3*'s ancient ruins constructed with massive stones like the monolithic walls at Ollantaytambo and Sacsayhuaman in Peru, where the smooth stone walls looked extruded using unknown ancient technology.

Construction went on around the clock under the watchful eye of Ibecci paratroopers, the *Vorian* and its five spacecrafts flying continuous defence patrols.

16 SQUABBLES

The United Nations, New York

"Hi, Laura, how may I help you?" Maj.-Gen. Arias said as the face of Laura Bonte appeared on the video link.

"Do you have a few minutes to discuss the last message from Viceroy Marel?"

"I knew you were going to call right after we received the second message from the aliens, just to gloat."

"It's a moot point, now."

"Okay, fair enough. What can I do for you, then?"

"Right now, it's even more important to communicate with them and prove Viceroy Marel wrong. To do this, I need to disclose all the information you have to the Security Council. Those members don't much care or believe what the aliens may have to say, but our intelligence briefings will."

"Their last message actually has ratcheted things up and increased tensions, Laura. We are now dealing with a more complex issue beyond peaceful negotiations after the Chinese attempt to engage the aliens from their space station."

"Why?"

"China always acts in its own interests. You know as well as I do that for the last thirty years, the Chinese have been doing what they want without regard to international law. Their expanded two hundred–mile territorial claims in the South China Sea and their annexation of the Spratly and Paracel Islands are just two examples."

"I know all this, Maria. I still don't understand how this is related."

"At this moment, there are two carrier battle groups racing to the Kerguelen Islands. One is ours, and the other is Chinese from their South Sea Fleet, so the risk of international incidents can become very real. To make things even more complicated, French Special Forces are on their way and scheduled to make landfall sometime tomorrow. They are being followed by the French Rapid Reaction Force departing from Brest aboard one of their amphibious assault ships. We may now have to face the Chinese and the aliens."

"That does not surprise me, but surely our side will be less hostile toward the aliens."

"Is not just the Chinese who have doubts about the aliens, Laura. We do too. Think for a moment; how much do we really know about them? We don't even know what they look like."

"And whose fault is that, Maria? Go back and listen to the second message from Viceroy Marel. She knows about the squabbling that is going on at the Security Council."

"Laura, there are too many examples throughout history of deceit perpetuated by invaders, starting with the Greek deceit at Troy with the infamous Trojan horse. Or, if you prefer a more recent historical event, Stalin's deceit of the West during the Second World War that led to the USSR's eventual oppression and occupation of half of Germany, Eastern Europe, and the Baltic States that lasted fifty years. And let's not forget Russia's brutal invasion of Ukraine forty years ago and their claim that the massing of troops at Ukraine's border that had gone for months and months was just a military exercise. What if the aliens are just playing a deception game, and they take over as soon as they have a foothold?"

"A little theatrical with the history lesson, aren't we? But to clarify, I have never said we would open our door and lay down the welcome mat. I simply said we should start communicating with them, ask the tough questions, and see how far we get. The more we talk to them, the more intel we would get, which is better than the vacuum we find ourselves in at present."

"We do really want to communicate with the aliens in order to gather intelligence and understand them better. And if things go well, even establish relations. Who knows, maybe get some technology transfer. If they turn out not to be who they say they are, at least we will be somewhat prepared. It's not common knowledge, but when the small alien spacecraft performed its reconnaissance mission, its pilot communicated with us while we shadowed her. So, we have unofficially started communicating with them."

"Do you realize that your aim to communicate and establish relations with them is partisan? The NAU cannot unilaterally establish relations with the aliens. It's up to the United Nations," an annoyed Undersecretary Bonte replied.

"Laura, the Ibecci pilot contacted us first. Let me also emphasize that in the military, we don't make decisions by committee. We often need to make quick decisions as the situation may warrant. I can send you the transcript of the event. This transcript would be for your eyes only."

"Thank you. It would be helpful to see the transcript, but you still haven't answered my original question."

"That decision is still not up to me, Laura. I can put some pressure on my superiors and that's about it."

"I truly fail to understand the reason for keeping the information on the failure of the probe classified. It's old news. We now have more important events unfolding. How long do you think it will take news agencies to get to the Kerguelen Islands? In the meantime, we keep waffling and refuse to talk to the aliens. This would actually be the best time."

"You still seem to be ignoring the latest risks. China is vehemently opposed to establishing relations with the aliens, and, as I said earlier, they are sending a battle group to the Kerguelens. They already tried attacking the aliens once, and the likelihood of another confrontation is a forgone conclusion. Right now, things are fluid. For the moment, we don't want to appear to be taking sides. Wide distribution of the transcript of the probe's failure might be interpreted by the Chinese as the NAU providing intelligence to the Security Council in order to facilitate establishing relations with the aliens."

"For God's sake, Maria, when has the NAU, or the former United States for that matter, cared about what other members may think or withheld information when dealing with the UN on Seurity Council issues?" blurted an exasperated Undersecretary Bonte.

"We are dealing with the Chinese, Laura, who historically have never complied with a UN resolution if it was not convenient or suited their own interests. In the end, someone will be in the firing line. Who do you think that would be now that we and the Chinese are rushing toward the Kerguelens?"

Undersecretary Bonte looked at Maj.-Gen. Arias and said nothing for an uncomfortably long period.

"You know . . . before the Ibecci arrival, I spent my time at the Security Council dealing with issues on climate change, water rights, pollution, deforestation. Basically, the irresponsible human activities ruining our planet and causing countless regional conflicts. We have been trying to get a handle on these issues for the last fifty years in order to avoid a collapse of the ecosystem. The reality is all these meetings have always been sideshows, and nothing ever gets accomplished, just like the climate change conferences to curb carbon dioxide emissions that have been ongoing for just as long. Global temperatures have continued rising, together with the related side effects that will eventually lead to humanity's demise, perhaps fifty or a hundred years from now, but as a species, we are definitely on our way out. In the end, we are just like the inhabitants of Easter Island, fully aware there are only a few trees left yet cutting the last tree and not caring. Now it seems we are doing it again. I am running this sideshow, and all we need to do is to agree to talk to one entity sent to us by Divine intervention to help save us from ourselves. But we just don't want to agree to move forward. Oh, they won't be able to help with things like the will of governments, but maybe they have magic solutions that will absorb the carbon dioxide in the atmosphere, you know? Like a benign Grey Goo that can also magically transform into trees. But we just don't know because we have yet to talk to them."

"I do truly understand where you're coming from, Laura."

"Do you really? Look at you and me and the members of the Security Council and how we live compared to the rest of the population on this planet. Are those of us who are in charge too comfortable to care? There are so many things in the world off-kilter, but maybe the Ibecci can help fix some of them. They offered their knowhow in exchange for a place to live. It's that simple. And we know they can undertake mega-engineering projects such as the terraforming of Mars, so for them, restoring our planet might be child's play."

"You make a compelling argument, but for the moment my hands are tied."

"What did Jared Diamond say was one of the symptoms of collapsing societies in his forty-year-old book *Collapse*? Oh yeah, it was a 'failure of group decision-making, where societies end up destroying themselves through the sheer act of making disastrous decisions coupled with idleness in the face of disaster.' That neatly sums up where we are right now."

"Laura, I am asking you to trust me and have faith things

will work out," Maj.-Gen. Arias replied.

"How can I when all I have witnessed throughout my career are failures. Right now, inaction is the biggest mistake, and I hate to sound alarmist, but the collapse of human civilization is just around the corner. What worries me even more than our present inability to take any decisive action is the thought the door might eventually close and the Ibecci offer to help will disappear."

"Laura, I will make things right. I will send the team that first talked to Seren *Capac* to the Kerguelen Islands in the hope we can start a dialogue with her, and then I'll bring you in. Please believe me. I want this as much as you do."

It was a tone of conviction that encouraged Undersecretary Bonte. Even though Maj.-Gen. Arias had good intentions, Undersecretary Bonte knew she had no real power to change things.

17 CONTEST FOR RESOURCES

***Soul-T* Mining Spaceship, Asteroid Belt**

The *Soul-T* had been on the asteroid for three months out of its planned six. Jan extracted a full load of platinum ore in record time and started preparations for the flyback.

She went outside in the robotic quadruped to collect the mining equipment. It was something Jan could have done from the spaceship, but she wanted to go outside one last time before the long flight back. She stepped out of the service garage onto the pitch-dark surface, turned-on the quadruped's powerful flood lights, and walked down the lane demarcated by ground lights to the open pit about a hundred metres away.

The mining equipment was scattered like toys in a sandbox. Jan walked around the circumference of the pit and illuminated the equipment.

She stopped next to a ten-ton tracked ore hauler. Through the head-up-display, she commanded it and three others to return to the ship and power down. She then turned her attention to the walking excavators and rock driller located further down the shallow pit. Jan illuminated them from the edge and commanded them to retract their attachments and climb up the pit. The machines complied by moving down the lit lane, zombie-like, and entered the service garage to park themselves.

Her job now complete, Jan looked through the reinforced carbon nanotube canopy at the black vault of space. Jupiter and Mars were visible, together with billions of twinkling stars. She never grew tired of the breathtaking view that, for an astrophysicist like herself, revealed the incomprehensible vastness of the universe with its two trillion galaxies each containing billions of stars. Time seemed to slow down as she gazed in fascination, but a slight shaking of the ground disturbed her zen moment.

"What the . . ."

She instinctively looked at the three axes of motion in her head display, thinking she had started floating away from the asteroid, but the instruments confirmed she was on the surface and motionless. "Ella, has the asteroid attitude changed? I felt the ground shake."

"Hold on, lemme see. Yep, tiny Delta-V, as if we got a nudge. Course appears altered. Too early to give you a new bearing."

"Ella, do any of the sensors show something that could explain it?"

"Nothing. No objects nearby that could affect our gravity, and we're still too far away from Mars to be affected."

"Okay, Ella . . ." Jan replied with hesitance in her voice. "I'm done here. I'm coming in."

"Copy that."

Jan walked back to the *Soul-T* as fast as she could while trying to remain calm. She thought that maybe an Ibecci tugboat got behind the asteroid. But that made little sense, as the asteroids they had been rounding up were V-type asteroids. Just balls of ammonia and ice to rebuild the planet's atmosphere.

Hers was an M-type metal-rich asteroid that couldn't be used to terraform the planet.

And it was her asteroid! She had found it and claimed it. Jan wasn't about to give it up. She had plans, big plans, to buy a large chunk of Detroit's inner city where she grew up and rehabilitate it. Build schools and parks and make it safe and clean where those she knew could live free of crime, poverty, and misery. And her asteroid held riches beyond belief. She stood to make billions, as multiple ships could mine the asteroid for five years or more. This trip alone would yield anywhere from three to five tons of platinum, with a market value of some $700 million, and 7 percent would be hers. And that was only the start!

Jan arrived at the service garage, closed the airlock, and dismounted from the quadruped. She then methodically checked all the mining equipment was secured at their berths and opened the airlock to the command module.

"Ella, send Frankie up to recon the asteroid. I want to see if an Ibecci ship got behind us and is trying to highjack our asteroid," Jan said, referring to a surveying drone she had christened Frankenstein because of its utilitarian ugliness.

"Okay, Jan, commanding Frankie to recon the asteroid."

The fridge-sized drone, designed to operate in the harsh environment of space, climbed slowly from its pad next to the command module using its LOX/LH maneuvering thrusters. It reached a height of thirty metres, made a complete rotation to orient itself, turned on its flood lights and high-definition cameras, and flew toward the far side of the asteroid.

"Is Frankie up yet?" Jan asked as she floated through the command module airlock.

"Just reaching the far side."

"Anything?"

"Yep, the featureless spaceship we saw weeks earlier is kissing the asteroid, and our Delta-V is changing. The tugboat is definitely pushing us."

Jan reached the command module and looked at the video feed from Frankie.

"Argh! Ella, open communications! All channels!" Jan snapped, staring at the monitor while clutching a grab-hold.

"Done."

"Alien spaceship. This is the Outer-World Mining spaceship *Soul-T.* We are currently on the surface of the asteroid. Please respond."

Jan waited. She knew they would understand her, as the Ibecci had proven they could communicate in multiple languages.

She tried again.

"Alien spaceship, my drone is less than a kilometre from you. You must surely have it on your radar. My spaceship is at the other end of the asteroid. I repeat, my mining spaceship is at the other end of the asteroid. This is my asteroid. I claimed it first before you arrived in our solar system. We were here when your flotilla flew past Mars some ninety days ago. I have already been mining it, so take your paws off it!"

After a brief delay, a response came.

"*Tiwan* spaceship. We do not have paws. We possess dextrous hands with opposable thumbs. We were not aware of your presence."

"You are now. And like I said, I claimed it first and have been mining it. Go find another asteroid. With your advanced technology, you can find an equally rich platinum asteroid deeper in the belt and haul it wherever you need to."

"We understand, *Tiwan* spaceship. We will comply with your request."

"One more thing. We are preparing to lift off and fly back to Earth with a full load of ore, but we will be back in a month to continue mining. I have set locator beacons on the asteroid showing it's already claimed by the *Soul-T.*"

"We recognize your claim."

As the Ibecci spaceship said this, Frankie's high-definition camera confirmed the spaceship backing away from the asteroid.

"Well, that was strange, but easy. Maybe too easy," Jan said.

"Yeah. Like shooing a rabbit away from the garden. The question is whether they will come back as soon as we're gone."

"You know, Ella, sometimes your comments are spot on. Stuff I consider really basic goes over your head, but then you come back with this insightful observation."

"Wow! Was that a compliment? Hard to tell. Must be 'cause I'm so dense, but hey, I appear bright sometimes."

"Moving right along, Ella. Our asteroid is just too valuable, and on Earth we would definitely have to be vigilant. But with the Ibecci, I just don't know. Maybe they really didn't know we were here. As you said months ago, the asteroid metal content masked our presence."

"And there it is again! Sometimes I make good calls."

"You always do, Ella. Enough nonsense. I want to get going. Retrieve Frankie, turn on locator beacons, and start the pre-flight checklist."

"Roger."

Ella went through the checklist while Jan ticked off items on her electronic clipboard as she floated around the command module.

Jan then looked at the main status boards, all in the green, and strapped down in the pilot's seat.

"Ella, bring reactors to full power."

"Roger, Jan. Ramping reactors to full power."

"Ella, ready?"

"Ready."

"Grapples off. Maneuvering thrusters only. Separate from the asteroid. Bring us up nice and gentle."

"Roger, Jan. Separating from the asteroid. Maneuvering thrusters only."

The *Soul-T* lifted off slowly until it was a couple of kilometres away from the asteroid.

Jan checked that all beacons were active.

"Okay, Ella, we are clear. Find us a nice ice asteroid to

fill up."

"Roger, Jan. Scanning."

"Found a target asteroid. Course laid in."

"Go for maximum acceleration."

"Okay, Jan. Go for 0.4G acceleration."

Ella ramped up the VASIMR engines with power from the spaceship's Prometheus nuclear reactors and hydrogen stored in the gigantic cryogenic tanks.

Not counting the detour to replenish the LH tanks, the fly back at a continuous acceleration of 0.4 G and equal deceleration at the midway point would allow the *Soul-T* to reach Griffin Base in less than 8 days.

"Ella, get the FD computer to calculate the asteroid's new velocity vector and store it."

"Done."

Jan then queued an extended version of Dire Straits's 1978 "Southbound Again." She loved its bluesy rock style and made it a tradition to play it on her return flights. She started composing the daily report as she thumped her foot and moved her head in rhythm.

Soul-T Mining Ship. Asteroid belt. 93 days in space. Have reached a full load of 203 tons of ore. Just departed for Griffin Base. En route to fill up LOX and LH tanks. No malfunctions. This morning, before departure, an Ibecci tugboat latched on to our asteroid and started directing it toward Mars. The tugboat backed off as soon as we raised it on the radio, advising we had already claimed it. Have beacons in place. Hope they will honour our claim.

As the rate of acceleration increased, the ship vibrated imperceptibly from the VASIMR engines' electromagnetic field even though the engines were shielded and almost fifty metres aft.

The *Soul-T* was moving forward slowly, accelerating at 4 m/s/s. Jan saw the blip of the Ibecci tugboat on the radar. It was crossing behind her present course some twenty kilometres away. She sneered, thinking they were moving away too promptly.

She debated going down toward Mars to get closer to the Ibecci and study them, as her curiosity kept increasing. Maybe on her next trip, she thought . . . assuming she would find her asteroid when she returned.

18 LONELY HEART

The Brinnan Manor, Killiney, Ireland

Cate Brinnan woke up in her bed at the Brinnan Manor. It was 7:30 a.m. on a beautiful Sunday morning in June.

She had enjoyed a good night's sleep but was still tired from her intense post-graduate research at Trinity College's Department of Astrophysics and Space Physics. She was searching for the elusive Planet Nine, a planet theorized by astronomers at the beginning of the twenty-first century responsible for the strange and tilted orbits of trans-Neptunian objects.

Since her return from Chile three months earlier, Cate had immersed herself in her work with the university's planet-hunting team, racing against other teams worldwide to be the first to confirm the existence of the super-Earth planet believed to be deep in the Oort cloud.

Its discovery had eluded astronomers for some forty years and Cate kept an almost inhumane and excruciating pace, stubbornly determined to be the first one to pinpoint its location. But the super-Earth planet did not seem to want to reveal itself due to its extreme distance, which made it over eight hundred times fainter than Pluto.

Carlos's arrival two weeks earlier had created a welcome distraction, but after his departure, she had found it difficult to apply herself with the same level of intensity.

Her thoughts invariably drifted to the memories of her time in Chile and the few days they spent together in Dublin. This irked her because the memories made her triste, grudgingly acknowledging the handsome Catalonian had really gotten under her skin. Only one other former boyfriend had done that, but it had ended badly because he had been intimidated by her intelligence and driven personality. The lovable Spaniard, on the other hand, admired and appreciated her talents to the point of near worship.

So here she was, awake, still tired and miserable, well aware she was part of the wealthy 1 percent of the population who had it easy, thanks to her great-aunt Elia's music success from seventy years earlier and the royalties from her songs. Yet feeling gloomy because she missed Carlos.

It wasn't as if she did not have the opportunity to go out with other men. She was an undeniably beautiful, intelligent, and well-educated woman who had men lining up for her. She chuckled at the thought that love was strange. It immediately reminded her of the old Huey Lewis and the News song "The Power of Love." She sang a few lines aloud, changing the words to suit her situation, and chuckled at her impromptu reworking of the lyrics.

She got up and went to the bathroom to take a shower, hoping it would wake her up. She stepped into the large, well-appointed en suite and started singing the 1980s song "If I Could Be Where You Are" by her great-aunt.

Cate sang the entire four verses while in her mind she reviewed her work schedule and decided to go to see Carlos.

She figured she needed maybe three weeks to finish the latest numerical simulations. Afterward, she would let the rest of the team continue while she went to Chile for a couple of weeks. She needed to see Carlos, hoping her instincts would tell her what to do.

Above all, she wanted this relationship to be more than an infatuation for someone who was handsome, had a cute accent, and happened to like and admire her.

The thought made her tingle, so with the decision made, she happily got dressed and went downstairs to have breakfast.

Who knows? She thought. Between the intimate moments she was planning, she might actually help him find the Ibecci's home planet.

19 SHARED KNOWLEDGE

NAUS *Enterprise* (CVN-80) Aircraft Carrier, South Indian Ocean

"It's all about optics and leveraging any advantage we may have, Major Krol," Maj.-Gen. Arias replied as she discussed his and Capt. Dini Flanders's deployment to the *Enterprise* aircraft carrier.

The *Enterprise*, together with Carrier Strike Group 3, was now steaming south at thirty knots from the Gulf of Oman toward the Kerguelen Islands, some 7,200 kilometres away.

"But, Maj.-Gen., with all due respect, I only spoke to Seren *Capac* for less than ten minutes. How much of advantage is that over some navy analyst who will be more familiar with his surroundings and the navy's operational procedures?" Maj. Krol replied.

"You are forgetting, Major, we still have very little information about these aliens. For all you know, they might really treasure relationships, irrespective of how insignificant they may seem to you and me. Seren *Capac* is, after all, a stranger in a strange land, and perhaps your familiar voice may be reassuring."

Maj.-Gen. Arias looked at Capt. Flanders and continued.

"In a similar manner, your early analysis proved spot-on, Capt. Flanders, so I like your analytical capabilities to be at the disposal of the team. You will both pack right away and leave this afternoon for Diego Garcia. There you will transfer to a carrier air transport that will deliver you to the *Enterprise*. Understood?"

"Yes, sir," the two officers replied in unison.

"You should also be aware the PLA's navy nuclear aircraft carrier *Liu Huaqing* and its task force are steaming south at full speed from the South China Sea. But they have slightly more distance to cover. We have a four days' advantage over them. Do either of you speak French?"

"I can understand perhaps 50 percent, if spoken slowly, and can read some of it, but that's it, Maj. Krol replied.

"What about you, Capt. Flanders?"

"I can function at a working level and make myself understood Maj.-Gen.," Capt. Flanders asserted.

"Good, because you might need to interface with French Special Forces parachuting onto the island. Their rapid reaction task force is also on its way aboard one of their Epée-class amphibious assault ships. There is additional information in the briefing packets. At this point, the situation is very fluid. Your principal task will be to serve as a liaison with the aliens. Godspeed to both. Dismissed."

That afternoon, Maj. Krol and Capt. Flanders left from Vandenberg Air Force Base aboard a military Hermeus, Halcyon, hypersonic transport that flew to London and then, with a fresh crew, continued south to Johannesburg and finally to Diego Garcia. It was a relatively fast eight hours of total flying time, flying in relative comfort compared to what it would have been flying aboard a C-17 or worse yet, the old venerable C-130J *Super Hercules*. Both aircraft were still operational because of the limited military budgets that long ago had resulted in the cancellation of the C-X *Next Generation Airlifter* intended to replace the older aircraft.

Capt. Flanders kept quiet throughout the entire trip,

reading documents on her tablet. She appeared relaxed, while Maj. Krol tried to keep busy on administrative tasks, reviewing background documents including the transcripts from the 614 AOC surveillance of the convoy of alien spaceships that landed on the Kerguelen Islands.

The transcripts contained synthetic renderings and photographs of the spaceships that were significantly larger than the spaceplane flown by Seren *Capac* during her first incursion. There were also small and strange-looking teardrop-shaped spacecraft escorting the convoy that were smaller than Seren *Capac*'s spaceplane. He concentrated on assimilating the additional information, but it wasn't enough to keep him fully occupied. He finally turned toward Capt. Flanders.

"Hey, Flanders, since we left, all you have been doing is reading on your tablet nonstop. Something entertaining, I hope?"

"Oh . . . just want to brush up and prepare myself as best as I can for our potential interaction with Seren *Capac*, sir. I am reading background information on the various South American tribes near Lake Titicaca, including the Paracas and Wari cultures, with special emphasis on their folklore."

"Okay, I am listening. May as well get up to speed on this stuff."

"Yes, sir. Well, the Paracas was a culture that existed around 800 BC and had extensive knowledge of irrigation and water management, as well as textiles. We know very little of this culture, and so a lot of the information I am gathering is from questionable studies. When you join the dots, some interesting things become obvious. For example, some textile designs appear reminiscent of printed circuit boards, although I confess this information is speculative."

She continued in an animated voice, "Then, there's the odd practice of cranial deformation, which produced elongated skulls. According to anthropologists, the Paracas people believed that individuals with elongated skulls could get closer to their Spirit Gods. Some documents suggest the practice followed the so-called Path of Viracocha from southeast of Lake Titicaca to northwest of Peru. And . . . this is the really interesting part; many of the skulls excavated near Lake Titicaca appear to belong to an extinct human race with elongated heads that were a natural condition and different from man. Wouldn't it be amazing if Seren *Capac* had an elongated skull like the examples from the anthropological digs?"

"Hmm . . . didn't see that one coming. Thought when you said you were brushing up on the subject, it would be on the Tiwanaku and Puma Punku ruins and everything related to them. But I suppose exobiology would also be an important subject."

"Well, sir, the language is a problem because there is not much to go on. Anthropologists speculate the language of the inhabitants was possibly Puquina, but it is extinct, and I haven't had enough time to review the available references. I actually started a few days ago, but then we got these orders, and I had to rush to transfer all documents to my tablet. Anyway, I am finding more interesting connections to unrelated items that fit with some of the folklore, surrounding the writings about the God Viracocha who, history tells us, came down from heaven to teach men the basics of civilization. If you will allow me, I'll illustrate what I mean by using llamas and alpacas as an example."

"You mean the animals from the Andes where alpaca wool comes from?"

"Yes, sir. They're classified as camelids, and paleontologists postulate they originated in North America about forty million years ago and migrated to South America about three million years ago. Then they inexplicably disappeared only from North America about ten thousand years ago. Why is their disappearance confined to only North America?"

"I don't know, but I assume you do."

"No one knows, but it's an interesting mystery that allows us to consider a very different explanation. These animals mostly live at high altitudes in the Andes, which is a very specific habitat. Their physiognomy is also unique, particularly for the llamas, and different from other Earth camelids that are larger and have heavier legs. Exobiology tells us that creatures from a planet with a lesser gravity would have less muscle and be slender and tall, which describes the shape and proportions of Llamas. Based on what Viceroy Marel stated, their race is taller than ours. Isn't it possible that when the Ibecci first visited our planet and founded Tiwanaku, they also brought flora and fauna? It would explain why Llamas only existed in South America but not in North America ten thousand years ago. Condors, or more specifically the new-world condors, were most probably also introduced by the Ibecci, as they are unique and totally unrelated to the old-world vulture family. The aforementioned examples are consistent with the folklore that states Viracocha brought knowledge and also gifts from the heavens," Capt. Flanders said. She paused, trying to read Maj. Krol's face.

He remained expressionless, so Capt. Flanders continued as if giving a dissertation.

"What is immediately useful to us, assuming the previous questionable hypothesis is correct, is that the Ibecci are an enlightened civilization that believes in aiding and educating those with whom they come in contact rather than acting as conquerors and subjugating them. In effect, they are true creators, which fits the folklore of how Viracocha is described. There are other interesting contributions such as the origin of potatoes and corn, or maize as it is known in South, Central America and Mexico. Even quinoa was first domesticated over 7,000 years ago around Lake Titicaca and became the principal stable of the Incas. The lowly potato, in particular, is probably the most obvious gift from the Ibecci. Just like quinoa, the potato is indigenous to the Andes and specifically to the regions of modern-day southern Peru and the most northwestern region of Bolivia. Widespread cultivation as a food staple was started somewhere around 8000 BC in extreme environments at high altitude and poor soil conditions. These facts alone are an absolutely amazing coincidence of time and location, which fits perfectly with the Ibecci establishing their settlement at Tiwanaku."

"Okay, Flanders, you are the historian and linguist, but the stuff you are outlining is pretty bizarre. But we have no precedent to draw from, so I guess I'll trust your instincts on the research you are conducting. You made an interesting point about the Ibecci being benevolent. Really hope it's true."

"I hope so too, sir."

And with that, they both fell into silence. By the time they arrived at Diego Garcia, the *Enterprise* and its strike group were approximately eight hundred kilometres north of the island. A V28 tilt-rotor carrier transport was dispatched from the *Enterprise*.

The pair washed up and changed clothes as the carrier transport arrived and quickly boarded for the last leg of the trip. Thankfully, the benign May weather, with light southeasterly winds, made the two-hour flight to the *Enterprise* agreeable.

Aboard the *Enterprise*, things were different. Steady rain had been falling continuously for the past two hours as the strike group entered a low-pressure tropical storm with clouds at a thousand metres. Mercifully, the sea was relatively calm with one and a half-metre waves.

CAP and ISR operations were ongoing handled by F47 UCLASS.

The flight deck was not the usual smelly place with the characteristic stench of jet fuel and fumes. Instead, the steady rain had washed away and filtered the air, but it also raised the level of humidity, and, coupled with the +35°C temperatures, made it oppressive.

As soon as the V28 touched down, an ensign greeted Maj. Krol and Capt. Flanders.

"Welcome aboard. Please follow me and watch your

step. Someone will look after your bags and bring them to your assigned quarters. In the meantime, Cmdr. Phelps, the CCSG would like to greet you," the ensign stated.

"Commander Phelps?" Maj. Krol inquired with a puzzled look.

"Yes, sir. He does not like to be addressed as admiral unless the circumstances require it. I am told he is a Louisiana boy whose father was a shrimp fisherman, and this shaped his unassuming personality. You will see him doing his regular rounds and sometimes, especially with the maintenance crew, go back and give them a hand if they are working on something particularly vexing. Loves people and machines and spends more time away from the flag bridge than in it. But he expects a lot from everyone."

"Never heard of a general who did not want to be addressed as such."

"Everyone is looking forward to working with you, sir. My understanding is that you will work directly with the CCSG and the other commanders."

The ensign led them into the island, down a narrow corridor, and then up a set of stairs to the flag bridge below the main bridge. The ensign entered and approached the CCSG who was peering out through the bridge's angled windows with large binoculars.

The CCSG stood-up and approached Maj. Krol and Capt. Flanders. He was what one would expect an admiral to look like, complete with a chiselled square jaw, short-cropped white hair, and grey-blue eyes that instantly conveyed authority. He was a tad shorter than Maj. Krol would have expected him to be, but made up for it with muscular arms and a chest that reminded him of a body builder.

Maj. Krol now understood what the ensign had meant. The CCSG had grown up on fishing boats and was accustomed to hard, physical work.

"Welcome aboard, Major Krol and Capt. Flanders. I trust you had pleasant flights. We are looking forward to your contributions. Are you up to a briefing with our Commanders?" the CCSG asked with hardly any of the Louisiana drawl Krol had assumed would be present.

"Yes, Admiral, absolutely. We are here to help in any way we can," Maj. Krol replied.

"Good, I'll let the Commanders know and will arrange our meeting for an hour from now. How does that sound? Don't worry about an agenda, major. This first briefing will be informal. More of a meet-and-greet to give us a bit of background on what you know. One last thing. Around here, you can address me as Cmdr. Phelps. Ensign Wainwright will bring you to your quarters and tell you how to get to the flag officers briefing room."

"Thank you, Cmdr. Phelps." And with that, Maj. Krol and Capt. Flanders saluted and followed the ensign out.

An hour later, Maj. Krol and Capt. Flanders entered the well-appointed flag officers briefing room furnished with high-back leather chairs placed around a large rectangular wooden table that would not have been out of place at a law firm.

A steward dressed in formal whites was setting up coffee and tea. Maj. Krol and Capt. Flanders sat themselves at what they hoped was the opposite end of where the CCSG normally sat.

There was a holographic projector on the table and Maj. Krol connected his tablet to it. He established a link to the 614 AOC theatre through the secure military network and went through the multi-level authentication. A window appeared floating in midair with the face of IMCO, who greeted him with a big smile.

"Hi, Maj. Krol. How are things in the Indian Ocean?

"Pretty quiet at the moment. Who's the acting shift senior officer?"

"Maj. Parker, sir. I'll transfer your feed to one of the primary screens."

The video link then changed, and Maj. Krol found himself staring at Maj. Parker, who was sitting in the AOC theatre command chair.

"To what do I owe the honour of this call from the south Indian Ocean? Is it mai tai hour yet?" Maj. Parker said merrily.

"You bet. And in about five minutes, I need to be on my best A game, answering questions posed by the admiral and his commanders on what we know about the aliens' intentions and their spaceships beyond what has already been provided in briefs."

Maj. Parker's jovial demeanour changed right away, and immediately sat straight up in her chair.

"How can I help?"

"Not sure yet, but we may want access to any real-time feeds, so meanwhile stand by."

"Roger that," Maj. Parker replied and then continued.

"Be advised our latest satellite images show three of their spaceships grounded on the southwest side of the island, essentially opposite and furthest away from the French outpost. The fourth spaceship appears to be keeping station and motionless about a hundred nautical miles out and due west from the island at an altitude of one hundred fifty metres, just floating like a weather balloon. The escorts identified when the convoy of spaceships entered the atmosphere appear to be performing CAP operations. We are also keeping an eye on two Divine Eagles. At this moment, they are just passing over Indonesia at 22,000 metres on a southwesterly course and ahead of their own strike group. I don't think the Divine Eagles are actively searching for the *Enterprise*, but hazard to guess they are trying to acquire the aliens' spaceships as early as possible and designate them for targeting with their DF-29 ASBMs. The Chinese seem to know the *Enterprise* is travelling south from Diego Garcia. They changed the orbits of their recon birds to cover that area of the ocean. Right now, there is a lot of traffic passing over your position. I assume the *Enterprise*'s warfare officers are aware of this, as we have passed along the information."

"Excellent." And as Maj. Krol replied, the CCSG filed in followed by four of his commanders.

"Captain Flanders and Maj. Krol, I would like to introduce you to the *Enterprise*'s Commander Air Group (CAG), Tanis Konstantinos, Capt. Parisa Nalbandian, our surface warfare commander (AS) and the Captain of the *Enterprise*; Joe Oliver, our air warfare commander (AW) who flew in from his destroyer; and Samantha DesRosiers, our electronics warfare commander (AQ). Our undersea warfare commander (AX) is a little busy now, so you will meet him later," the CCSG said.

He continued, "We are really interested in what you can tell us about the aliens. What I am looking for is your personal impressions and gut sense beyond what is available in the transcripts. We need to figure what kind of threat they pose, as I frankly don't want to get in a firefight with them. I suspect we would be severely outgunned. There is nothing I would like more than to turn around and go back to our operations in the Gulf of Oman, but the French may need our help."

"Yes, sir. I also have my colleague, Maj. Pamela Parker from the 614 AOC on the video link. She may help with information above and beyond what I can provide."

"I see that, Maj. Krol. Well, I am always one for encouraging initiative, so welcome to the meeting, Maj. Parker."

"Thank you, sir."

Maj. Krol took over and continued, "As you know, our exchange with Seren *Capac* was limited. However, my impression is she appeared by the book, kept communication to a minimum, and was at all times cordial. She showed flexibility to adjust her flight path to match the flight performance of our SR-72. Above all, what I believe is important is that Seren *Capac* initiated communications first and emphasized her appreciation of our willingness to respond and cooperate with her. As far as your statement of a potential confrontation, at no time was Seren *Capac* hostile. Her behaviour was consistent with the general posture conveyed in the message from their viceroy that they do not wish to quarrel with us. My opinion, keeping in mind the very limited interaction we had with them, is that the likelihood of confrontation is small. Capt. Flanders has been doing indirect research beyond the current analysis. She has been trying to profile their behaviour based on information from when the Ibecci first came to Earth and established their outpost at Tiwanaku. You might consider her analysis somewhat unusual, but I ask you to keep an open mind. Capt. Flanders?"

On cue, Capt. Flanders sat straight in her chair and spoke as if delivering a scholarly paper to a university audience.

"The problem we have with the Ibecci is that we know very little about them or their operational doctrine. We cannot even say they will abide by the rules of the Geneva convention, and we can't just take the words from Viceroy Marel at face value. What I have done is look to their past, or more accurately, our past, for hints of their possible behaviour. From a profiling perspective, we know conquering races typically leave a significant imprint on defeated foes, including their DNA through rape and intermingling, as the Spanish conquistadores did to the Incan and Aztec Empires. In the case of the Ibecci, the available anthropological information from excavations near Lake Titicaca shows elongated skulls of an extinct human race, different from ours. There is no evidence of the Indigenous population exhibiting these physiological traits. The conclusion one can draw from this is that the Ibecci either did not interbreed with the Indigenous inhabitants, or could not, but did not attempt to exterminate them either," Capt. Flanders said and then paused, looking around the room.

No one spoke.

"If we look at the limited information available on Tiwanaku and the Puquina language, including their God

Viracocha, we see that Viracocha was revered as someone who brought knowledge from the heavens. The literature rarely depicts him as a Warrior God or a vindictive and angry God who would bring wrath onto the inhabitants, as so many ancient Gods are typically depicted. Past evidence, therefore, tells us they kept to themselves and eventually became extinct. This is, in some ways, consistent with their actions to date. They asked for a place to live and offered knowledge and technology in exchange, and because of our unwillingness to communicate with them, they will now simply settle in areas away from us."

"What you've just described is not much to go on, Capt. Flanders, and seems based mostly on conjecture," the CCSG said.

"You are absolutely right, sir. But keep in mind the analysis and briefing documents compiled to date are just a summary of events, with some occasional sprinkling of opinions provided by analysts, including myself, but all of these opinions have no precedents to draw from. This is further compounded by the fact the Ibecci first settled on Earth anywhere between ten and fifteen thousand years ago. This is an incredibly long time ago and at the end of the last known ice age. As a result, the little information we have on them is more folklore than anything else. This called for thinking outside the box," Capt. Flanders replied.

"I concur with you. This is an atypical situation. We lack the usual profiles on their operational doctrine, their strength, and even their weapons. Is there anything you can tell us about the composition and details of the spaceships that are now on the Kerguelen?" the CCSG asked.

Maj. Parker answered this time.

"Not much more from what is contained in the briefings. The spaceship currently stationary at an altitude of one hundred fifty metres is about the length of a *Zumwalt-2* destroyer, perhaps a bit larger. It has the same signature as the spaceship that entered our atmosphere to escort Seren *Capac* back to their fleet, and it appears to be similar to four other spaceships photographed by the *Xpace Explorer* probe. It has advanced ECMs, as we were unable to track them. They also appear to possess a direct EMP or cyber weapon that is target-specific and disrupts computer hardware and software, similar to our HPM missiles, but likely more capable. We are trying to determine the true nature of the weapon based on the counterintelligence we are slowly gathering from the temporary failure of the *Tiangong4* space station computers when the Chinese attempted to engage the Ibecci. Additionally, these spaceships—" But the CCSG interrupted Maj. Parker.

"So, we can't track, target, or shoot at them, and if we try, they'll fry our electronics. And on top of all that, they have four of those spaceships. Not a very comforting thought."

"Yes, sir, that is a very succinct way of putting it. We also believe the spaceship performing picket duties has a complement of five small spacecraft that escorted the convoy on their way down to the Kerguelen.

"If I may ask, major, how do you know the spaceplanes are attached and supported by the larger spaceship?" the CAG asked.

"As this point, commander, it's pure speculation. The spaceship performing picket duties is about 180 metres in length but is very wide with a beam we estimate to be about seventy-five metres. Our analysts speculated the reason for the width was to accommodate an internal hangar running the length of the spaceship. At the moment, the small escorts also appear to be running CAP operations, so they would need a larger vessel to provide support services. The large spaceship would be the logical candidate."

"Do we have any information on the capability of these escorts?" the CAG asked.

"Not much. The escorts differ from the spaceplane flown by Seren *Capac* on her first incursion. Their radar signature is smaller, but we have not been able to get a good look at them. Their infrared signatures are certainly cooler, so we don't think they use chemical propulsion, but they are definitely spacecraft that can operate both in the atmosphere and in space," Maj. Parker finished.

"Hmm . . . not much to go on, and still we know little about the enemy, assuming they are the enemy," the CCSG declared, looking at the faces of those sitting around the table.

There was no reaction, so he continued.

"Now I know how Nimitz felt at the beginning of the Battle of Midway, and even then, he had more information to work with and knew the capabilities of the Japanese navy. We are still too far away to gather any data on them. But in another sixteen hours, we will be close enough for the Trackers to acquire them on their radars provided they have not enabled their ECMs. At that point, we can hopefully start gathering additional intel. I know more or less what to expect from the Chinese, so let's hope your assessment and my gut instincts are correct and these aliens have no interest in waging war. Still, we need to be cautious. Suggestions, anyone?"

"We could have two of the DDGs move ahead, sir, rather than staying in tight, and provide a picket for what we may face from the aliens," the AW suggested.

"Agree, Cmdr. Oliver. Let's have the *Stout* and the *Fitzgerald* move ahead. I also want the *Ross* and the *Trudeau* to veer east to provide a barrier between the Chinese carrier group and us. This will unfortunately stretch us thin. Above all, our standing orders are to remain neutral and not take sides. A small comfort, considering the Chinese and we are converging at the same location. Hopefully, our own airborne early-warning radars and the French Special Forces may give us more information. On the upside, if things go well, we might do some crab fishing in the Southern Ocean. Good briefing, all."

20 RECONNAISSANCE

1er RPIMa, Special Recon Patrol, Atop Peak Les Deux Frères, Kerguelen Islands

Sixteen hundred kilometres further south from the *Enterprise*'s current location, Lt. Patrice Mimieux of the French 1st Marine Infantry Parachute Regiment (1er RPIMa) was with his five-man recon squad atop Peak Les Deux Frères. He was observing the Ibecci's construction site in the middle of Vallée des Sables from about 2.4 km away.

Four hours earlier, the squad had performed a night HALO parachute jump after a twenty-hour flight aboard an A400M-300 *Atlas* military transport, successfully landing on a relatively flat riverbed east of Les Deux Frères.

Their equipment included military spec. electric hoverbikes plus two armoured robot-ape combat support units (RCS), designated G1 and G2, equipped with remotely operated MG7 machine guns in 7.62x51-mm NATO. The squad was otherwise lightly armed with only their standard-issue HK416F assault rifles, chambered in 6.8x51-mm NATO, plus one squad member equipped with a Steyr IWS2000 anti-matériel rifle chambered in 15.2x169-mm armor-piercing APFSDS ammunition.

What they lacked in firepower, they compensated with their Paladin P7 carbon nanotube passive exoskeletons. The P7 was a Swiss-German design in the tradition of Swiss mechanical timepieces and a marvel of human kinetics. Power assist was provided via clever mechanical joints with spiral torsion springs at each joint together with elastic and dampening devices and a deep understanding of human kinetics. The result was an exoskeletons more reliable, less complex, and quieter than heavier powered exoskeletons.

The squad's orders were to observe and collect data from a distance that would not appear threatening. They had prepared for harsh winter conditions based on the islands' proximity to Antarctica and the month of June being in the middle of the Southern Hemisphere winter.

Surprisingly, the average daytime temperatures were a mild 3°C, while nighttime temperatures dropped to just below freezing. These moderate temperatures made the recon patrol's surveillance job easier.

It was the middle of the morning, overcast, but with good visibility. Lt. Mimieux had placed G1 and G2 at the centre of their position. He was in a prone position, looking at the feed from the robot apes' head-mounted 20X cameras in his helmet-mounted HUD.

He could see a beehive of activity from what looked like bipedal and multi-legged construction bots milling around the site.

There were too many to count. Some were going in and out through the ramp of a large spaceship grounded about a hundred metres to the south of the main construction area. The spaceship had few external features that made it look more like a gargantuan rectangular metal box with smooth sides than an interstellar-capable spaceship.

Lt. Mimieux could also see the silhouette of two other spaceships in the distance and far away to the north of the site. He zoomed in to maximum magnification and still had to look hard to distinguish the spaceships as their grey hulls blended with the rocky landscape. He was reassured he could account for all the spaceships, knowing the fourth was west of the island performing picket duties.

As he continued surveying, he looked up the opposite hill and found himself staring at Ibecci soldiers. He was sure they were also looking at him, but it was difficult to tell from their strange-looking full-face helmets. He could also see other soldiers dressed in full battle gear walking around in skier-like strides. They were imposing even from a distance of over two kilometres, and they were definitely carrying barrelled weapons, but it was anyone's guess whether they were projectile or energy weapons.

He then noticed faint movement in the distance and further west on L'Aiguille Noire, which was at a higher elevation and almost five kilometres away.

He commanded G1's digital zoom to its maximum magnification. The Ibecci appeared to be erecting treelike structures Lt. Mimieux guessed were fractal antennae. He assumed they were part of a high-resolution surveillance radar.

"Henhouse, Weasel. Activity on the construction site continues. The three spaceships previously accounted for are still grounded. There is recent activity in the distance atop L'Aiguille Noire. Looks like fractal antennae being erected that may be part of a tracking radar. We are sending a two-man team with G2 to get a closer look. Over," he reported to his superiors aboard the *Foudre*.

"Weasel, Henhouse. Understood. Over."

Cmdr. DesRosiers aboard the *Enterprise* was fluent in French and jumped in.

"Weasel, Henhouse2. Please be advised in twelve hours we should be in range to send birds up to survey the site. Over."

"Roger, Henhouse2."

Suddenly, Seren *Capac* jumped onto their supposedly secure frequency, just as she had done with the 614th AOC the first time she came to Earth.

"Warrior Weasel, this is Seren *Capac*, the squadron leader of the fliers aboard our frigate, the *Vorian*. I am Viceroy Marel's appointed ambassador to establish diplomatic relations with France. You can come and inspect the emplacement of our detection and surveillance arrays you seem interested in," she said in French.

Lt. Mimieux could not respond. He waited for a response from Lt. Col. Henri Leclerc, the commander of the rapid reaction force aboard the *Foudre*.

After a full minute of silence, he addressed the *Foudre*.

"Henhouse, this is Weasel. Do you copy? Over."

Everyone waited for a response.

Lt. Col. Leclerc finally spoke.

"Seren *Capac,* I am Lt. Col. Henri Leclerc. I have been instructed by my government to communicate with you. I am aboard one of our ships en route to the Kerguelen. We accept your offer, but we are still six days away. Lt. Mimieux can go to your site in my place until we arrive. He is a member of our 1st Marine Infantry Parachute Regiment currently observing your site."

Seren *Capac* searched her neural translator for the ranking of Lt. Col. Leclerc in Ibecci and learned the ranking was equivalent to an *Iovian*. It made sense, as the French officer was appointed to communicate with the Ibecci. She was relieved to learn a lower ranking officer would meet her and replied.

"Friendship is good, Lt. Col. Leclerc and Lt. Mimieux. We are aware of your surveillance team watching from a distance. We can meet at a location of your choosing, or you can come down to our site."

"Very well, Seren *Capac*. Lt. Mimieux will come down to your site. In the meantime, please pass along the message to Viceroy Marel. France understands the Ibecci's need for a place to live, but France needs to set certain conditions. As a result, we want to discuss the specific logistics of living in French territory, together with unrestricted access to your site," Lt. Col. Leclerc said with a tone he hoped was as delicate as possible.

"Lt. Col. Leclerc, I'll pass along your message to our Core Command to ensure that upon your arrival, our senior officers are present to discuss your requests. In the meantime, I'll inform our paratroopers to allow Lt. Mimieux to enter our perimeter. I am currently flying defence patrols with the rest of our fliers, but I am on my way. Lt. Mimieux, please do not fear our paratroopers. They are instructed to use force only in self-defence."

"Seren *Capac*, this is Lt. Mimieux. I'll come down to your site alone in one of our hoverbikes. Mimieux out."

Lt. Mimieux got up and walked down the slope to where the squad had left the hoverbikes.

Sergeant Clement Bouquin, the squad's second in command, stopped him.

"Lieutenant, take George1 with you," Sergeant Bouquin said, referring to one of their robot-apes. They were affectionately named after the monkey from the Curious George book series.

"Best if I go unarmed," Lt. Mimieux replied. "Besides, you know that our briefings indicated they have advanced cyberwarfare systems capable of disabling computers and electronic systems. If they decide to show aggression, they will surely disable G1 right away. And if we get in a firefight, I don't think its machine gun can do much damage to those paratroopers we can see in the distance. Maybe Simard could with well-placed shots," referring to Corporal Chantal Simard, the squad's sniper. So, I'll go unarmed except for my personal weapon."

He turned around and continued walking down the slope. At the bottom of the hill, he climbed onto his own hoverbike, checked the Li-air battery charge, showing over 90 percent charge, and started it.

The two slightly offset and superposed one-metre diameter blades in the front housing started to rotate, followed by the two blades in the aft housing. As Lt. Mimieux applied the throttle, the blades' speed increased, and the 270 kg, 3.6-metre long hoverbike lifted about a metre off the ground.

The controls and steering were a mix of those of a motorcycle and a Segway. He pushed the handlebar gently to the right to turn the hoverbike around and then pushed on it to advance.

The hoverbike had a top speed of eighty kilometres per hour, but in the interest of caution, he was going at a slower speed. It took almost fifteen minutes to go around the north side of Peak Les Deux Frères and come down to the Vallée des Sables.

He did not know exactly where to go, as the construction site now stretched over three hundred metres in all directions. There was a large pit in the middle of the site that kept increasing in size because of the nonstop excavation, so he kept travelling south, with his every movement broadcasted in real time to the *Foudre* and the *Enterprise*.

At the southern edge of the site and to his right, he could see six Ibecci paratroopers. Peak Les Deux Frères and his squad were on his left. He looked up toward his squad and signalled he was going in.

"Weasel2, you are in charge until I come back. Make sure you continue to relay my real-time feed plus your feed to Henhouse and Henhouse2. Over."

"Copy that, Weasel," came the response from Sergeant Bouquin.

In his helmet HUD, Lt. Mimieux then clicked the comm. options drop-down menu to mute the communication to the *Foudre* and the *Enterprise* in order to speak to Sergeant Bouquin privately.

"Clem, keep your cool, okay?" He clicked back to all channels.

"Weasel out."

He turned the hoverbike to the right toward the six paratroopers who appeared to be the welcome party.

As soon as he got to within a hundred metres, the paratroopers positioned themselves in two rows of three each, facing toward him, but with their weapons slung casually over their shoulders. At a scant thirty metres, he slowed down to the equivalent of a brisk walk, figuring there was no sense in rushing his arrival.

He stopped about ten metres short of their location and then settled the hoverbike on the ground and turned it off.

Aboard the *Foudre*, personnel monitoring his vital signs noted his stress levels. His heart rate had jumped to 170. Pressure was up, but respiration was within normal parameters. The *Foudre* did a quick status check.

"Weasel, Henhouse, what's your status? Over."

"Henhouse, Weasel. Have shut down the hoverbike. I am about to dismount and walk the last ten metres to meet our new friends. Over"

Although what he really wanted to say was *I'm going in to face six armoured brutes each over two metres tall with weapons that can probably vaporize me. So, what do you think?*

"Weasel, Henhouse, roger. Over."

"Henhouse, are you getting my video feed from the back-up camera and audio? Over."

"Weasel, Henhouse, your video and audio are crystal clear. Over."

"Understood, Henhouse. Hope I don't disappoint our visitors for not bringing a housewarming gift. Make sure Lt. Col. Leclerc doesn't forget. Out."

21 KEEPING AN EYE

NAUS *Enterprise* (CVN-80), Kerguelen Islands

In the *Enterprise* Combat Direction Centre (CDC), Cmdr. Samantha DesRosiers, the AQ, was monitoring the RPIM team in the Kerguelen Islands as well as the progress of the Chinese Divine Eagles.

"Sir, the Divine Eagles are advancing on a southwesterly course, but I think they'll soon change their course to a heading of 180 degrees. They have not yet detected us, but we will soon be within range," the AQ said.

"That's immaterial, Cmdr., as I'm sure the Chinese satellites most probably have our position already," the CCSG said.

"Yes, sir. We also have noticed a change of status and activity around the DF-29 mobile launchers on the Spratlys."

The AQ pointed to the holographic tactical sphere in the centre of the CDC. The sphere was set to a diameter of 6,000 km and an altitude 30,000 metres, with the Kerguelen Islands at its centre. The Divine Eagles appeared as two tiny red specs at the edge of the sphere. The *Liu Huaqing* carrier task force with its complement of four Type 057 *Shenyang* destroyers was at the eastern edge of the sphere and still some 5,800 km from the Kerguelen Islands.

"Have the Divine Eagles detected the Trackers yet?" the CCSG asked as he looked at two blue and four green dots positioned over the strike group.

The E-5A Tracker AEW aircraft were performing airborne early warning (AEW) and surveillance together with four F47 unmanned drones.

"Don't think so, sir. We are keeping them beyond the range of the Divine Eagles. We need a bit more room to maneuver and would like to recommend we veer southwest to a position west of the island and behind the Ibecci spaceship. That way we will have the island in front of us and won't get caught in any crossfire," the AQ said.

"Yeah, that will keep us out of harm's way from whatever the Chinese plan to send toward the Ibecci, but it also brings us awfully close to the Ibecci spaceship. It will also leave the *Trudeau* and the *Ross* on their own," replied the CCSG, referring to the *Zumwalt-2* guided missile destroyers, NAUS *Ross* (DDG-1025) and NAUS *Trudeau* (DDG-1026).

"Yes, sir, I know. My thinking is that if the Ibecci are lying, it makes little difference how much distance we have between us and their spaceships."

"Yeah . . . planning to face the known threats while ignoring the unknown. You and I are going to look real bright if this situation goes sideways."

"It is a calculated gamble, sir."

"That remains to be seen, Cmdr." said the CCSG soberly. Any objections to a westerly course change, Capt. Nalbandian?" the CCSG asked the AS, also present in the CDC.

"No, sir."

The CCSG then spoke up.

"Come to a new heading of 220 degrees."

A communications petty officer standing next to them relayed the message to the Bridge.

"Bridge, CDC. Come to a new heading of 220 degrees."

"Aye, aye, new heading of 220 degrees."

The Carrier Strike Group with its two remaining *Zumwalt-2* DDGs, the NAUS *Fitzgerald* (DDG-1023), the NAUS *Stout* (DDG-1027), and the supply ships started turning as a group.

"Cmdr., please inform the CAG and AR I want another Tracker up, supporting the two DDGs to the east of us, together with a complement of F47s."

"Yes, sir."

"Where is the *Foudre* and its escort?" the CCSG then asked.

"About 3,200 km north from the Cape of Good Hope, sir."

"All right then. We don't need to worry about them yet."

The CCSG then turned his attention to Cmdr. James "Jimmy" Weng, the AX and Lt. Cmdr. Isabel "Izzy" Urbina, the submarine element coordinator (SEC). Both had been busy getting their assets in position to track the two Chinese Qin-class attack submarines presumed to be in the south Indian Ocean and ahead of the *Liu Huaqing* task force.

"Cmdr. Weng, how much longer before we have the Mantas in position?"

"Probably another eight hours, sir," the AX replied.

The Mantas were all-electric underwater gliders with a shape similar to a manta ray albeit with narrower wings and an overall size slightly larger than a fighter jet. It was a complete departure from the shape of a conventional submarine. The fully autonomous submersibles relied on the change in their buoyancy for propulsion, gliding silently up and down to a maximum depth of 1,200 metres by emptying and filling their ballast tanks. It was a silent propulsion method, making a Manta quieter than any attack submarine. This was their primary means of propulsion when operating on silent ISR mode, but the speed was limited to a maximum of eleven knots. Mantas were also equipped with pump jet propulsors buried inside their hull.

The active propulsion was used to transit quickly to and from assigned surveillance areas or to outrun threats during emergencies.

"What is their current speed?"

"I am running them at their tactical speed to get them in position quickly, sir," the SEC replied.

Twenty-four hours earlier, she had instructed the pack of four Mantas to travel southeast in order to lie in wait at the Geelvinck fracture zone.

"Hmm … We run slow and maybe miss the Chinese boats passing through, or we run fast and risk being heard. What's your opinion, Lt. Cmdr.?"

"The various scenarios we ran show the Chinese subs unable to reach the Geelvinck fracture zone before the Mantas. The last four hours will be dicey. At that point, the most optimistic scenario has the Chinese subs and two of our Mantas converging, but this is extremely unlikely," the SEC replied.

It was a big ocean, and the Chinese attack subs had the option to continue southwest, never coming close to Geelvinck fracture zone. Even if they chose this route, they would eventually need to turn due south and hopefully be acquired by the sonars of the Mantas.

"All right, Lt. Cmdr., I'll meet you halfway. Let's increase their speed for the next four hours and then go back to their tactical speed."

"Yes, sir."

The SEC prepared a set of commands she would transmit next time the Mantas came up to a depth of sixty metres for their periodic updates. The message would be sent using the quantum key distribution (QKD) communications laser and received by the Manta's photonic sensors.

"What about the *Grenville*?" the CCSG asked, referring to an improved *Virginia* class attack submarine, one of the two attack submarines attached to the *Enterprise* strike group.

"Quiet as a mouse, sir. She is just keeping station about a hundred miles northeast from the *Trudeau* and the *Ross*," the SEC replied.

"Good. She can give the DDGs some protection in case the Chinese decide to get adventurous, but I am hoping they will simply ignore us."

22 INTRODUCTIONS

Vallée des Sables, Kerguelen Islands

Lt. Mimieux was ten metres from the Ibecci paratroopers. Every movement he made was measured. Slowly, he reached behind his back for his HK416F and placed it upright next to the hoverbike.

He removed his helmet, placed it on the seat, and started walking toward the imposing Ibecci paratroopers with only his sidearm for protection. His action was against the most basic military training of never letting go of one's personal weapon, but this was no ordinary situation.

He approached the closest paratrooper, which he gauged to be over two metres tall. The paratrooper was dressed in a charcoal-grey battle suit with a glass-like polished surface. It shimmered in the light, just like the lustre of a pearl.

Lieutenant Mimieux guessed the effect was from the material being made of hundreds of thin translucent layers that reflected and refracted light like Earth's Dielectric/Bragg Mirror technology intended to disrupt lasers. He thought it was not something suited for ground combat because the surfaces would get dirty and lose their ability to reflect an incoming energy beam. Strange symbols were etched on his chest and left shoulder that probably identified his name and rank.

The Ibecci paratrooper was standing with his arms relaxed and in front. His body proportions looked wrong. His arms appeared longer than the arms of a human of the same size. But the most striking feature was the elongated helmet that was reminiscent of the teardrop aerodynamic helmets worn by professional track cyclists.

Lt. Mimieux stopped in front of him and slowly extended his gloved hand, greeting the Ibecci paratrooper in French.

"I am Lieutenant Pat Mimieux from the 1st Marine Infantry Parachute Regiment," he said as he looked up.

Lt. Mimieux was 1.93 metres tall, but the Ibecci paratroopers towered over him by a full thirty centimetres. He looked down at Lt. Mimieux and extended his hand in the same gesture.

"I am Bracon *Patros*. My classification is equivalent to a sergeant. Seren *Capac* has asked that I relay to you and your Lt. Col. Leclerc that you can go anywhere you want on the construction site. We will escort you and answer questions you may have. Friendship is good, and you can consider us your family under your philosophy of fraternity. Seren *Capac* is on her way," the Ibecci paratrooper concluded while simultaneously shaking the lieutenant's hand.

"Your French is good, Bracon *Patros*."

He was unsure if the voice was the paratrooper's or computer generated, but the French accent was good, not perfect, but it was good.

"Our neural interface and aural device allow us to speak in any language. We simply formulate what we want to say in our mind and our neural interface, with its built-in translator, sends our thoughts to the aural device. The speech is then delivered in the native language of the receiver as naturally as possible."

"Hmm . . . a direct neural interface. Pretty impressive. We are just getting close to figuring out that it can be done, but we are probably twenty-five years away from finally developing a robust working interface, and this on top of forty years since we started working in this field," Lt. Mimieux replied.

Lt. Mimieux had a master's degree in science with specialization in applied physics from Ecole Spéciale Militaire (ESM) Saint-Cyr, the French military's equivalent of West Point, and his mind was buzzing with dozens of questions regarding the Ibecci technology. He wanted to know about the multilayer construction of their iridescent battle suits, their direct neural interface, and their big long-barreled personal weapons.

Aboard the *Foudre* and the *Enterprise*, people were having the same thoughts as live-stream video was collected through Lt. Mimieux's back-up chest camera.

Lt. Mimieux did not know where to start, so he took a stab at asking questions while they waited for Seren *Capac*.

"Bracon *Patros*, do you mind if I ask you about your personal weapon?"

But before the Ibecci could answer, a small spacecraft approached silently from the southwest.

While the spacecraft flown by Seren *Capac* on her first incursion to Earth looked little different from Earth's hypersonic spaceplanes, the small spacecraft she was in now looked positively alien.

It appeared to have a slender teardrop shape with the pointed end facing aft and a flat bottom. There were no visible control surfaces or even a discernable canopy. To a trained aerodynamicist, the shape was not optimal for hypersonic flight, and it just looked like it was flying backward. The surface was glass-like with no visible seams and highly polished, as light reflected and refracted, making it difficult to determine its true colour. The effect was like the iridescence of the paratrooper battle suit.

The spacecraft moved silently except for a very low frequency hum Lt. Mimieux could feel in his jawbone. He immediately thought that it was just like the popular accounts of alien abductions. He would eventually learn the hum was from the graviphoton field generators (GFGs) that created an intense magnetic field.

The spacecraft approached slowly, descending almost vertically. As it got closer, Lt. Mimieux saw the spacecraft's surface was steel blue. It finally settled down fifteen metres away on three support legs that extended just before touchdown.

Initially, nothing happened. After a couple of minutes, the hum stopped, and a stepladder extended down at the front of and beneath the spacecraft.

A figure came down the ladder. Lt. Mimieux could only see flat boots that looked like snowboarding boots and the bottom portion of a jumpsuit in the same steel blue colour. The jumpsuit material had hundreds of horizontal folds. Lt. Mimieux thought it was a pressurized suit designed to handle high-G maneuvers, similar to Earth's G-suits.

The torso of the pilot finally emerged. It bent down to come out from under the spacecraft and then straightened. The upper portion of the jumpsuit had similar horizontal folds as the lower portion. The jumpsuit had no symbols nor lettering that Lt. Mimieux could see except for a small tag on the left side of the chest with the depiction of a bird with individual feathers at its wingtips, just like those of a Condor. Despite the folds, it was easy to see the pilot was female.

She was tall and slender and had the same long arms as the paratroopers. She was not wearing a helmet, and her head was shaved. Her skin was reddish pink, like the colour of a bad sunburn. But the most striking feature was her elongated skull, which took some getting used to. Otherwise, her facial features were not much different from those of a Caucasian and not at all unpleasant. She walked with a self-assured gait, and Lt. Mimieux judged she was perhaps five centimetres shorter than he was.

As he looked at her, he thought he saw a flash of something emerging from the spacecraft. It promptly revealed itself as a floating sphere that came behind the pilot, rising about one and a half metres above her head and then moving in unison with her.

The sphere was bigger than a basketball, perhaps sixty cm in diameter, and made of the same highly polished steel blue material as the spacecraft. It was clearly equipped with an antigravity device that allowed it to float silently.

The pilot stopped in front of Lt. Mimieux. She took her gloves off and extended her reddish pink hand, showing an opposable thumb and four humanlike fingers. She then flashed a smile, revealing perfect white teeth.

"I am Seren *Capac,* Viceroy Marel's appointed ambassador to establish diplomatic relations with France," she said, but her lips did not move, the sound instead emanating from a speaker hidden within her body. She then immediately added in her own voice, but at a slightly different pitch.

"Friendship is good," enunciating the phrase slowly to make sure she would be understood.

Lt. Mimieux looked at the extended hand and the sphere above her head, hesitating for a couple of seconds, but then recovering quickly. He also removed his right-hand glove and shook her hand.

"Lt. Pat Mimieux from the 1er RPIMa. On behalf of France, I would like to welcome you on French territory," he said while simultaneously trying to process everything.

He then looked at her more closely. Seren *Capac* did the same, as if trying to read his mind. She raised her almost nonexistent eyebrows and then spoke through her neural interface and hidden speaker.

"I am not very different from you. As you can see, I am female. I am also slightly shorter than our average females. Our males are about thirty centimetres taller." She then turned toward Bracon *Patros* and spoke a few words to him.

The paratrooper promptly removed his helmet, showing the same elongated and shaved head with Caucasian features and reddish pink skin.

The linguists aboard the *Foudre* and Capt. Flanders aboard the *Enterprise* noted several words in the brief exchange between Seren *Capac* and Bracon *Patros*. The words appeared to have a Latin root. *Caputus* was one such word, which was awfully close to *caput*, or head. And so was the name *Patros*, which was close to *patronus*, or protector.

This deepened the mystery because the assumption, up to this point, had been the Ibecci language would have shared commonalities with the Puquina language, not Latin.

After the brief exchange with Bracon *Patros*, Seren *Capac* turned back to look at Lt. Mimieux, who was studying the sphere.

She again answered the questions she thought were in his mind.

"It is my companion orb. Every flier has one. It has multiple capabilities, ranging from serving as a beacon for downed or stranded fliers to helping them survive and navigating unfamiliar locations on the surface of a planet or in space. It is also designed to protect the flier. It has a neural link, keyed to its flier so that commands can be given with no need to speak." And as she said this, the orb came down in front of her and moved closer to Lt. Mimieux.

She continued, "It is equipped with a small graviphoton field generator and a coherent energy beam you call a laser. It is now tracking you, your squad, and the six paratroopers next to me."

She paused, looking at Lt. Mimieux for any reaction.

He simply nodded and swallowed hard.

"I am sure you and your superiors have many questions in need of answers. I will answer them in as much detail as I can. Is this satisfactory?"

"Yes, that would be fine," Lt. Mimieux said.

"Then let's begin. Our first convoy that landed five days ago comprises four spaceships. You can see three of them here, and the fourth, the Frigate *Vorian*, is over the western Indian Ocean. It is performing surveillance and defence duties together with its complement of five spacecraft, which are identical to mine. I assume your superiors are aware of this. The *Vorian* is one of five identical spaceships designed to provide fleet defence. As such, it lacks offensive weapons. Our frigates are about 30 percent larger than your latest Aconit-class frigates or the *Zumwalt-2* destroyers from the NAU battle group that is on its way."

As she spoke, the surveillance personnel aboard the *Foudre* and the *Enterprise* took notice. The Ibecci were very good at intelligence gathering.

Seren *Capac* continued.

"The *Vorian* has an approximate mass of 140,000 metric tons because of the composition of its hull."

The orb then projected a hologram of the *Vorian* in front of them, with cutaways and descriptive notes in French. Seren *Capac* continued.

"The hull has a thickness of 1.8 metres and is made of an engineered element that, in our language, is known as *reterit*. Its atomic number is 159, which places it in what your physicists call the second island of stability in your periodic table of elements. The name of this engineered element given by your physicists is unpentennium, a group 7 transition metal and a close analog of iridium. It shares some of its physical properties while being 45 percent denser. *Reterit* is not naturally occurring. It is manufactured on a material's accelerator. It is a noble metal with a high melting point and designed to withstand lasers. Its high density also makes it an ideal shield against radiation. The thickness also serves the purpose of protecting the interior of the spaceship from space debris during our long interstellar journey. I can provide additional information, but in the interest of expediency, we have created a repository of information in your open data network you call the World Wide Web. We located the information at the address www.Ibecci-race.net. You can find information on the *Vorian*'s capabilities, including its multilayered defensive weapons. Our Viceroy hopes this information will act as deterrence."

"I guarantee you the French and the NAU navies will be impressed, but I am part of the French Army, so less able to appreciate what you are saying. I find your technology fascinating, and I'm especially curious about your paratrooper's personal weapon, but I need to know your strength here on the ground."

As Lt. Mimieux said this, Bracon *Patros* moved forward two steps and presented his weapon while Seren *Capac* looked on.

Lt. Mimieux immediately noticed it was a projectile weapon, as the paratrooper had pushed back the slide to open the breech for inspection. He looked up at the paratrooper, who gave an imperceptible nod, and the lieutenant took the weapon. It felt much heavier, although not uncomfortably heavy, thanks to the power assist of Lt. Mimieux's exoskeleton. The barrel was much thicker and longer than the traditional forty-five to forty-eight centimetres found on most of Earth's assault rifles. He looked up at the paratrooper inquiringly.

"What kind of ammunition does this weapon fire?"

The Ibecci paratrooper then handed him what appeared to be a caseless round slightly smaller than a 12.7×99-mm (.50-BMG). It looked to be ten millimeters with a length of some fifty millimeters. It felt much heavier than a 12.7×99-mm though.

"What's the projectile made of?" Lt. Mimieux asked.

"It is a tungsten jacket with an iridium core. Most of our kinetic weapons fire projectiles at 1,500 m/s and higher velocities, so we need a hard exterior jacket. The iridium core gives the projectile a high mass, resulting in maximum kinetic energy," Bracon *Patros* said.

"How do you keep the barrel from eroding?"

"The barrel is finished in a super-hard crystalline material similar to what you call nanocrystalline diamond. It offers a very high wear resistance. The ultra-high polish of the barrel is an indication of its hard crystalline finish," Bracon *Patros* said, and Lt. Mimieux noticed the exterior surface finish of the black barrel was glass-like.

"May I keep this round?" Lt. Mimieux asked.

The Ibecci paratrooper again nodded imperceptibly.

In his head, Lt. Mimieux had roughly estimated the muzzle energy of the ammunition used in Ibecci personal weapons would be maybe twice the energy of a 12.7×99-mm round. He wondered about the recoil of the weapon and the chamber pressures needed to propel the projectile to such high velocities. He also thought about their heavier weapons, which they surely had, and shuddered at the thought of having to get in a firefight with the Ibecci.

He then turned to Seren *Capac*.

"Would you mind describing your strength on the ground and the construction plans of your settlement?"

"I was going to answer those two questions next. Please walk with me."

They started walking toward the large excavation at the centre of the construction site, which was growing by the hour.

"We have a cohort of two hundred paratroopers that came down to the surface in the IIC *Utios*, a dedicated military transport. Please do note I said military transport. It is not an assault spaceship. What is left of the IIC Fleet is simply the five frigates previously mentioned, plus Viceroy Marel's Flagship, which is the last of the Eberon class dreadnoughts and much less capable than the newer frigates. These two hundred paratroopers have the responsibility to set up a defensive perimeter during construction. Some paratroopers have heavier weapons, and we have deployed an eight-*crelon* squad with heavy weapons to the detection and surveillance antenna emplacement until permanent point defence batteries are installed. These will comprise of two coherent electromagnetic energy batteries and two quad electromagnetic projectile batteries. Your civilization possesses similar weapons, so you know they are strictly defensive in nature. We categorize their range to be less than forty kilometres for effective interception of incoming threats."

"Electromagnetic rail guns have much longer ranges and could be used offensively," Lt. Mimieux replied.

"Yes, you are correct, but I stated point defence batteries so they would be used strictly for interception of threats that cannot be much further than forty kilometres away. At much longer ranges, predicting and achieving reliable intercepts becomes very difficult, even with high velocities kinetic projectiles. Our quad rail batteries fire kinetic projectiles at a maximum initial velocity of some 5,000 m/s. The flight time to intercept an incoming threat forty kilometres away would be eight seconds. This is a long time-delay to intercept maneuvering threats travelling at high velocity."

"But your rail guns could be used offensively on slower moving or stationary targets," Lt. Mimieux asserted.

"Using our quad rail batteries as offensive weapons is not possible because the projectiles are expressly designed for threat interception. Each 50x150-mm iridium projectile fired by the batteries contains 220 fin-stabilized darts, each with a diameter of three millimeters. The darts disperse radially near the target based on guidance and proximity inputs. The kinetic energy of each dart is too small to inflict much damage to a target such as one of our spacecraft or your large watercrafts," Seren *Capac* replied, incorrectly assuming the NAU and French ships, just like her own spaceships, were heavily armoured and able to stop iridium armour-piercing fléchettes.

"I wouldn't be able to judge your statement one way or another, but the people watching and listening will."

Seren *Capac* once again looked at him, but this time with a piercing gaze. She was annoyed at his reply. Based on the biometric data from her orb, she received implied skepticism and suspicion emanating from Lt. Mimieux.

For the moment, she let it go, as the *Viracoh* had drilled into her that diplomacy required restraint in one's reactions, so she continued with her briefing.

"These batteries plus three additional sets are currently aboard the *Utios*. The other three are to be installed in three perimeter defence towers that will guard the settlement."

As she said this, the orb projected a hologram that enveloped them, showing how the settlement would look when completed.

Lt. Mimieux was immediately mesmerized by the effect. He was inside the projection and saw a curved translucent dome over his head, perhaps fifteen metres high, and an enormous lush garden with flowers and open spaces and paths. The realistic vista surrounded him and, in the distance, as he looked through the translucent roof, he could see the fuzzy outline of multistorey towers. He pivoted to take in the entire projection and could see three towers that looked like high-rise apartment buildings.

"Wow, this is impressive! A truly immersive experience that requires real wizardry," he said, almost childlike.

"You are inside a holographic projection of the settlement as it will look standing in the large central atrium. The atrium will have a diameter of almost three kilometres with a roof of translucent material similar to Earth's aerogel material but reinforced with carbon nanotubes. It will provide leisure spaces and meet our food needs via large vertical aeroponic gardens. The multistorey buildings you see in the distance will house twenty-five thousand Ibecci families with their young. There will be three towers located around the atrium. Finally, further out, there will be three slimmer defence towers. A more detailed description is available in the repository of information within your open data network."

"This a lot to take in," Lt. Mimieux replied.

"There are pictorials and renderings of the settlement, including aerial views in the information repository, that show how the buildings will be arranged and connected."

"How long will it take to build what you just described and house twenty-five thousand of your people?" Lt.

Mimieux asked.

Seren *Capac* looked at him for a couple of seconds and then replied.

"The name of our people in our language is *crelon*. As far as your question regarding the duration of our construction activity, the initial plan is to build the atrium and one housing building for an initial group of ten thousand *crelon*. The plan is to complete these two buildings in forty-five days. This is not difficult, at least for the construction of the buildings, which is being done using a building printing process similar to your own technology, albeit more advanced. You can see the construction gantries being erected to the south of the large excavation. They will dispense sintered rock and other material continuously to complete the shell of the buildings in twenty-five days, with most of the raw material extracted from the site. Small fusion plants will then be installed. The more time-consuming step is the growing of food, which I have been told will take about seventy to ninety days before the first harvest is ready. Construction will continue for another hundred and twenty days, and the entire settlement will be completed in approximately one hundred and fifty days. The *Vorian*, together with its five spacecraft, will remain here until the settlement is complete and we've had time to assess the level of threats we may be facing."

"Lt. Col. Leclerc and his team will have more questions when they arrive," Lt. Mimieux replied.

"We are expecting this. After we are done here, I will arrange for senior staff from our Command Operations or possibly, more senior staff from our Core Command to come planet-side, together with Seldik *Centor*, the commander of the *Vorian*. This will be arranged by the time your Lt. Col. Leclerc arrives. I trust this is satisfactory."

Lt. Mimieux simply nodded.

23 TOGETHER

The Extremely Large Telescope (ELT), Cerro Armazones, Chile

After a nonstop fifteen-hour flight from Heathrow and just before arriving at the Pudahuel International Airport in Santiago, Chile, Cate Brinnan went to the first-class washroom to get refreshed and change into fresh clothes. She seldom wore luxury designer labels but wanted to look her best when Carlos saw her.

She did her makeup and put on an expensive emerald silk blouse that showed a bit of cleavage, complementing it with an equally expensive tailored and neatly pressed grey skirt made of high-end merino wool. The skirt was short but not too short, allowing her to show her shapely legs with comfortable white canvas flats. The flats did not detract from her overall stunning look, as men and women in first class equally turned their heads when she walked back to her seat.

As it was winter in the Southern Hemisphere, with average temperatures of 0 to 5°C in Santiago and colder in Cerro Armazones, she wore a tan half-length leather coat matching her carry-on bag and purse.

She disembarked quickly to catch the connecting domestic flight to the city of Antofagasta, thirteen hundred kilometres north and closer to Cerro Armazones. It was a two-hour flight, but the anticipation made the time pass quickly.

Cate got off the plane and proceeded to the baggage claim area where Carlos was waiting.

As she walked toward him, she could see him smiling with that childlike grin she loved so much. He kept looking straight into her eyes and greeted her.

"*¡Hola, mi bella Irlandesa!* I don't think there are words to describe how beautiful you look," Carlos said. He then kissed her on both cheeks and on her lips, softly and briefly.

That's my lad, she thought. *We are making progress.* She grabbed him by both shoulders and pulled him down toward her, kissing him hard, but briefly. It was an intimate kiss, and to her delight, Carlos responded with the same intensity.

"I've missed you, sweetie," Cate replied, looking straight up at him and then running her eyes up and down to check him out.

"That's good then," Carlos said, grabbing her hand as they continued walking to the baggage carousel.

He still looks good, smells good, and is as adorable as always, Cate thought to herself as she watched Carlos effortlessly snatch her heavy suitcase from the carousel.

He was casually dressed in worn-out but clean jeans with an equally worn-out wide brown belt and an ESO-issue grey T-shirt under a bomber-style brown leather jacket. The T-shirt was neatly tucked into his jeans and showed the European Southern Observatory logo and the name *de Cevedes* printed on the breast pocket. It was not tight, yet it outlined his well-built chest and flat stomach. He was the antithesis of what a stereotypical astronomer was supposed to look like, and it was the reason Cate was attracted to him.

The incongruously dressed pair left the airport and walked to the parking area. They got into a grey all-electric extended range VW Amarok pickup truck marked with the ESO logo and left for Cerro Armazones about three hours away.

Carlos drove south on the B-70 two-lane highway that crossed the desolate desert of the Antofagasta region.

Once they left the city boundaries, the landscape turned to an unchanging arid and bleak vista, devoid of any vegetation, similar to the hyper-dry Atacama Desert. He then started chatting about his work.

"Your timing to come visit is very good, as I'm really struggling. Well . . . All observatories tasked with imaging Barnard's Star b are struggling to locate it. I was thinking . . . Your search for Planet Nine shares some similarities. Maybe you have some ideas?" Carlos asked as he drove, looking straight ahead at the almost deserted highway.

Cate initially said nothing. His shoptalk annoyed her because she had consciously made the effort to look good and had expected he would look at her more than he had. But then, that was Carlos, and given the drive through the desert was far from entertaining, she simply resigned to join in the conversation, at least for the duration of the trip to the ELT.

"Yes, I am running into similar problems," she replied curtly.

Carlos continued, somewhat hesitantly, turning his head to look at Cate and smile.

"I know one reason we cannot easily detect the Ibecci planet is because it likely crosses the plane of the Milky Way, where light pollution from the galactic core would make detection difficult."

"I can see that. We have a similar problem. Planet Nine's aphelion also crosses the plane Sof the Milky Way. But for us, the key stumbling block is that we think the planet is surrounded by a cloud of objects hiding it. That wouldn't be your problem though. Your problem is simply related to the low luminosity of Barnard's Star, or else Barnard b's orbit is inclined. But you already knew that, so I'm not really telling you anything new."

This went on for a bit as they discussed strategies of how to overcome the difficulties they were facing with their respective projects. They eventually exhausted the discussion, so Cate changed the subject.

"Are you still getting together with staff from other observatories? It's been a while since I've talked to the guys at the VRO, and I wondered if Peter and Jürgen were still there?" she asked somewhat more animatedly, shifting her weight and turning her body slightly toward Carlos.

"Ah ... Yes, most emphatically," he said, looking straight at her and then glancing quickly at her shapely legs.

"Recently?" she asked smiling, pleased Carlos had finally given her a once-over, even if it was fleeting.

"We actually got together the day the ELT captured decent images of the flotilla of Ibecci ships passing through the orbit of Mars. Peter and Jürgen came over to celebrate the discovery, and I opened my best Rioja. I think I mentioned this when I visited you in Dublin. Maybe not. Anyway, we don't get together as often since you left, but we can now that you are here!" Carlos said excitedly.

"I'd like that very much."

They continued reminiscing for a bit, finally arriving at the large and well-appointed Spanish style staff house about three kilometres below the ELT main telescope building.

It was just after 6:00 p.m. and dark by the time Carlos parked the truck in the circular laneway. They got out and entered through the main entrance, crossing the large foyer to one of the two wings where bedrooms were located. The building was almost empty, as the staff was already gone to the telescope to start the night shift, except for four employees who were in the kitchen. They were noisily preparing dinner to be served around 8:00 p.m.

Carlos brought Cate's suitcase to one of the empty bedrooms that looked like a typical hotel bedroom with two double beds and its own washroom. He deposited Cate's luggage on a luggage rack while she removed her leather coat. He then turned to look at her, appreciating her beauty in an uninhibited way, and spoke.

"Cate, I just want to say you look absolutely stunning. I don't recall ever seeing you dressed up so beautifully."

"Do you like it?" she asked, looking straight at him with hunger in her eyes while slowly undoing the buttons of her silk blouse, showing she was not wearing a bra.

Carlos moved toward her. He tenderly held her face in both hands and gave her a long and slow kiss.

Cate returned the kiss with urgency. She rushed to undo all the buttons of her blouse and then helped Carlos take off his jacket and T-shirt.

Carlos carefully placed her blouse and his T-shirt on one of the beds. He turned around to close the door of the room and then turned back to look at Cate, who now wanted him more than ever.

She slipped off her canvas flats and stepped barefoot toward him, pushing him onto the other bed. In one swift move, she removed her panties, lifted her skirt, and climbed onto the bed, straddling Carlos. Cate pressed herself against him while kissing him with unbridled lust.

Carlos reached to the back of her skirt and undid the zipper while Cate stopped long enough to do the same by undoing his belt and removing his jeans. She then resumed straddling him, holding him in a tight embrace, feeling his skin against her soft skin as they coupled. Cate then started rocking back and forth with increasing speed until they both climaxed.

It was short and intense lovemaking. Afterward, Cate continued kissing Carlos slowly now that her initial hunger had been satisfied.

"I wanted you since the first time I saw you," Carlos said, looking straight into her eyes with an intense gaze.

He then took the initiative to explore every inch of her body. Cate let herself be carried away as Carlos methodically kissed and caressed her.

They made love unhurriedly, afterward basking in the

afterglow of intimacy.

Cate placed her head on Carlos's chest and spoke.

"That was really wonderful, sweetie. You hid your fiery romantic passion."

"Eh . . . I was just being polite, but not anymore, *amor*," Carlo replied as he gently caressed the side of her leg, which she had placed on top of his.

In response, Cate just squeezed him and replied, "Glad to hear it, sweetie."

They stood there for a few minutes in an embrace, and then Carlos spoke. "I'm curious and haven't really asked you, but what made you change your mind to come visit me? I mean, I am thrilled, especially after . . ." He let the words trail off.

"You mean, after my not-too-subtle advance followed by our delightful lovemaking?"

"Yes," Carlos replied simply.

"Hmm . . . I still need to work on your shyness, but then, that's what makes you so lovable," she stated in her captivating Irish accent. "Anyway, to answer your question, I kept thinking about you after you came to visit me in Dublin. Decided I needed to know if what we had was more than just a friendship. Plus, I could not concentrate fully on my work," she replied, and to emphasize her point, ran her finger up and down his chest and rippled stomach.

"I am so glad," Carlos said.

He continued, "Remember when I asked you to come with me to the Canary Islands to see Pepe Astrade at the GranTeCan? At the time, I couldn't stop thinking how great it would have been for you to be there. I am sure we would have found time for this, but the wait to be with you was worth it."

"I agree, sweetie." Cate said, tilting her head up to look at him.

"Are you hungry?" Carlos asked.

"I could have a bite and a cup of tea," Cate replied. She then got up to go to the bathroom while Carlos looked at her stunning, naked figure as she walked away. When she returned, she went to her suitcase and pulled out casual clothes in which to get dressed.

On cue, Carlos followed suit. Then they both went to the kitchen, where supper was ready.

They grabbed plates from the well-appointed cupboard and served themselves from trays and pots sitting on the large black granite central island. As they filled their plates, Cate turned toward Carlos.

"Hey, it just occurred to me that maybe the reason you can't detect the planet is because the Ibecci might have hidden it."

"What do you mean? They can't hide a planet," Carlos replied.

"No, not physically, but they could optically."

"I still don't follow what you are saying," Carlos said.

"When I was doing my undergrad, I remember one class that dealt with the physics of transit photometry. The professor then started going on a tangent about advanced alien civilizations that might want to cloak their planet from the prying eyes of other civilizations by placing large lasers in orbit. The lasers could be tuned to the brightness of the star. As the planet shadow crosses its star and the field of view of, say, an alien civilization, the orbiting lasers would compensate for the loss in brightness, essentially making the planet undetectable."

"Hmm . . . a very bizarre idea. But then, we are under so much pressure, and everyone is coming up empty-handed, I suppose it is worth considering. Wouldn't such a cloak require huge lasers and vast amounts of power?"

"Apparently not. I can't quite remember the name of the astronomer who proposed the idea at the beginning of this century, but I remember my professor stating it would require something in the order of fifty megawatts of power. I wouldn't think that kind of power would be a problem for an advanced civilization."

"Intriguing," Carlos said as he exited the kitchen and

went to the enormous dining room table that sat sixteen people. They sat down with the other staff members, exchanging pleasantries.

Two of them recognized Cate and welcomed her while giving Carlos approving looks. Cate continued the discussion.

"So, the next move for you would be to talk to your bosses at the ESO and have them link with the UN or maybe the military to talk to the Ibecci and have them ask the question. You might consider talking to other astronomers first to see if the same thought has occurred to them or if they can entertain the notion of such an unconventional idea. That way, you won't look like a fool when you approach your bosses at the ESO. I would avoid talking to Peillinger at the GMT, as he wouldn't be objective at all, but I am sure you know this," Cate said.

Carlos just looked at her and smiled.

"You still amaze me on so many levels, you know. They practically drill into our brains that astronomers are supposed to be objective, but your creativity and thinking outside the box is unparalleled. I doubt very much anybody has thought about this possibility."

"It helps that I have musical talent and I'm a lefty," Cate replied, turning her head and smiling at Carlos.

Carlos just smiled back, paused for a second, and then spoke.

"I wish I could stay and spend more time with you, but I have to go to the observatory with the rest of the team. I know you've been travelling for almost a day and you might be tired."

"Oh, I'd like to go with you, if you don't mind. My body is still on Dublin time anyway, so I might manage to sleep a bit, but I'll probably be awake after midnight. Plus, there is the added advantage we can come back together and resume from where we left off," Cate replied with a mischievous look.

They went to the main observatory building together.

Carlos knew Cate truly loved her profession and would be at home at the observatory, especially one like the ELT, the most powerful ground-based telescope in the world.

They arrived at the gargantuan observatory building that was larger and taller than the Roman Colosseum. Carlos immediately went to his desk and started creating a project entry for the hypothesis Cate had suggested, which was necessary in order to talk to other astronomers.

Carlos did not know it then, but Cate's hypothesis was not a bizarre idea at all. The Ibecci had, in fact, cloaked their planet long ago from the prying eyes of the *Grisamirs*.

24 FACE-TO-FACE WITH A BALISTRO

L'Aiguille Noire, Kerguelen Islands

"I believe you also wanted to inspect the detection and surveillance antenna arrays we are erecting on L'Aiguille Noire. We can go there next unless you wish to inspect the construction activities here," Seren *Capac* said.

"Yes, I'm interested in inspecting your radar emplacement."

"Very well, Lt. Mimieux. I'll go back to my flier. Unfortunately, it is a single-seat flier. I assume you will use your small flying vehicle to get there?"

"Yes, I'll meet you there."

It was now early afternoon, and while sunset was at 5:30 PM, Lt. Mimieux wanted to make sure he would be back with his squad by dusk.

They started walking back to where they had originally met with the entourage of six Ibecci paratroopers with the orb still floating over Seren *Capac*'s head.

They walked quietly for about five minutes. As they reached Seren *Capac*'s spacecraft, she grabbed his arm and looked at him, meeting his gaze and speaking with her own voice rather than the translator.

"Lt. Mimieux . . ." And then she paused. "The Ibecci do not wish any harm to your people despite the distrust I detected from you in my biometrics," she said, speaking slowly, clearly trying to enunciate each word carefully.

"We are being open, and everything I have said and shown to you is factual. My race just wants a place to live after so many years of living in the confines of our spaceships. In exchange, we will give you any information and technology you want," she said almost pleadingly.

After she spoke, Lt. Mimieux wanted to say a couple of words of reassurance offline but did not have his helmet to access the HUD and mute the audio feed, so he simply responded by repeating what Lt. Col. Leclerc had stated earlier.

"France understands your plight and the need for a place to live. The distrust you sensed from me is a very human trait, and it stems principally from fear of the unknown. We know so little about you, yet you know so much about us. This in itself is a worry for all the governments on Earth. I hope you can understand that. We are all trying to develop mutual trust, but this will take time."

"Yes, of course. We are the first extraterrestrials humanity has encountered," Seren *Capac* said slowly in her own voice and smiled briefly.

"You are absolutely correct about that. I am going to my hoverbike now. It'll take me longer to reach L'Aiguille Noire. You will have to wait for me," he said and continued walking the additional fifty metres to the hoverbike.

Lt. Mimieux drove as fast as the terrain permitted, covering the five kilometres to L'Aiguille Noire quickly. He dismounted at the base and needed fifteen minutes to reach the top.

Seren *Capac* was already waiting for him.

Autonomous construction bots were connecting equipment with power cables to the fractal antennas. These were mounted in what appeared to be freshly poured concrete bases.

Paratroopers were settled in two forward emplacements oriented toward the east. They appeared to be similarly equipped to the paratroopers Lt. Mimieux met earlier, except for two, wearing heavier battle suits and carrying what looked like a twenty millimeter or larger four-barrel auto-cannon. The gun rested on a mount attached to the right side of the battle suit at waist level. On the opposite side, there was a large rectangular box. Lt. Mimieux guessed it was the ammunition storage even though he couldn't see an ammo belt running from the box to the gun. He thought it probably contained over five hundred rounds.

As he kept studying the arrangement, he wondered if the off-centre design was due to the need to balance the weight of the heavy gun and the large ammunition box. He thought it remarkable the basic design of infantry weapons of an advanced interstellar civilization was no different from those used on Earth, albeit more deadly. But then, the evolution of machine guns on Earth had seen little change in almost a hundred and fifty years, given the current MG7 standard-issue machine gun of the French Army was simply an evolved version of earlier weapons like the Hotchkiss M1914 used in WWI, but not much different.

Seren *Capac* noticed Lt. Mimieux studying the paratroopers with the heavy weapons and once again volunteered an answer before Lt. Mimieux could ask.

"They are our heavily armed and heavily armoured paratroopers. In terms you can understand, you could consider them to be 'heavy gunners,' but in our language they are known as a *Balistro*," she said. She then spoke to one of them who came over from the emplacement.

As the paratrooper ambled toward them, Lt. Mimieux could see the gun was motion stabilized and the mount gave the weapon complete freedom of motion because the paratrooper pivoted the barrel straight up. He stopped in front of Lt. Mimieux, showing little deference to Seren *Capac.*

"You are not as fearsome-looking as a *Grisamir*," the

paratrooper said directly to Lt. Mimieux.

"I don't know what a *Grisamir* is," Lt. Mimieux replied, looking at the enormous paratrooper. He was taller and his battle suit was bigger than any of the other paratroopers.

"This is Arcal *Decanu*, the most veteran paratrooper of the Ibecci Imperium Field Army (IIFA) and one of a few remaining Ibecci paratroopers who served in the last campaign against the *Grisamirs* just before the solar flare of 1998. His rank is equivalent to a master sergeant," Seren *Capac* said.

Arcal *Decanu* simply stood for a few seconds looking down at Lt. Mimieux and then turned around back to the emplacement.

Lt. Mimieux looked at Seren *Capac* after Arcal *Decanu* walked away.

"He doesn't look like he has great mobility."

"*Balistros* are the last line of defence, so by definition, they do not need mobility except to retreat when fighting a defensive battle. *Balistros* keeps fighting until the enemy advance has been stopped or they die trying. They are volunteers screened for their suitability to meet their primary responsibility. While there is no shortage of volunteers, few can meet the demanding physical and psychological requirements, which include the requisite to continue fighting while badly injured and still retain over 90 percent of their lethality. They accomplish this through significant artificial enhancements. They are by far the most enhanced of the Ibecci military personnel and are technically cyborgs. This makes a *Balistro* the most lethal weapon of the Imperium Field Army while still keeping the essence of a sentient *crelon(e)*."

"I saw little sentience in Arcal *Decanu*'s behaviour," Lt. Mimieux countered.

"Don't judge him by his conduct. He has seen terrible things during multiple campaigns against the *Grisamirs* and lost thousands of paratroopers he had trained against the unrelenting *Grisamir* hordes. He knows his job well, is fiercely loyal, and follows the command structure without question."

"Couldn't you accomplish the same job with robotic weapon systems as we do? Such systems would keep performing their duty until damaged or destroyed without the loss of life."

"We learned long ago while fighting the *Grisamirs* that autonomous and even semiautonomous weapon systems carry a significant liability risk. At best, an enemy can disable them as we did with the small Chinese space station. At worst, the enemy can take over their control and operate them against you. We learned this painful lesson long ago, paying a heavy price with countless *crelon* lives. In the battlefield, all our weapon systems have a sentient *crelon* operator so that a *Balistro* cannot be compromised via a cyberattack, or an autonomous flier performing defence patrols cannot be disabled. There are only two exceptions. One is the sentient ship entity (SE) aboard our defence frigates. The other is a flier's orb. The orbs are keyed through a special neural interface more advanced than the standard neural interfaces used by all other *crelon(e)*."

"You and Arcal *Decanu* keep mentioning the *Grisamirs*. Who are they, exactly?"

"The *Grisamirs* are a most implacable non-biological organism. They are extremely evolved, cybernetic machines. They are a formidable foe that at first glance appears barbaric because of the way they fight, giving no quarter, destroying and harvesting everything in their path. However, this is wrong, as they are simply machines that behave more like bacteria or a virus with a predetermined set of instructions. Your army ant would be another example of an organism that exhibits a very similar behaviour to a *Grisamir* horde. At least, that is how the lowest elements of their hierarchy behave. They feel no pain and have no feelings of fear, anger, or despair. They simply follow their programming to take over new terrain and resources, removing any barriers immediately in their path while ignoring the flanks of a battlefront, or the spaceships at the edge of the battle."

Lt. Mimieux looked at her but said nothing

She continued, "The Ibecci Imperium has been fighting them for about six hundred of your years, although containing their advance is a more appropriate way of describing the conflict. It started as a contest for resources within our own planetary system when they first appeared on asteroids at the edge of the *Perfal* system and started mining metal and any other valuable elements from the asteroids. Initially, they were simple mining machines designed to extract resources. We tried to communicate with them to no avail and attempted to develop a better understanding of who they were, including finding out their original creators. We followed them in our own spaceships toward the cold dwarf star we call *Frigun*. You know it as WISE 0855-0714, which is approximately three light-years from *Eder*. We hoped to communicate with higher levels of their hierarchy, but it was too long a voyage and our spaceships were attacked. It wasn't an overt or intentional attack. To them, our ships appeared as a source of rich, dense metal. Some of the crew were able to escape, but there was a significant loss of life. We took steps to safeguard our operations and started destroying their mining machines wherever they appeared. At first, it was relatively easy to destroy them, but within fifty of your years, they evolved into hybrid mining and war machines with the ability to react and respond to an attack. Their latest evolved *Ardreker,* as we call them, are heavily armoured multi-legged mining machines equipped with powerful energy weapons. They can only be disabled with multiple hits from high-velocity kinetic projectiles. Our weapons evolved in order to defeat the *Ardreker* and the higher battle organisms we call *Irascilin,* which are nearly invulnerable. The twenty-five millimeter autocannon carried by a *Balistro* was purposely created to destroy the *Irascilin,*" Seren *Capac* concluded.

"All this sounds surreal, like in a science fiction movie

where I still don't know the ending. First we meet you, and now we find out there are other threats. From your description, the *Grisamirs* sound all too terrifying, so the question for Earth is, and believe me, you will be drilled by Lt. Col. Leclerc and others about this: Are the *Grisamirs* following you, and will they invade our solar system like they did yours?"

"A very unlikely scenario for several reasons. Their known rate of expansion is such that it will take over three hundred of your years, likely more, before they have completely consumed *Eder* and all the bodies in the *Perfal* system. Based on their behaviour, there is no reason they would venture into empty space where there is nothing to harvest. This applies to most of the space between our planetary system and yours, which is empty until you get to the edge of your Oort cloud. In addition, during our voyage of twelve years, we continuously monitored for any signs of the *Grisamirs*. We also have a fast armoured scout ship that stayed behind for the equivalent of three of your months after the convoy of spaceships left *Eder*. It performed surveillance duties to see if the *Grisamirs* sent anything after the convoy. It then sprinted forward to catch up and repeated this maneuver for the first half of our voyage until we determined the convoy was in the clear. The *Nike*, as it is called, is currently keeping station at the edge of your Oort cloud at a distance of about 120 AU. It is deploying sentry buoys in an arc that extends for five AU on either side of the path, followed by our convoy. These buoys will remain in place as sentries."

"So, they did not follow, but you are setting up surveillance, which tells me there is a possibility they might show up."

"Yes, in two or three hundred years they will start expanding once they have mined all the resources in the *Perfal* system. They could choose to expand in this direction. More likely, though, they will travel toward two binary stars you call Alpha and Proxima Centauri. There is potentially more matter revolving around that binary system as well as the brown dwarf binary system you call Luhman 16, which is in the near vicinity of the Centauri binary system."

"You will probably need to bring your own experts when you meet with Lt. Col. Leclerc to further elaborate on the *Grisamirs*, as I am sure those listening in see them as a potential threat to Earth.

"Our senior personnel will be able to provide more detail as you request."

"Good. Sunset will be in about two hours, and I want to be back with my squad before then. Your current readiness both here and at the construction site is as if you are certain of hostilities against you."

"You should not be surprised at our preparations. We believe they are very much warranted given the Chinese watercraft that are on their way here. Our monitoring of the communications of the NAU watercraft confirms there is a very high probability the Chinese are intent on striking our site. That is one reason we are flying defence patrols and the *Vorian* is positioned where it is," Seren *Capac* concluded.

Lt. Mimieux looked at her and said nothing. He then turned around and started walking toward his hoverbike.

25 CONVERGENCE

NAUS *Enterprise* (CVN-80), Kerguelen Islands

Jimmy Weng, the Undersea Warfare Commander (AX), and Lt. Cmdr. Izzy Urbina, the Submarine Element Coordinator (SEC), were in the *Enterprise* CDC tracking the advance of the Mantas.

The Mantas were about three hours away from their assigned surveillance area. They reported a weak sonar contact far away and to the south of their position.

"Flag bridge, CDC. Mantas report possible contacts due south."

"CDC, flag bridge. The CCSG is on his way."

The CDC was two levels down from the flag bridge, and Cmdr. Phelps got there quickly.

"What have you got, Lt. Cmdr?" the CCSG asked.

"The Mantas are reporting a weak sonar contact due south from their position."

"Is it one of the Chinese subs?"

"Pretty sure. Signal is weak, but it's from a Type 097, all right. Sounds like it's travelling beyond flank. We can make out the noise of the cooling pumps, so it must be doing thirty-seven, maybe thirty-eight knots, right, chief?" Lt.

Cmdr. Urbina asked the warfare specialist who was sitting at a nearby console analyzing the data stream.

"Affirmative, sir. The Type 097 is balls to the wall," the warrant specialist said in navy speak.

"How far away?" the CCSG asked.

"Hard to say, but if I were a betting woman, I would say three hundred kilometres south from the Mantas. I think they detached from the task force and went straight south to get around us. We're still working on a better fix, but it looks like they are travelling on a heading of 220 or maybe 270 degrees," the SEC replied.

"Damn! They wanted to bypass anyone sitting on the east side of the island, or maybe their recon satellites saw the *Trudeau* and the *Ross* and did not want to risk meeting them head-on."

"Agree, sir."

"We could get the *Olympia* to go around the south side of the island to track them," the CCSG said.

"I wouldn't recommend it, sir. The Kerguelen plateau is too shallow. Easier to just reposition the *Grenville* further south," the AX said, referring to the two improved *Virginia* class attack submarine supporting the strike group.

"Yes, that's an option, but we still have another Chinese sub out there. I want to keep the *Grenville* where it is right now," the CCSG said.

"We could instruct two of the Mantas to follow it, sir. They won't be able to catch up, but at least they will stay with it," the SEC replied.

"I think that would be best. In the meantime, we need to understand why this attack sub is so far ahead of the strike group," the CCSG said and then turned around toward the holographic table in the centre of the CDC.

The holographic sphere was now reduced to a nineteen hundred–kilometre radius and thirty thousand–metre altitude, but it contained all the known Chinese battle group assets. The type 097 Chinese subs were now shown at their presumed locations, plus the Divine Eagles, some eight hundred kilometres from the island and the *Liu Huaqing* task force, just inside the sphere.

"Opinions?" the CCSG asked.

As he did this, the AQ and the AS, together with Maj. Krol and Capt. Flanders, entered the CDC.

"Maybe their plan is simply to get their assets in position as quickly as possible and then wait for the rest of the strike group," the SEC volunteered.

"But why so close? Their CJ-30A has a range of at least two thousand kilometres, and the sub is probably much closer by now," the CCSG said.

"I would guess that at this moment the sub is probably around a thousand to sixteen hundred kilometres from the island," the SEC replied.

"The Chinese know we don't want to get into a confrontation. Right now, their thinking is they're essentially unopposed and can get as close to the island as they want. This way they can launch their LACMs really close, giving the Ibecci essentially no time to react," the AS said.

"It would explain why their task force let their subs get so far ahead. The question now is how close do they want to get?" the CCSG asked.

"Who knows, maybe within three hundred kilometres? At such a short distance, the Ibecci would have little time to react," the AS replied.

Everyone looked on, so she continued.

"The Chinese probably want to get this operation completed quickly and out of here before the French arrive. That way they won't have to explain firing into French territory. I figure in approximately forty-eight hours they'll be within range to launch their aircraft and hit the island with a combined strike of air-launched, ship-launched and submarine-launched LACMs, together with a salvo of DF-29 ASBM from the Spratlys. I bet they'll probably fire over a hundred missiles, thinking their saturation attack will overwhelm the Ibecci. We'd do exactly the same thing," the AS finished.

"Cmdr. DesRosiers, are the two Divine Eagles in range to provide targeting information to their strike group?"

"Yes, sir, they are."

"Well then, I guess the Chinese now have all their ducks in a row, so we just wait for hostilities to commence. What do you think, major? Should we alert the Ibecci about the Chinese subs?" the CCSG asked Maj. Krol.

"They know the Chinese are coming. I would guess they should have no problem tracking and targeting all surface- and air-launched missiles fired at them. It's anyone's guess whether they know about the subs. We warned them the first time, so warning them this time will show consistency on our part. I understand from my orders we were to remain neutral though," Maj. Krol replied.

"We are cooperating with the French, major. We will send a message to the *Foudre* and Lt. Mimieux to warn them two Chinese attack subs are approaching the island with the intent to fire LACMs into their territory. We can't help it if Seren *Capac* overhears this information," the CCSG replied with a sly look on his face.

"I must remember to never accept an offer to play poker at your table, Cmdr. Phelps," Maj. Krol replied.

The CCSG gave Maj. Krol an amused look.

"I think it is a good way of warning the Ibecci, but I also don't want to get on their bad side," the CCSG replied. "I keep remembering Viceroy Marel's words that Earth will find them to be a formidable opponent. We still don't know how they will react to hostility, and I really don't want to find out if their bite is worse than their bark. Cmdr. DesRosiers, after we are done here, please send a message to the French."

"Yes, sir."

"I also think it might be prudent to move the *Ross* and the *Trudeau* a hundred kilometres north from their current position. Please inform Cmdr. Oliver to do so. In the meantime, I'll communicate with NAVCENT and the vice chief of naval operations to coordinate a meeting with the

Chinese UN representative at the diplomatic level to tell them we know what they are up to. This will add legitimacy to our warning to the French. I suggest we all get some rest because in two days, maybe sooner, we are in for some real fireworks," the CCSG concluded.

He did not say it, but he was praying for the strike group not to get drawn into a confrontation with the Chinese while also having to look behind his back for potential reactions from the Ibecci.

Cmdr. DesRosiers advised the RPIM five-man squad to expect hostilities in forty-eight hours with potential use of submarine-launched LACMs at close range.

As predicted, the Ibecci overheard the message because the RPIM squad noted additional Ibecci paratroopers on the ground.

26 LOGIC SELDOM PREVAILS

The United Nations, New York

News leaked to the media that the French military had met with the Ibecci in the Kerguelen Islands and were allowing them to build a settlement.

Demonstrations started almost immediately in France and around the world. From Manila to Caracas to Lagos, people came out into the streets by the thousands chanting, "Leave our planet" and "Earth belongs to the human race."

Chaos spread faster than when the aliens first arrived four months earlier. The disorder grew in intensity at an alarming rate, although it wasn't difficult to agitate people already at the end of their rope and desperate for better living conditions. The demonstrations simply gave people an excuse to turn their attention away from their meagre existence.

At the UN, an emergency session of the Security Council was called by Undersecretary Laura Bonte to discuss the news and worldwide unrest.

As soon as the session started, Yongrui Xu from China requested the floor.

"Distinguished members of the Security Council. We

need to unite as one voice, as one planet, to take action and expel the aliens from Earth. You have witnessed the unrest across the globe. We are entering a dangerous phase and the potential for widespread anarchy because of the foolishness by France to grant the aliens permission to settle in their territory."

He paused to see the reaction of the members. Murmuring immediately started but died down soon after.

"We cannot take the alien's message of friendship at face value. China believes it is better to err on the side of caution before it is too late. China will take a stand against the aliens and do what's needed."

Alain Trouchette, France's representative, was not present to respond to the Chinese insult, and no one seemed to be willing to speak up in support or opposition.

This went on for a short time until Gabriel Medina from Argentina finally requested the floor and voiced a forceful riposte.

"Members of the Security Council, the aliens stated they came in peace, searching for a place to live. Yet China, with no basis or evidence, is telling us the aliens cannot be trusted. We know better, should know better."

Medina then paused and looked around the room for a reaction.

"Our duty is to give the aliens the benefit of the doubt and trust them until proven otherwise. Throughout history, man has done exactly the same thing China wants us to do. To persecute and label those seeking refuge. Yet, over and over, strangers coming to a new land have invariably allowed societies to advance and become better. Diversity has always enriched societies. I don't need to provide examples because all of you know human migrations have been going on since the dawn of our own civilization and are the catalyst for growth," Medina said and paused.

Some members nodded.

"Planet Earth has reached its limits of growth. Our civilizations are in a crisis of immense proportions, and our future seems uncertain. We are simply hobbling along without really knowing what our next steps should be. At this juncture in our evolution, we are in dire need of new blood and new ideas to continue moving forward. I say the Ibecci can provide this. They may prove to be our salvation. France showed courage and leadership by being the first to welcome the Ibecci, taking the risk and allowing them to settle in their territory. Argentina and all the South American nations are willing to do the same and grant the Ibecci sanctuary. After all, their first settlement was on my continent. I implore members to become united, not to expel them, but to welcome them and assist them. *Viva la diferencia.*"

The same members who had nodded earlier now applauded vigorously, while the vast majority remained impassive.

Within a few minutes, Undersecretary Bonte adjourned the meeting, as no one seemed interested in expressing opinions or bringing forward any motions.

Thirty minutes later, in her office, Undersecretary Bonte reflected on the day's events.

"Well, another useless session, but this time the Chinese stoked the fire now that things around the world are getting more unstable. We might have also broken the record for the shortest Security Council session ever held." Undersecretary Bonte said to her assistant, Jennifer.

"Maybe the Council Members are preoccupied with what is happening at home and are being reserved, Madam Undersecretary."

Undersecretary Bonte said nothing as she looked out from her office window to the East River.

It was now late May and all the trees along the river were in full bloom. Summer was just around the corner, and with it, the thoughts of warm temperatures and long, lazy days should have been utmost in the minds of everyone.

Instead, all she could see was police and military presence, as the UN building had been cordoned-off to prevent demonstrators from getting too close. Her mind drifted away, and she started softly singing the old George Gershwin song "Summertime."

She was no Ella Fitzgerald nor Norah Jones, but she had a melodious voice good enough to sing at any nightclub in New York. She crooned, and the drowsy melody helped soothe her frayed nerves. After just four bars, she came back to reality and spoke.

"Most of the Security Council members are simply irrational, Jen. That's why no one spoke except for Argentina. Meanwhile, the Chinese are behaving like children. No, scratch that. Like bullies . . ."

Just then, her ruminations were caught short by a call. The main screen in her office lit up and she found herself staring at Maj.-Gen. Arias and a high-ranking NAU navy admiral, judging from the stripes on his sleeves.

"Good afternoon, Undersecretary Bonte. I hope we are not calling at a bad time. We have an urgent matter to discuss with you. This is the vice chief of naval operations, Admiral Harry Shear," Maj.-Gen. Arias said.

"Undersecretary Bonte, I wish the circumstances were different and we had time for pleasantries, but time is of the essence," Admiral Shear said, wasting no time.

"What can I do for you?"

"As you know from an earlier conversation with Maj.-Gen Arias, a Chinese navy task force is on its way to the Kerguelen, and, unfortunately, it is not to welcome the Ibecci. There is a very high probability the Chinese will fire their weapons at the Ibecci settlement on the island. We need to impress upon the Chinese government the NAU and France don't think it's advisable for them to fire into sovereign French territory."

Undersecretary Bonte raised an eyebrow, conveying puzzlement.

"You are joking, right? While I like the idea of applying pressure to get them to back down from this action, the success of trying to change their mind on any issue is less than stellar. It would be difficult in this case, given that at today's Security Council meeting, China essentially warned all members they plan to take hostile actions against the Ibecci."

Maj.-Gen Arias and Admiral Shear looked at each other. She ignored their reaction and continued.

"But I am sure you are aware of their poor track record taking advice from other nations or complying with UN resolutions. At any rate, what do you need from me?"

"We want to talk to China through back channels rather than having France go through the normal diplomatic route of recalling their ambassador. There are several reasons for this. First, the world doesn't need more discord, pitting one nation against another nation. The second reason is partly partisan and meant to keep the peace. We want to ensure China does not view the NAU as siding with the Ibecci, which could precipitate a more widespread worldwide conflict."

"It's pretty widespread right now. Hard to imagine getting any worse," Undersecretary Bonte said cynically.

Admiral Sheer ignored the comment and continued.

"By going through the UN, we appear neutral and simply coming to the aid of France. We need your help to set up a meeting with Yongrui Xu. We want you to meet with him while accompanied by someone from the State Department who will give the Chinese information gathered in the Kerguelen."

"What you are asking is something that should be handled by the State Department. I can set up the meetings, but in my current position, I cannot get involved."

"That's why you will be accompanied by Phil White from the State Department."

"Phil White? That's cute. Couldn't State come up with a better name, or are they running out of creative people? But I digress; I still don't see why my involvement is needed."

"We figure you know the Chinese member, and since time is of the essence, you may be able to arrange a meeting quickly."

"Okay, if you can have your G-Man here in thirty minutes, I'll have my assistant set up an appointment with Mr. Xu to meet in the next two hours."

Right after the video call concluded, Jennifer called the offices of the Chinese UN delegation and immediately ran into trouble trying to get an appointment.

"Madam Undersecretary, the assistant to Mr. Xu is refusing to grant us an appointment, saying Mr. Xu is too busy for the next three weeks, even after I stated it's an urgent matter."

"Well, if they won't come to us, we will go to them. As soon as Phil White arrives, we will go down. Let's see if they'll ignore us then."

About forty-five minutes later, Undersecretary Bonte, trailed by Phil White dressed in a tailored three-piece navy suit , entered the offices of the Chinese delegation.

The reception area was furnished with opulent Chinese rosewood furniture made of burgundy-black Dalbergia and all-but-extinct ebony-coloured Diospyros. Armoires and credenzas were arranged around the perimeter of the room, and ornate Qing Dynasty–style couches and low-back armchairs were placed around an exquisitely carved coffee table. It was like entering the special events office at the Peninsula in Hong Kong.

A tall and striking Chinese administrative assistant wearing a red dress was standing next to a holographic terminal, answering incoming calls. She turned toward Undersecretary Bonte and smiled, recognizing her right away.

"Good afternoon, Madam Undersecretary Bonte. How may I help you?" the assistant asked in perfect English.

"Hi, Peizhi. We are here to see Yongrui Xu. It is an urgent matter. We just need thirty minutes of his time, but likely less."

"I am really sorry, Madam Undersecretary, but I already informed your assistant Mr. Xu's agenda is fully booked for the next three weeks."

"Yes, Peizhi. I am aware of that. That's why I came down instead. Mr. Phil White, here from the State Department, has information of the utmost importance that we need to bring up with Mr. Xu. So, we will wait here until Mr. Xu comes out of his office, as I imagine he has to at some point. Your choice. You can tell him we are here, or you can ignore us, but we are not going anywhere."

The assistant, still smiling politely, looked at Undersecretary Bonte for a couple of seconds but said nothing and turned back to the holographic terminal, likely to inform Yongrui Xu the undersecretary was in their offices and wasn't going away.

After thirty minutes, two Chinese officials in grey suits entered the Chinese offices and promptly opened the door to the meeting room.

"Excuse me, Madam Undersecretary, Mr. Xu will now see you," the receptionist announced.

"Well, thank you, Peizhi! That is much appreciated," Undersecretary Bonte replied with all charm she could muster.

Undersecretary Bonte and Phil White entered the spacious meeting room decorated with the same opulent armoires and credenzas. A highly polished burgundy-black table that could seat thirty people occupied the centre of the room. Mr. Xu was already standing to the side of the table and greeted Undersecretary Bonte in his accented English.

"Good afternoon, Madam Undersecretary Bonte. I had to rearrange some of my schedule to meet you regarding this urgent matter that I am assuming is somehow connected to the Chinese UN delegation and—"

"Come, come, Yongrui. We are not children. Give me the decency of not insulting my intelligence. You know what this is all about. Pretending to be naïve is not something that suits you," Undersecretary Bonte replied bluntly.

"Very well, Madam Undersecretary, but truthfully, I can give you a maximum of thirty minutes."

"We won't need that much time. Mr. White is from the State Department and brought some information to my attention. Normally, I don't deal with such issues since this is not the purview of the UN, but it was impressed upon me things might get out of control. We want to prevent this, ideally through quiet channels. To save time, I will not skirt the issue," Undersecretary Bonte said, locking eyes with the Chinese official.

She then sat down in a high-back chair.

Phil White followed suit and sat down next to Undersecretary Bonte. He then presented his business card, followed by an envelope he took out from a soft black leather briefcase. He placed both in front of Mr. Xu.

Undersecretary Bonte then spoke.

"In the envelope, you will find information gathered by the *Enterprise* aircraft carrier task force. I am sure you know the *Enterprise* left its regular patrol area in the Gulf of Oman and is now near the Kerguelen Islands, ostensibly to lend support to France as needed. The data gathered includes images, maps, and an analyst's summary. I'll give you the highlights. The *Liu Huaqing* task force, with four of their destroyers, is about thirty-six hours from the island. One of two Qin-class attack subs normally attached to the task force is way in front, and as of eight hours ago, about a thousand kilometres from the eastern side of the island, and it seems to be in a hurry to get to the island. In case you are unfamiliar with the Kerguelen Islands, the eastern side of the island is where the main French outpost of Port-aux-Français is located. Maybe the crew of the sub is planning to do some sightseeing on the Kerguelen Islands and dock at their main port. If this were the case, I would think the Chinese government would have alerted the French government of their impending goodwill visit, but I understand this is not the case," Undersecretary Bonte added sarcastically.

To his credit, Yongrui Xu's expression remained placid, which deflated Undersecretary's Bonte intended insult, so she continued.

"And finally, this photo shows the DF-29 long-range anti-ship ballistic missiles in the Spratly Islands being readied. So, my question is do you know the meaning of all this activity?" Undersecretary Bonte asked.

"I am aware of the deployment of warships from the PLA's navy to the south Indian Ocean, but I don't know any specific operational details given that I am simply an official of the Chinese government assigned to the UN," Yongrui Xu replied.

"Okay, fair enough. Then I'll volunteer a hypothesis put forward by the State Department. They conclude there is a high probability the PLA navy is planning to launch a combined attack against the Ibecci who arrived on the Kerguelens less than two weeks ago."

"You are making inflamed accusations with no basis and implying China is planning a pre-emptive strike. What if we are just being cautious and simply deploying our forces as a precautionary measure to prepare ourselves for unknown eventualities? After all, there is still much we don't know about the aliens," Yongrui Xu said in a composed manner.

"Strangely enough, this morning at the council meeting, and let me make sure I get this straight, you said that 'All the nations of the world should unite to expel the aliens from our planet, and China will stand against them.' So, you can tell me whatever you want, but your speech from this morning tipped your hand, and the evidence is in front of you. I said earlier we wanted to bring this up through back channels, which I now have done, rather than through the more public display of France getting into a diplomatic row with China. We will be watching your every move. The NAU is there to lend a hand to France, and an unprovoked attack on French sovereign territory, regardless of the reason, will be dealt with the full weight of the UN Security Council."

"Are you threatening China, Madam Undersecretary?"

"Yongrui, first of all, and this is a cultural lesson, I have

Italian heritage from my father while my mother was Black American. Italians do not make threats, they get even. Second, and this really is more important, I am here in the capacity of the undersecretary of the UN Security Council, who answers directly to Federico Escabeche, the secretary general of the UN. As such, I am simply upholding the primary mandate of the UN and looking after the safety and security of all nations on Earth," Undersecretary Bonte concluded while looking at Yongrui Xu with a relaxed gaze.

Yongrui Xu stared at Undersecretary Bonte for a moment, blinked, and then spoke.

"Unless you have something else you wanted to discuss, I think we are done here, Madam Undersecretary," he replied with a controlled voice as he tried to hide his rage.

"Yes, I believe so. Look at the time! We got our business completed in eleven minutes. Always a pleasure, Yongrui."

She then stood up, followed by Phil White, and turned around toward the meeting room door. She waved goodbye to Peizhi on her way out.

Despite what had been implied by Undersecretary Bonte, the Chinese did not have plans to fire their weapons into French territory because of the international complications such an action would create.

The Chinese simply wanted to blow the *Vorian* out of the sky. This they hoped would make the Ibecci reconsider their plans to settle on Earth.

27 HOSTILITIES

***Liu Huaqing* Carrier Task Force, South Indian Ocean**

The *Liu Huaqing* nuclear super carrier and its four Type 057 *Shenyang* destroyers was now less than eighteen hundred kilometres from the Kerguelen Islands and within range to strike the Ibecci.

Two Type 097 nuclear attack submarines normally attached to the carrier battle group were rushing forward to get to within three hundred kilometres from the island to launch LACMs at close range.

Admiral Shen Hsu was in the flag bridge of the Type 004 nuclear super carrier that became operational in 2034 as the first nuclear super carrier of the PLA's blue-water navy.

His battle group was ready, but there were uncertainties. He did not know whether he could inflict any damage to the Ibecci, given the nonexistent information on their defensive capabilities. But knew the Ibecci could launch effective cyberattacks such as the one that temporarily crippled the *Tiangong4* space station.

He was also worried about the French and the NAU forces. But it was not his job to question the decisions made by the PLA navy. He was simply a second-generation navy commander tasked with obeying the order of his superiors, just like his father before the MERS pandemic of 2027 took his life and the lives of his mother and younger sister.

Providence seemed to be on his side as the Ibecci repositioned the spaceship tasked with defending their settlement out at sea. This made Admiral Hsu's job much easier. He could now direct his attack toward the spaceship and avoid firing missiles onto the island.

The tempo aboard the *Liu Huaqing* increased as the operation got underway. Flight crews rushed on the carrier deck to prepare a flight of thirty *An-Jian3* unmanned combat aerial vehicles, each carrying a single CJ-30K medium-range ASCM as the first wave of the attack.

Admiral Hsu watched through the flag bridge's angled windows as electromagnetic catapults launched the UCAVs in rapid succession. The force of thirty *Dark Sword* UCAVs, as they were known in the West, were to fly toward their target, release their ASCMs, just two hundred kilometres away from the carrier and return.

This was a deception intended to light up the Ibecci's radars, distracting and hopefully misleading them into thinking the Chinese attack would be small while the destroyers simultaneously launched the much larger wave of ASCMs from behind.

Fifteen minutes after the last *An-Jing3* left the carrier, a junior lieutenant entered the flag bridge to inform the admiral of the progress.

"Admiral Hsu, the UCAVs are approaching their release point."

"Thank you, lieutenant. Are the destroyers and the DF-29 launchers ready to fire the second salvo?"

"Yes, sir. Standing by."

"Good."

The Admiral got up and walked to the CIC to watch the operation. As he entered the CIC, the four *Shenyang* destroyers fired a volley of anti-ship missiles. The destroyers were deployed around the carrier one kilometre away, but the sound was still deafening as the combined barrage of 112 medium-range anti-ship missiles left their vertical launch system cells.

The white-painted missiles sprinted upward, emerging from a blanket of acrid grey smoke temporarily obscuring the destroyers.

The missiles reached an apex in an almost choreographed precision. They quickly pivoted to a horizontal sea-skimming flight, accelerating to Mach 3 toward their target. One missile failed to pivot to a horizontal flight, instead continuing straight up and had to be destroyed midflight. Another missile plowed straight into the ocean after transitioning to a horizontal flight, exploding on impact. This left 110 missiles on their way toward the Ibecci spaceship.

At the same time, four DF-29 ASBM on mobile launchers were fired from the Spratly Islands some six thousand kilometres away. The four missiles were to follow a ballistic trajectory travelling at Mach 10.

There were now thirty air-launched, 110 ship-launched, and four ASBM missiles airborne.

The missiles flew to their target following a preprogrammed flight, continuously updated via BeiDou satellite guidance. This was augmented with real-time information transmitted by the two Divine Eagles flying ahead of the battle group.

Admiral Hsu watched the advancing missiles in the holographic sphere inching closer and closer to the island. They would fly past it and reach the spaceship, keeping station out at sea, in thirty minutes.

28 IN THE LINE OF FIRE

NAUS *Ross* (DDG-1025), Kerguelen Islands

Some five hundred kilometres northeast of the island, an E-5A Tracker, airborne early warning aircraft, together with four F-47 UCLASS drones, provided air cover to the *Ross* and *Trudeau*.

The E-5A was tracking the advance of the *Liu Huaqing* task force about 400 km further east from their position. It's AN/APY-12 radar detected the 140 supersonic sea-skimming cruise missiles within seconds of their launch.

Aboard the *Ross*, the air detection console in the CIC lit up as the data was instantaneously downloaded via the cooperative engagement data (CED) link.

The holographic tactical sphere in the centre of the CIC also updated, showing the missiles as glowing red dots, each with a leading red ribbon projecting toward the island.

The air detection tracking (ADT) warfare specialist spoke in a calm voice as the general quarters bells rang outside the soundproofed CIC.

"Quails inbound. Large force of quails inbound. Computer confirms 140 supersonic cruise missiles in two groups separated by one hundred kilometres. Heading of two hundred fifty degrees. Warning white," the ADT announced as the missiles would pass approximately one hundred kilometres south from the current location of the Ross.

"Please catalogue the contact data into the NTDS, chief," the detection tracking supervisor (TRK SUP) said.

"Yes, sir."

"Can we make out the type?"

As the TRK SUP asked, a second screen on the air detection console above the active screen changed status and started blinking angrily. The screen showed four ballistic missiles on their boost face fired from the Spratlys that had been detected by the NAU Space Tracking and Surveillance System (STSS).

"Sir, STSS reports four scuds launched from the Spratlys," the ADT announced in a more excited voice.

"Type and trajectory, chief?"

"Possible DF-29 ASBMs in boost phase. Computers still working on their trajectory, sir."

At the same time, the CIC watch officer (CICWO) arrived at the air detection console.

"Chief, what is the estimated flight time to the Kerguelens?"

"Computer says about thirty minutes, sir."

The DF-29 hypersonic anti-ship ballistic missiles (ASBM) travelled at Mach 10, so the decision to intercept had to be made quickly. The missiles could be intercepted during their midcourse flight or during their terminal phase if the first attempt failed. The time depended on their ballistic trajectory, so the first task was to figure out how much time they had to make a decision.

"Set interception time to seven minutes from now chief," the CICWO said.

More information on the trajectory of the missiles was needed before the strike group could commit to take action against the Chinese missiles. The CIC team waited for three agonizing minutes.

"Chief, need a trajectory update," the CICWO requested in an urgent tone.

"Predicted trajectory is still only approximate. STSS is projecting a two hundred nautical–mile cone enveloping the island with the strike group inside it, sir."

"Yeah, figured as much," the CICWO replied, knowing it was too early to determine a reliable trajectory given the ASBMs were still in boost phase.

The CICWO pivoted around toward the centre of the CIC to look at the holographic tactical sphere. It now showed the four missiles as four arcs coming down from the top of the sphere. The arcs then transformed into a transparent crimson cone that enveloped the island, the *Enterprise*, its two destroyers, and the *Vorian*.

"Please catalogue contacts into the NTDS, chief."

The CICWO then looked up at the video screen in front of the CIC consoles.

By now, all the ships in the Carrier Strike Group were in direct video link with the *Ross*.

"Recommend starting evasive actions and have the *Enterprise* move further west from where the ASBMs are projected to land," the CICWO announced.

"Agreed," replied the CCSG.

The CCSG then turned to Capt. Nalbandian.

"Capt. Nalbandian?"

"I concur, sir."

Capt. Nalbandian could then be heard in the background, giving the order to have the *Enterprise* increase its speed to flank and turn to a westerly course, away from where the missiles were projected to land.

"Sir, I recommend we intercept," Joe Oliver, the AW stated.

The CCSG remained silent.

He was mulling it over and weighing his options while keeping an eye on the clock. He was 99 percent certain the Chinese were targeting the Ibecci's spaceship, their future settlement, or both, but there were still dangers in the form of malfunctions that might end up changing a missile's targeting or trajectory. He could not simply assume the missiles would aim true or the aliens would destroy them, so the danger was very real.

"Bring them down!"

"Copy that, sir," the AW replied and then continued.

"CICWO, you are lead."

"Yes, sir! TAO, please transfer targets to fire control and designate targets," the CICWO said to his tactical action officer responsible for weapons' deployment.

"Transferring targeting data to fire control and designating four incoming DF-29s as Skunk1 through Skunk4! SWC, please assign Skunk1 to the *Ross*, Skunk2 to the *Trudeau*, Skunk3 to the *Fitzgerald*, and Skunk4 to the *Stout*, and confirm," the TAO said.

"Assigning targets SK1 to the *Ross*, SK2 to the *Trudeau*, SK3 to the *Fitzgerald*, and SK4 to the *Stout*, sir," replied the ship's weapons coordinator.

Her hands danced in the air with blinding speed in front of the holographic tactical sphere as she typed on a floating virtual keyboard. She first named the targets as requested and dragged each radar contact to the assigned destroyer in a seamless operation that integrated all assets within the strike group.

As the SWC performed the task, labels appeared next to each DF-29 ASBM in the tactical sphere, and those of the other ships.

The targets were now transferred to the tactical weapons control system of each destroyer. All that remained was assigning the appropriate weapon system to each target and the weapon control system would do the rest.

"Assign targets to SM-5, two interceptors per target."

"Assigning targets to SM-5," the SWC replied.

She highlighted the four targets and then clicked on a pull-down menu to select the Standard Missile SM-5 midcourse antiballistic missile (ABM) from the options, assigning two missiles to each target.

"SWC, you are cleared to engage," the TAO said.

In an almost anticlimactic action, the SWC clicked the *Missile Launch* option in one of the drop-down menus and then confirmed by clicking *Yes* in a dialogue box.

"SM-5s away, sir. Weapon's control confirms eight successful launches," the SWC replied as each destroyer fired two SM-5 hypersonic antiballistic missiles from their VLS cells.

The missiles climbed straight up at Mach 15 to meet their designated targets above the atmosphere, hopefully before the DF-29 warhead separated into two independent and manoeuvrable kinetic re-entry vehicles.

Everything had happened in less than sixty seconds from the moment the CCSG gave the order, and now the equivalent of over $350 million dollars of sophisticated medium-range antiballistic missiles were racing toward their targets.

The hypersonic missiles were being guided with real-time course updates from the destroyer's AN/SPY-3C radar and augmented with data from the STSS to intercept the incoming DF-29 missiles.

This was a feat equivalent to hitting a bullet with a bullet, and those witnessing the events were aware of the extraordinary danger because a single conventional kinetic vehicle carried enough energy to obliterate a navy ship.

The tension in the CIC of every destroyer and the *Enterprise* CDC was palpable. Both the CICWO and the TAO aboard the *Ross* were glued to the screens of the missile tracking consoles.

"Flight status, SWC?" the TAO asked in a tense voice.

"All missile readings are nominal, sir."

The holographic 3-D tactical sphere showed the eight SM-5 ABMs as eight thin blue lines arching up in a northeasterly direction to intercept the DF-29 near the apex of their ballistic trajectory at an altitude of some two thousand kilometres.

"Time to intercept?" the TAO asked next.

"Slightly less than ten minutes, sir," the SWC replied.

"ADT, current flight profile of the DF-29s?" the CICWO asked.

"Still in boost phase and climbing, sir."

This was good because the midcourse intercept needed to be done as early as possible to assess success or failure and the extent to which a terminal intercept would be needed.

At least the guidelines called for this procedure, but the operational reality was different. Carrier strike group admirals preferred to execute both intercepts without verification of the success of the midcourse intercept because of the extreme danger anti-ship ballistic missiles, also known as carrier-killers, posed to large warships.

The CICWO and TAO were already thinking ahead to initiate the terminal intercept. They needed to wait until those DF-29s that got through were close enough for the SM-10s terminal phase interceptor to take care of them.

It was, however, impossible for a human to react fast enough and make the split-second decision to launch the terminal intercept missiles. Instead, the weapons control system calculated the optimal time for intercept and autonomously fired the short-range SM-10.

The TAO gave the order to proceed with the terminal intercept autolaunch.

"SWC, enable weapons control system to fire terminal phase interceptors when in range."

"Yes, sir," the SWC replied.

Once again, her fingers danced through the virtual keyboard in front of her and clicked a menu to authorize the weapons control system to automatically launch the SM-10 when in range. She then confirmed the order she had been given.

"SM-10s are now hot and on standby for autolaunch, sir."

They had now done as much as they could to protect themselves against the incoming DF-29 anti-ship ballistic missiles. All they could do was wait for either the SM-5 and SM-10 interceptor missiles to take care of them or the *Vorian* to destroy them.

29 PROBING

IIC *Vorian*, Kerguelen Islands

The *Vorian* was keeping station at an altitude of one hundred *passu*, out at sea on the western side of the island.

Her six graviphoton field generators allowed the two hundred–*passu* interstellar *liburnia* to stay suspended in midair, just like a weather balloon. Its polished grey-blue hull gleamed in the sunlight and, depending on the angle of view, blended with the colour of the sky or appeared as an ungainly mass.

The *Vorian* was far from graceful. It was wide and tall to accommodate eight operating decks. The wide beam was also needed for a hangar running the entire length of the spaceship to handle five small combat spacecraft.

Aesthetics had not been a criterion to build a capable, yet beautiful, fleet defence *liburnia* like the spaceships of the defunct Ibecci Imperium *Classis,* of which the *Imperator Eberon* was the only survivor.

The *Vorian* and her sister spaceships were constructed with survivability and toughness as their prime design objectives. They were ugly fighters that could withstand pounding after pounding to protect the priceless lives of the last remnants of the Ibecci race. She proudly wore the badge in honour of *Balistro* Vorian *Decanu*, who gave his life eons ago defending the Imperium against packs of *Irascilin* battle machines.

Spacecraft under the command of Seren *Capac* could be seen leaving and entering her hangar as they performed around-the-clock defence air patrols.

"Seldik *Centor, THRAVES* show 140 missile threats with a closing rate of two thousand *mille passu/jore* flying just above the surface of the sea. Targeting is still uncertain," Craefin *Junct* announced.

"I see them, Craefin," said an annoyed Seldik *Centor*.

He looked at the room-sized holographic sphere in front of and below the command deck and reflected on the fact the hostility of the *Tiwan*'s inhabitants toward his race was becoming a reality.

"*Centor*, there are four other threats further away. We became aware of these because of the four watercraft from the NAU faction that launched missiles to intercept them."

Seldik *Centor* said nothing. He was thinking about the possibility his race would be marred in a prolonged conflict. The thought unsettled him deeply, as he was tired of being constantly at war with something or someone, but then it was all he had known his entire life. Still, he managed a cynical grin.

Craefin *Junct* looked up and to his right at his commander.

"*Centor*, how should we deal with the threats?"

Again, Seldik *Centor* said nothing. He stood next to the command deck railing, looking down at the holographic sphere showing the NAU projectiles rising straight up from their watercraft not too far away. He knew the *Vorian* could deal with the threat of 140 missiles easily, and any future ones, and reflected on the inevitable fact lives were going to be lost on both sides.

His orders were explicit though. He could not harm the *Tiwan* inhabitants unless in self-defence, so he was going to do the next best thing and destroy as much of *Tiwan*'s military hardware as he could.

As he considered his options, Craefin *Junct* called his attention again.

"*Centor*, the threats are now some twenty *glosils* from the settlement. Should we move up to battle readiness and prepare to destroy them?"

"SE, infiltrate and map the missile circuits," Seldik *Centor* said to the ship's sentient entity while still looking at the realistic holographic image of the beautiful but nearly dead blue ocean in front of him.

The *Vorian*'s biometric sensors had detected large amounts of synthetic polymers the inhabitants called plastics floating and decaying at the bottom of the ocean. More alarmingly though, the sensors had also charted vast areas where there was little life, higher levels of acidity, and strange areas near landmasses where the water was devoid of any oxygen while containing high levels of nitrogen and phosphor. The available *Tiwan* information on their worldwide network stated these areas were known as Dead Zones, accounting for some 30 percent of the total surface area of their oceans. But Seldik *Centor* had no time to reflect on the problems of the planet's failing ecosystem.

"*Gubernum*, bring the *Vorian* to a defensive stance and move us closer to the island," Seldik *Centor* ordered.

"*Aien, Centor.*"

Seldik *Centor* then sat in the command chair and secured himself with a four-point restraint.

The *Vorian* pitched forward, bringing the nose of the spaceship to a 45 percent down angle. This maneuver exposed the top of its hull to the incoming threats, together with its complement of coherent energy (CE) and quad electromagnetic projectile point defence batteries.

In space, the concept of a close-in weapon meant ranges over five thousand *mille passu*. But on Earth, this range was reduced to a maximum of ninety *passu* at best because of atmospheric distortion and gravity. The *Vorian* was going to have to adjust and place more emphasis on cyber warfare to disable the threats by exploiting the weakness of their opponents' own circuitry, as it had done with the Chinese space station.

"Comm, order the fliers to deploy to the island and maintain defence patrols," Seldik *Centor* then ordered.

"*Aien, Centor.*"

"Craefin, is the SE's infiltration and mapping complete?" Seldik *Centor* asked next.

"Yes, *Centor,* but at this point the mapping of the missile's circuitry is only partial—" Craefin *Junct* said, but was cut off midsentence by the SE as it came online.

"Warning. Assessment has determined the incoming missile threats are targeting the current spatial coordinates of the *Vorian.* Destruction of the threats is recommended, followed by repositioning to a higher altitude beyond the reach of future threats."

The SE had ascertained this after it had successfully infiltrated the missile's signal receivers and read the targeting coordinates stored in the guidance hardware using quantum probabilistic techniques that relied on non-locality, tunneling, and entanglement. This cyberwarfare activity could only be described as "spooky action at a distance" and very different from more traditional cyberwarfare attacks. It was also beyond Earth's technology.

"Noted. I want to erode their numbers slowly to test the behaviour of the Chinese aggressors. What are our options?" Seldik *Centor* asked.

"The missiles are fully autonomous, and their circuitry is robust. The intrusion agent could access and map the circuit network only up to a point. They have triple redundant guidance that includes satellite guidance, real-time feed from two surveillance and targeting drones flying ahead of their battle group, and inertial guidance. The missiles are also equipped with a terminal guidance assisted by a self-contained radio emissions array. My ability to control them is limited to the signal receiver that can accept new targeting coordinates while in flight, or I can enable an autodestruct. This last option would be the most expedient way to destroy all missiles," the SE said.

"Leave this option for last. We don't know what their reaction will be to a total and sudden neutralization of their attack. They might decide the only way to get through our defences might be to use fission weapons."

"How do you wish to proceed?"

"Let's go along with their plan and only take small steps to thwart their attack."

"How do you wish to proceed?" the SE asked again.

"Could you disable the guidance systems of three missiles and force them to go on terminal guidance? Seldik *Centor* asked.

"The satellite and real-time guidance signal receivers can be disabled in several ways, but I cannot disable the inertial guidance. The missiles would simply continue on their current programmed course."

Seldik *Centor* thought it over while looking at the advancing threats in the holographic sphere. He wanted his response to be measured.

"Can you pick three missiles that are ahead of the pack and change their targeting coordinates to veer away? Then change the coordinates again. Have the missiles cross through the pack, and enable the autodestruct to take out any nearby missiles?"

"That is possible."

"Proceed," Seldik *Centor* said.

The threats were now at the midway point, and the SE changed the targeting coordinates of three of the leading missiles. The missiles then veered to the right and away from the pack.

30 HOSTILITIES 2

Liu Huaqing Carrier Task Force, South Indian Ocean

"Sir, we have three missiles veering to a new course of 270 degrees," announced a warfare specialist monitoring the flight of the 140 anti-ship supersonic cruise missiles, now some seven hundred kilometres from their target.

Cmdr. Jia Ning, the on-duty CIC senior officer, and Admiral Hsu looked at him and the holographic sphere. Three of the missiles were turning slightly to the right and away from their programmed course.

"What's the reason for the change in course?" Admiral Hsu asked.

"Unknown, sir. Current diagnostics show the status flags of the BeiDou guidance, and the real-time feed from the Divine Eagles, all green."

Just a few minutes earlier, he had learned of the antiballistic missiles fired by the four NAU destroyers to intercept the DF-29s launched from the Spratlys. The NAU ABMs were climbing in a ballistic trajectory to meet the DF-29s high in the atmosphere, and Admiral Hsu resigned himself to the fact some of his missiles would be shot down. He did not blame the NAU for their reaction. He would have done exactly the same thing in order to protect his battle group. Now he had three missiles acting erratically that might reduce the strength of his attack before the aliens even engaged him.

"Verify the missiles' targeting coordinates," Cmdr. Ning ordered.

"Targeting coordinates do not match initial entries, sir."

"What's the location of those coordinates?" Admiral Hsu asked.

"In the middle of the ocean and north from the island, sir."

"I can safely assume, Cmdr. Ning, the aliens somehow accessed and altered the missiles' targeting coordinates."

"How could they do that without getting a warning the quantum key distribution communication was breached? And why only three missiles, assuming that's what's going on."

"Maybe they are playing a cat-and-mouse game and want to test us, Cmdr.," Admiral Hsu said.

"Re-enter the correct coordinates," Cmdr. Ning ordered.

"Sir, I have sent commands to the missiles to accept the latest coordinates of the alien spacecraft's location, but the coordinates are overridden right away."

"Admiral Hsu, we can command the missiles to autodestruct. Their current path will take them close to the two NAU destroyers, and when the missile's terminal guidance goes active, they will target the destroyers," Cmdr. Ning volunteered.

Admiral Hsu mulled it over. On one hand, he did not want to get in a confrontation with the NAU, but the intel he could gather from the NAU's defensive capabilities could prove valuable.

"No. Let the NAUS deal with those three strays. After all, they claim the air defence capabilities of their *Zumwalt-2* destroyers are unmatched, so let's see if their claim is true."

31 UNEXPECTED

NAUS *Ross* (DDG-1025), Kerguelen Islands

Aboard the NAUS *Ross*, ten minutes had elapsed since the launch of the SM-5 antiballistic missiles to intercept the Chinese DF-29 ASBMs.

The holographic sphere in the CIC showed the thin blue lines of the SM-5s and the red lines of the DF-29 converging high in the atmosphere. Two of the blue and red lines merged and then faded away slowly.

"SK1 has been trashed! SK4 has been trashed!" the ADT announced.

There was no rejoicing. There were two DF-29 starting their terminal descent.

"ADT, what's the status of SK2 and SK3?" the TAO asked.

"SK3 is entering terminal phase. SM-5s assigned to it missed. SK2 trajectory appears to have changed after we lost telemetry from the SM-5s assigned to it, sir."

"SWC, can you confirm status of the SM-5s assigned to SK2?" the TAO asked the ship's weapons coordinator.

"Confirmed, sir. No telemetry from the two SM-5s assigned to SK2," the SWC replied.

Despite the relative success of two confirmed intercepts and one probable, the mood in the CIC was sombre. They now had to wait to see if SK2 was still a threat and for SK3 to release its two re-entry kinetic vehicles, which would be intercepted by the short-range SM-10.

There was no time to sit and wait as another threat emerged.

"Gophers inbound! We have three supersonic gophers inbound! Heading of 270 degrees and two hundred kilometres out. Warning red," the ADT announced.

"Can you make out the type, chief?" the TRK SUP asked as he looked at three large red dots in the holographic sphere with pulsating trailing red lines.

"Probable CJ-30K, sir. They appear to have detached from the pack."

This threat was more severe than the remaining antiballistic missiles because the *Ross* and the *Trudeau* had less than three minutes to engage.

"Okay, chief, catalogue contacts into the NTDS."

"Transferring contacts to NTDS," the ADT replied.

"TAO, they are now yours," the TRK SUP announced.

Aboard the *Trudeau*, they were running through the same procedure in order to engage the Mach 3 anti-ship cruise missiles.

"Copy that," the TAO said.

"Transferring NTDS data to fire control and designating three incoming CJ-30K as Quail1 through Quail3! SWC, assign targets to RIM-188s," the TAO ordered, referring to the medium-range rolling airframe missile designed to counter anti-ship missiles.

"Targets assigned to RIM-188s," the SWC replied and the holographic sphere updated with the new assignments.

The destroyer's forward RIM-188 box launcher pivoted from its resting cradle in the direction of the incoming missiles and angled up, waiting for the command to fire its seaRAMs.

"SWC, you are cleared to engage."

"RM-188s away. Weapons control confirms three successful launches."

In a simultaneous action, the *Trudeau* also fired three RIM 188 missiles.

Now all six rolling airframe missiles were flying toward the three supersonic CJ-30K ASCMs. They were closing the distance at a combined hypersonic speed of Mach 7, with the intercept calculated to occur in less than a minute.

If the RIM-188s missed, given the CJ-30K built-in maneuvering capabilities, the two destroyers had their laser area defence system (LADS).

The LADS were the last layer of defence that was more reliable, nearly impossible to defeat and cheaper to operate compared to the cost of $15 million for each RIM 188.

All NAU navy LADS comprised twin-collimated infrared lasers with a combined power of two hundred kilowatts and a range of up to eight kilometres, depending on the amount of atmospheric distortion and haze. LADS were essentially autonomous as most engagements occurred in the last five to ten seconds before impact.

The *Ross*'s and *Trudeau*'s AN/SPY-3C electronically scanned array radars were already sending targeting information to their respective LADS while they powered up.

The CIC watch officer gave the bridge the last order she could to minimize the ship's profile seen by the terminal guidance of the ASCMs.

"Bridge, CIC, come to a heading of ninety degrees."

The two destroyers watched the advancing ASCMs get closer and closer praying either the seaRAMs or the LADS would take them out.

32 GRADUAL ATTRITION

IIC *Vorian*, Kerguelen Islands

Aboard the *Vorian*, enough time had elapsed to change the targeting coordinates of the missiles previously diverted.

The ship's sentient entity changed their course due south. The missiles crossed the path of the larger pack, and the SE enabled the autodestruct.

The missiles exploded in midair, engulfing and detonating another missile nearby. This secondary explosion damaged a fifth that started to fly erratically, finally plowing into the ocean below.

The SE then spoke.

"Five missiles neutralized. How do you wish to deal with the remaining threat?"

Seldik *Centor* ignored the SE but smiled at the results. He could have not asked for a better outcome. He had wanted a subtle attack with minimal damage to baffle the Chinese aggressors and got precisely that.

Satisfied, he turned his attention to the airborne targeting drones.

"Comm, order two fliers to destroy the surveillance drones."

Seren *Capac* and her wingman Grifer *Junct* immediately replied.

Moments later, the two small teardrop-shaped spacecraft were vectored toward the Chinese unpiloted drones flying at high altitude east of the island.

Seren *Capac* and her wingman punched their field propulsion engines and accelerated toward their targets until they were hypersonic.

On their way, they detected four NAU drones protecting a manned surveillance aircraft. The fliers ignored them, as their orders had been specific, and continued flying northeast.

As they neared their targets, the two fliers climbed to eighteen thousand *passu*. They powered up their hard X-ray coherent energy (CE) beams capable of near instantaneous and destructive superheating and dove straight down toward the surveillance drones.

33 FIRST LOSSES

***Liu Huaqing* Carrier Task Force, South Indian Ocean**

"Sir, the two NAU destroyers launched seaRAMs to intercept the stray ASCMs," a warfare specialist announced in the *Liu Huaqing* CIC.

Admiral Hsu grunted. "Let's see how they do."

Moments later, the warfare specialist spoke. "The course of the strays is changing due south . . ."

"I . . . just lost them plus two other missiles, sir. I only show 135 active missiles."

"What's going on?" Admiral Hsu demanded, quickly pivoting toward the holographic sphere just in time to see five green dots fade.

"Was it the NAU seaRAMs that destroyed them?"

"No, sir, those are still on an intercept course . . . Correction, sir, the seaRAMs have also disappeared from my screens."

On cue, Admiral Hsu glanced at the holographic sphere and saw the red lines of the NAU seaRAMs fade.

"Check your telemetry on those missiles," Cmdr. Ning ordered.

"Sir, I don't have any telemetry available. They are no

longer transmitting and don't appear on radar. Our count is down to 135 missiles, sir."

Admiral Hsu smiled at what the aliens had done. They had taken control of his missiles, maneuvered them at will, and then used them against him by commanding the autodestruct near other missiles.

He now had a new respect for these aliens. Clearly, they were sly and calculating. They could have stopped his attack in a single blow, but they took control of just three missiles, perhaps to taunt him or test his reaction.

It was an intriguing puzzle, and he became more interested in the alien's next move. In the meantime, he needed to act fast to preserve the missiles he still had.

"Well played, *Tongzhi* alien," Admiral Hsu whispered and then looked at Cmdr. Ning.

"Lock the target coordinates, disable the autodestruct and command the missiles to go on inertial guidance," he ordered.

The action he requested would fuse the coordinates into a onetime programmable non-volatile memory (OTP NVM), making it impossible to change the target coordinates.

"Yes, admiral, but may I point out we are not dealing with a static target, sir. If the Alien spaceship moves away from its present location, we lose the ability to update the coordinates. The missiles may not be able to acquire it on terminal guidance."

"I realize that, Cmdr. Ning, but the alternative is to allow the aliens to continue highjacking our missiles. This may happen all at once or slowly, as we just witnessed, and I want to prevent this. Comply with the order!"

"Yes, sir."

Suddenly, things in the CIC got busy with additional threats.

"Sir, two hostile aircraft are flying toward the Divine Eagles. Hostiles are hypersonic and climbing beyond the reach of the four *An-Jiang3* escorting the Divine Eagles," another warfare specialist announced.

"Any details on the hostiles?" Cmdr. Ning asked.

"Yes, sir, the Divine Eagles are sending streaming video, which shows two teardrop-shaped wingless aircraft." the warfare specialist replied, directing the feed to one of the CIC screens.

"Hmm . . . small and, I dare say, not menacing at all," Cmdr. Ning said offhandedly.

"They'll dive from above," Admiral Hsu said, glancing at Cmdr. Ning with a disapproving look.

In another area of the carrier, drone pilots were at their consoles and commanded the four *An-Jiang3* UCAVs escorting the Divine Eagles to climb toward the hostile spacecraft on full afterburner.

The arrow-shaped *An-Jiang3* had a thrust-to-weight (T/W) ratio of 1.3, and the four UCAVs were now flying almost vertically at a speed shy of Mach 1.5. They would then engage the alien spacecraft with their one hundred and fifty kilowatt solid-state infrared lasers when in range and shoot them down.

Admiral Hsu could see the *An-Jiang3* climbing in the holographic sphere, knowing the fate of the two Divine Eagle was in the hands of the drone pilots.

34 AIR SUPERIORITY

The Skies East of the Kerguelen Islands

Seren *Capac* and Grifer *Junct* dove toward the Chinese surveillance drones and immediately detected four delta-wing combat drones.

Three drones were climbing toward them at one and a half times the speed of sound, illuminating the Ibecci fliers with a weak coherent energy beam. The beam was too weak and was simply reflected by the fliers' iridescent multilayer skin.

Seren *Capac* had a split-second decision to make. She could either try to control the drones or destroy them. She opted for the latter.

She powered up her 0.5 *Tz* CE beam at a distance of 3,800 *passu* and targeted the lead combat drone. A visible coherent violet beam laced with the destructive, but invisible, hard X-ray beam fell squarely on the nose of the lead combat drone. Seren *Capac* kept the CE focused for three *punctums* until the beam burned through the aluminum fuselage, searing and melting the electronics, wiring, and a fuel line.

The drone lost control and exploded in midair. Two

other drones behind it rolled and shifted laterally to the left and right of Seren *Capac*'s dive.

This maneuver brought the left drone in direct line of sight of Grifer *Junct,* who illuminated it with his CE beam for about the same amount of time, destroying it just like the first one.

Seren *Capac* continued her dive toward the larger surveillance drones, leaving Grifer *Junct* to deal with the third combat drone.

As she got closer to the surveillance drones, she decelerated and focused her CE on the high aspect ratio wing of one drone, almost point-blank, burning through a noncritical location of the wing with no effect.

She dove past the drone and pulled up hard into an inverted loop, pushing just over 9Gs. Her vision greyed out, so she instructed her orb to perform the maneuver and position the flier behind the drone while her flight suit did its job to keep her conscious.

The flier completed the loop, slowed down to subsonic, rolled, and was now flying horizontally and positioned behind the surveillance drone.

Through her neural link, Seren *Capac* ordered the orb to illuminate the target with the CE beam. She focused the coherent violet beam on the tail of the drone. The beam burned through the entire length of the fuselage, burning electronics and wiring in its path. The drone lost control and dove into a spin, breaking apart before hitting the surface of the ocean below.

Seren *Capac's* vision was now fully restored, and she was about to go after the second surveillance drone, which had gone into an evasive maneuver, when the fourth combat drone came straight at her in a shallow dive at a scant five hundred *passu.*

The drone was quickly reducing the distance between the two of them, travelling at nearly two times the speed of sound, while illuminating her flier with its weak energy beam. She pulled up slightly to get her nose lined up, switched her CE beam to pulse mode, and illuminated the drone with a series of pulses, burning through the fuselage in several locations.

Instinctively, she then pulled to the right to avoid colliding head-on. She was only subsonic, and her evasive maneuver was too slow relative to the fast-approaching drone, which did not appear to be flying in a controlled fashion anymore.

Her orb knew this and punched the field propulsion engine faster than Seren *Capac* could react, accelerating the flier in a hard, evasive climb to avoid the impending collision.

The combat drone passed underneath her flier but still made slight contact, suffering further damage, as it did not possess the same structural integrity and armoured exterior of the Ibecci flier. It then pitched forward, finally falling from the sky in a flat spin and crashing into the ocean.

The hard evasive maneuver subjected Seren *Capac* to high Gs on several axes, causing her to go into a g-force-induced loss of consciousness.

Her spacecraft did not suffer any structural damage, and her orb took over and went into level flight while it simultaneously monitored Seren *Capac*'s vital signs. She regained consciousness soon afterward but experienced short-lived post G-LOC convulsions.

Her orb made Grifer *Junct* aware of the mishap, who recriminated himself for not having been able to destroy the last combat drone fast enough.

He communicated to check on her condition using his neural link.

"*Capac*, are you okay and able to continue flying?" he asked.

"What happened, Grifer?" she replied in a confused tone, a normal aftereffect of G-LOC.

"You went unconscious when you pulled up hard in order to avoid colliding with the drone you destroyed."

"Yes, that is the last I remember. The drone was coming

toward me fast. I set the CE on pulse mode and punched holes through its fuselage and then tried to pull up frantically."

"Your orb took over to avoid a head-on collision. We will have to review the full image stream from your orb, but you can see the orb had concluded the drone was in a deliberate collision course."

"Yes," Seren *Capac* said simply while she reviewed the orb's information through the neural link.

She then cursed in anger.

"We had trained against this! It should have been all but instinctive for me to recognize the intent of that drone!"

"*Capac*, no time for recriminations. The intelligence assessment established the *Tiwan*'s military had a few fliers to waste that way."

"We can review what happened when we get back. Let's finish our task. Please lead," Seren *Capac* said.

She then instructed her orb to place her in the wingman's position behind and off the right wing of Grifer *Junct*.

Grifer *Junct* quickly acquired the remaining surveillance drone that was trying to escape, flying as close to the surface of the ocean as its design permitted.

The two fliers approached from above, and Grifer *Junct* illuminated the drone with his CE beam, easily punching holes through its fuselage. The drone could then be seen losing stability, pitching its nose forward and crashing into the ocean.

With the last drone now destroyed, they turned around to head back to the island, accelerating until they were hypersonic.

As they were flying back, their orbs alerted them of a small force of Chinese combat drones racing toward them, but the drones were too far away and too slow to pose a threat.

Both pilots flew back in silence, thinking this time they had been lucky, aware events could have turned out differently.

35 ONWARD

***Liu Huaqing* Carrier Task Force, South Indian Ocean**

"Sir, we lost the Divine Eagles along with their four escorts," the warfare specialist announced.

The update was unnecessary. Admiral Hsu had watched the dogfight in the holographic sphere and observed firsthand how his less capable combat drones could not match the flight performance or weapons of the alien spacecraft.

He had nothing in exchange for the losses and right now, he had to continue with the operation and safeguard his 135 ASCMs, now less than ten minutes from the target.

He needed early warning and control aircraft up in the air. He also needed to appear reactive to the destruction of the Divine Eagles, so he gave a useless order.

"Send four *An-Jiang3*s to chase after the hostile spacecraft. I also want an EAW up with escorts to replace the downed Divine Eagles."

"Yes, admiral, but it is unlikely the *An-Jiang3*s will catch up," Cmdr. Ning replied.

He ignored Cmdr. Ning.

"Are the ASCM's target coordinates now locked?"

"Yes, sir, they are," the warfare specialist replied.

"Are the submarines standing by to launch their ASCMs?"

"Affirmative, admiral."

The *Hu sha* and *Hai lang* Qin-class attack submarines had been lying in wait three hundred kilometres southeast from the island. They were now counting down the time to come up to a missile launching depth and fire their CJ-30A salvo just eight minutes before the ASCMs already in flight were expected to reach their target.

Admiral Hsu was hoping the additional ASCMs suddenly appearing from a southwesterly course would be a surprise that would get through the Ibecci defences.

At the designated time, the *Hu sha* rose to launch depth and fired. The missiles rose straight up, then pivoted to a horizontal flight and updated their targeting coordinates with the latest location of the alien spaceship.

Within minutes, the *Liu Huaqing*'s main search and targeting radar reported the launches, and the tracks of the missiles were automatically added to the holographic sphere.

"Tracking has confirmed twelve successful launches from the *Hu sha*, sir."

"Why hasn't the *Hai lang* fired her salvo yet?" Admiral Hsu asked.

"Unknown, sir."

The *Hai lang* was one hundred kilometres further north from the *Hu sha*, but there had been no sign of activity from her.

"What's the latest status of the *Hai lang*?"

"She was running silent because she was close to the NAU destroyers. It's possible she might be trying to evade one of the NAU subs attached to the two destroyers," Cmdr. Ning said.

"Unlikely, major, but you should be able to see for yourself. If one of the NAU subs was after her, we would see coordinated activity from their destroyers, would we not?"

"There's been little movement from the NAU destroyers, sir."

"Well then, there's your answer. The NAU would avoid getting into a confrontation with us at all costs unless it was to come to the aid of the French. I am sure they have been shadowing the *Hu sha* and the *Hai lang* with their underwater drones. Their subs might know where she is, but they would keep at a respectful distance, just like we would."

"A malfunction then?" Cmdr. Ning continued.

"Your guess is as good as mine, Cmdr."

The orders given to the captain of the *Hai lang* had built-in redundancies. Unless the submarine had suffered a serious malfunction or come under attack, the *Hai lang* was expected to come to launch depth and fire her twelve anti-ship missiles on her own. It would not be as perfectly synchronized as the original plan, but it would be executed nonetheless.

In the meantime, Admiral Hsu would have to content himself with a force of slightly less than one hundred and fifty anti-ship missiles targeting the *Vorian*.

It was still a considerable number, and no warship on Earth could stop such a barrage.

36 INVINCIBLE

IIC *Vorian*, Kerguelen Islands

"Warning. Threats are a few *glosils* away," the *Vorian*'s SE announced.

It then took matters in its own hands and sent an autodestruct command to all the incoming missiles but could destroy only twelve missiles launched by an underwater craft at the southern edge of the island.

Next it executed a series of alternate commands and spoke.

"Ship's close-in weapons now active."

The SE performed the tasks autonomously, without consultation or approval, using advanced algorithms originally conceived by its designers long ago.

Seldik *Centor* and the command crew simply stood by and watched the SE take over, as its decision-making and reactions were much faster than the *Vorian*'s crew.

Moments later, ten electromagnetic projectile batteries came to life. The Chinese missiles were some one hundred *mille passu* out, and the SE fired short bursts of 0.034 *passu*-hypersonic iridium projectiles to calibrate their aim under the influence of *Tiwan*'s gravity and air friction.

As the projectiles left the quad-rail batteries, they created bright ionization trails due to their hypervelocity. Even under full daylight, the trails resembled a meteor shower accompanied by a deafening sound. It started as a high-pitched *whoosh*, similar to the noise made by multirocket launchers, followed by a series of thunderclaps that turned into one long, deep rumble.

Despite their hypervelocity, the projectiles still took twenty-four *punctums* to reach their targets. The SE considered the closing velocity of the missiles and the effect of gravity, but it underestimated air friction, resulting in the projectiles arriving a little late. Hitting a missile travelling at several times the speed of sound and one hundred *mille passu* was challenging even for a Type 1 Civilization.

The SE made targeting corrections and fired a second burst. This time the *Vorian*'s surveillance arrays confirmed interception. Each projectile was packed with 220 fin-stabilized iridium darts designed to disperse radially in front of a target. The intercepted Chinese missiles were shredded by the ultrahard, needlelike iridium darts. It was just a few at first, but by the time the Chinese missiles were at sixty *mille passu* from the *Vorian*, they found a wall of iridium darts.

In all, the ten electromagnetic projectile batteries fired almost five thousand projectiles that dispersed over one million darts.

The SE then turned its attention to the only remaining long-range kinetic projectile that was not intercepted by the NAU fiefdom. The projectile was in a ballistic trajectory travelling at fifteen times the speed of sound, and the SE assigned the two remaining batteries. They fired continuously for close to one hundred *punctums*, but the kinetic projectile was a solid bolide that simply fragmented and continued in its flight path with close to its original mass and kinetic energy.

The SE reacted to this and moved the *Vorian* away from its path, but fragments still rained down on top of the hull.

The loud clangs from the fragments hitting the armoured hull could be heard by the crew on the command deck, but the fragments did not penetrate the thick *reterit* armour.

One CE battery and two antenna arrays were damaged, and the hull suffered scaring and gashes, which the *Vorian* would display proudly as its first battle scars.

As Seldik *Centor* observed the engagement, he thought that if this was a measure of what the humans could throw at the Ibecci, then he had nothing to worry about.

He was thankful the construction site had suffered no damage, but more importantly, that there had been no loss of life.

As he considered the events, twelve new threats appeared from the northeastern corner of the island that were launched by a second underwater craft. The threats were hardened to cyber intrusions, so the SE dealt with them the same way as it had done with the other hundred and fifty missiles.

Afterward, the SE spoke in an impassive tone.

"All threats have been nullified. SE is now relinquishing command."

Seldik *Centor* simply took over and wasted no time in turning the tables on the Chinese.

He went after their ability to launch another assault just as he had done against the Chinese space station. This time, however, he went much further.

"SE destroy all the Chinese network circuitry, save for their propulsion, navigation, and environmental controls."

"Do you wish to target all five watercrafts?"

"Target the four smaller watercrafts that launched the missiles. Leave the drone-carrying watercraft untouched."

The SE complied and broadcasted a complex high-energy electromagnetic pulse in a focused beam directed at the four smaller watercrafts.

The signal was laced with a powerline carrier wave that entered through the communications and data system receivers. The signal travelled through cabling and morphed into an EMP-like high-voltage electric field, permanently damaging all circuits. It was a cyber warfare technology indistinguishable from magic.

Seldik *Centor* assumed this last action would ensure the Chinese fiefdom would not bother the Ibecci again. Unfortunately, he was wrong.

37 SOME JUST DON'T GIVE UP

***Liu Huaqing* Carrier Task Force, South Indian Ocean**

They were so close, yet so far.

Admiral Hsu's large missile force was destroyed at some seventy-five kilometres from the alien spaceship.

The long-range tracking radars aboard the *Liu Huaqing* and the airborne EAW saw individual patches of fog appear in front of each missile. The fog patches grew and merged into a large cloud, and, one by one, the missiles exploded, stopped reporting and simply disappeared in the holographic sphere.

It could have been missiles, but he doubted it, as their radar signature would have been well defined. It could have been lasers. But lasers that could maintain a focused beam at such a long range would be something he would have to see. And lasers would not display the fog-like radar signature.

Regardless, his operation had failed miserably, even if it was against a technologically superior opponent. His superiors would not consider technological superiority as an excuse.

Now Admiral Hsu needed to shake off the sense of

doubt creeping in his mind.

He was about to turn his attention to his back-up plan but was distracted by a message from the *Hai lang* attack submarine, which was keeping station to the north of the island.

The message came in at the submarine communications console.

"Admiral Hsu, the *Hai lang* apologizes for being late to the party. Her captain had to deal with two pesky NAU underwater surveillance gliders that got too close to his boat, and could not fire his salvo on queue with the *Hu sha*. He is launching them now and hopes it's not too late," Cmdr. Ning said.

Admiral Hsu grinned as his battle group achieved a minor victory against the NAU. It gave him a small sense of comfort to know his super-quiet Qin-class submarines were more than a match for the NAU. He could almost see the incredulous look on his NAU counterpart's face, Admiral Joe Phelps that the Qin-class sonar technology was good enough to acquire, track, and destroy the supposedly undetectable NAU autonomous underwater gliders.

It was ironic though because he was not even fighting the NAU. The news and information would be valuable for later analysis, but his priorities were now elsewhere.

He looked toward the holographic sphere showing the twelve lonely ASCMs launched by the *Hai lang* flying west toward the Ibecci spaceship. The missiles flew for just a few minutes and then disappeared from the sphere, just like his earlier force.

He had already concluded they would not get through and was about to give orders for the second phase of the operation when the video screens in the CIC lit up and showed the faces of the commanders of the four destroyers.

"Now what?" he asked, visibly infuriated.

"Admiral Hsu, our computer systems have been destroyed, and a few of the crew have minor burns from electrical arcs. It looks like some sort of EMP," the commander of the *Zhuhai* said.

"I don't understand, commander. If all your computer systems were destroyed, how come your video communication systems are still operating?" Admiral Hsu asked with a confused look.

"The navigation, propulsion, environmental, and communication were untouched, admiral. The EMP was very selective and only crippled the computers operating the combat systems," the commander of the *Zhuhai* replied.

"We were equally affected, admiral," the commander of the *Guangzhou* added.

The other commanders nodded in agreement.

"All of you?" Admiral Hsu asked. He then looked at Cmdr. Ning inquiringly to see if the *Liu Huaqing* had also been affected, but she shook her head in the negative.

"Affirmative, sir," the commander of the *Zhuhai* replied.

"Can you undertake repairs?"

"We have some spares, but not in sufficient quantities to replace all the hardware, and we would have to upload software because the main servers were also destroyed. So, the short answer is no, admiral."

"All right then, since your combat systems are out of commission, I suggest you turn around and head back to Zhanjiang at your best speed to get repairs started as soon as possible. The engineering and science team can also start looking at what happened and figure out how to defend against it next time."

"But, admiral, that will leave you without an escort and totally unprotected."

"What would you suggest then? You have no functioning combat systems, so how useful are you to me? You don't have any air defence capabilities, sonar to track enemy submarines, or capable of launching a second wave of ASCM."

Admiral Hsu waited for a response but only received silence, so he continued.

"The *Hai lang* and *Hu sha* will stay with me. We will send them a message informing them of the latest events as soon as we can. I figure in about two days' time we will also head back," Admiral Hsu concluded.

The four commanders acknowledged the order and signed off.

Admiral Hsu then turned around and spoke to Cmdr. Ning.

"Nothing changes. We move to the next phase of the operation."

"Yes, admiral."

She then prepared a message for the *Hu sha*.

Four hours later, the *Hu sha* travelled westward carrying a special operations submersible with ten *Hailong* (Sea Dragon) Special Forces and enough demolition explosives to blow up half of the island. Its destination was a sandy cove called Plage de la Possession near the southwestern tip of the island and about seven kilometres south from the Ibecci construction site at Vallée des Sables.

The shallow Kerguelen Plateau, with a depth of only thirty metres, surrounded the island, and the *Hu sha* could not get too close to shore. It deployed the submersible out at sea about three kilometres away. The submersible covered the distance slowly, finally reaching the postcardlike sandy beach with fine black sand and tranquil waves, evocative of a cove on a tropical island.

The *Hailong* SFs set foot on the beach just as the sun was setting in the west. They deployed with orders to destroy everything at the Ibecci construction site and get out before they were discovered. A truly impossible order.

The squad split into two four-man teams and moved up the left and right flanks of the Vallée des Sables, while two other SFs veered east in order to move up the riverbed on the east side of Peak Les Deux Frères.

The three teams quickly advanced thanks to their *Jianhuren-* (Guardian-) powered exoskeletons despite their heavy weapons and scores of portable loitering munitions. They also had two quadruped *Z-Luozi* robotic mules, each equipped with 10x72-mm caseless heavy machine guns.

The robotic mules were advancing fifty metres ahead of each team.

Small reconnaissance quadcopters were also deployed to scan ahead in the valley and surrounding hills. The real-time feed from the quadcopters was sent to the HUD of each *Hailong* SF, and their built-in tactical 3-D map updated with the location of the Ibecci forces and their construction site seven kilometres away.

The *Hailong* SF were under strict instructions to avoid engaging the small contingent of French forces known to have landed on the island. Unfortunately, the French forces did not appear in their 3-D tactical map.

This might become an issue once the *Hailong* started engaging the Ibecci. But time to scout ahead looking for the French was something they did not have. Either the Z-L scouts or the quadcopters would eventually detect them, or the French would give away their position when they started firing on the *Hailong*.

The squad, though, was too small to complete the operation successfully, despite being heavily armed and one of the best in the world at conducting counterinsurgency and demolition operations.

For the second time, the Chinese had ignored the warning from Viceroy Marel not to underestimate the Ibecci.

Admiral Hsu was aware of this and feared he was sending his Special Forces on a suicide mission.

In the end, he knew his superiors were playing by Sun Tzu's rule book, which stated, *He who wishes to fight must first be willing to accept the cost.*

38 MOMENTARY CALM

NAUS *Enterprise* (CVN-80), Kerguelen Islands

"What are they doing?" the AQ said while looking at the holographic sphere in the CIC. The *Liu Huaqing*'s four destroyers could be seen leaving the aircraft carrier behind and turning on a northeastern heading.

"It's a puzzle to me also, Cmdr. DesRosiers," the CCSG replied.

"Maybe we are reading all this wrong and the *Liu Huaqing* will also start heading back?"

"It's plausible, but unlikely. A carrier group moves in unison, so what they are doing doesn't look right. You're also assuming they are done, Cmdr."

"Well, sir, they fired some 170 missiles toward the island and the Ibecci spaceship, and not a single one got through."

"Think for a moment, Cmdr. If an order had been given to us to neutralize the aliens, would we just launch one attack and then give up and go home without trying again if our assets were still intact?"

"Not sure, sir. This is an atypical situation, but I assume they don't have an appetite for sending ground forces into the island, given that it is French territory, so their only option would be a repeat of the last strike."

"A fair assessment, Cmdr., but not applicable to the Chinese. You know just as well as I do the PLA's Joint Chiefs of Staff would disregard any international boundaries. They won't be squeamish about sending troops to the island if that is their back-up plan. They will continue engaging the Ibecci until they exhaust their ordnance or suffer enough losses and unable to continue operations. I am sure they are now working on their back-up plan, whatever that is. So, keep an eye on those destroyers."

"Understood, sir."

The CCSG then turned around to speak to the SEC at a nearby station.

"Lt. Cmdr. Urbina, any more news on the two Mantas that have not reported back?"

"Nothing, sir. It's puzzling, and the lack of IUSS coverage does not help."

"Seems today is a day for mysteries, Lt. Cmdr. How close were the Mantas to the Chinese sub on the northern side of the island?"

"We figure about sixty kilometres, sir."

"What about the *Grenville*?"

"It had the Mantas's latest position and knew the Mantas were trying to get closer to the Chinese sub, but the *Grenville* sonars reported nothing out of the ordinary. Her captain is just as puzzled as we are."

"Any chance the Chinese acquired the Mantas in their sonar, got nervous and dealt with them?"

"I doubt it, sir, given our knowledge of the capabilities of the Type 097, plus the *Grenville* would have heard something."

"Hmm . . . Wouldn't be the first time the Chinese caught us by surprise with their capabilities. Frankly, Lt. Cmdr., I find it improbable we lost two of our Mantas to wide system failures. I can accept one, but two is unlikely."

"Yes, sir."

"Until we get any more concrete information about what

really happened, I'll assume they were destroyed by the Chinese sub. It is important we get to the bottom of this. As of right now, we potentially have a situation where the Mantas assumed stealth to conduct ISR operations is in question."

"Understood, sir."

The AX was nearby and had remained silent during the exchange, letting Lt. Cmdr. Urbina update the CCSG.

"Sir, we got word from the *Olympia*. Their sonars detected noise from the southwestern tip of the island, matching the signature of a Type 097. The sound was fading in and out, as the Kerguelen Plateau is shallow. It may have reflected and travelled, making it look like the sub was travelling west."

"What's your guess, Cmdr.?"

"We are currently assessing, but odds are even the Chinese sub is now travelling due west, sir."

"What about the two Mantas shadowing it?"

"They are too far east and in deeper waters, sir."

The CCSG then turned back to the AQ.

"Cmdr. DesRosiers, what is the shoreline south from the Ibecci construction site like?"

The AQ zoomed in the holographic sphere toward the shoreline immediately south from the Ibecci construction site.

"There is a small beach called Plage de la Possession that looks ideal for an easy landing, sir."

"Hmm . . . I don't believe in coincidences, so I'd say this is possibly the start of the Chinese's next phase of the offensive. Probably a small contingent of Special Forces delivered by the Chinese sub travelling west. Opinions?" the CCSG asked.

"What would be the point of a small group of Special Forces? I would think they would be overwhelmed by the Ibecci ground forces," the AQ replied.

"Agree, but the Chinese have either little information on the Ibecci forces on the ground, which is doubtful, or else they are being foolish. Something I would have not expected either," the CCSG said.

"Another missile strike at point-blank range, then?"

"Your guess is as good as mine, Cmdr. In the meantime, please notify the French forces on the island of the submarine travelling west and a possible missile strike or landing of Chinese Special Forces of unknown strength. Hopefully Seren *Capac* will hear this message."

"Yes, sir."

"And since we are obliged to assist the French, please have a team of MSFs assembled to deploy to the island soonest," the CCSG ordered, referring to the Maritime Security Force (MSF) aboard the *Enterprise.*

It was a symbolic gesture more than anything else, as the carrier security forces were lightly armed and not up to the task of confronting heavily armed Chinese Special Forces.

"Right away, sir."

"Also have Maj. Krol and Capt. Flanders report to the flag officers' briefing room," the CCSG said next and then turned toward the AX.

"Cmdr. Weng, please commence ASW operations. I want that sub to know we have a fix on him."

Yes, sir," replied the AX, fully aware the stakes for confrontation were now rising.

Hunting and getting a fix on the Chinese sub could become deadly if her captain took defensive actions to neutralize the helicopters and the destroyers hunting it. It would become a question of whether the sub's captain could stay calm and not shoot first.

Thirty minutes later, a V28V carrying four MSFs left the *Enterprise.* The tilt-rotor aircraft was flying toward the Kerguelen Islands to meet with the French RPIM squad.

Maj. Krol and Capt. Flanders were also aboard after meeting with the CCSG and ordered to go to the island because their knowledge and expertise might somehow be needed. The CCSG was not one to keep his team benched, even if Maj. Krol had argued he was unsure of what kind of contribution he could make. He had tried to explain he was simply an Air Force major with expertise in astronautics and orbital mechanics and not trained to go out with ground forces to shoot the bad guys.

This did not go well with the CCSG, especially because Capt. Flanders showed instant eagerness at the opportunity to go to the island to meet the Ibecci.

The flight took just under forty minutes. During the flight, Maj. Krol kept reviewing the events that led him to where he was right now. He laughed at the incongruity of it all and how destiny always pulled him in a different direction. All he had ever wanted was to be a fighter pilot, but he never made it because of his height and that pesky inner ear problem. So, he contented himself with tracking threats in orbit and talking to the jocks that flew SR-72s. Now here he was with ground pounders going up against Chinese Special Forces.

He also found it hard to reconcile how badly he had misjudged Capt. Flanders. He had assumed she would have been out of her element going to the island because her areas of expertise were linguistics and history. Yet there she was cradling the pump-action shotgun she had asked for and been given after patiently explaining and demonstrating she had grown up with them hunting grouse, ducks, and geese with her maternal grandfather and knew how to use them. This had earned the approval and nods from the MSF team after they saw how she unloaded, disassembled, and reassembled the shotgun with expert dexterity.

The V28V took the long way around, coming in from the north and arriving at the base of Peak Les Deux Frères on the eastern side just as the sun was setting down.

Maj. Krol, Capt. Flanders, and the MSF team got out quickly and started the climb to the top of the hill to join the RPIM team. As they were climbing, Krol figured Capt. Flanders would somehow surprise him again. And indeed, as he watched her, it was clear she was at ease walking in rough terrain while carrying a loaded weapon.

Damn. A brainiac with two PhDs who is also a hunter. It doesn't get any weirder than this, he thought. He put it out of his mind and continued climbing up the hill.

39 PICKING UP THE PIECES

1er RPIMa, Special Recon Patrol, Atop Peak Les Deux Frères, Kerguelen Islands

The RPIM squad was at the same spot where they had landed almost three days earlier and now on full watch for the Chinese Special Forces that just landed.

"Visitors coming up the laneway, and it doesn't look like they are interested in socializing," Cpl. Chantal Simard whispered through her comm. link.

The RPIM squad knew, however, there was nothing funny about heavily armed Chinese Special Forces wearing *Jianhuren*-powered exoskeletons with nearly indestructible carbon nanotube ceramic armour.

The Chinese SFs were now advancing quickly up the Vallée des Sables in two columns about two kilometres south from the Ibecci construction site.

Cpl. Simard was on top of Peak Les Deux Frères, about one hundred metres further south from the rest of her squad in case she needed to engage the Chinese SFs with her fifteen-millimeter antimatériel rifle. It was something she desperately wanted to avoid.

It was almost fully dark, and she was tracking them

through the infrared imaging of G1.

G1 was sitting on its hind legs next to Cpl. Simard in what looked like a Norman Rockwell postcard image. Its head was turned south toward the Chinese Special Forces while the tall, redheaded, part-time amateur bantamweight UFC fighter, was in a prone position with her rifle at the ready.

"Probably Sea Dragon SFs," she continued.

"They are split into two four-men teams, advancing on the east and west flanks of the valley with two of their robot mules in front and quadcopters scanning ahead. Can't see their backs, but I'm sure they're carrying loitering munitions in quad tube launchers. Everybody, stay low and don't make any sudden movements. On the plus side, there are only eight of them."

The *Enterprise* MSF team heard the warning relayed in English in their comm. link translators and picked up their pace to reach the top of Peak Les Deux Frères quickly, knowing full well they were heavily outgunned.

Cpl. Simard took control of G1 and guided it down the slope slowly to place it between them and the Chinese. It was tricky because the quadcopters might detect the movement. Thankfully, the German-designed semiautonomous robot apes had an almost nonexistent thermal signature and were quiet and tough to spot if operated expertly.

Meanwhile, Lt. Mimieux was scanning in the Ibecci's direction. He saw the same reception group that had welcomed him plus a *Balistro* in front of the six paratroopers.

"Heads up, everyone. The Ibecci are coming out to receive the visitors and are standing casually with their weapons shouldered," Lt. Mimieux said.

"Hey, who's the brute with the big gun in front of the reception group?" Cpl. Simard asked.

"A heavy gunner. Same four-barrel autocannon as the paratrooper I met at L'Aiguille Noire."

"Oh yeah, I remember! The chatty fellow you couldn't

shut up. Real charmer, that one," Simard continued with her wisecrack banter.

"Seren *Capac*, be advised the Chinese are advancing toward your paratroopers. They will fire on them and try to destroy your construction site," Lt. Mimieux announced.

As Lt. Mimieux said this, the *Enterprise* MSF team arrived at the top of the hill near Simard's position.

The Chinese quadcopter scouting ahead on the east flank must have detected the movement or heard noise even though it was some five hundred metres away. It altered course and climbed toward the top of Peak Les Deux Frères at high speed.

"Everybody, drop to the ground and freeze," Cpl. Simard whispered in a calm voice over the comm. link as she tracked the quadcopter in her HUD.

Capt. Flanders was in front of the *Enterprise* MSF squad and reached the top of the hill first. She immediately saw the quadcopter barely illuminated by the fading light on the western horizon and instinctively raised her pump-action shotgun. She fired twice at the drone that was fifty metres away and slightly above her line of sight.

The shots reverberated through the surrounding hills, and the drone dropped out of the sky like a mortally wounded game fowl.

Flanders then spoke enthusiastically to the MSF assigned to her.

"Chief, you ever done quail hunting at dusk?" But all hell broke loose, and the MSF pushed her down to the ground.

"Oh . . . bad move," Cpl. Simard said over the comm. link as automatic weapons fire from the closest robot mule started to pepper their position.

She commanded G1 to lower itself to present the smallest profile.

"G1, weapons free," she voiced. Then through her HUD, she simultaneously pressed the command to release the safety on G1's MG7 medium machine gun mounted on its back and tagged the robot mule as the target G1 was to engage.

The Chinese robot mule was below in the valley and roughly one thousand metres away. The 7.62x51-mm rounds from G1's MG7 simply bounced off its carbon nanotube ceramic armour.

Cpl. Simard knew this would happen. She had intended it as a distraction to get the robot mule to stop firing on the MSF's position and instead engage G1.

She had little time for her next move because the lightly armed 130-kg robot ape was no match for the Chinese's bigger and heavily armed robot mule.

"Stay low and keep your heads down," Cpl. Simard said over the comm. link. She then crawled slowly between the rocks, being careful to remain concealed, and shifted ten metres further south in case the Chinese had somehow pinpointed her position. She needed to disable the robot mule fast before she lost G1.

While the Chinese's 10x72-mm armour piercing caseless ammunition from the robot mule's machine gun could not penetrate the superhard carbon nanotube armour of G1, the kinetic shocks from repeated impacts would eventually damage its internals.

Cpl. Simard got in position, raised her fifteen-millimeter antimatériel rifle and aimed toward the robot mule. She placed the scope's reticle squarely on the head of the robot mule, hoping to disable its imaging and IR sensors. She then pressed the EXACTO smart-ammunition target lock and fired, keeping the rifle steady. At a distance of a thousand metres and with a muzzle velocity of 1,500 m/s, it took 0.65 seconds for the 15.2x169-mm armor-piercing, fin-stabilized discarding sabot (APFSDS) tungsten dart to reach the target.

Aided by the Extreme Accuracy Tasked Ordnance (EXACTO) guidance technology, the tungsten dart scored a hit and penetrated the thinner armour of the robot mule's head, pushing it back against the body. The head then partially exploded as the dart transferred twenty thousand joules of kinetic energy similar to the older 12.7x99-mm NATO (.50-BMG) ammunition.

It stopped firing, but after a momentary pause, the quasi headless robot mule resumed engaging G1.

Simard figured it had back-up imaging or one of the SFs was now guiding it.

She quickly shifted her aim to the centre of its body and fired again. The tungsten dart again found its target. The robot mule was violently pushed back a couple of metres, but the dart failed to penetrate the robot mule's armour, which was equivalent to 150-mm RHAe.

Simard knew chances were good it would get up and continue engaging G1. She crawled to reposition ten metres further south in order to keep firing until she disabled it.

In her HUD, she checked the condition of G1. Although G1 was semiautonomous, it had advanced self-preservation routines that activated. G1 had stopped firing, retracted its MG7 machine gun, and switched to a defensive stance, tucking its head in and lowering itself as low to the ground as its design permitted. Now its slanted, heavily armoured light brown back was the only portion exposed to incoming automatic weapons' fire.

The Chinese SFs, realizing they had been detected, stopped and hurriedly launched multiple loitering munitions toward the main construction site and the two spaceships grounded north of the site.

The high explosive, loitering munitions flew a high-speed, erratic path toward their designated targets to thwart any attempts to shoot them down.

In the dark, muzzle flashes and tracers could be seen as the *Balistro* engaged them with his twenty-five-millimeter four-barrel autocannon that radially dispersed hundreds of iridium darts. Some loitering munitions were successfully intercepted right away, exploding midair in brilliant fireballs.

The Chinese SFs kept advancing and were now only eight hundred metres from the Ibecci. Two squad members, carrying the same caseless heavy machine gun as the robot mules returned fire, engaging the *Balistro* head-on.

The robot mule on the west flank was also commanded to fire on the *Balistro,* who was now coming under simultaneous fire from three Chinese heavy machine guns.

The *Balistro* was busy intercepting the loitering munitions and could not return fire. Under darkness, it was hard to see if the rounds from the heavy machine gun were causing any damage.

Ibecci paratroopers deployed at his flanks opened fire with their personal weapons that fired high velocity ten-millimeter iridium caseless ammunition, delivering three times the kinetic energy of Earth's weapons.

The two Special Forces carrying the heavy machine guns were hit multiple times and stopped firing, falling down hard. The Ibecci rounds did not penetrate their armoured exoskeletons, but the SFs were rendered unconscious from the hydrostatic shocks.

Suddenly, another Chinese SF fired a MAWS toward the *Balistro*. The rocket flare could be seen streaking toward the Ibecci paratroopers, but the sixty-millimeter antiarmour missile, known in the West as the Hidden Blade, was intercepted by the *Balistro* just before it reached the Ibecci position, exploding in a fireball.

Another bright explosion was also seen further north, where the two Ibecci spaceships were grounded, and a second and third explosion over the main construction pit occurred as the three loitering munitions found their targets.

"That's going to leave a mark!" Cpl. Simard said above the noise of gunfire as she raised her head at an alternate firing position.

Through her scope, she saw the robot mule on the east flank advancing toward the Ibecci's position. Once again, Cpl. Simard placed the scope's reticle on the centre of its body and fired. She again scored a hit. The impact kicked the robot mule sideways a couple of metres, but this time, it stayed down.

At the Ibecci's position, the muzzle flashes from the

Balistro autocannon suddenly stopped. The Ibecci paratroopers continued firing on the advancing Chinese Special Forces, who fired a second MAWS, hitting the *Balistro* head-on and viciously throwing him back.

Over the comm. link, Lt. Mimieux ordered his squad to open fire on the Chinese position. He then commanded G2 to advance down the slope to close the distance between itself and the Chinese, simultaneously firing its MG7, while the NAU MSF joined in with their small arms.

Lt. Mimieux knew the attempt from the French and NAU contingent to engage the Chinese Special Forces was useless. This was confirmed by the lack of attention paid by the Chinese to the weapons fire coming from Peak Les Deux Frères.

As Lt. Mimieux was thinking this, he felt the same low-frequency hum in his ears and jawbone he had felt the day before.

Suddenly, a bright violet laser beam laced with a destructive, high-energy beam fell on the lead robot mule. The beam came down from the sky and behind the Ibecci's position.

Through his helmet-mounted thermal imaging, Lt. Mimieux could see the spot on the exterior armour of the robot mule where the beam was focused momentarily glow white-red, deform and buckle inward, finally exploding as the ammunition and Li-air internal batteries caught fire.

In response, the Chinese fired another MAWS toward the location of the laser beam. The glowing rocket flare climbed toward the beam but exploded at the halfway point as it crossed the laser's path.

Unfazed, the Chinese SFs continued firing and advancing.

The Ibecci spacecraft laser then illuminated one of the Chinese SF, but only for a moment. He must have felt the sudden heating as he stopped firing and dropped to one knee. After a momentary pause got up and started firing again.

It was the wrong move, as he was illuminated again. This time, the laser beam stayed focused until it burned through his exoskeleton, and the Chinese SF fell to the ground with a gaping hole in his torso. The beam then shifted to another Special Forces, who suffered the same fate.

Now, there were only four Chinese SFs left at some three hundred metres from the Ibecci position, with no robot mules to give them fire support. They stopped firing and took cover in a small depression.

In the lull that ensued, everything went quiet as the Chinese SFs reassessed their situation. The low-frequency hum from the Ibecci spacecraft also stopped.

Lt. Mimieux then heard the *whop-whop* sound of helicopter blades coming from the direction of L'Aiguille Noire in the distant west, hoping it was an attack helo.

As the helo got closer, Lt. Mimieux recognized the characteristic sound of an Eurocopter *Tiger2*. He figured it had been dispatched by the *Foudre* while still about eight hundred kilometres out at sea.

The helo was coming toward his position fast, and then the comm. link crackled.

"Weasel, Weasel, this is Rooster. Heard your party was getting out of hand and you needed help. The *Foudre* is also sending a platoon of marines. Over."

"Man, am I glad to hear your voice, Rooster! The Ibecci took care of the rowdies. We just need to round them up and kick them out. Some of them may need medical attention. Over."

"Will be on standby. Over."

"Roger, Rooster. Weasel out."

In the night sky, the attack helicopter was all but invisible and from its sound. Lt. Mimieux could tell the high-speed hybrid attack helicopter had swooped over the valley, then turned north and got in a firing position.

Lt. Mimieux then addressed the Chinese SF using the two speakers of G1 and G2.

"Chinese soldiers, you have entered French territory.

Lay down your weapons. If you do not, the Ibecci will fry you with their lasers, and if they don't, we are authorized to use deadly force."

There was no response.

Through his thermal imaging, Lt. Mimieux could see some movement and thought they might comply. Then he heard the thump of mortar fire directed at the construction site. Two rounds exploded in quick succession. An SF then got up, fired a third MAWS toward the Ibecci position, and started advancing again. It was obvious their orders had been to complete their mission at all costs.

During the pause, two *Balistros* had moved in. Both opened fire with their autocannons. First, they shot down the MAWS and then started advancing toward the Chinese position.

It was impressive to watch them amble forward like fictional mechanized warrior machines with their long twenty-five-millimeter multi-barrel autocannons firing away. They concentrated their fire on the lone Chinese SF still moving forward and quickly cut him down. They then switched to the other three remaining SFs before they could lob any more mortar rounds.

"What a waste." Cpl. Simard's voice was heard over the comm. link.

She then got up, slung her antimatériel rifle over her shoulders and whistled to G1.

"Okay, G1, secure weapons and come to me."

It was mesmerizing to see the robot ape walking toward her on its four limbs with the gait of an ape, then sit on its hind legs, raise its head to look up at Cpl. Simard, and wait for her next command.

She did a systems check. Through her HUD, she accessed its software interface and found its armour grid intact and all systems in the green. it was a credit to the robustness of its design.

She then turned around and started walking to join the rest of the squad.

"G1, follow."

The robot ape fell in step next to her, or, depending on the terrain, followed behind just like a dog following its master. They were effortless, natural-looking movements that had taken over forty years of biomechanical research and millions of lines of computer code, starting with the Charlie robot ape. Charlie had originally been conceived for space exploration back in the first decade of the twenty-first century under the German Intelligent Structures for Mobile Robots' program. Its design then changed in the mid-2020s to a robotic infantry support unit when NATO was forced to re-arm to counter Russia's reignited expansionism during the Ukranian War of 2022-2024.

Lt. Mimieux meanwhile watched for any signs of movement from the Chinese SFs. He figured some of them might still be alive, but injured.

"Weasel2, go down with the medi-kit and attend the injured," Lt. Mimieux said to Sergeant Bouquin.

"Roger, lieutenant."

Lt. Mimieux then got on the comm. link to advise the Ibecci.

"Seren *Capac*, our squad will come down to the valley to see if there is anyone left alive who might need medical attention."

There was no response. He noticed the Ibecci were dealing with their own injured. He could see movement through his thermal imaging around the *Balistro* that had been hit.

A floating flatbed transport and strange-looking robotic units were hovering around. There were also scores of paratroopers facing the Chinese SFs. He tried again.

"Seren *Capac*, do you have injured paratroopers? I see movement near the *Balistro* that took heavy fire. Anything we can do?"

Seren *Capac* responded right away.

"Krato *Patros*, one of our *Balistros,* is injured, not severely, we hope, but he needs medical attention. We will take him to the medical facilities aboard our military transport."

"Do you need assistance?"

"We can manage. The *Utios* has a fully equipped medical suit to look after his injuries," Seren *Capac* lied, as the trauma unit aboard the military transport was incapable of handling the serious injuries Krato *Patros* had suffered.

The *Balistro* was placed in an induced cryogenic stasis in order to transport him to the *Imperator Eberon*'s better-equipped medical facilities.

"Understood," Lt. Mimieux replied.

The *Tiger2* attack helicopter was still loitering above, and Lt. Mimieux ordered it to land in the middle of Vallée des Sables.

He then turned his attention to the progress of his squad descending to the valley and saw five people trudging down the hill. He could not make out who they were, as visibility was poor since it had started to snow.

"Weasel2, who is accompanying you?"

"Weasel, Capt. Flanders, and Maj Krol asked to come down. They are being escorted by personnel from the *Enterprise*. Over," Sergeant Bouquin replied.

"Seren *Capac*, please be advised, Capt. Flanders and Maj. Krol are coming your way."

"This is good! I will finally meet Maj. Krol. Friends and friendship are good," Seren *Capac* replied in a cheerful tone.

Lt. Mimieux said nothing and got back to Sergeant Bouquin, who was now checking the four Chinese SFs closest to the Ibecci's position.

They were confirmed casualties, and Sergeant Bouquin walked south to where the other four SFs were located. He found two still alive.

"Henhouse2, Weasel. Request assistance with transport of two injured Chinese SFs in need of medical attention. Over."

"Weasel, Henhouse2. Roadrunner1 is still grounded on the eastern side of Peak Les Deux Fréres and can assist.

Over."

"Henhouse2, Weasel. Thank you. You probably have better facilities aboard your carrier to deal with injured combatants compared to our hospital at Port-aux-Français."

"Roger, Weasel. We are glad to lend support until the *Foudre* arrives. Over."

"Roadrunner1, Henhouse2, please assist Weasel as required. Over."

"Copy that, Henhouse2. We are on our way. Please advise where you would like us to land. Over."

Through the joint tactical battlefield system, Lt. Mimieux simply tagged the location of Sergeant Bouquin in his HUD and then instructed the V28V pilot to fly toward his position.

Sergeant Bouquin was busy removing the powered exoskeletons of the two SFs. It was a slow and methodical task. Afterward, and as soon as the V28V arrived, the two injured and unconscious Chinese SF were strapped in stretchers and the V28V left for the *Enterprise.*

Sergeant Bouquin now had to continue collecting the six casualties to be handed over to the Chinese.

Lt. Mimieux hoped this would be the last of the Chinese incursion into the Kerguelen Islands and wished for the promised French marines to get to the island quickly.

The direct assault he had just witnessed did not sit well. He changed the frequency on the comm. link to address only his squad.

"Bouquin, Simard, stay sharp. I have a feeling we are not done yet."

"What ... !" Sergeant Bouquin exclaimed in a questioning tone.

"Simard, get G1 to scan south for any hostiles. I'll command G2 to do the same and scan on the eastern side of Peak Les Deux Frères in case there is another contingent coming up behind us. They would need to go north and around. Maybe they are still down there."

"Roger that," Cpl. Simard replied.

"Rooster, what's your fuel status?"

"We have enough to loiter for fifteen minutes. Over."

"Standby. We may need you airborne in a hurry to deal with a second wave."

"Understood."

Lt. Mimieux then started running down the hill to warn the Ibecci discreetly in case his hunch was wrong.

40 MAKING FRIENDS

Vallée des Sables, Kerguelen Islands

It was just before 8:00 p.m., and wet snow was still coming down on Vallée des Sables.

Maj. Krol had had enough excitement and wanted nothing more than to go back to the *Enterprise*, warm up, and eat a hot meal.

Unfortunately, it was not his call to make. Back at Vandenberg AFB, Maj.-Gen. Arias had given him and Capt. Flanders specific orders to meet the Ibecci.

The *Enterprise* CCSG had reiterated this before sending them to the island and instructed his MSF squad to make the meeting possible. Capt. Flanders's eagerness and go-getter attitude made the outcome a forgone conclusion.

So here they were, in the middle of the night, on an inhospitable, remote island, trudging through the mud and wet snow after having survived a firefight with Chinese Special Forces.

Capt. Flanders was in front leading the group to meet the Ibecci like an excited teenage girl going to meet her best friend.

The cheerful tone from Seren *Capac* seemed to support

Maj.-Gen. Arias's hypothesis that friendship might be something the Ibecci treasured, perhaps because they felt isolated and needed a sense of belonging after having lost their home planet.

What Maj. Krol and Capt. Flanders did not know was this sense of isolation was deeply felt by the young Seren *Capac.*

As they got close, they could see strange-looking multilegged bots milling around and illuminating the Ibecci position. The Ibecci appeared busy and simply ignored them. Capt. Flanders took a stab, raised her hand, and greeted the Ibecci.

"*Salve,*" she voiced forcefully, using the casual Latin greeting, hoping to convey friendship.

Some Ibecci paratroopers reacted and looked toward her. One slender and slightly shorter Ibecci who was not wearing a bulky battle suit, turned toward her, catching Capt. Flanders's eye.

"*Salvius,*" the Ibecci female replied and then waited.

Capt. Flanders kept walking and smiled at the Ibecci female, who she assumed was Seren *Capac.*

Unexpectedly, the Ibecci female ran toward Capt. Flanders, wrapping her long arms around and hugging her in a humanlike gesture of greeting. She then blurted something rapid fire that Capt. Flanders failed to understand, only catching a few words like *circulus ex amicis.*

Capt. Flanders returned the hug and then pulled back and looked up to take a good look at the tall Ibecci female.

She then said, "*Confusa perplexus*" to indicate she did not fully understand what Seren *Capac* had said. She was truly dumbfounded with the Ibecci language that had some commonalities with Latin but were slightly different or else pronounced differently. Then again, no one really knew how Latin, or Archaic Latin, had been spoken in antiquity.

The biggest mystery though, was that she couldn't understand the Latin connection with the extinct Puquina language associated with the culture that built Tiwanaku.

Seren *Capac* realized what was going on. Her facial expression changed to disappointment at the prospect of conversing casually with the human female. She recovered quickly, smiled at Capt. Flanders, and then spoke, but her lips did not move. The synthesized sound instead came through a hidden speaker within her body.

"I am Seren *Capac* and am happy we finally meet. You came with Maj. Krol who showed friendship when I first entered your planet," she said, taking a good look at Flanders and then looking at Maj. Krol, who was next to her.

On cue, Maj. Krol quickly introduced himself.

"Major Frank Krol. A pleasure to meet you, Seren *Capac*. This is Captain Daniela Flanders."

"A pleasure as well. You can call me Dini *Capac*," she said to establish a connection and give Seren *Capac* a sense of ease.

"Dini . . . I like your name. Yes, Dini *Capac*, friendship is good. If you are with Maj. Krol, then together we are friends," Seren Capac said, visibly pleased.

She then moved to the left and with her longer arms reached out to Maj. Krol to embrace them both.

It was easy to understand why Seren *Capac* thought of Maj. Krol as a friend. He had shown concern by warning her of the danger coming from the Chinese *Tinagong4* space station during her first trip. But Seren *Capac*'s warm reception also stemmed from her outward personality.

"I am a linguistics expert and wish I could speak your language, but I am really confused about it. It has some Latin words, and yet most words I do not recognize. And very few seem to have the structure associated with the Puquina language," Capt. Flanders said.

"I too would like to converse naturally and with no aids," Seren *Capac* replied slowly in an accented English, using her own voice.

She then smiled, knowing that for the time being, she wouldn't be able to do so, and switched back to her neural interface to answer Capt. Flanders's question.

"Our language shares commonalities with your Latin, because Latin is a descendant four times removed. Your open data network states Latin descended from Vasconic languages, or possibly proto Basque, but you will only be able to ascertain this if you go back far enough. The oldest group of languages on the European continent are the Vasconic languages, which morphed into an Iberian language, followed by Tartessian, Phoenician, and Etruscan. Etruscan being the accepted closest ancestor of Latin," Seren *Capac* stated.

Capt. Flanders paused with a confused look, trying to digest what she had just been told, and then answered.

"Hmm . . . I understand the connection with ancient Phoenician and Archaic Latin since the widely accepted premise is that Latin derived from Etruscan, Greek, and ultimately Phoenician. But the link to the older languages is less clear."

"Remember, all these languages are the most recent examples of your known history dating back to three thousand of your years. The first Ibecci expedition came to your planet thirteen thousand years ago. You undoubtedly recognize the similarities of the word *Iberian*, as in the Iberian language, with the name of our race. The Iberian language is in fact the language spoken by the Ibecci explorers who came to your planet thirteen thousand years ago, and which shares its script with Latin," Seren *Capac* further explained.

"Wow! This is fascinating, as it points out to the origin of our civilizations differing greatly from what we think we know," she responded excitedly and then continued.

"So, all our ancient languages like Vasconic, Basque, and Phoenician were actually brought to our planet by your race But I still don't follow the connection between Phoenician and the Puquina language. I don't recall scholars stating that Puquina resembled an Iberian, Phoenician, or Latin root."

"Your assumption the builders of Tiwanaku spoke the

Puquina language is incorrect. Your worldwide information network indirectly points to this by stating the language spoken by the ancient inhabitants of Tiwanaku cannot be verified, as there are no inscriptions.

"Hmm . . . I agree what we know is based on speculation because of the long time scales," Capt. Flanders replied.

"The only accurate piece of information regarding Tiwanaku is its name. The ancestors of the Puquina and Wari cultures came up with the name," Seren *Capac* continued.

"The name is not Ibecci?"

"No. The colony was actually known as *Tellus Coloniam*, which you should easily recognize, but after the first transmissions received in *Eder*, the name changed to Tiwanaku. This is believed to have occurred as the small Ibecci expedition befriended the Indigenous people to help with the construction of the settlement. I can explain more fully if you come to the *Utios*, our troop carrier, as I am getting cold, even if my flight suit is designed for extreme environments. We can travel together on one of our transports and continue our conversation. Yes?" Seren *Capac* asked with a pleading look.

"That sounds like a wonderful idea," Maj. Krol exclaimed He had remained silent because the conversation was beyond his depth.

"Oh, yes! I would love to continue our conversation! There are so many things you are telling us that differ from what we think we know. Obviously, much of our history is not even ours!" Capt. Flanders said.

Seren *Capac* suddenly turned around and faced her paratroopers. She then started looking east, then north, and spoke.

"Lt. Mimieux is running toward us."

She continued, "One of our fliers performing defence patrols has also informed me of two unknown humans travelling on foot, moving north and parallel to us, but on the other side of the hill. Perhaps more Chinese combatants."

The Ibecci paratroopers turned around to face north while a *Balistro* and three paratroopers started advancing toward the northeast in order to confront the Chinese SFs at the edge of Peak Les Deux Frères.

In the dark, Lt. Mimieux could now be seen faintly some fifty metres away, running toward them in long strides thanks to the augmented power provided by his exoskeleton leg extremities.

It was a clever recuperative passive design relying on the motion and mass of the wearer to store energy and then release it, propelling the leg forward at each stride. Just like a human body naturally relies on a pendulum-like leg motion to walk.

As Lt. Mimieux approached, he slowed down, simultaneously taking off his helmet and hurriedly addressing Seren *Capac*.

"There is a possibility of more Chinese Special Forces coming up on the other side of Peak Les Deux Frères," he blurted out in English without bothering with pleasantries.

"I have just been made aware of two unidentified humans moving north on the other side of the hill—" But Seren *Capac* could not finish her sentence.

Explosions rocked the construction site just a hundred metres from where they were standing, momentarily lighting up the night sky.

Simultaneous explosions muffled by the falling snow could also be heard further north, where the Ibecci spaceships were grounded.

Instinctively, everyone ducked and their position started coming under automatic weapons' fire.

Lt. Mimieux immediately ordered the *Tiger2* attack helicopter in the air to deal with the threat. As he did this, another explosion went off, perhaps thirty metres away from them.

Thankfully, the *Balistro* and paratroopers that had advanced north blocked the explosion and shrapnel, but the proximity of the blast overpressure threw everyone back. Seren *Capac* had her back toward the explosion and fell into the arms of Capt. Flanders, both falling into the mud and wet snow.

Lt. Mimieux and Maj. Krol were also thrown back.

Without thinking, Lt. Mimieux rolled over on top of Seren *Capac* and Capt. Flanders to protect them with his exoskeleton.

"Are you okay?" he shouted in English above the noise of automatic weapons' fire.

Capt. Flanders lifted her arm, making the universal thumbs-up sign to show she was okay, and then wiggled out from under Seren *Capac*, who was slumped and motionless on top of her.

Lt. Mimieux gently pushed Seren *Capac* off to the side, rolled her on her back, and cradled her exposed head in his arms.

He had removed his helmet earlier and could not use the built-in diagnostics to check her vital signs, and, in any event, it may have been useless because of her unique physiology.

He felt uncomfortable holding her and was expecting an Ibecci paratrooper or medic to come barreling down and push him out of the way.

But it was humans who had attacked the Ibecci, so he felt obliged to help. So, he held her, unaware her companion orb was directly above him, monitoring her condition.

He took a small backup flashlight affixed to the exterior hard shell of his exoskeleton and rapidly flashed it on her face for any signs of movement. The light triggered some fluttering of her eyelids, and gradually, she opened her eyes. For just a moment, he looked at Seren *Capac*'s fine features as she slowly moved her head left to right, trying to shake off her confusion. Then she looked at him and imperceptibly held on to him, uttering a single word.

"*Gratiae*," but Lt. Mimieux could not hear it above the noise of automatic weapons' fire.

Seren's companion orb, aware she had regained consciousness, took action. It dashed at high speed past the *Balistro* and paratroopers to destroy the two Chinese SFs using its built-in high-energy laser.

Within a few minutes, the deafening noise of automatic weapons fire ceased as the Chinese SFs were neutralized by the combined action of Seren *Capac*'s orb and Ibecci *Balistros*.

All that was left was a crater and scorched earth where the two remaining Chinese SFs had made their last stand.

Lt. Mimieux helped Seren *Capac* sit up. Two Ibecci paratroopers came to her aid, accompanied by what appeared to be another pilot dressed in the same steel blue flight suit with horizontal folds and the emblem of a condor on his left breast pocket.

He was taller than Seren *Capac* but shorter than the paratroopers and featured the same elongated and fully shaven head. He was also accompanied by an orb floating above his head. It was clear this was his first time coming in close contact with humans because he studied the group carefully and spoke.

"I am Grifer *Junct*, Seren *Capac*'s wingman."

"Grifer *Junct*, I have asked our friends to come along with us to the *Utios*, where I can answer more of their questions," Seren *Capac* said.

She stood up and smiled at Lt. Mimieux and Capt. Flanders. She moved closer and then stretched her long arms to embrace all of them to emphasize her point.

"Yes, *Capac*, but I think we should first look after you. We can exchange information later."

At this moment, diplomacy was the last thing on Grifer *Junct*'s mind. He urgently wanted to resume defence patrols around the construction site in order to avoid a repeat of what had just happened. He felt guilty thinking he had not done a good job protecting their site, resulting in repeated attacks, the death of one *Balistro*, and damages to the construction site.

"I am fine, but cold. Our friends must also be, and it is dark, late, and the falling snow shows no signs of stopping. We should show our friends some hospitality. They stood with us side-by-side during the battle and have now twice protected me. I believe it is appropriate to offer them shelter for the night," Seren *Capac* said.

"As you wish, *Capac*. I would like to resume defence patrols right way."

"Granted," Seren *Capac* responded simply and watched him walk away toward his spacecraft grounded some fifty metres away.

"Will you and your personnel come to the *Utios* for shelter from the snowfall?" Seren *Capac* asked Lt. Mimieux and the others.

"Your invitation is kind. Unfortunately, my squad and I have work to do to recover all the bodies of the fallen Chinese soldiers, and the wounded need to be transported to the NAU aircraft carrier But I cannot speak for Capt. Flanders or Maj. Krol," Lt. Mimieux replied.

As he said this, Sergeant Bouquin spoke over the comm. link.

"Lieutenant, Roadrunner1 is en route to the *Enterprise* with the two wounded Chinese SFs. We are almost done here collecting the casualties and could ask for another V28 to be sent to collect them. I wouldn't mind going to a warm place and getting out of my exo," Sergeant Bouquin chimed in.

He spoke on the open frequency, so everyone heard it. It was not something Lt. Mimieux was thrilled about, but he knew where Sergeant Bouquin was coming from.

"Me too, boss! Would love to get to know some Ibecci boys . . ." Cpl. Simard quipped merrily.

Even though the RPIM squad had prepared for cold weather and their exoskeletons provided protection from the elements, the squad was now on their third day of operations, sleeping outdoors inside their exoskeletons. They were tired and in dire need of a shower, a soft bed, and a decent meal, so the prospect of going into a warm place was alluring.

Lt. Mimieux understood this and was not about to muzzle those under his command for making a reasonable request.

As he reflected on this, the comm. link crackled with a message from the *Foudre*.

"Weasel, Henhouse. Please be advised a Panther is about one hour away from the island, carrying eight marines and Lt. Col Leclerc."

"Roger, Henhouse," Lt. Mimieux replied happily.

"Upon arrival, they will relieve you and bring back the Chinese casualties. Your orders are to accept the Ibecci invitation and continue gathering intel. Lt. Col Leclerc will meet you at the Ibecci spaceship. Over."

"Understood Henhouse. Weasel out," Lt. Mimieux replied and then turned toward Seren *Capac*, who was smiling.

"I am glad you can come," a visibly pleased Seren *Capac* replied, who felt an urgency to foster a relationship with the humans. A task now more critical because of the events of the last twelve hours.

But for Seren *Capac*, it was more than following orders from Marel *Viracoh*. She needed to belong and make friends. From the age of six, when she was taken away from her family and selected as a survivor, she learned to make friends fast to avoid the pain of separation. She became very social, with a strong collaborative spirit, in order to feel connected. And right now, she desperately needed to feel connected to the humans rather than be portrayed as a threat.

41 IBECCI HOSPITALITY

Vallée des Sables, Kerguelen Islands

The Ibecci, together with the French and NAU military personnel, arrived at the *Utios* military transport.

In the dark and with the limited visibility from the unrelenting snowfall, it was impossible to appreciate its length of over a hundred and fifty metres and height of ten storeys resting on the ground like a beached ocean liner.

But as Lt. Mimieux remembered, it was shaped like an elongated box with smooth sides. Not the way fictionalized interstellar spaceships were supposed to look.

Everyone followed Seren *Capac* and her omnipresent orb, floating above her head, up a large ramp, which could have been at the front or the back of the spaceship.

Lighting with an amber hue illuminated the interior. It was bright, but with a tinge reminiscent of candlelight. It had a calming effect compared to the sterile quality of Earth's cool LED lighting technology, giving the interior of the spaceship a decidedly nineteenth-century Victorian steampunk feel where time seemed to pass more slowly.

They walked a short distance through two sets of pressure doors and entered a sort of locker room of generous dimensions with a high ceiling that could accommodate tall *Balistros*.

There were endless bays at both sides of the room that went on as far as the eye could see. Lt. Mimieux remembered Seren *Capac* had said the *Utios* carried a cohort of two hundred paratroopers, so he figured maybe each paratrooper had an assigned bay, but that was just a guess.

Each bay had a niche with shelves and a larger empty space with straps possibly designed to hold a combat-ready paratrooper during rough landing operations. The niche with shelves contained neatly arranged battle suits, torso plates, helmets, and a personal weapon that looked like the ones paratroopers carried on the field. Above each bay there were distinct symbols that were probably the name of each paratrooper. A few were empty, and there were bigger bays with larger components Lt. Mimieux assumed were probably for *Balistros*.

Sitting benches made of a metal resembling brushed aluminium sat in the middle of the long room at regular intervals. They were crafted with fine scroll metalwork reminiscent of nineteenth century wrought ironwork and taller than one would expect a sitting bench to be.

As Lt. Mimieux appreciated the ornate metalwork, he realized it was present everywhere inside the spaceship, instantly reminding him of Captain Nemo's *Nautilus* submarine depicted in books and movies. He then had the ridiculous thought that maybe Jules Verne had been a descendant of the Ibecci.

One by one, the Ibecci paratroopers in front of the group stopped at their respective bays, placed their weapons in a cradle, and started removing their gear. Seren *Capac*, shadowed by her orb, motioned the humans to follow her further down to where there were empty bays.

"Please make yourself at home. You can remove your gear and use these niches to store your personal weapons, helmets, and outfits. The cleansing chambers—I believe in your language they are referred as showers—are in the adjacent room through the doorway you see on the opposite side. I will need to help each one of you to operate the cleansing chambers because their physical and medical scanners may trigger alarms," Seren *Capac* said.

"A shower! Oh yes, that would really be wonderful after three days inside my personal coffin. Hope they are toasty and clean," Cpl. Simard said, prompting a disapproving look from Lt. Mimieux.

"Simard, exercise a little more tact," Lt. Mimieux snapped.

"My apologies, lieutenaaant . . ." she replied, enunciating the word slowly.

Lt. Mimieux simply ignored the implied insult, knowing Cpl. Simard was a chatterbox difficult to muzzle, always saying what was on her mind.

"The cleansing chambers will warm you up and go through repeated cycles of cooling and heating to relax tired muscles. They are also clean and devoid of any bacteria, if I understand your comment, Cpl. Simard. Disinfection is an implicit feature due to the way they operate, which includes the use of UV radiation plus bathing the user with low levels of ionized air to eliminate airborne bacteria," Seren *Capac* declared.

"Sounds different, like a cross between a tanning bed and a shower," Cpl. Simard replied.

"The cleansing chambers are not the same as your idea of a shower. They are cylindrical alcoves that fit one individual. A design that is necessary in space. They do not use water as is your concept of a shower, based on information I extracted from your worldwide information network. In space, the use of large volumes of water for cleansing is an extravagant luxury. The chambers also perform physical and medical scans that require the user to be in proximity to the scanners."

"I haven't been in the field for as long as the French marines, so I'll pass on your kind offer," Maj. Krol said.

"Please trust me. You will feel energized and relaxed.

Unfortunately, it is also a requirement for your safety, and ours, because of the skin microbiota and bacteria we carry, which may affect you, and the ones you carry, which may affect us. The cleansing, therefore, serves the purpose of decontamination," Seren *Capac* asserted.

She had failed to mention it was more of a safety feature for the humans since Earthbound Ibecci had already been inoculated with wide spectrum antibiotics as a prerequisite before entering the planet.

"Yes, of course! It would be like what happened when the conquistadores arrived in Mexico and brought smallpox with them," Capt. Flanders declared.

Seren *Capac* delayed responding for a few seconds, likely to look up the historical reference, and then answered.

"Yes, Dini *Capac*, that is a very accurate example," she replied smiling.

"I guess that settles it! I really want to get out of my exo and clean myself, 'cause I know I stink. Then I'm going to relax and maybe get something to eat," Cpl. Simard said.

She walked up to the nearest locker, placed her sniper rifle bag in the niche, and removed her exoskeleton.

Sergeant Bouquin quietly went to the adjacent locker and started doing the same.

Lt. Mimieux followed, together with the remaining RPIM squad.

Maj. Krol and Capt. Flanders went to empty lockers across the room and were joined by Seren *Capac*.

She offered Maj. Krol help since he was the senior-ranking human. As she was doing this, Cpl. Simard turned to speak to Lt. Mimieux.

"Hey, lieutenant, I have a problem. I left my personal kit with clean undies at my hoverbike," she announced deadpan.

Lt. Mimieux grimaced at her candid and ill-chosen statement and braced himself for more to come.

"That's the least of your problems Simard, 'cause you really smell!" Sergeant Bouquin quipped as she was half done removing her exoskeleton.

"That's why I was the first one to say yes to a shower, genius! And the whiff drifting toward me tells me you don't smell like roses either, you overgrown ape!

"It's probably your own. You just don't know it," Sergeant Bouquin replied mockingly.

She glared at him with a look that was more jest than anything and replied, "After I'm done taking my luxurious bubble bath, I'm going to break every bone in your body! And don't think I can't do it, because I have wrestled bigger brutes than you and hurt them real bad."

"Hey, you two knock it off!" Lt. Mimieux exclaimed.

The exchange had been in French, and Maj. Krol did not catch the clowning, as he had removed his translator earpiece, but he saw Capt. Flanders smiling.

"Flanders, what's so funny?"

"Oh . . . Cpl. Simard and Sergeant Bouquin are just horsing around, and their comments are hilarious."

Seren *Capac* joined the conversation and answered Cpl. Simard's concern, not really knowing Cpl. Simard was just fooling around.

"You will find our use of undergarments differs from yours. The cleansing chambers will apply undergarments tightly to the body of the user, depending on his or her preferences and the diagnostics of the stations. You don't need to fret," Seren *Capac* said.

"That's pretty awesome. Can I pick the colour and the style? I don't want something practical and ugly. After all, I need to maintain my reputation," Cpl. Simard continued.

"What reputation is that?" Sergeant Bouquin asked, still mockingly.

"Pretty like a flower, but strong like a bull, of course," Cpl. Simard replied straight-faced, which garnered snorts and chuckles from the RPIM squad and Capt. Flanders.

Not that it was inaccurate, as the tall, good-looking redhead from the region of Alsace had a sensuous but muscular body that she had developed over years of intense training as an amateur UFC fighter. The laughing was more due to her nonstop comedic wit.

"You know, Simard, if you don't make it in the UFC, you can always try comedy," Lt. Mimieux exclaimed.

"What . . . ? Are you saying I'm not strong, or pretty or both?"

"Give it a rest, Simard," Lt. Mimieux replied.

Seren *Capac* was clearly having difficulty following the back and forth between Cpl. Simard and the others, so she simply answered Cpl. Simard's question.

"I am sorry, but there is no option to choose a colour. The undergarments are functional and only available in grey. They meet several functions beyond basic hygiene. They are a tight-fitting garment made of thin synthetic fabric with similar properties to wool. The fabric is also impregnated with silver nanoparticles. Together, the wool and the silver nanoparticles provide effective antimicrobial and antibacterial properties to control skin bacteria and infections. The cleansing chambers will also apply the same material as a pressure binding around sore extremities requested by the user or to support sprains detected by the scanners."

"So, we are going to look like mummies," Cpl. Simard quipped as she finished removing her boots. She was now standing barefoot at her station, just wearing her army-issue olive drab sports bra and bottoms.

Seren *Capac* delayed responding for a few seconds, likely to look up the reference to mummies, and then answered.

"There is some flexibility for the user to specify the width of the undergarment. I, for example, prefer a tall bottom undergarment because I am a spacecraft pilot and need support in the lower abdominal area beyond what my flight suit provides. Other Ibecci prefer narrower undergarments," Seren *Capac* replied with the sound now emanating from her orb as she had finished undressing.

She was standing in front of Cpl. Simard, showing underwear tight against her body and halfway to her navel.

She also had bandages around her thighs and no bra. Her body was tall, with essentially the same anatomy as a human except for her arms and legs that were very thin, with no muscle definition. It was a little unsettling as her thin extremities made her look almost malnourished, like a female marathon runner, and yet endowed with average-sized breasts.

"Hmm . . . pretty utilitarian. You said we could specify the width, right? What's with the bandaged thighs?" Cpl. Simard asked.

"I am still getting used to the higher gravity of your planet, and the bandages help during flight to deal with high G-forces. They also help with walking, as your gravity is twice what I have experienced my entire life. Ibecci don't have the same amount of muscle mass as humans, as our life in space changed the composition of our bodies," Seren *Capac* replied, looking at Cpl. Simard and the others who were now down to their undergarments.

Her expression was not one of approval as she looked at the well-developed muscular male and female bodies in front of her, although it could have also been due to the humans' body and facial hair, which were in striking contrast to the hairless Ibecci. Yet, she clearly attempted to keep her expression neutral.

"Ah . . . that explains why you are so thin. You work with me, girl, for three, maybe four, months and I'll get you in great shape, just like me. Your struggles with our higher gravity will be over. I guarantee it," Cpl. Simard declared while simultaneously doing a 360-degree pirouette to emphasize her point.

"Simard, please . . . just stop," Lt. Mimieux implored.

"What boss? I am just offering to train her. You know I'm also a fitness instructor, right?" Cpl. Simard replied with a serious tone.

"Please do not fret, Lt. Mimieux. I welcome the dialogue as part of getting to know each other. My orb is telling me you and others are uncomfortable with the discussion, although Cpl. Simard appears at ease. Highlighting the physical differences between our species is an important step to show you we are not that different despite the shape of our skulls and the colour of our skin. In fact, we share the same lineage," Seren *Capac* replied through her orb.

With her standing there, it was hard to see much difference, especially because under the orange interior illumination, the red colour of her skin was washed away, instead appearing a pleasing honey brown. It made her look like a topless and tanned sun worshiper from Santorini, Lefkada, or the beaches along Spain's Costa del Sol, rather than an alien from another planet.

"What do you mean when you say we share the same lineage?" Capt. Flanders turned toward her and asked.

"That we have a shared origin. Our DNA is very similar and points to a common ancestor. I believe you call it Homo sapiens. We don't know much more than that. It is a great mystery we have been trying to solve since our race first came to your planet."

"That's unbelievable, but how is that possible?"

"We do not know. There is not much more I can add because there is no history or anthropological references to help, and so Ibecci scholars find themselves at a dead end. From what I have studied of your history, your race finds itself in a similar situation in the sense that Homo sapiens appeared from nowhere. And from the perspective of history, you have few historical records that go back beyond 4000 BC. Because of this, a significant amount of your past seems to be based on conjecture and folklore more than on accurate records," Seren *Capac* said.

Capt. Flanders simply smiled and nodded, thinking about how just a few days ago she had given Cmdr. Phelps the same speech in the flag officers' briefing room of the *Enterprise*.

"Yes! You are so . . . right. We know little of our ancient history and lost so much of it over millennia to war, barbarians, and accidents like the fire of the Great Library of Alexandria, which was reputed to contain the records of ancient history. But as you correctly state, a significant amount of what we take as facts is just folklore and speculation. The Great Library of Alexandria is a perfect example because it is believed to have contained records of such wonders as the Hanging Gardens of Babylon and even Atlantis if the accounts from ancient Greek historians are to be believed. But there is no hard evidence to back this up except for the writings of Plato and the lesser-known Athenian statesman Solon. A better tangible example, though, is the Great Sphinx of Giza, which is a widely recognizable ancient monument. Most archeologists date it to approximately 2500 BC. But not all archeologists agree. A few suggest it is at least five thousand years old, as evidenced by water erosion, so the basic piece of information related to who built it and when is a total mystery."

"At least your historians know where Atlantis was located. Your worldwide information network states two locations. One at the site of the ancient city of Tartessos in Andalusia, near what the Spanish fiefdom calls the Doñana National Park. The remnants supposedly exist beneath the mud. One document we accessed states that high-altitude satellite images show parts of several rings that match Plato's description of the city's ring system. And a second location at the Richat Structure in Africa. This appears to be the more likely location as the ring structure is visible and the location is more in line with ancient accounts Atlantis was past the Pillars of Hercules.

"Why would you say those places are the actual location?" Capt. Flanders asked.

"Because we think it is probably our second settlement, but we did not know this until our scholars started reviewing your own history records to get clues about what might have happened to Tiwanaku. As they did this, our scholars stumbled on the myth of Atlantis. However, it is still a theory based on conjecture, given that most of your information on Atlantis is speculative as a result of the Young Dryass Impact event that occurred 10,000 to 12,000 years ago, erasing all the history of previous civilizations. We can talk about this later if you don't mind, as I see most of you are now undressed. Now I would like to bring you to the cleansing chambers," Seren *Capac* announced through her orb, first in French and then in English.

Capt. Flanders just looked at Seren *Capac,* speechless, with eyes as big as dinner plates. She had to summon all her self-control to stop asking questions.

Cpl. Simard spoke first, just like a child wanting to be the first to go on a ride.

"Me first! I want to try these cleansing chambers and take a relaxing snooze."

Seren *Capac* went through the doorway she had shown earlier, followed by Cpl. Simard and the rest.

They entered another long room with tiled floor as long as the change room and parallel to it. It was illuminated with the same orange lighting as the change room, but appeared brighter because of the light-coloured tiling on the walls and floors.

There were benches and countless enclosed glass cylinders sitting on the far wall with the same ornate metalwork.

The cylinders were about one metre in diameter and three metres in height and looked like fictional suspended animation chambers. They were arranged in groups of four, continuing to the far end of the room.

Lt. Mimieux figured there were as many as fifty cylinders. Seren *Capac* walked up to the first one. It detected her proximity, and the entire glass cylinder rotated to expose an opening. She then turned toward Cpl. Simard and addressed her.

"I'll help you first. You will have to remove your bottom undergarment and chest support," Seren *Capac* announced.

Cpl. Simard did as she was told.

"Where can I put them?" she asked unabashedly

standing naked in front of Seren *Capac* while holding the two items in her hand.

"I am afraid we will have to destroy them. I will show you," Seren *Capac* replied.

"Ah . . . it's only army-issue. Not like the pretty stuff I wear going out on the town."

Lt. Mimieux shook his head from side to side but said nothing.

Seren *Capac* went to the side of the glass cylinder and placed her hand on the glass surface. A touch screen with cyan-coloured symbols appeared on the glass that moments earlier had been totally transparent. She tapped a few icons and a small trapdoor opened at the back and near the bottom of the chamber. Another small panel slid open at head height.

"Please enter the chamber and throw the items through the bottom opening. At the top, you will see a smaller opening. Reach in with your hand, and you should find eye protection with an adjustable elastic band you can hopefully adjust to fit your narrowly shaped head. Then turn around and face the front."

Cpl. Simard complied, then adjusted the goggles and put them on.

"Does the eye protection fit?" Seren *Capac* asked.

"Yes," Cpl. Simard replied with no rambling commentary.

"Good. Please widen your stance slightly and lean back. Do not be alarmed, as I will close the glass door. The cleansing chamber will go through a series of cycles. First, you will be bathed in UV light. You will also feel jets of ionized dry air on your body warmer than the room temperature. The UV light and ionized air will eliminate airborne and skin surface bacteria and pathogens. As you feel the air jets, you can raise your arms and legs to get the air to strike specific areas. After a minute, the chamber and jets of ionized air will get progressively warmer, and at this point you can lean back. The cycle will then reverse, and the temperature inside the chamber will drop quickly to below zero and then back to room temperature. Once this first cycle is complete, you will be bathed in warm moist air, which is the closest equivalent to your notion of a shower. This will be followed by a third cycle. Do you have questions?"

"No. Seems simple enough."

"The last thing the cleansing chamber will do is apply a lower undergarment via two arms that will come down and rotate around your body. I have selected a slim undergarment based on your request. I have also specified an upper chest support to be applied in a similar manner. It requires that you raise your arms. I'll close the door now," Seren *Capac* stated, almost as a question, to which Cpl. Simard replied with a simple nod.

Seren *Capac* then moved to a second cleansing chamber nearby that opened just like the first one. She turned toward Maj. Krol.

"Maj. Krol, would you like to be next?" she asked in English.

"Sure thing," he replied. He stepped forward and disposed of his underwear just as Cpl. Simard had done moments earlier. He then turned around to face the front of the chamber wearing the goggles.

"Dini *Capac*, would you mind watching how I enter commands to configure the cleansing cycle so you can help others?"

"Yes, I'd be glad to help," Capt. Flanders responded eagerly.

Seren *Capac* repeated the explanation of the cleansing cycle stages to Maj. Krol in English to make sure he knew what to expect. A few moments later, the chamber closed to start the cycle.

The two went through the procedure one more time, first helping Sergeant Bouquin and then splitting to help the others.

When it was time for Lt. Mimieux to go through

decontamination, Capt. Flanders took care of him. As he entered the chamber, she couldn't help noticing Seren *Capac*, glancing at him with the same difficult-to-read expression but perhaps with an imperceptible hint of approval. He was an ectomorph, but with muscular arms, and, at 1.93 metres tall, much shorter than an Ibecci male. But from Seren *Capac*'s perspective, maybe similar enough in physiognomy that she seemed attracted to him.

Capt. Flanders couldn't help an inner chuckle at the preposterous idea of an interspecies romance, but then there was that moment between the two after the explosion at Vallée des Sables, so maybe such a possibility was not far-fetched. She put it out of her mind and instead concentrated on helping the remaining members of her team go through decontamination.

She was the last one to go through.

After emerging from the chamber, she sensed the pleasant trace of humidity that lingers right after a shower and felt energized, just as Seren *Capac* said they would.

"Ah . . . that felt good!" Capt. Flanders exclaimed, somehow amazed that a nearly waterless shower would be just as satisfying.

"I am glad you feel refreshed," Seren *Capac* replied.

She then addressed the entire group, still using her orb. "We have long shirts, which you can use as temporary clothing to cover yourselves. They should suffice, as I am sure you have by now noticed we keep the interior of the spaceship at a comfortable temperature."

As she said this, an Ibecci male handed out the shirts from a cart brought to the shower room.

"Hey, Seren *Capac*, could we get some water and maybe something to eat?" Cpl. Simard asked in her characteristic direct style. "I left my rations at Peak Les Deux Frères."

"Certainly! I was going to offer you nourishment. You will recognize some of our foodstuffs, especially the potatoes and quinoa. We also have corn, but the varieties we consume are red and black, the original colour of the corn the Ibecci brought to Tiwanaku. I believe you know it as heirloom corn. We prepare these starches simply, but they will quell your hunger. Now please follow me."

"I knew your race introduced food staples to our planet!" Capt. Flanders exclaimed as the group followed Seren *Capac* down the shower hall further into the bowels of the spaceship.

She was eager to resume the conversation regarding the first voyage of the Ibecci to Earth, their language, and especially the history of Earth's first civilizations.

The tantalizing bits of information Capt. Flanders had learned in the last few hours were remarkable and mysterious, and her mind raced as she joined the dots.

It all fit. The Incan and Mayan jewelry in the form of delta wing aircraft, and their images and renderings of men with strange-looking headgear reminiscent of a pilot's helmet. The flying vehicles of Atlantis. Gilgamesh, the alien-hybrid warrior king created by the seven Anunnaki who themselves, just like Viracocha, came from the heavens to teach Sumerians how to build their great cities. The Lady of Elche with her elongated head and strange headgear that looked like oversized headphones, who was more than likely an Ibecci female pilot. They were all linked to the Ibecci, and their arrival had made a worldwide impact. History would have to be rewritten, and the assumption of Mesopotamia being the cradle of civilization revised with the Ibecci race added as the catalyst for the emergence of Earth's past civilizations.

As Capt. Flanders reflected on all of this and walked toward what was probably an alien mess hall, the snow outside continued to fall relentlessly, fueled by an intense tropical cyclone forming in the middle of the Indian Ocean, south from Diego Garcia.

They were safe inside the Ibecci spaceship, and the NAU and French navy ships near the island were also safe, as the water was too cold to fuel the cyclone.

In contrast, the *Liu Huaqing*, with her four *Shenyang*

destroyer escorts, were now travelling on a northeastern course toward the cyclone. They were only at the edge of the cyclone but already facing three-metre swells. As they continued on their set course, the seas were bound to get rougher, and the *Liu Huaqing* carrier task force would soon face sustained winds of one hundred to one hundred and sixty kilometres per hour and much bigger swells.

It was ironic the confrontation had thankfully been mild and resulted in limited loss of life and matériel. But it appeared maybe Mother Nature might have the last word.

42 DISTORTING THE FACTS

The United Nations, New York

"China's actions cannot be tolerated! No nation has the right to enter the sovereign territory of another nation," Alain Trouchette, the representative from France, said in his opening remarks.

He was speaking at the emergency meeting of the UN Security Council.

He continued, "A small contingent of Chinese Special Forces landed on the Kerguelen Islands, a recognized French Territory, and fired their weapons at the Ibecci. Furthermore, they fired at a small reconnaissance team of the French forces that arrived on the island to observe the Ibecci and report on their activities. France and the NAU have submitted a formal protest along with evidence detailing the Chinese incursion and aggression," he concluded, locking eyes with his Chinese counterpart.

After a few minutes and as the whispering among members subsided, Undersecretary Laura Bonte gave the floor to Yongrui Xu to respond to the accusations.

"China vehemently disputes the claims made by France and the NAU," Yongrui Xu said while looking straight at

Alain Trouchette with a look that could only be interpreted as disdain.

He looked down at his notes.

"China did not invade the French Kerguelen Islands. As a nation focused on the well-being of our people and that of other nations, China made the unilateral decision to safeguard our planet from the Invaders when no one else was willing to do so. China's PLA navy fired missiles at the military spaceship of the aliens defending their beachhead!"

He raised his head and looked around to all the members in the semicircular amphitheatre to let the statement sink in.

"Yes, make no mistake, China considers their landing site a beachhead from where they will mount a full-scale invasion of our planet, and China wants to prevent this!"

Members immediately started murmuring. It slowly grew in intensity until the room erupted into chaos.

"Ladies and Gentlemen, please allow the Chinese member to continue," Undersecretary Bonte pleaded over the noise.

On cue, Yongrui Xu resumed his speech.

"The conniving aliens also inflicted damage to the Chinese carrier group, including the destruction of our surveillance drones and the combat drones protecting them. They also attacked four Chinese destroyers. These actions clearly show these aliens are not as peaceful as they profess. And on top of this, China's efforts were thwarted by the traitorous NAU and French Ibecci sympathisers!"

His words immediately triggered an outcry, and members started shouting. But there were also nods and smiles from members who shared China's view.

It was unofficially accepted China invaded French territory, yet a large contingent of members sided with China.

Tim Laurier, the French-Canadian representative from the Northern States and Canada (NSC), asked for the floor and provided a rebuttal. He first spoke in French and then impassionedly repeated the statement in English.

"Members of the Security Council, I believe it is my duty and responsibility to point out the honourable member from China is distorting the facts. The Chinese carrier group, in fact, fired first. The Ibecci simply defended themselves. The so-called attack that damaged their destroyers was simply a measured cyberattack that crippled the computer systems of the Chinese destroyers, sparing the lives of all Chinese sailors. The Ibecci could have inflicted significantly more damage if they had wanted, including sinking the entire Chinese carrier group," Laurier stated in his polished delivery.

The choice of words and the cadence had a calming effect, and members happily listened to the well-liked, bilingual, French Canadian.

Laurier continued, "While there still are dissenting views regarding the true intentions of the Ibecci, it is imperative humanity begin a diplomatic dialogue instead of resorting to force, given we have yet to respond to their first message. I ask of all members to heed the conciliatory voices of those who wish to put diplomacy first. We still need to find out their true intentions, and sending an overdue message of welcome and opening a dialogue are the best ways to establish a common ground. Please reflect on the fact that for the first time in history, we have discovered humanity is not alone in the universe."

He looked up to gauge the effect of his words as the chamber went dead silent. He then turned his head toward Alain Trouchette, giving him an imperceptible nod, and then at Yongrui Xu with a conciliatory expression meant to bring the two nations together.

"We, as an enlightened civilization, should try to build a friendship with our newfound neighbours. The alternative path we seem to be following might plunge our planet into an internal conflict; something no one wants. China may, in fact, find itself at war, not just with the Ibecci, but with other nations of Earth. Divisiveness is the least thing our planet needs right now. Thank you."

43 GETTING NOWHERE

It was the second week of Cate Brinnan's stay at the ELT.

She and Carlos had been enjoying each other's company beyond the mutual attraction. They also shared the common ground of astronomy, and Cate happily went with Carlos to the Colosseum-sized observatory.

It was after midnight, and the two were examining the latest computer images around Barnard's Star in an open area next to the telescope's behemoth Naismith mount.

Carlos's mind was elsewhere as he kept glancing at Cate.

"Stop looking at me! Focus on the work at hand!" she said sternly in her thick Irish accent.

"I'm sorry, *amor*! I still can't believe my luck!"

"Your luck is going to change if we don't find their planet before someone else does!"

Carlos smiled and started singing the ninety-year-old song by Billy Preston "You Are So Beautiful," which she thought corny and snorted.

"You don't like my singing?"

"Carlos, sweetie, please stop. I promise you we will take a break and I'll give you all my attention," she said with a mischievous grin.

"Really?"

"Really. Now get to work."

"Okay, but we are wasting our time. If the planet had transited in front of Barnard's Star, we should have seen it by now, especially with the coronal filter. I'm thinking the planet's orbit is not aligned with our line of sight."

"Or . . . we are looking at this all wrong," Cate replied.

"How so?"

"Maybe there is no planet where we think it should be."

"Based on what?"

"Well, the more I think about this, and the more we look at the data, the more I'm inclined to side with past research that concluded the star's unaccounted perturbations are from a second planet further out."

"Well, yes, that was the widely held assumption until the Ibecci arrived, so I don't follow where you are going with this."

"Think about it. We keep looking for a habitable planet closer to the star and inside the orbit of Barnard's Star b, but we are coming up empty. That shouldn't be because a planet that close will probably have a period of forty to sixty days. It should have already transited in front of the star. Agree?"

"Yes, that's why I suggested it's not aligned with our line of sight."

"True, but hear me out. Previous analysis also tells us Earth-sized planets in the habitable zone are pretty well ruled out. Yet we are ignoring this because we understandably believe the Ibecci planet must be there, even though existing data tells us differently. Right?"

"Yes, I guess so."

"That leaves us with Barnard b, which is at the edge of the habitable zone, but is it? So, once you eliminate the impossible, what remains, however improbable . . ."

"You are saying Barnard b is their planet?"

"Could be. Who knows? Have we bothered to imagine

it to check surface conditions?"

"Well, no, we haven't. The general assumption is that it's too frigid and too big."

"We don't know for sure, and as for size, it's only three Earth masses, so not that big. What we need to do is find the planet further out, responsible for the perturbations in the data. Then model the system. See if it agrees."

Carlos remained silent. He looked way up past the open roof of the observatory at the clear night sky, showing millions of twinkling stars, and then fixed his gaze on Cate.

"So, we look for the planet further out, which is the opposite of what everybody else is doing."

"Yes. Trust me on this. It's like the problem I've been wrestling with in my search for Planet Nine. Essentially looking for a planet, not knowing where to look and then modelling the system until you get agreement."

"I admit they are logical arguments, even if it's going against what all other observatories are doing."

"The benefit of right hemisphere thinking, sweetie."

"I thought that was a myth."

"Who is the more unconventional thinker? Who's the better singer, and, most importantly, who's the better kisser?"

"You on all counts?"

"That's right, sweetie," she said, looking intently at Carlos.

She moved toward him, gave him a slow, sensual kiss, and then grabbed his hand.

"Come. Let's go to the upper catwalk and look at the night sky."

Cate got up, pulling Carlos toward the access walkway that led to the top of the telescope's tower.

There was no elevator, so they climbed the equivalent of twelve storeys up yellow-painted metal stairs that wound around the telescope, reaching the highest point of the access walkway.

It was a dizzying height, made worse by the open

catwalk, despite tall, protective railings. Not a place for someone with a fear of heights looking down through the open grating or up to the curved roof deck.

Cate, though, found it calming from the activity down below.

She looked up through the open roof at the indescribable beauty of the night sky that almost glowed from the dense star count.

"Isn't it breathtaking?"

They both gazed in silence and with a deeper understanding. There was intelligent life out there. Humanity was not alone. This knowledge somehow made the universe more mysterious, even if scientists had known for over a hundred years—intelligent life in the universe was a given since Frank Drake developed the Drake equation.

Cate moved toward Carlos and kissed him, slowly at first. Her respiration then quickened, and she kissed him more intensely, pressing herself against him.

Carlos reciprocated, holding her face and kissing her passionately.

As Carlos kissed Cate, her knees gave way, reminding her the damned Catalonian was the only one who could affect her that way.

She came up for air and pulled back.

"This is a sample of what awaits you later when we go back to the house. In the meantime, let's go back down and start thinking about our alternate approach and how you are going to sell it."

"You are a tease, you know, but passionate love is supposed to be exciting, and in that department, you are off the scale."

"Oh, that's so sweet. Are you looking for extra favours?

"Eh no, simply stating the obvious, *mi bella Irlandesa.*"

"Well, flattery will get you everywhere, sweetie."

Cate started going down the metal stairs, smiling back as she always did.

They went to work right away, outlining their research

approach, unaware other observatories were reaching similar conclusions.

The difference, however, was the other observatories were thinking the Ibecci came from further away, discounting Barnard's Star altogether as their place of origin. Two strong contenders being considered were Teegarden's Star b and Luyten's Star b, both about twelve light-years away and with significantly higher ESIs. Others even suggested Proxima b, only 4.2 light-years away, even though it was essentially uninhabitable.

While some alternatives made sense, the naysayers were conveniently ignoring that it would be counterproductive for the Ibecci to lie about the true location of their planet if they wanted to develop trust with Earth.

But every story always has two sides, and so there was the other unsavory alternative.

For the time being, the mystery of the Ibecci race's true origins deepened. And with the frantic pace now somewhat reduced, Cate and Carlos had more time for intimacy, which suited them both.

44 TRY, TRY AGAIN…

Ministry of National Defence (August 1st Building), Beijing

"We all know Planet Earth is doomed! The climate is changing at an alarming pace. The concentrations of methane continue to climb at an ever-increasing rate," Brigadier Jun Liang said.

He was addressing the PLA navy's joint staff and the Central Military Commission after Admiral Hsu's failed attempt to destroy the aliens.

"Let me remind all those present that after 2080, our weather models and the ones from the West will not tell us what the planet's weather will be like.

"In the last twenty years, we had to invest trillions to safeguard low-lying areas from the rising sea levels around Shanghai, Macau, Xiamen, and all along the shores of the Zhujiang Estuary.

"All throughout the world, we are seeing the same flooding and destruction. Venice is gone, and that after China spent over half a trillion Euros buying up and rehabilitating most of it.

"New York City, Boston, and London won't be around

much longer. And that applies for other low-lying coastal areas where 40 percent of the entire world population lives."

"We've known this for over thirty years. We took steps to build our space infrastructure to colonize Mars. As we speak, the development pace of our space transportation systems is accelerating. Our scientists are now doubling their efforts to engineer spaceships beyond those currently in use by Griffin Space Systems."

Brigadier Liang delivered his opening remarks in a calm but firm voice. Something people who knew him were not accustomed to. He took a sip from a glass of water and continued.

"Now we face this unknown threat from the aliens. The threat is very real, as witnessed by Admiral Hsu's carrier task force. Their technology is superior, and despite our best efforts, we were unsuccessful at inflicting any damage.

"Thankfully, Admiral Hsu broke off the engagement relatively unscathed, as the aliens were unwilling or unable to strike back."

Brigadier Liang paused and looked around the theatre.

"From the start, I had advocated to stop them before they got a foothold on Earth. The threat has now doubled. They are here while simultaneously working toward the terraforming of Mars and its eventual colonization.

"It's time to flex our muscles, but this time in space and free from the confines of Earth's atmosphere.

"If we are to survive, we must strike a decisive blow in order to protect China and our right to colonize Mars.

"The PLA's Space Forces will do what needs done."

Two days later, a *Shenlong* spaceplane, carrying the *Jiantou* second stage, rose slowly from the ultralong seven-thousand-metre runway at the Dongfeng Space Centre in Inner Mongolia.

The fully loaded, eighty-seven-metre, twin rudder delta wing *Shenlong* lumbered off the runway, gaining altitude slowly. Even though it carried the *Jiantou* second stage affixed to its nose, the highly swept ogival delta wing spaceplane looked like a single vehicle reminiscent of the 1978 Rockwell's Star-raker.

The spaceplane's six turbo-aided rocket-augmented ram/scramjet engines initially accelerated it to Mach 3 and an altitude of twenty thousand metres. The engines then transitioned from turbine to ramjet/scramjet operation and the spaceplane accelerated and continued climbing, more steeply, to an altitude of thirty-four thousand metres and Mach 7.

At that altitude, the rarified air contained almost no oxygen to sustain the ramjet/scramjet mode. The TRREs switched to their oxygen-kerosene rocket mode for the final leg of the ascent to one hundred kilometres and an orbital velocity of Mach ~22.

The smaller arrowhead-shaped *Jiantou* then separated, fired its two oxygen-kerosene rocket engines, and continued ascending to rendezvous with the *Tiangong4* station in GEO. There it refueled, and after a brief delay, separated, fired its engines, and its two taikonauts set a course toward L2, approximately 1.5 million kilometres away.

Free from gravity, the *Jiantou* easily accelerated and shut off its engines.

Now the OTV and its two taikonauts were on their own, running dark, travelling at a velocity of 11 km/s and carrying its deadly cargo of two nuclear-tipped CJ-30 missiles in its internal bay.

The journey was expected to take thirty-five hours, and just before arrival, the *Jiantou* would fire the two nuclear-tipped missiles as close to the Ibecci fleet as they dared, turn around, and return home.

45 THE STAKES KEEP RISING

614th Air and Space Operations Centre (614 AOC), Vandenberg AFB

"AIDA, has the Chinese OTV fired its engines yet?" Maj. Krol asked as he looked at the main holographic display in the AOC theatre.

"It did just now."

The main holographic display showed the *Tiangong4* station in GEO and the arrow-shaped *Jiantou* spaceplane with its nose pointed up. The moon was also framed further to the right, together with L2 shown as a point in space at the top right corner of the display.

Maj. Krol stood next to his chair with his eyes focused on the display. But so was everyone else in the overcrowded AOC theatre.

"AIDA, please add the most likely trajectories from the *Tinagong4* station to the Chinese moon base and to L2," Maj. Krol requested.

AIDA complied, and two amber lines appeared in the holographic display with the likely trajectories to the moon and L2.

"AIDA, what's the probability the OTV is headed

toward L2?"

"Greater than 70 percent."

Maj. Krol kept watching the main holographic display intently. He now had a better appreciation of who the Ibecci were after his return from the Kerguelen Islands. And despite his initial reluctance to meet the Ibecci, he now fully realized how useful the trip had been to help him understand that the Ibecci were naïve.

As he watched the events unfold, he knew the stakes were rising dangerously because the Chinese OTV's probable mission was to strike the Ibecci fleet with nuclear weapons.

He turned around, looked up at the railing just outside the glassed meeting room. Maj.-Gen. Arias and others were standing there watching the developments.

"Maj.-Gen. Arias, we need to warn the Ibecci. Up till now, they have been playing defence and we know they're good at it. But if the Chinese are carrying nuclear missiles and inflict serious damage to their fleet, the Ibecci might decide to go on the offensive, and we don't know how angry they will get."

"Concur," Maj.-Gen. Arias said.

"IMCO, patch us through to the *Enterprise* in the Kerguelen Islands and ask them to link us with the French Special Forces on the island. Hopefully Seren *Capac* will hear us."

A few seconds later, IMCO nodded once communications had been established.

"Seren *Capac*, this is Maj. Krol from the North American Union. There is a small Chinese spacecraft just leaving their space station. It's likely headed toward the Ibecci fleet stationary at L2. We believe it's carrying nuclear missiles. They will fire as close to your spaceships as they can. You must alert your fleet and deal with the threat. Please understand the Chinese are acting alone. We have tried to dissuade them many times, but we cannot control their actions. Do you understand?"

There was no response.

"IMCO, please have the *Enterprise* and the French Special Forces acknowledge our message.

"They have, sir."

"Okay then. Let's try again," Maj. Krol said and repeated the message.

He waited a few minutes and then looked at IMCO, who shook her head in the negative.

"Well . . . they did the same thing when we warned them last time," Maj. Krol concluded.

Maj. Krol hoped the Ibecci heard the message but did not count on a rebellious space miner from Elliott Rusk's Outer-World Mining coming to the aid of the Ibecci.

46 UNFORESEEN

***Soul-T* Mining Spaceship, Beyond the Orbit of the Moon**

The *Soul-T* had been travelling for a few weeks and was nearly at the end of its trip back to Griffin Base.

Jan was reading the latest e-book on political and socioeconomic decline, foretelling an impending worldwide downfall and a New Dark Age, when Ella chimed in with something interesting besides the daily updates from Griffin Base.

"Hey, Jan, we got a small spaceship on the long-range radar. It's small, below us, and translunar. Pretty sure it's headed to L2.

"Another alien spaceship or one of ours?"

"Not alien and not GSS. It's a Chinese OTV."

"That's odd. What's it doing beyond the orbit of the moon?"

"You asking me?"

"Ella, who else is in here?"

"Um . . . just you and me?"

"Well, then?"

"Okay, okay, don't get testy. Just because you are bored

and grouchy is no reason to snap at me."

"So now you can read my mood? When did you get this upgrade?"

"'Tis part of my brilliant and awesome personality, as I can deduce things, you know."

"Really?"

"Absofreakinlutely!"

"Okay, Ella. If you say so. In the meantime, we were talking about the Chinese OTV."

"Oh yeah. Yes, I think maybe they want to get close enough to the aliens to collect data. But the OTV is running dark with no electromagnetic emissions."

"That's weird."

"That's what I was thinking."

"Scan it."

Ella complied and scanned the OTV with the hyperspectral 3-D sensors.

"Nothing out of the ordinary except for two small lead spheres in their cargo hold. Can't make much more than that," Ella replied.

Jan thought it over. The spheres could be used for many things, including shielding for nuclear reactors to power electric propulsion technology. But she was well aware of other unsavory uses.

"Is there a crew on board?"

"Yes, two crew members."

"What's their plan?" Jan voiced and then remained silent. She did not like the potential implications.

By now, Jan had made up her mind the aliens were just a bunch of refugees in search of a place to live. And she didn't buy the crap from most governments on Earth they were dangerous invaders. Else, there wouldn't be a reason for the terraforming of Mars. The hauling and injecting of huge ice and ammonia asteroids into the planet was just too much trouble when Earth was available.

"Ella, scan the news from Earth for any clues on why the Chinese OTV is in a translunar flight path toward L2."

After a short time, Ella responded.

"Various sources report China is officially at war with the Ibecci."

The news had all but confirmed her fears the OTV was likely carrying nuclear weapons. There was no other explanation why a small orbital transfer vehicle designed to travel between Earth and the moon should be way out here. Especially when the Chinese were now building spaceships much bigger than the *Soul-T* and built expressly to colonize Mars.

She wanted to help the Ibecci, but was not sure what to do, so she gave Ella a rash order.

"Reverse course and fire up the engines! We are going after them."

"What did you say?"

"You heard me!"

"Jan, I must point out we are hauling a lot of ore. That's a significant course alteration requiring a huge delta-V."

"Ella, don't argue with me; just do it!"

"Fine. But why do you want to go after the Chinese OTV?"

"You tell me," Jan snapped back.

"You just don't know, do you?" Ella said.

"Don't give me any of your psychobabble!"

"Well then, answer the question. But my guess is you haven't formulated an action plan. You just got mad seeing the lonely OTV that's maybe up to no good. You feel a sort of kinship toward the Ibecci and want to help. So, what is it you think you can do?"

Jan remained silent.

"I'm waiting for an answer."

"Ella, just do what I ask ... please," Jan said with a pleading tone.

"Okay then. Glad we had this talk. Strap in and prepare for deceleration," Ella said finally.

Ella then rotated the mining spaceship using small attitude thrusters. Next, she fired the spaceship's four

VASIMR engines.

The *Soul-T*, with its full load of platinum ore, was travelling inbound at a velocity of 27 km/s. Now it needed to decelerate quickly and speed up in the opposite direction, a maneuver that required a huge delta-V. But VASIMR engines were designed for such maneuvers.

"Ella, check the status of the ore."

"Secure and loaded in the mass drivers."

"Ella, go for maximum acceleration."

"Okay, Jan. 0.4Gs it is, but I want it on the record that I'm objecting to this action."

"Ella, object all you want."

"I have, and it's on the record."

Ella then ramped up the VASIMR engines.

The deceleration built up slowly, and Jan strapped into the pilot seat. She settled down for the long and boring two hours it would take to decelerate, went back to her book, and queued her hip hop music. The 1967 hit song "Chain of Fools" by Aretha Franklin began playing from speakers all over the ship.

Sometime later, Ella spoke.

"We are almost dead stop. Shall I continue firing the engines at their present rate and build up speed going the opposite way?"

"How fast is the Chinese OTV travelling and how far away?"

"Travelling at a leisurely 11 km/s and about 300,000 kilometres from us."

"How long will it take to catch up?"

"Depends how fast you want to go, but we need a minimum velocity of 25 km/s to catch up, and it will take another two hours. Any slower and we essentially arrive at L2 at the same time as the OTV. I'm assuming that's not what you want."

"How far from the Ibecci fleet will we be when we catch up?"

"About 200,000 kilometres away, give or take."

"How we doing with our LH and LOX supplies?"

"We got oodles. Enough to intercept the Chinese OTV, then go back to the asteroid belt and come back."

"Good. That's what I thought."

The cryogenic hydrogen and oxygen supplies were mostly for the VASIMR engines but also for production of water and breathing air, as Outer-World Mining spaceships were designed for extended deep-space missions that could last up to a year. By necessity, the spaceships were equipped with huge cryogenic tanks with a supply five times larger than needed.

"What are you planning to do when we catch up?"

"Haven't thought that far ahead."

"You know you could blast them with R & B music and hope they'll turn around."

"That's not a bad idea, Ella, but no. We'll probably need more persuasive measures in order to prevent them from blowing themselves up, assuming that's what they intend to do. First, though, we need to get real close. Continue at our present acceleration."

"Okay, Jan, continue accelerating to a final velocity of 25 km/s."

All this time, the *Soul-T* had kept its powerful LIDAR pointed toward the OTV to gather range and speed.

And if it hadn't been for the fact the Chinese OTV had been travelling under a total blackout, its radar warning receivers would have detected the *Soul-T* illuminating them.

Meanwhile, Jan kept listening to her music as the 1967 R & B song from Jackie Wilson titled "Your Love Keeps Lifting Me Higher and Higher" started to play.

47 STAY THE COURSE

Jiantou OTV, En Route to L2

The _Jiantou_ OTV had been designed as an orbital transfer vehicle to ferry personnel and supplies to the _Tinagon4_ station and the Shensheng-Gong lunar base at Mons Rümker. Not for deep-space missions.

Not surprisingly, it was cramped with very little in the way of creature comforts except for a zero-gravity toilet. Yet it had travelled for more than twenty-four hours toward deep space, covering nearly 1,000,000 km without active navigation guidance and under total radio silence.

It was still about 500,000 km from L2 and needed to update its position.

In space, where distances were measured in millions of kilometres, a 0.1 percent drift could mean a difference of a thousand kilometres and a total miss. This was an issue even for the two-hundred-kiloton nuclear-tipped missiles carried by the OTV as a nuclear explosion in the vacuum of space was less effective since kinetic energy dissipated quickly.

The _Jiantou_ taikonauts activated their navigation and guidance and sent a narrow radar pulse to the Shensheng-Gong lunar base to update their position.

As they did this, their navigation radar alerted them of a radar signal illuminating them from far behind and above the ecliptic. In their urgency to go back to running dark, they ignored it.

Six hours later and at a distance of 250,000 kilometres from L2, the taikonauts activated their radars to do one last course update. Right away, they got audible warnings from contacts ahead and behind.

The radio then crackled with a female voice trying to reach them using the common space VHF frequency for ship-to-ship communications.

"Chinese OTV, this is the Griffin Space Systems mining spaceship the *Soul-T*. I am 8,000 kilometres behind you and trying to catch up. Please respond Over."

The *Jiantou* radars confirmed the source of the transmission to be the radar echo behind them, but the taikonauts ignored the radio call.

"Chinese OTV, you're way past the orbit of the moon and travelling toward deep space. Are you in need of assistance? Please respond. Over."

The taikonauts kept ignoring the radio transmissions. They had more urgent things to worry about.

The radar echo in front was at a distance of 10,000 kilometres. It was bigger than the one behind and it matched their velocity vector. They figured it was an Ibecci spaceship. This meant their effort to avoid detection had been useless. Now they needed to decide whether to keep running toward the Ibecci fleet, hoping the spaceship would allow them to pass, or fire their missiles.

The taikonauts decided to play it cool and follow their original orders. In the meantime, there was no point running dark anymore. They sent a short transmission to the Shensheng-Gong lunar base to advise they had been detected and were now being tracked.

They settled down to wait for the Ibecci spaceship to make the first move, aware the odds of returning home now looked dim.

As they did this, they kept an eye on the fast-approaching GSS mining spaceship.

48 CRAZY

***Soul-T* Mining Spaceship, Near L2**

"Can't say I expected a reply," Jan said.

"What do you want to do now?" Ella asked.

"I don't know, but their refusal to respond confirms they are not planning to go to L2 to pay a social visit. They could also be unconscious. Who knows?"

"You better decide what you want to do real quick, because unless we start decelerating, we'll blow past them inside of an hour, and in another two, we'll be knocking on the door of the Ibecci spaceship 10,000 kilometres away from us."

Jan thought it over for a few seconds.

"Match the OTV's velocity."

"Okay, Jan. Firing up the engines to match its velocity."

The *Soul-T* had started decelerating much earlier, but was still travelling at 14 km/s compared to the Chinese OTV's velocity of 11 km/s.

Ella ramped up the VASIMR engines to slow down further.

Moments later, Ella spoke again.

"We are now decelerating at 0.4Gs. Range to target is

6,000 kilometres and forty minutes."

Jan looked at the flight dynamics screen showing her projected trajectory relative to the OTV.

"We'll overshoot the OTV."

"I got this, Jan. We'll fly past them, reduce our velocity below theirs, and allow them to catch up. Easy-peasy."

Matching the velocity of the Chinese OTV was straightforward, as the *Soul-T* had been expressly designed for chasing and capturing asteroids. And this maneuver was easy since the Chinese OTV was not tumbling on multiple axes like most asteroids did.

The *Soul-T* was soon matching the speed of the OTV, slightly behind and about three kilometres from the OTV's starboard side.

Jan tried hailing it.

"Chinese OTV, this is the Griffin Space Systems mining spaceship the *Soul-T*. I'm matching your velocity and will come alongside. Please respond. Over."

No response.

"Ella, bring us in close."

Ella complied and fired maneuvering thrusters. The *Soul-T* then started moving sideways at a velocity of three metres per second to cut the distance to the Chinese OTV gradually.

After fifteen minutes, the *Soul-T* was one hundred fifty metres from the OTV, and Jan tried hailing them again.

"Chinese OTV, this is the Griffin Space Systems mining spaceship the *Soul-T*. I'm currently matching your velocity and at a distance of one hundred fifty metres from your starboard side. Permission to dock. Over."

Still no response, yet this last hail should have generated a response.

Jan tried again.

"Chinese OTV, this is the Griffin Space Systems mining spaceship the *Soul-T*. Do you copy? Over."

Nothing.

"I'm going to try one last time, and then we are going

in," Jan said.

"Good luck." Ella replied with a hint of human sarcasm.

"Chinese OTV, please come in. Over."

Still nothing.

"Ella, bring us in and commence docking,"

"Okay, Jan. Slowing down to one metre per second and positioning for final docking."

Ella then rotated the *Soul-T* by ninety degrees, placing it perpendicular to the direction of travel and ahead of the OTV. This was necessary, as the OTV's docking port was on its nose.

The *Soul-T* was now fully visible through the cockpit windows of the OTV, and the radio finally crackled.

"Mining spaceship, ABORT your docking operation immediately! I repeat, abort your attempt to dock immediately," a Chinese accented voice said.

"Ella, hold position."

Ella immediately fired maneuvering thrusters to cancel their forward velocity.

"Okay, Jan. Holding position. Approach velocity zero metres per second."

"Chinese OTV, nice of you to respond to our hails. Do you need assistance? Over."

"Negative. We DO NOT need any assistance," the Chinese accented voice replied testily.

"You are way past the orbit of the moon and going toward deep space. How is your fuel status? Are you able to get back? Over."

"Our fuel status is good."

"Just curious. Where are you going? After all, your OTV is a small spacecraft not designed for deep space. Over."

Silence.

"How are your food and water supplies?"

A reply came after a long delay, but it wasn't an answer to Jan's question.

"Mining spaceship. Move out of our flight path and allow us to continue on our way."

"Roger that. Just one last question. My hyperspectral sensors detected two lead spheres in your cargo hold. Perhaps shielding for small nuclear reactors that are part of a new propulsion system? Are you intending to test it out here? Just curious. Over."

It was the wrong question to ask. The OTV immediately fired small attitude thrusters and started moving sideways and away from the *Soul-T*.

It then fired its RP-1-oxygen rocket engines and accelerated away toward L2.

"Hey, Jan, those are just old-fashioned chemical rockets."

"Nah. Really! You know, the bit about an implied new nuclear propulsion system was a test to see how they would react."

"Ah . . . Definitely missed that."

"Ella, please prepare to deploy grapplers."

"Um . . . You realize the OTV is not a hunk of space rock we can just grab. Right?"

"Ella . . . Get ready to deploy the goddamned grapplers and chase after it!"

"All right, all right. But the grapplers will probably damage the OTV's exterior thermal protection. It will be unable to survive a re-entry," Ella countered while simultaneously maneuvering to chase after the OTV.

"Ella, their plan never included returning to Earth. They likely never had sufficient fuel to return to the moon, let alone Earth."

"I suppose that makes sense."

"Okay then. Now that we have established their true intentions, let's chase after them and prevent them from doing what they came here to do."

"Okay, Jan, firing up the VASIMR engines and ramping up to maximum acceleration. The OTV is pulling away from us at 5Gs. Distance is currently two hundred kilometres and increasing."

"I see that," Jan replied as she looked at the projected

flight trajectories of both spacecraft in the flight dynamics screen.

Jan was not worried, though, because the OTV acceleration would likely be a short burn of only one hundred and twenty seconds or less, at which point it would be travelling at sixteen, maybe eighteen, kilometres per second. The *Soul-T*, in contrast, could continue accelerating for a long time and achieve much higher final velocities.

The OTV burn lasted as Jan had predicted. After twenty minutes of chase at a continuous acceleration of 0.4Gs, the *Soul-T* was one hundred fifty kilometres away from the OTV and gaining rapidly. Ella then spoke.

"Throttling down. We will be within capture range in three hundred seconds."

The distance between the two spacecrafts continued decreasing rapidly.

Ella then maneuvered the *Soul-T* to decelerate and match the velocity.

"We will be within capture range in one hundred seconds."

The radio then crackled with the Chinese accented voice.

"Mining spaceship, ABORT your pursuit."

This time, it was Jan's turn to ignore the call.

"Ella, scan the OTV and tell me if they have any fuel left."

"Hyperspectral sensors detect only small traces of hydrocarbons. Their RP-1-oxygen tanks are empty," Ella replied.

Jan then radioed the Chinese OTV.

"Chinese OTV, this is the *Soul-T*. Our sensors show your fuel tanks are empty after your last burn. You do not have any fuel to decelerate and then return home as you previously stated. Over."

A reply came after a brief delay. "That is not your concern."

"Chinese OTV, you know very well it is my concern and responsibility. All space faring nations of Earth, and this includes China, follow the same maritime and space laws. It is my duty to help any distressed vessel. You have no way of getting back home," Jan replied.

Silence.

"Chinese OTV, do you copy? Over."

Still silence.

"Chinese OTV, we will come alongside, secure your spacecraft with our grapplers, and tow you. Over."

The OTV then fired attitude thrusters and started to roll to make it difficult for the *Soul-T* to grab it. But a rotation on a single axis wasn't much of a challenge for the *Soul-T*'s flight dynamics computers.

"All right, Chinese OTV. We can do it the hard way. You are simply wasting time. Be forewarned, your action may cause damage to your fuselage, as I'll be more forceful capturing your spacecraft."

"Okay, Ella, bring up the expanded capture screen on the FD computer and go for capture."

"Okay, Jan, but their roll rate is 60 degrees per second. Matching it may place loads on the berths beyond design," Ella replied, pointing to the fact the OTV's roll rate, while not uncomfortably high, would be difficult to match with the *Soul-T*'s present load.

"We'll soon find out, won't we—" Jan stopped midsentence. "What's that?" she said, looking at the visual images of the OTV on her screens.

Jan saw the OTV's cargo bays open in one of the spacecraft's rolls. Then, halfway into the next roll and hidden from view, two bright streaks emerged at the front of the OTV. The streaks continued toward the general direction of the Ibecci spaceship, still holding station some ten thousand kilometres away.

"Shit, Ella. Are those missiles? Jan asked.

"Radar confirms two small objects emerging from the OTV and accelerating away," Ella replied.

"Hold capture. We need a better visual," Jan said hurriedly.

"Okay, Jan. Slewing LIDAR toward the objects."

Within scant seconds, computer screens showed the detailed image of the two objects, confirming Jan's initial guess.

"Ella, we need to warn the Ibecci spaceship and get the hell out of here. Open the radio on all frequencies. Hopefully, they are listening."

"Ibecci spaceship, this is the Griffin Space Systems mining spaceship the *Soul-T*. We are at a distance of ten thousand kilometres from you. We are pretty sure you have been tracking us and the small Chinese orbital transfer vehicle. We mean you no harm. I repeat, we mean you no harm. The Chinese orbital transfer vehicle just fired two missiles we believe are carrying nuclear warheads. I repeat, the OTV fired two nuclear missiles aimed at you. You need to protect yourself."

Jan felt a real urgency and repeated the message twice, hoping for a sign the Ibecci understood what was coming.

Her mind was now racing, and all she could think of was the Chinese were bent on destroying the aliens and no different from the racial profiling and unjustified use of force she had known during her childhood years.

She racked her brain to figure out what else to do besides warn them. She could use the mining lasers. They were powerful enough, but those lasers did not have targeting software for aiming as a long-range weapon. The *Soul-T* would need to get very close to nuclear missiles that were most likely set to detonate on proximity. Not the smartest thing to do. Then there was the problem the *Soul-T* likely appeared to the Ibecci as being part of the hostile action against them, even if she had tried to warn them.

Feeling powerless, she put it off her mind and spoke.

"Ella, grab that goddamned OTV and let's get out of here fast! Hopefully, the aliens can destroy those missiles, but we need to get away."

"Roger. Go for capture, decelerate, and then reverse course at best possible acceleration," Ella replied.

The *Soul-T* matched the roll of the OTV and extended its four gargantuan grapplers that looked like oversized buckets of a backhoe.

Surprisingly, the OTV fired its attitude thrusters, slowing down its roll rate, allowing itself to be hurriedly captured.

Ella then fired the VASIMR engines to decelerate, pushing the rate of deceleration to 0.42G; it was the maximum the *Soul-T* could go.

Jan strapped into her seat and queued the old R & B song "Mustang Sally" by Mack Rice, cranking up the volume to its highest level, as fear of what was coming crept into her mind.

49 INTERDICTION

IIC *Inilian*, Near L2

"*Centor*, THRAVES has detected two missiles fired by the smaller spacecraft. They are approaching at thirteen *mille passu/pu*," the bridge *Junct* announced.

"SE, threat analysis," Taris *Centor*, the commander of the IIC *Inilian*, ordered the spaceship's sentient entity while standing on the upper command deck.

"The missiles carry a fusion warhead. Explosive yield is at least ~150 *Tz*."

Taris *Centor* looked at the approaching missiles projected in the room-sized holographic sphere. She looked down and to the right at the helmsman on the lower deck and barked a second order.

"*Gubernum*, maintain our distance relative to the threats!"

"*Aien, Centor*." Maintain distance relative to the threats."

The *Inilian* immediately increased its speed as it continued retreating toward L2.

It wasn't a maneuver that suited Taris *Centor*'s temperament, as she had really wanted to neutralize the threats right away. But Marel *Viracoh*'s orders had been clear when she instructed the *Inilian* to intercept the two *Tiwan* spaceships.

"*Centor*, the mining spaceship is broadcasting a warning message in multiple frequencies," the bridge *Junct* announced.

"SE, translation and analysis!" Taris *Centor* barked.

"A courtesy warning of the incoming threats while claiming not to be part of the action against us."

"It may explain its behaviour, but it may also be a deception. Will see," Taris *Centor* remarked dismissively.

"SE, infiltrate the missile circuits and give me options to control or destroy them."

"The missiles appear to be fully autonomous. There are no access points through which I can gain entry."

"What about a high-energy electromagnetic pulse?"

"It may destroy its radio emissions array, but the missiles will continue travelling still containing a live warhead."

"Bring up the CEs," Taris *Centor* snapped.

The *Inilian*, just like its sister *liburnia*, had twenty-four coherent energy batteries, each with a power output of one *Tz*, an effective range as high as 30,000 *mille passu*, and only limited by the ability to target small threats at extreme distances.

"Two CE batteries energized and assigned to the threats," the SE replied.

Taris *Centor* studied the movement of the mining spaceship that moments earlier had snatched the smaller spacecraft and was now decelerating to get away. She temporarily put them off her mind, instead focusing on the immediate threat.

"Destroy the missiles," Taris *Centor* barked.

Right away, two violet coherent energy beams, laced with a destructive and invisible X-ray-directed energy beam, leapt forward from the CE batteries like long iridescent lances. The beams touched the two missiles 6,000 *mille passu* away.

Within scant seconds, the spots on the missiles illuminated by the beams started glowing red-hot.

The missiles' casing then buckled and crumpled inward from the sudden superheating, finally exploding in silent and brilliant flashes of light, just like a tiny man-made supernova that faded slowly.

The explosion released vast amounts of gamma rays that did not pose a threat to the *Inilian* thanks to its thick *reterit* hull. The energy release and destructive compression shockwave present in an atmospheric blast was much smaller in the vacuum of space. As a result, the remnants of the blast dissipated quickly. Within less than ten *glosils*, all traces of the nuclear explosion had simply vanished.

It was a feeble and laughable attack against a *Vorian*-class Ibecci *liburnium* and more akin to a Roman trireme going against a modern-day destroyer.

But the underlying intention to harm the Ibecci was not lost on Taris *Centor*'s easily angered temperament.

"*Gubernum*, pursue the *Tiwan* spacecraft!"

50 TRYING TO SURVIVE

***Soul-T* Mining Spaceship, Near L2**

The *Soul-T* was still decelerating, trying to come to a stop and then reverse course, while the Chinese missiles continued travelling mercilessly toward the Ibecci spaceship.

Jan looked at the flight dynamics screen and thought they were still too close, so she attempted to communicate with the Chinese OTV to no avail.

"Ella, slew all instruments toward the location of the Ibecci ship—" She was cut off by audible alarms.

The *Soul-T* radiation sensors responsible for monitoring background gamma and X-ray radiation registered a short, bright flash as the missiles detonated, simultaneously discharging some ten MeV of energy as gamma rays, X-rays, and neutrons.

There was no way to outrun the radiation discharged within nanoseconds of the explosion.

Thankfully, the *Soul-T*'s command module was shielded to minimize radiation exposure during long-duration missions.

"Did the missiles detonate before reaching the Ibecci

spaceship?" Jan asked.

She looked at the flight dynamics screen, which moments earlier had shown the missiles still eight thousand kilometres from the Ibecci spaceship.

"Looks that way, but we have bigger problems. The Ibecci spaceship is now coming after us."

"Shit, Ella."

"Consequences, consequences. You can't stir a hornet's nest without angering the wasps."

"Oh, shut up, Ella!"

Jan then did the only thing she could do. The thing that had always helped her when things got really bad growing up as a teenager in Detroit's inner city slums. She found the appropriate hip hop music and piped it through the radio on all frequencies as it if were a distress call.

51 NO MERCY

IIC *Inilian*, Near L2

The *Inilian* pursued the two *Tiwan* spacecraft for a short time at the maximum acceleration its graviphoton field generators could produce, which for this part of the universe was one and a half times *Tiwan*'s gravity.

Taris *Centor* wanted to get precise targeting and cripple the *Tiwan* spacecraft beyond recognition. This, despite the direct orders from Marel *Viracoh*.

She was about to give the order to fire on the *Tiwan* spacecraft when the command deck *Junct* called her attention.

"*Centor*, there is a transmission from the larger spacecraft. It appears to be a general distress call, but it doesn't appear to be a regular transmission."

"They know we are coming. Is it a cyberattack?" Taris *Centor* asked.

"Unknown, *Centor*."

"SE, analysis."

"It's a song. The *Tiwan* worldwide information network states it was created almost one hundred *anni* ago by a female singer named Aretha Franklin."

"Not a cyber weapon?"

"There are no embedded complex low-frequency or ultra-high-frequency carrier signals that can be detected. The electromagnetic signal is clean. Its spectrum is in the audible range only."

"What's the purpose of the broadcast if it is not a cyber weapon? SE, explain."

"The large spacecraft is a mining spacecraft with no offensive or defensive weapons. The logical explanation is that its pilot surmised that since we ignored her first transmission, claiming she was not part of the attack against us, we would ignore a second message and plea for mercy. Thus, aside from running away, she is likely using unconventional means as her only option to appease us."

"Let's hear it," Taris *Centor* ordered.

The SE complied, and the speakers on the bridge started to play the song.

It had a melody played by a stringed instrument similar to an Ibecci *lutee* and a rhythm that was pleasant even for the distinct music style of the *Tiwan* culture.

Taris *Centor* listened to the music for a short time, reflecting on the lyrics her neural interface translated. The lyrics "Save me / Somebody save me" repeated multiple times.

Taris *Centor* looked at the magnified image of the two *Tiwan* spacecraft looming larger and larger in the holographic sphere as the *Inilian* gained on them.

She knew the rudimentary mining spaceship had been in the asteroid belt near *Tiwan4* going about its business and then, with a small load of ore, returning to *Tiwan3* without bothering the Ibecci.

In contrast, the smaller spacecraft from the Chinese fiefdom was hostile from the start.

So why did the mining spaceship come back and chase after the smaller spacecraft? Was it truly trying to stop it? Was its pilot simply gallant toward the Ibecci? This was certainly consistent with its behaviour, so she made up her mind.

"SE, I want the small spacecraft that fired those missiles damaged beyond repair. I want pinpoint burn-throughs until its life support is fully compromised. Leave the mining spaceship untouched. Understood?"

"*Aien, Centor.*"

The *Inilian* was now at some three thousand *mille passu* from the *Tiwan* spaceships. It continued accelerating and reducing the distance rapidly while the SE directed one CE to fire on pulse mode, strafing the small spacecraft held in capture clamps.

52 HIGHER GROUND

Soul-T Mining Spaceship, Near L2

"They're shooting at us!"

It was like watching a silent movie. All Jan could see were rapid purple flashes on multiple monitors in the command module. Perfectly round burnt holes appeared on the white fuselage of the OTV.

"Jesus, they're strafing the OTV!"

"Yep, they'll turn it into Swiss cheese, and then they'll do the same to us."

"Ella, not helpful! Make a useful comment or shut up!"

"Sorry, Jan, that's all I got. We are gonna be fried, and that's the truth. I suggest you don your pressure suit."

"Oh my God, Ella. Shut the fuck up!"

Jan knew Ella was right. As the thought crossed her mind, alarms started ringing throughout the ship, and the interior lighting shifted to emergency red.

"We've been hit!"

"Yep, it's our turn now. Closing hatches to all modules. Please don your pressure suit. Hope my core stays intact, and I can be revived after they salvage the wreckage."

"Ella, for the love of God, stop with the fucking

cynicism! Give me a damage report!"

"Okay, Jan, I'll stop. The hangar and connection to the hab module have been punctured. Fully depressurized. Pressure in the command module in the green. Multiple hits on the structure and clamps holding the OTV. Still holding. Oxygen tank #3 losing pressure, likely punctured. Other hits on noncritical areas. Please don your pressure suit."

As Ella reported the damage, Jan became strangely calm. It wasn't courage or resignation. It was conditioned behaviour she had learned as a child watching the senseless violence in Detroit's inner city. So, she uttered words she remembered hearing her mother say.

"We will be okay."

"Okay, Jan, if you say so, but you're nuts. And while you keep on believing we will be okay, don your pressure suit, please?"

"Ella, you are so right! Soldiers keep on warring and believers keep on believing."

"Jan, I think you've lost it. Don your suit, pretty please?"

Jan ignored Ella, and as alarms continued beeping, she cued Stevie Wonder's "Higher Ground" and transmitted it on all frequencies.

As the music played, Jan floated to one of the control panels, turned off the audible alarms, and waited for the inevitable outcome as the Ibecci continued strafing the OTV, now a complete wreck.

Then the purple flashes stopped.

"Ella, did the Ibecci stop firing?"

"Looks like it. Might be a momentary calm. Please don your pressure suit."

"Ella, stop telling me to don my pressure suit! If we go, we go. Is that clear?"

"Crystal clear, but you're still crazy. What do you want to do? The Ibecci spaceship is cutting the distance fast."

"Ella, we keep decelerating as hard as the VASIMRs will go and build up speed going the other way. Give me a damage report on the OTV."

"What's left of it is still in holding clamps. Gaping holes and scorched marks everywhere. Some are visible through the windshield. It appears fully depressurized."

"Okay, Ella. Let's see if we can raise them on the radio. Chinese OTV, please respond."

Nothing.

"Chinese OTV, please come in."

No response.

"Chinese OTV, please come in. Over."

Still no response.

Jan mulled over her options. She looked up toward the remote sensing computer monitor, but the ship was too close to scan it with the hyperspectral sensors, and doing an EVA was suicide.

"Ella, send Frankie up to inspect the OTV and peer through the windshield. I'll keep trying to raise them on the radio."

"Roger."

Ella commanded the surveying drone and maneuvered it along the fuselage of the OTV.

Jan watched the feed intently and was amazed by the hundreds of burned holes. The drone reached the front of the OTV. It shined its high-intensity floodlights through the windshield. The fully suited astronauts could be seen strapped to their seats with visible burns on their spacesuits and debris floating everywhere.

"There's nothing we can do for them. Bring back Frankie," Jan said in a shaky voice.

"Roger, Jan. Please note the Ibecci spaceship is decelerating hard and altering course. Distance is now just under four hundred kilometres."

"Probably repositioning to finish us off."

"Jan, would it be wrong of me to point out I'm not allowed to be cynical, but you just did?"

"Captain's privilege, Ella," Jan replied drily.

"Of course, how silly of me. You exercised the 'Rules for thee, but not for me' clause."

Jan grinned inwardly at Ella's cheeky remark and strapped down. She started composing her last message to the Griffin Base, advising of the current events and impeding destruction of the *Soul-T*. She was about to send it when Ella spoke.

"Jan, the Ibecci spaceship is portside, 'bout fifty kilometres away."

Time seemed to slow down. Jan looked at the flight dynamics screen. The *Soul-T* was still decelerating. Her velocity was down to 0.6 km/s, roughly two minutes away from a dead stop, while the Ibecci ship matched the *Soul-T* speed and decel.

Jan slued the SAR toward it. An image of a rectangular spaceship appeared, travelling upright, with its long axis on the vertical.

At this distance, the *Soul-T*'s instruments resolution was down to less than two metres.

"Look at it! Bristling with laser cannons or whatever those things are. There must be over a dozen batteries."

"Radar shows two small spacecraft coming out. They are moving toward us."

"Coming to deliver the knockout punch, Ella."

53 SURVEY THE DAMAGE

IIC *Inilian*, Near L2

Taris *Centor* ordered fliers launched to inspect the *Tiwan* spacecraft up close.

As she waited for the fliers to move in, she examined the damage on the Chinese spacecraft looming large in the command deck's holographic sphere.

Wisps of smoke and gas rose from its fuselage, now pockmarked with hundreds of burn-throughs.

"SE, scan the small spacecraft and report!"

"No electromagnetic emissions. Fully exposed to vacuum. No life support. No vital signs from its occupants."

Satisfied, she turned her attention to the primitive mining spaceship.

"SE, what's the condition of the mining spaceship?"

"Minimal damage. Their command module is intact. Losing oxygen from one of five tanks."

"What about the crew?"

"Its single female crew member appears uninjured."

"What about propulsion?"

"Appears undamaged. Still decelerating."

"Can the spacecraft continue to its final destination?"

"Yes, they have sufficient fuel to reach *Tiwan3*."

As she studied the mining spaceship, Taris *Centor* struggled to see how such a crude spaceship could travel much further than the orbit of the gas giant *Tiwan5*, and worse, with only one crew member.

She kept examining the spacecraft as the *Inilian* and the fliers shadowed it.

This went on for a bit.

"*Centor*, your orders?" the command deck *Junct* asked.

Taris *Centor* ignored the question, still undecided what to do next.

54 THANK YOU

***Soul-T* Mining Spaceship, Near L2**

"What are they waiting for?"

Jan considered whether to raise them on the radio. It didn't seem logical, as the Ibecci had just spent the last fifteen minutes catching up to the *Soul-T* and the last five firing at her.

"I don't know, Jan. I don't have a crystal ball, even if I'm the smartest AI in the whole GSS. Besides, those small spacecraft look too small and cute to be dangerous."

"Okay, genius; humour me. On what are you basing your statement of cute?"

"Well . . . they're shaped like a teardrop and have a smooth, seamless iridium surface. I mean, look at them; they're cute as a button."

"It's alien technology, Ella. For all you know, those small spacecraft could vaporize a large asteroid."

"Maybe, Jan, but you don't know that for sure, do you?"

"Exactly, Ella. We don't know for sure. We are at their mercy. Looking at the Devil."

The *Soul-T* and the Ibecci spaceships came to a stop in unison. Then, together, they started moving in the opposite direction.

After a short time, the Ibecci ship and its escorts fell behind. This happened slowly at first. Then more rapidly.

"Jan, methinks we survived our encounter."

"Maybe."

After five minutes, the distance between the *Soul-T* and the Ibecci increased to some 850 kilometres. The flight dynamics screen said the Ibecci spaceships were accelerating away at 1.5Gs.

"We can breathe easy now, Ella. Get Frankie up. See if we can fix the leak on oxygen tank #3 and the punctures on the hab module."

"Roger, Jan."

"I want to deliver our ore asap, Ella. We continue accelerating at our current rate."

"You got it, Jan."

Jan cued the 1969 Sly and the Family Stone song "Thank You (Falettinme Be Mice Elf Agin)" and transmitted on all frequencies.

Then she rewrote the message to Griffin Base.

Soul-T Mining Ship. Asteroid belt. 104 days in space. On the fly-back to Griffin Base, long-range radar detected a Chinese OTV flying toward L2. Witnessed the OTV firing two nuclear-tipped missiles toward an Ibecci spaceship. The Ibecci fired back, disabling the OTV and killing its crew. Detoured to recover it. Flying back to Griffin Base at best possible speed

55 BENEVOLENCE

IIC *Inilian*, Near L2

Taris *Centor* ordered the *Inilian* back to the fleet, leaving the *Tiwan* mining spaceship unharmed.

She figured she owed the pilot a debt of gratitude and respected her for her fearlessness going out alone in the harsh environment of space in such a primitive spaceship. It was a complete disregard of life by the *Tiwan* race. But apparently, a normal behaviour.

After all, the Chinese had just tried to wipe out her race with fusion weapons. A barbaric behaviour consistent with what humans were doing to their home planet, and this scared her. Not something that happened often. She then scoffed at the ludicrous thought she preferred fighting the *Grisamirs*. At least she always knew where she stood with them.

As the mining spaceship travelled toward *Tiwan3*, it kept broadcasting music. This time, it was a song with a thank-you message imbedded in its lyrics.

Aboard the *Imperator Eberon*, Marel *Viracoh* had watched the unfolding events.

"*Nens puberen*," she uttered, as it was all too clear humans behaved like immature children.

Clearly, the Chinese fiefdom was not willing to yield and accept the Ibecci unless they were taught tangible lessons. She hoped the badly damaged remains of the small spacecraft and the failed attempt to destroy her fleet would convince the Chinese fiefdom of the futility of their hostile actions and accept the inevitability of a stalemate.

She was sure humans would eventually accept the fact the Ibecci were not a weaker tribe that could be eliminated and were here to stay just as they had done twelve thousand years earlier.

She returned to the more pressing tasks to manage the overdue relocation of *crelon(e)* to the Kerguelen Islands and commence operations for a second settlement in the fiefdom of Argentina, which seemed friendly to her race.

She also had the formidable task of dealing with the dire state of the planet's ecosystem. Her *crelon(e)* needed to live on planet Earth for a hundred years. So, like it or not, the Ibecci were forced to fix the mess its inhabitants had created.

Quietly, the Ibecci went to work with environmental clean-up near their enclaves. Their efforts would be limited, as they could not reverse the rise in ocean levels, the loss of ice at the poles, nor could they control the increasingly violent and unpredictable weather or deal with the accelerated extinction of species.

As the Ibecci tackled the environmental clean-up, humanity would eventually realize that the Ibecci were, in fact, humanity's salvation.

56 SENTINEL: IIC NIKE

Edge of the Oort Cloud, 120 AU From Earth

The *THRAVES* operator aboard the IIC *Nike* turned toward the holographic sphere in the centre of the command deck and saw another sentry buoy fail. The buoy started blinking red in a field of hundreds scattered deep inside the Oort cloud.

It was the fourth to fail in the last one hundred *jore* in proximity to others. It stopped transmitting, with no warning of impending danger or failure, even though it was designed to monitor the surrounding space up to 100,000 *mille pasu.*

The operator was a *crelon*-cyborg, still sentient, but with suppressed emotions that made his behaviour machine-like. In a detached, monotone voice, he addressed the ship's sentient entity.

"SE, confirm time of failure."

"560 *jore.*"

The operator raised his hand at his station and typed a command on a floating keyboard to acknowledge the failure. He then entered the time it took the signal to travel back from a distance of 4,000 AUs inside the cloud.

This should have caused alarm, as the probability of four buoys failing in rapid succession without warning was nearly impossible.

Looking at the holographic sphere from the upper command deck, the *Nike*'s *Centor* calmly addressed the SE in the same detached manner.

"SE, provide explanations for the multiple failures."

"Unable to answer."

"SE, is there any astronomical activity near the failed buoys that can explain the failures?"

"Insufficient data. Unable to answer."

The *Centor* pressed on.

"SE, state probability of the failure of four random buoys in one hundred *jore*."

"Higher than one in ten million."

"SE, state probability of the failure of four buoys in close proximity and in one hundred *jore*."

"Higher than one in a billion."

"SE, project a path of a *Grisamir* incursion through the field of failed buoys and extend to the *Perfal* system."

The SE complied, and the holographic sphere expanded from a 10,000 AU bubble inside the cloud to a six-light-year logarithmic bubble reaching the *Perfal* system. A straight cyan line then appeared from the centre of the failed buoys to the *Perfal* star.

The *Centor* remained impassive.

In the next twenty *jore*, three more buoys failed just like the others.

The *Centor* knew he needed to investigate. It was a bleak proposition even for the unemotional cyborg crew of the *Nike*.

"SE, send a priority message to CC advising something unknown is taking out sentry buoys. The *Nike* is leaving station to investigate. Dispatch a *liburnium* to lend support."

The Dromon-class fast scout with its sensor suite and stealthy chondrite hull left its station in the Heliopause and accelerated to 1.5Gs. The journey, even under continuous acceleration, would take half an *anni*. As the spaceship left, the *Centor* prayed the failures had not been caused by a *Grisamir* incursion.

GLOSSARY OF ACRONYMS AND TECHNOLOGY

9 RW: 9th Reconnaissance Wing.

14th: AF: Fourteenth Air Force.

614th AOC: 614th Air and Space Operations Centre is part of the Joint Space Operations Centre (JSpOC) located at Vandenberg AFB. Both the 614th AOC and JSpOC fall under the command of the 14th Air Force (14th AF) and the Air Force Space Command (AFSPC). The primary responsibility of the 614th AOC is to provide space situational awareness and the command and control of joint space operations on behalf of the AFSPC.

ABM: Antiballistic missile.

ACC: Air Combat Command.

Aconit-class air-defence frigate: Follow-on to the FREMM (European multipurpose frigate). The Aconit-class exhibits a clean, stealth superstructure typical of the era in order to minimize radar cross section. It is equipped with 32 VLS cells, a 50-mm OTO Melara Inferno naval railgun system replacing the 76-mm SR (Super Rapide) naval gun. A laser area defence system (LADS) replaces the OTO Melara Dart/Strales 76-mm inner layer defence system.

Single hangar with two H410 X3, high-speed transport helicopters. Displacement of 7,000 metric tons and length of 144 metres. The first ship of it class, the *Finistere* entered service in 2034.

aerogel: A microporous, ultralight solid material that is 99 percent air and exhibits an ultralow density and high thermal resistance. It is also translucent. Silica based aerogels are the most common type of aerogels.

AESA: Active electronically scanned array radar is a type of phased array antenna.

AEW: Airborne early warning.

aeroponics: An indoor farming technique that grows plants on vertical shelves to optimize the use of space and water. It can be ten times more space-efficient than traditional farming. Plant growth is also significantly faster, achieving harvests twenty times a year compared to the usual two or three. Aeroponics can achieve overall yields that are two hundred times greater than traditional farming.

AFSPC: Air Force Space Command is part of the NAU Air Force. The headquarters are located at Peterson Air Force Base, Colorado. Its primary responsibility is to support NAU military operations worldwide using reconnaissance satellites, launch systems, and cyber operations.

AIOIDAS: Artificial Intelligence and Omnipresent Information and Data System. An omnipresent AI system of the NAU Air Force Space Command. Informally known as AIDA (pronounced *IDA*).

Airbus A400M-300: Four-engine, turboprop military transport used by EU member countries. Manufactured by Airbus Industries. Entered service in 2013. The stretched three hundred-series entered service in 2032, featuring a 15 percent lighter airframe, a six-metre longer body, and increased range. Maximum cargo capacity of thirty-nine metric tons.

Alexander Lippisch: German aeronautical engineer credited for making significant advances in aerodynamics during World War II, including delta wing and flying wing designs. His most significant design was the Messerschmitt Me 163 *Komet* rocket fighter. His most radical was the Lippisch P.13a supersonic ramjet-powered fighter and the lesser known, but still unusual, P.13b, which was also a supersonic ramjet-powered fighter.

An-Jian3 UCAV: The *An-Jian3*, or *Dark Sword*, is a carrier based blended wing unmanned combat aerial vehicle (UCAV) with a wingspan of fourteen metres, a length of eleven metres, and a maximum takeoff weight of 17,000 kg. Maximum speed of Mach 1.7+ and thrust-to-weight ratio of 1.3. Armament includes a 150-kW solid-state laser. Similar in design and performance to the NAU's navy F47. The *An-Jian3* predecessor was the *Lijian* UCAV. Entered service in 2039.

AN/APY-12 Radar: Latest generation of active electronically scanned array (AESA) airborne radar. The E5A Tracker airborne early warning aircraft attached to the Ford-class carriers uses this radar. The APY-12 replaces the older APY-9 used by the E2E *Hawkeye* AEW.

AN/SPY-3C Radar: X-band active electronically scanned array (AESA) radar used in the Ford-class and *Zumwalt-2* destroyers.

anthropomorphic computer algorithms: Advanced computing algorithms designed around the attribution of human traits and emotions to nonhuman entities.

AOV: Autonomous orbital vehicle. Refers to the unmanned X-87 spaceplane, the successor of the X-37 spaceplane that was active until 2026.

AQ: Command and Control, Space and Electronic Warfare Commander (C2W) is a member of a Carrier Strike Group. Responsible for electronic warfare and as such, responsible for monitoring and gathering intelligence from multiple sources (organic and electronic means). Develops operational battle plans including deception and counterattack in conjunction with the CCSG. Call sign AQ.

AR: Air Resource Element Coordinator (AREC) is a

member of a Carrier Strike Group. Provides availability of aircraft and aircraft resources as requested by the Warfare Commanders. Call sign AR.

arcology: An architectural design concept for a group of buildings that are self-contained, self-sufficient, and designed to minimize human environmental impact. The concept was developed by architect Paolo Soleri.

AS: Surface Warfare Commander (SUWC) is a member of the Carrier Strike Group responsible for planning and executing both offensive and defensive war-at-sea strikes. The AS is also the commander of the CVN. Call sign AS.

ASBM: Anti-ship ballistic missile.

ASCM: Anti-ship cruise missile.

ASM: Air-to-surface missile.

ASW: Anti-submarine warfare.

astronomical unit: See AU.

ATT: Anti-torpedo torpedo. Lightweight 324-mm diameter torpedo designed for the role of anti-torpedo torpedo. Current examples of operational ATTs include the NAU Mark 60, the European Union's MU 90D Hard Kill, and the Chinese YU-13 lightweight torpedoes.

AU: Astronomical unit. An AU is equivalent to the distance from Earth to the sun; approximately 150 million km.

AUG: Autonomous underwater gliders are unmanned small- and medium-sized winged submersibles that propel themselves by gliding downward and upward through filling and emptying their ballast tanks. Their propulsion method generates very little noise, making them ideal for surveillance and reconnaissance where they can glide undetected. A drawback of this propulsion method is a maximum speed of eleven knots (twenty kph). Military AUGs are typically titanium double-hulled submersibles because of the need to glide from shallow depths to depths of approximately 1,200 metres. Their typical crush depth is 1,800 metres.

Aurora reconnaissance aircraft: Alleged secret

hypersonic reconnaissance aircraft developed in the late 1980s and early 1990s by Lockheed Skunk Works to replace the retired SR-71 *Blackbird*. Believed to rely on PDE propulsion based on accounts of "donuts on a rope" contrails reported by eyewitnesses. Speed believed to be in the Mach 5–6 regime and maximum ceiling of +27,000 metres.

AW: Air Warfare Commander (AWC) is a member of a Carrier Strike Group And responsible for inner defence of the Carrier Strike Group. The AWC is usually in the CIC of an AEGIS Cruiser or an AEGIS Destroyer. Call sign AW.

AX: Undersea Warfare Commander (UWC) is a member of a Carrier Strike Group responsible for surface and undersea warfare. Call sign AX.

AXO: Auxiliary information officer.

BACCC: Beijing Aerospace Command and Control Centre. The Chinese equivalent of JSpOC. Responsible for space launches.

Barnard Star: A low mass red dwarf star in the constellation of Ophiuchus, approximately six light-years away from Earth. Today, it is the fourth closest known individual star to the sun, but it has one of the largest apparent motions of any star and gets as close as 3.8 light-years from our sun. It was at this distance some 12,000 years ago when it was the closest start to *Sol* and will be again in another 10,000 years. Barnard is a small star one-fifth the size of *Sol* with a mass of only 15 percent that of *Sol*. It is also a very dim star due to its approximate age of ten billion years. Its measured luminosity is less than 1 percent that of *Sol*. Not visible with the unaided eye. It is also considered to be one of the oldest stars in the Milky Way. In 1998, Barnard experienced a very energetic stellar flare that produced large X-ray and UV emissions.

Barnard b: A planet orbiting Barnard's Star discovered in November 2018. Its existence was inferred using the radial velocity method. The planet is estimated to have a diameter about 1.5 times and a mass about three times that of Earth. It is estimated to be located about 0.4 astronomical units from Barnard's Star with an orbital period of 233 days.

BeiDou satellite guidance: Chinese global position satellite system that serves both commercial customers and the Chinese military.

BFST: Brigade des Forces Spéciales Terre (French Army Special Forces Brigade).

BPC: Bâtiments de projection et de commandement is the French navy's term for *amphibious assault ship.*

C3I: Command, control, communications, and intelligence; colloquially also known as *C Cubed Eye.*

CAG: Commander Air Group is a member of a Carrier Strike Group and the most senior naval flight officer of a carrier air wing. The CAG can also assume the responsibilities of the strike warfare commander.

CAP: Combat air patrols.

carbon nanotubes: Carbon nanotubes (CNTs) are the strongest and stiffest materials yet discovered due to their chemical bonds being stronger than diamonds. Their tensile strength is ninety times greater than steel and about thirty times greater than Kevlar. There are single-walled carbon nanotubes (SWNT), double-walled (DWNT), multi-walled nanotubes (MWNT), and finally, superhard carbon nanotubes (SCN). Despite their impressive physical properties, molecular scale defects will significantly reduce their tensile strength. Manufacturing methods to produce defect-free long fibres of CNTs that could be weaved into yarn were not perfected until the late 2030s. By 2050, MWNT became the principal component of ballistic armour and CNT-ceramic composite armour, replacing KM2 (Kevlar).

CCSG: Commander Carrier Strike Group is a fleet admiral in command of a Carrier Strike Group. The AQ, AS, AW, AX, and CAG report to the CCSG. He is also known as the Composite Warfare Commander (CWC).

***Chang Qiang* EKV:** The Chinese "*Long Spear*" exoatmospheric kill vehicle (EKV) deployed aboard the

Tiangong4 space station.

CDC: Combat Direction Centre. Located aboard an aircraft carrier.

CEP: Circular Error Probable. Ballistics term to denote the accuracy of a projectile landing within a circle of a given radius.

Charlie robot ape: See RSC.

CIC: Combat Information Centre.

CIWS: Close-in weapon system is a ship defence system against anti-ship missiles.

CJ-30A: Chinese submarine-launched supersonic land attack cruise missile (LACM). It is an evolved version of the older CJ-10 LACM. Reported to be equipped with a suite of guidance systems including BeiDou satellite guidance, inertial guidance, terrain contour matching, and terminal active radar homing. It has an estimated CEP of one to three metres, a range of 2,000 km, and speed of Mach 3. Entered service in 2029.

CJ-30K: Air-launched version of the CJ-30A.

CMC (China): Central Military Commission is considered the supreme military policy–making body of the Peoples Liberation Army (PLA).

Corps de Reaction Rapide (CRR-FR; France): Rapid Reaction Corps-France is a military unit of the French Armed Forces and NATO that has a contingency of four hundred men. Its primary task includes reconnaissance, initial entry, and stabilization operations. It can deploy within forty-eight hours' notice.

CSG: Carrier Strike Group. Typically used by the NAU's navy for their carrier groups.

CTF: Carrier Task Force: Typically used by the PLA's navy for their carrier groups.

CWC: Composite warfare commander is the overall commander of a Carrier Strike. The AQ, AS, AW, AX, and CAG report to the CWC. The CWC is a fleet admiral.

DDG: Hull classification for guided missile destroyer of the *Arleigh Burke* and the *Zumwalt-2* class destroyers.

DF-29: The next generation of the Chinese DF-26 carrier killer missile. The DF-29 is a long-range, anti-ship ballistic missile (ASBM) with a range of just over 8,000 km and a CEP of one to three metres. Entered service in 2031.

Dielectric or Bragg Mirrors: Mirrors composed of many layers of highly reflective insulating material with precise spacing between each layer. The layers that make up a Dielectric Mirror can be engineered to give it a reflectivity of up to 99.99 percent, allowing it to effectively reflect the coherent light from high-intensity lasers.

Divine Dragon **spaceplane:** See *Shenlong* spaceplane.

Divine Eagle: A Chinese high-altitude long endurance (HALE) unmanned aerial vehicle designed to provide airborne early warning, tracking, and targeting of surface and airborne targets. The twin-boom, twin-engine high–aspect ratio aircraft can operate up to a maximum ceiling of ~25,000 metres. Their AESA radars are reported to have a range of 900 km. The first generation entered service in 2017.

E-5A Tracker AEW: The all-weather airborne early warning (AEW), command and control version of the F39 *Hellcat* sixth-generation fighter that entered service in 2033. It was developed under the F/A-XX next generation air dominance program. The E-5A predecessor was the E-2E *Hawkeye* AEW.

ECM: Electronic countermeasure.

ecophagy: The total consumption of an ecosystem. This could occur via out-of-control self-replicating nano-bots that consume entire ecosystems. However, it can also be triggered by events that lead to massive species extinctions such as the unrelenting growth of the human population that is currently triggering the sixth great extinction, eventually leading to a lifeless planet.

EKV: Exoatmospheric kill vehicle; an antisatellite weapon system.

ELT: Extremely Large Telescope. The telescope saw first light in 2024. It has a primary mirror that measures 39.3

metres with an angular resolution of 0.001 arcseconds.

ELINT: Electronics signals intelligence.

Epée class amphibious assault ship: The Epée class is the next generation French amphibious assault ships replacing the Mistral class. The Epée BPC (bâtiments de projection et de commandement) class has a length of 189 metres with a fully loaded displacement of 19,000 metric tons. It has a capacity to carry 450 combat troops, eighteen transport and attack helicopters, and two LCACs. Entered service in 2036.

EMP: Electromagnetic pulse; a burst of electromagnetic radiation that damages electronic equipment.

ESA: European Space Agency.

ESAC: European Space Astronomy Centre is located near Madrid and is an arm of ESA responsible for analysis of all data collected at ESA's observatories worldwide.

ESI: Earth Similarity Index. The degree to which an exoplanet is similar to Earth on a scale from zero to one with one being the most Earth-like. ESI depends on the planet's radius, density, escape velocity, and surface temperature.

ESO: European Southern Observatory headquartered in Munich, is an intergovernmental European astronomy organization supported by fifteen EU member nations. The agency provides state-of-the-art research facilities and observatories in Chile at La Silla, Paranal, Chajnantor, and Cerro Armazones.

ESSM: Evolved Sea Sparrow Missile. Also known as the RIM-162 ESSM. Designed to protect ships from maneuvering supersonic anti-ship missiles. In service until 2027.

Eurocopter *Tiger2*: The Eurocopter *Tiger2* is the next generation attack helicopter used by NATO members. It was originally developed from the Eurocopter X3 experimental high-speed compound helicopter (H3 concept). The *Tiger2* is a four-blade twin-engine high-speed hybrid attack helicopter that exhibits increased horizontal speed thanks to short span wings and tractor propellers. Entered service in 2029.

EXACTO Smart Ammunition: Extreme Accuracy Tasked Ordnance (EXACTO) is a guided ammunition. It relies on remote guidance tied to the optics of a weapon in order to achieve sub-MOA accuracy at extreme distances. The technology is integrated into the .50 BMG (12.7x99-mm NATO) ammunition and larger calibers including the 15.2x169-mm anti-matériel ammunition used in the Steyr IWS2000.

exoskeleton: Armoured suit that provides augmented power to legs and arms, giving infantry soldiers increased mobility and the ability to carry heavier loads and weapons. Consists of a body framework and struts connected to mechanical joints at legs and arms. Powered exoskeletons rely on servomotors, onboard computer processors, and a power supply to actuate the joints. Artificial muscles have also been tested, but as of 2050 were still considered immature technologies.

Passive exoskeletons on the other hand, rely on clever mechanical joints together with elastic and dampening devices (springs) and a deep understanding of kinesiology. Multiple technologies developed early in the twenty-first century were perfected to produce passive exoskeletons with a high degree of freedom of motion that mimic the energy-storage strategies of human movement. These strategies relied on the motion and mass of the wearer to store energy and release it to propel legs forward at each stride, just like a human body naturally relies in the pendulum-like leg motion to walk. Passive designs are capable of transferring as much as 80 percent of the load to the ground during the single support phase of walking while keeping the load away from the spine and legs at a fraction of the power of heavier powered exoskeletons.

All armoured exoskeletons built after 2050 featured a hard exterior layer of carbon fibers with layers of high tensile-strength carbon nanotube mesh plus a layer of interior formfitting foam for comfort and exterior ventilation ribs for dissipation of body heat. Heavier powered exoskeletons rely on a carbon nanotube ceramic composite armour in order to give the exterior shell more rigidity and additional mass for better kinetic energy dissipation. Some early exoskeletons used shear thickening or dilatant fluids to aid in dispersion of the kinetic energy of projectiles, but the technology never fully delivered on its promise. The US and China exclusively use heavier and more complex powered exoskeletons. The *Talos*-10 (T10) is the powered exoskeleton used by US Special Forces. The *Jianhuren* (Guardian) is the main powered exoskeleton used by Chinese Special Forces. In contrast, NATO adopted the lighter and more elegant Swiss/German made *Paladin* Mk7 passive exoskeleton.

F39 *Hellcat*: F39 *Hellcat* is a sixth generation wedge-shaped tailless fighter from the NAU navy. It entered service in 2036 to replace the F35C. Originally developed under the F/A-XX next generation air dominance program.

F47 UCLASS: An unmanned combat aerial vehicle from the NAU navy that entered service in 2029. It fulfills the dual roles of airborne surveillance and strike. Originally developed from the X47C prototype.

F80: The F80 was the first operational jet fighter of the United States Air Force. It entered service in 1946.

FIDO: Flight dynamics officer.

field propulsion: Field propulsion is the concept of spacecraft propulsion where momentum of the spacecraft is changed by an interaction of the spacecraft with external force fields such as gravitational and magnetic fields. Under the framework of quantum field theory (QFT), where space has a physical structure, it may be possible to deform the space around a spacecraft and create an area of high pressure and an area of low pressure. The differential pressure would cause the spacecraft to move forward. One theorized means of mediating this deformation proposed by quantum field theory and quantum electrodynamics would rely on creation of an electromagnetic zero-point field and a resulting Lorentz force that can accelerate the spacecraft. A second theoretical and more exotic field propulsion method is also based on creation of a strong magnetic field, which will cause graviphotons or their newer postulated particle, the chameleon, to emerge. These two particles are said to interact with matter (the spacecraft) via a postulated fifth force, creating attractive and repulsive forces. See Gravitons, graviphotons and chameleons.

GEO: Geosynchronous Orbit. Approximate altitude of 35,800 km (22,400 miles).

***Gerald Ford* Class Aircraft Carrier:** The follow-on to the *Nimitz* class aircraft carrier. Similar in size and displacement but employing technological improvements such as electromagnetic catapults that replace the standard steam catapults and new ship self defence systems (SSDS) that use laser area defence systems (LADS) in place of the old RIM-162 ESSM and Phalanx CIWS. Carries a complement of twenty F39 *Hellcat*, thirty F47 UCLASS, six E-5A AEW, and eight V28V.

GMT: Giant Magellan Telescope. The telescope saw first light in 2025. It has a primary mirror that measures 24.5 metres with an angular resolution of 0.21 arcseconds.

gravitons, graviphotons and chameleons: Postulated elementary particles that are responsible for giving mass to matter and capable of interacting with matter. The graviton is thought to be the elementary "force carrier particle" that mediates the force of gravity, just like electromagnetism is mediated by the photon, the strong force by gluons and the weak force by the W and Z bosons.

The graviphoton is another postulated, but more exotic particle that is a superpartner of the graviton, and under certain conditions, capable of interacting with matter to provide both attractive and a repulsive force or antigravity.

The chameleon (proposed in 2003) is a third postulated elementary particle that exhibits similar properties to the graviphoton. It is believed to be capable of interacting with matter with a strength equal or greater than that of gravity via a hypothesized fifth force. This force has roughly the strength of gravity with a range of anywhere from less than a millimetre to light-years.

These theorized particles and their interaction with gravity are in agreement with some of the obscure theoretical work by German physicist Burkhard Heim conducted in the 1950s and 1960s. In his work, Heim predicted two additional fundamental forces and a carrier particle (graviphoton) that could emerge under an intense electromagnetic field, in turn creating a gravity-like force through extraction of zero-point energy. He went on to propose a gravity/antigravity-induced propulsion concept based on a rapidly rotating torus that would create a radial magnetic field capable of transforming electromagnetic radiation into a gravity-like field through conversion of photons into graviphotons.

Grey Goo: Uncontrollable self-replicating nano-bots that consume everything in their path.

GTC: Gran Telescopio Canarias. It is also known as the GranTeCan. The telescope saw first light in 2007. It has a primary mirror that measures 10.4 metres.

H410 X3, Panther: Medium-lift transport compound helicopter used by NATO. This latest iteration of the Panther/Dauphin was developed from the Eurocopter X3 experimental high-speed compound helicopter (H3 concept) proposed in 2010. The H410 is a high-speed, long-range hybrid helicopter that exhibits increased horizontal speed thanks to short span wings and tractor propellers. Maximum speed of 510 kph, range of 900 km (560 miles), and capacity of thirteen passengers or 2,300 kg. Entered service in 2031.

Halcyon: Hypersonic business jet manufactured by a consortium including Hermeus and Lockheed Martin. The aircraft is designed to carry twelve passengers at a speed of Mach 5 with a range of 5,000 km. Entered service in 2038.

HALO: High-altitude low-opening parachute jump.

HK416F: The French armed forces standard-issue assault rifle with a 419-mm (16.5-in) barrel, chambered in 6.8x51-mm NATO; the replacement of the older 5.56x45-mm cartridge. The parent weapon is the NATO standard HK416 A5 assault rifle designed and manufactured by Heckler & Koch.

Hotchkiss M1914: Was the standard machine gun of the French Army in WWI. It was a gas-actuated and tripod-mounted medium machine gun with a rate of fire of 450 rounds/min. It was chambered in the now obsolete 8-mm Lebel cartridge.

hoverbike: All-electric personal flying vehicle similar to a motorcycle with four rotor blades. The military version has several names including Tactical Reconnaissance Vehicle (TRV) and High Mobility Personal Aerial Vehicle (HMPAV). Each rotor blade has a diameter of 1.2 metres, allowing the hoverbike to travel just above the ground at a height of 1.5 to 3.0 metres. The rotor blades are configured in pairs with two blades located in front in a slightly offset and superposed configuration, while the other two blades are located at the back. High-density Li-air batteries allow the hoverbike to operate continuously for approximately four to six hours. Length of 3.6 metres. The rugged military version has a weight of 270 kg. Top speed of 80 kph. Can carry a maximum load of 150 kg.

HPM missile: High-power microwave (HPM) missile is a nonnuclear electromagnetic pulse weapon designed to destroy electronic systems. Unlike a large EMP burst that saturates a large area, the HPM missile is a surgical weapon that can be target-specific. The platform of the HPM missile is the AGM-158 joint air-to-surface standoff missile. The HPM missile was developed from the counter electronics high-power microwave advanced missile project (CHAMP) in the mid-2020s.

HUD: Head-up display.

hyperspectral imaging: Remote sensing technology that belongs to the family of spectroscopic imaging. Remote hyperspectral imaging sensors collect images across a wide electromagnetic spectrum with each pixel containing full spectral information beyond visible wavelengths including near infrared and thermal infrared. Near and thermal infrared wavelengths are sensitive to the intra-atomic and inter-atomic bond strength of materials, in turn allowing the identification of the composition of materials and minerals.

hypervelocity: Normally considered to be greater than 2,500 m/s, or Mach 7.3.

IMCO: Information management and communications officer.

inconel 617: A high-temperature corrosion-resistant superalloy. It is a nickel-chromium-cobalt-molybdenum alloy originally developed and used in the cancelled X-33 *VentureStar* SSTO thermal protection system. Its excellent thermal characteristics and workability made it a logical choice for use in non-critical areas of the thermal protection system of the SR-72.

island of stability: Areas of the periodic table where a set of predicted, but as-yet undiscovered, heavier isotopes of transuranium elements would exist. These elements are theorized to be stable superheavy elements above element number 121. An example is unpentennium, a 7d transition metal with atomic number 159 that is theorized to exist in the second island of stability. Based on its molecular structure, metallic unpentennium would have a 45 percent higher density than iridium, its closest analog. This is believed to be one of the metals used by the Ibecci in the outer hull of their interstellar spaceships.

ISP: Specific impulse is a rocket engine measure of efficiency. It is defined as the total impulse (or change in momentum) delivered per unit of propellant consumed. ISP is expressed in seconds.

ISR: Intelligence surveillance and reconnaissance.

ITER: International Thermonuclear Experimental Reactor located in Cadarache, France. The program was the largest experimental fusion reactor that run from 2008 until

2036 when it shut down due to lack of funds after having spent in excess of $160 billion Euros.

IUSS: Integrated Undersea Surveillance System.

IWS2000: Semiautomatic antimatériel rifle produced by Steyr Mannlicher. The rifle is chambered in a unique 15.2x169-mm armor-piercing fin-stabilized discarding sabot (APFSDS) ammunition, capable of defeating the equivalent of 40-mm RHAe at one thousand metres. The rifle uses a smooth bore barrel and fires the 15.2x169-mm round at a muzzle velocity of 1,450 m/s. The thirty grams APFSDS exhibits a kinetic energy of 29,000 joules, which is 2.5 times greater than the comparable kinetic energy of a 12.7×99-mm NATO (.50-caliber) M903 SLAP. The IWS2000 was initially developed at the turn of the century. Entered service with NATO in 2026.

J-37 *Snowy Owl*: Carrier-based, midsize sixth generation fighter. The J-37 is a twin-engine air superiority multi-role stealth fighter and the successor to the J-31. Maximum speed of Mach 2.0+ and thrust-to-weight (T/W) of 1.2. Main armament consists of a 150-kW solid-state laser. Entered service in 2036.

J-37 EAW: The twin-seat all-weather airborne early warning (AEW) command and control version of the J-37 *Snowy Owl*.

JASSM: Joint-air-to-surface standoff missile.

***Jiantou (Arrowhead)*:** Small lifting-body orbital transfer vehicle (OTV) carried by the *Shenlong* (*Divine Dragon*) spaceplane. Its elongated and highly swept chevron shape is somewhat reminiscent of an F117. The shape is designed to affix seamlessly to the front of the *Divine Dragon*. Length of twenty-four metres with a fully loaded weight of 15,000 kg. Can carry up to five passengers or a maximum payload of 2,000 kg. The *Jiantou* predecessor was the WU-14 / DF-ZF.

JSpOC: Joint Space Operations Centre is subordinate to the 14th AF and the AFSPC. The primary responsibility of JSpOC is command, control, and orbit determination activities.

JTBS: Joint Tactical Battlefield System is a networked battlefield information system that allows integration (data fusion) of information from all sources. JTBS provides enhanced situational awareness in the form of a real-time composite picture of the battlefield. Its precursor was the network-centric warfare system developed at the turn of the twenty-first century with the goal to permit rapid and effective information sharing, rapid target assessment, and distributed weapon assignment.

KC-74: Military aerial refueling supersonic aircraft loosely based on the XB70 platform from the 1960s. Entered service in 2035 to support the SR-72.

LACM: Land attack cruise missile.

laser area defence system (LADS): The LADS is a ship self-defence system (SSDS) also known as a point defence system. The predecessor of the LADS was the high-energy laser area defence system (HELADS) developed at the beginning of the twenty-first century as a counter-RAM (rocket, artillery, and mortar). LADS entered service in the 2030s. Its primary component is a 150-kW laser that can shoot down anti-ship missiles and artillery, replacing the old RIM-116 SeaRAM and Phalanx CIWS. LADS are currently aboard the *Zumwalt-2* DDG and the *Gerald Ford*-class super carrier. LADS are also used by the French navy Aconit-class Frigates and the Epée class amphibious assault ships, replacing the older OTO Melara Dart/Strales 76-mm inner layer defence system. The Chinese navy Type 057 *Shenyang* destroyer and Type 004 *Huaqing* super carrier also rely on LADS.

Lagrangian points: The Lagrangian points are five locations in space around planet Earth where objects can achieve quasi stable positions relative to Earth. L2 is approximately 1.5 million kilometres from Earth.

LCAC: Landing craft air cushion.

LEO: Low Earth orbit. Extends to a maximum altitude of 2,000 km. Most spacecraft placed in LEO orbit at an altitude of 250 to 500 kilometres.

Li-air battery: Lithium air (Li-air) battery is a metal-air battery that has roughly ten times the energy density of lithium-ion batteries. It was finally commercialized in the year 2031 through a joint venture of NAU's billionaire Elliott Rusk and Norway's Statkraft and Statoil.

LIDAR: Light detection and ranging. Surveying and scanning sensor technology that uses a pulsed laser to measure distance to an object by illuminating it with pulsed laser light. The sensitivity of the laser return signal allows creation of detailed digital 3-D representations of the scanned object.

loitering munition: Miniature man-portable unmanned aircraft fitted with warheads intended for non-line-of-sight targets. Also known as lethal miniature aerial munition system (LMAMS). Typically carried in a backpack or by Special Forces in specially designed multitub backpacks integrated into their exoskeletons.

Manta AUG: A medium-sized winged autonomous underwater glider (AUG) with a size that is slightly larger than a conventional single-seat fighter jet. Maximum speed of eleven knots (twenty kph) on passive propulsion mode. Tactical speed with pump jet propulsion of twenty-seven knots (fifty kph) and maximum speed of forty knots (seventy-four kph). Operating depth of 1,200 metres. Crush depth of approximately 1,800 metres. Titanium hull construction. Carries two Mk 60 lightweight anti-torpedo torpedoes for self-defence. Typically carried and deployed by *Zumwalt-2* DDGs. Entered service in 2038.

Mark 60 Lightweight ATT: A 324-mm diameter lightweight torpedo developed from the Mark 54 and the EUs MU90 Hardkill ATT. The Mark 60 was especially designed for the anti-torpedo role.

MAWS: Multirole antiarmor weapon system is a man-portable missile that can be used against multiple light-armour targets.

metallic hydrogen: Metallic hydrogen is a highly

compressed state of solid hydrogen that is formed at very high pressure. Its density is theorized to be in the range of 0.7 to 1.3 g/cm³. This is about eight to sixteen times higher than the density of liquid hydrogen (0.08 g/cm³). As a propulsion fuel, metallic hydrogen would exhibit a theoretical specific impulse (Isp) of about 1500 sec. compared to 500 sec. for a conventional LH/LOX rocket engine. An oblique detonation engine (ODE) would achieve an even higher Isp. Metallic hydrogen is theorized to be stable at room temperature and pressure. Its much higher density would significantly reduce the size of a spaceplane's fuel tanks. This would reduce its empty weight, enabling the spaceplane to easily reach LEO and possibly GEO. Large scale production of metallic hydrogen is currently beyond the technological capability of planet Earth.

MG7: The Heckler & Koch MG7 is a general-purpose gas operated machine gun chambered for the 7.62×51-mm NATO. It entered service in 2028, replacing the less reliable MG5.

MOA: Minute of angle. Terminology that defines the accuracy of firearms. A grouping of shots inside a one-inch circle at one hundred yards is equal to one MOA.

molecular assembler: A theoretical human-made molecular scale machine that is programmed to manipulate atoms and molecules one molecule at a time to build complex molecules and larger devices in a Lego-like construction process. Ribosomes are an example of a biological molecular assembler. They are capable of assembling specific sequences of amino acids following a set of programming instructions from messenger RNA. Human-made molecular assemblers would be highly versatile, programmable, and capable of constructing and combining other molecules into more complex devices. Examples of such larger molecules include molecular motors, molecular gears, molecular rings, molecular switches, logic gates, molecular sieves, and molecular filters. Manufacturing of molecular assemblers is currently beyond the technological capability of planet Earth.

MPD thruster: Magnetoplasmadynamic (MPD) and VASIMR thrusters belong to the family of plasma or ion propulsion rockets. Plasma propulsion is a form of rocket propulsion that relies on an ionized gas or plasma to produce thrust. Plasma is first produced by subjecting an inert gas to an electric or magnetic field. The resulting electrically conductive high-temperature plasma can then be accelerated out the rocket nozzle by further application of electric or electromagnetic fields. MPD thrusters are in theory capable of producing high specific impulses (Isp) with an exhaust velocity as high as 50,000 m/s. This is about twenty-five times better than chemical rockets. MPD thrusters are also capable of high thrust levels. As a result, they can be used in applications requiring quick delta-V, such as chasing and landing on metal-rich asteroids. MPD thrusters can also be used for long deep-space missions such as travelling to Mars or the asteroid belt.

MRBM: Medium-range ballistic missile.

MSF: Maritime Security Force. Lightly armed navy master-at-arms personnel. Typically carried aboard a carrier. Its primary mission is force protection.

MU90D Hard Kill ATT: A 324-mm diameter lightweight torpedo developed from the EUs MU90 Hardkill ATT. The MU90 is specifically designed for the anti-torpedo role.

NAVCENT: NAU Naval Forces Central Command.

nanocrystalline diamond: Also known as hyperdiamond and aggregated diamond nanorods (ADNR). It is a denser form of diamond that is produced by compressing fullerite powder to a pressure of more than 20 GPa (1,400 tons/in^2). It exhibits twice the hardness and abrasion resistance of conventional diamond (Vickers hardness of ~300 GPa vs. 160 GPa for diamond) and about nine times that of other materials such as corundum (aluminum oxide) and titanium diboride. (Vickers hardness of 35 GPa).

NAU: North American Union is composed of the old United States and Northern States and Canada.

NAUS: North American union ship is a ship prefix used to identify a commissioned ship of the North American Union navy. Replaces the older United States ship (USS) prefix.

NNEMP: Nonnuclear electromagnetic pulse.

NOP: No Operation. An assembly language instruction.

NORAD: North American Aerospace Defence Command.

NRO: National Reconnaissance Office.

NSA: National Security Agency.

NSC: Northern States and Canada. The NSC is a breakaway portion of the old USA that includes California and the western states plus an enlarged Canada that had annexed most of the New England states.

oblique detonation engine (ODE): The oblique detonation engine is an advanced version of the pulse detonation engine. The ODE is used by the SR-72.

P.13a: The P.13a was a delta wing experimental interceptor designed in 1944 by Alexander Lippisch. The aircraft was to be powered by a ramjet engine and envisioned to achieve a maximum speed of Mach 1.5.

Panther H410, X3: Medium-lift compound helicopter used by NATO members. This latest iteration of the Panther/Dauphin was developed from the Eurocopter X3 experimental high-speed compound helicopter (H3 concept). The H410 is a high-speed long-range hybrid transport helicopter that exhibits increased horizontal speed thanks to short span wings and tractor propellers. Maximum speed of 510 kph, range of 900 km, and capacity of thirteen passengers or 2,300 kg. Entered service in 2032.

passive exoskeleton: See Exoskeleton.

PDE: Pulse detonation engines are a type of air-breathing engine that are more efficient and lighter than turbofan engines. Compared to all other engine types that perform best at specific speeds, PDE engines have a wide operating range from subsonic to Mach 10. PDEs outperform all other engine types at all speeds. They exhibit a specific impulse (Isp) of 4000 sec. which is 30 percent to 50 percent higher than a scramjet, about 15 percent higher than a SABRE engine, and about eight times higher than a rocket engine.

peak oil: Defined as the point at which all worldwide oil production (including unconventional sources) reaches a peak followed by an irreversible decline. The most recent available predictions, based on research published between 2010 and 2014, states that peak oil will occur sometime between 2010 and 2030. Other studies stated that peak oil for individual nations in the Middle East would occur before 2036 with the following individual dates: Iraq (2036), Kuwait (2033), Saudi Arabia (2027), Qatar (2019).

photonic communications: Photonic communication systems are submarine-based laser communication systems capable of transmitting and receiving communications from a submerged submarine. The technology was originally developed from experiments carried out in the 1980s, where lasers were demonstrated to be able to travel through air and water. After 2035, the technology became widely used in all modern submarines and autonomous underwater gliders (AUGs).

PLA: People's Liberation Army.

Prometheus Nuclear Power Plant: A nuclear fission reactor commercialized by Griffin Space Systems (GSS) for long-duration space missions. Similar, but more compact than the nuclear reactors carried aboard super carriers and optimized to maximize electricity production. The reactor relies on a Stirling radioisotope generator (SRG) design to generate electricity for electric propulsion systems. The early predecessors were its NASA namesake project from the turn of the twenty-first century and the more modest, 400 kW SAFE-400 experimental nuclear fission reactor developed in the 2020s. The Prometheus reactor is part of a nuclear-electric space propulsion system coupled to a

VASIMR ion propulsion.

QKD: Quantum key distribution is a communications technique that uses a shared random secret key known only to the sender and receiver to encrypt data. The technology also relies on the property of quantum entanglement to detect eavesdropping and guarantee secure communications.

QZJ-94 heavy machine gun: Successor of the QZJ-89 or Type-89 heavy machine gun used by the Chinese military. The QZJ-94 is a lighter version of its predecessor. It fires the high velocity 10x72-mm caseless anti-matériel ammunition. With a 19.44 g (300 grain) armour piercing round, the 10x92-mm ammunition has a muzzle velocity of 1,050 m/s and a kinetic energy of 10,700 J (7,900 ft/lbf).

RHAe: Rolled homogeneous armour equivalency is a term used to estimate the protective capability of armour or the penetrative capability of a projectile.

RIM-188: Rolling airframe missiles (RAMs) used to counter supersonic maneuvering anti-ship missiles. Primarily used for fleet area defence. It is the successor of the RIM-162 Evolved Sea Sparrow Missile (ESSM). The RIM-188 has a range of seventy nautical miles and speed of Mach 4. Entered service in 2033. Used by *Zumwalt-2* type destroyers.

robot ape: See RSC.

RPG: Rocket-propelled grenade.

RSC: Robot-singe de l'unité d'appui au combat. Robot ape combat support unit is a European developed multipurpose robotic combat support unit. RSC units are mission configurable. Known as "Rascals" by NATO forces with the exception of the French forces who refer to them as "Georges" in reference to the monkey from the Curious George book series. RSCs can be used as simple beasts of burden to help carry equipment and supplies or weaponized for specific applications, including general fire support and sniper fire support.

The RSC is a quadruped that can also stand and rise on

its hind legs to provide fire support over a low-rise wall, sandbags, or any obstacle that would block a quadruped. It is also capable of limited bipedal motion on even terrain. Its ancestor was the Charlie robot ape developed at the German Research Centre for Artificial Intelligence under the Intelligent Structures for Mobile Robots (IStruct) program. Charlie had originally been conceived at the turn of the twenty-first century as a robotic system for space exploration, but it evolved into a ubiquitous and standardized robotic combat support unit used by NATO. RSCs are heavily armoured with a hard carbon exterior plus layers of high-tensile-strength carbon nanotube mesh. Power is provided by Li-air high energy density batteries that allows continuous operation for seventy-two hours or longer, if conducting ISR missions. Weight of 90 to 130 kilograms depending on configuration.

SABRE engine: The synergistic air breathing rocket engine (SABRE) is a hybrid jet/ramjet air-breathing rocket engine. At speeds up to Mach 5.5 and an altitude of 30,000 metres, the engine operates as a jet engine and ramjet. At faster speeds and higher altitudes, it operates as an efficient rocket engine. In order for the jet engine to operate above Mach 3.0, the engine precools the combustion air using liquid hydrogen and helium. This increases the air density and allows the use of lighter materials, avoiding several of the common problems prone to hypersonic engines that compress the air and increase it temperature to 1,000°C. The SABRE engine offers a higher thrust-to-weight ratio compared to jet engines and scramjets. It also displays a specific impulse (Isp) of 3,500 sec. This is significantly higher than rocket engines.

SAR: Synthetic aperture radar.

SEC: The submarine element coordinator acts as principal advisor to AX for coordination with the attack submarines (SSNs) and autonomous underwater gliders (AUGs) assigned to the Carrier Strike Group. Also responsible for operational tasking of surface vessels conducting antisubmarine warfare (ASW).

***Shenlong* spaceplane (*Divine Dragon*):** A Chinese manned and unmanned large hypersonic spaceplane that can perform reconnaissance and precision strike missions as well as deliver personnel and cargo to LEO. Much larger than the NAUS SR-72 and similar in dimensions to the *Skylon*, but smaller than Rockwell's Star-raker concept from 1978. It can also be mated to the *Jiantou* (*Arrowhead*) reusable smaller second stage to serve as an orbital transfer vehicle (OTV). A turbo-aided rocket-augmented ram/scramjet engine (TRRE) provides propulsion. It consists of a turbine, ram/scramjet stage and an oxygen-kerosene-rocket stage. The turbine ram/scramjet breathing engine is used up to 34,000 metres. The spaceplane is able to continue to an altitude of 100 km with the help of rocket augmentation in order to reach an orbital velocity of 7.8 km/s. Length of eighty-seven metres (including the second stage) and maximum fully loaded weight of 420,000 kg. The *Shenlong* predecessor was the *Teng Yun* hypersonic two-stage spaceplane developed in 2030. The *Shenlong* entered service in 2048.

Shensheng-Gong (Divine Palace): Chinese moon base located at Mons Rümker in the northwest part of the moon's near side. This location was selected after the Chang'e 5 lunar exploration mission that landed at the site in 2019. The initial modules of the Shensheng-Gong base were brought in, starting in 2039 and buried under the lunar regolith. Modules were continuously added over the next fifteen years at an approximate rate of one module every three years to its current configuration, consisting of seven interconnected and buried modules.

SIGINT: Signals intelligence.

***Skylon*:** A large SSTO spaceplane that uses a SABRE propulsion system. It is designed to take off from a conventional runway and accelerate to Mach 5.5 and an altitude of 30,000 metres using a hybrid jet engine/ramjet and then continue to LEO in rocket engine mode carrying its own LH2 and LOX. The spaceplane is capable of delivering fifteen tons to a 300-kilometre altitude or eleven tons to an 800-kilometre altitude. Length of eighty-four metres and a fully loaded weight of ~320,000 kg. Entered service in 2032.

SM-5 midcourse intercept ABM: The standard missile (SM-5) is the latest generation of hypersonic antiballistic missile (ABM) used by the NAU navy *Zumwalt-2* destroyer. The SM-5 has a speed of Mach 15, a range of 4,000 km, and maximum ceiling of 2,500 km. Replaces the RIM 161 SM-3.

SM-10 terminal phase intercept ABM: The standard missile (SM-10) is the latest generation of terminal intercept hypersonic antiballistic missile. Replaces the RIM 174 SM-6 ABM.

Sopwith Camel: WWI single-seat biplane that entered service in 1917. It was the most successful WWI fighter credited with the most kills of any other allied fighter.

SOUTHCOM: NAU's southern command.

Spaceguard Foundation (SGF): Nonprofit organization that is part of the European Space Agency (ESA) Centre for Space Observation. The SGF primary responsibility is to discover, study, and observe NEOs. The agency headquarters are located in Frascati, Italy.

SR-72: The successor of the SR-71. The original concept relied on TBCC propulsion consisting of a turbine and scramjet engine and later revised to an oblique detonation engine (ODE), the successor of the pulse detonation engine. The ODE engine exhibits lighter design and better performance than the TBCC. Service ceiling of 34,000 metres and Mach 6. Length of thirty-six metres and fully loaded weight of 68,000 kg. Entered service in 2034. External skin made of Inconel 617 and critical areas coated with tantalum carbide (TaC) to withstand maximum surface temperature of 3,700°C.

SSDS: Ship self-defence system.

SSN: Hull classification of nuclear attack submarines.

SSTO: Single stage-to-orbit.

Steyr IWS2000: Semiautomatic antimatériel rifle produced by Steyr Mannlicher. The rifle is chambered in a specialized 15.2x169-mm armor-piercing fin-stabilized discarding sabot (APFSDS) ammunition. Capable of defeating the equivalent of 40-mm RHAe at 1,000 metres. The rifle uses a 1,200-mm, smooth bore barrel and fires the 15.2x169-mm ammunition at a muzzle velocity of 1,450 m/s. Muzzle energy of 29,000 joules for a thirty-five-gram APFSDS. This is 2.5 times greater than the comparable kinetic energy of the 12.7×99-mm NATO (.50-caliber) M903 SLAP. Entered service with NATO countries in 2028.

superhard carbon nanotubes (SCN): Single-walled carbon nanotubes can undergo a transformation to superhard phase carbon nanotubes through application of pressures greater than 30 GPa (~6,000,000 psi). The resulting material exhibits a bulk modulus of about 500 GPa (64 million psi), which is higher than that of diamond.

tantalum carbide (TaC): Refractory ceramic compound with one of the highest melting points, approaching 3,900°C. Its high temperature makes it a candidate for high-temperature aerospace applications such as hypersonic flight or rocket propulsion allowing the aircraft to reach speeds of Mach 6 where the stagnation temperature approaches 3,000°C.

TBCC: Turbine-based combined cycle engine. Combines a turbine jet engine and a scramjet engine. At speeds below Mach 2.0, the aircraft relies on the conventional turbofan engine. At high speeds, the turbine is bypassed and the engine operates as a ramjet, and as speed increases, as a scramjet. The TBCC is an evolution of the J-58 turbo-ramjet of the SR-71.

Tiangong4: The Chinese wheel-shaped, space station in GEO orbit. The main hexagonal wheel is composed of six modules. Each module has a diameter of 4.2 metres, a length of just under twenty-four metres, and a mass of forty-five metric tons. The wheel displays an overall diameter of around forty-three metres. Docking facilities are located in the central hub, which is connected to the outer ring with four spoke-like connecting modules. The station is powered by a compact nuclear reactor with an electrical output of 180 kW. Total mass of the station is approximately 600 metric tons.

***Tiger2* Attack Helicopter:** The Eurocopter *Tiger2* is the next generation attack helicopter used by NATO members. It was originally developed from the Eurocopter X3 experimental high-speed compound helicopter (H3 concept) designed in 2010. The *Tiger2* is a four-blade twin-engine high-speed hybrid attack helicopter that exhibits increased horizontal speed thanks to short span wings and tractor propellers. Entered service in 2028.

Topaz reconnaissance satellite: Follow-on to the KH-11/12 series of NAU reconnaissance satellites. The Topaz series was developed from the failed Future Imagery Architecture (FIA) and the Next Generation Electro-Optical (NGEO) programs. Topaz satellites feature advanced SAR imaging capabilities in addition to their high-resolution optical cameras. Capable of performing all-weather imaging.

TOPO: Trajectory operations officer.

TRRE: Turbo-aided rocket-augmented ram/scramjet engine. Propulsion engine used by the *Shenlong* spaceplane. It consists of a turbofan stage for subsonic/low supersonic flight, a ram/scramjet stage for the transition from supersonic to hypersonic flight and finally, a rocket engine to accelerate to an orbital velocity of 7.8 km/s in order to reach LEO.

t/w: Thrust-to-weight ratio.

Type 1 civilization: Based on Nikolai Kardashev's scale, a Type 1 civilization is capable of producing power at a rate of 10^{16} Watts. This is approximately 2,000 times greater than the current power production of planet Earth. Type 1 civilizations have the mastery of fusion power as well as matter-antimatter energy production and the use of nanotechnology including the design and deployment of molecular assemblers. Can manufacture and produce exotic materials such as elements in the second island of stability of the periodic table in commercial scale quantities, other exotic materials like linear acetylenic carbon (carbyne), and nanocrystalline diamond to name a few, as well as exotic fuels like metallic hydrogen. Type 1 civilizations are also capable of interplanetary travel, interplanetary communication, megascale engineering, planetary engineering and colonization, and finally, function with unified world governments, trade, and defence.

Type 004 super carrier: The Chinese Type 004 aircraft carrier is a nuclear-powered super carrier with a displacement of 90,000 metric tons. It is equivalent to the *Gerald Ford* class super carrier. The first commissioned carrier was the *Liu Huaqing*, named after the Chinese admiral credited for conceiving the future Chinese aircraft carrier program. Entered service in 2036.

Type 057 *Shenyang* class guided missile destroyer: Follow-on to the Type 055 *Renhai* class destroyer. The *Shenyang* class is a stealth guided missile destroyer. It uses next generation weapons including directed energy weapon systems such as laser area defence systems (LADS), and a 55-mm railgun that replaces the 130-mm H/PJ-38 gun. Carries a suite of ASW helicopters and UAVs. 128 VLS cells with a mix of land attack, anti-ship, anti-submarine, antiballistic, and SAMs. Displacement of 12,000 metric tons and length of 216 metres. Entered service in 2036.

Type 097 Qin class nuclear attack submarine: Follow-on to the Type 095 Feng class nuclear attack submarine. The Qin class is a fourth generation ultraquiet Chinese nuclear powered attack submarine. Uses a rim-driven pump jet propulsion significantly quieter than shaft driven pump jet propulsion. Entered service in 2035.

UAV: Unmanned aerial vehicle.

UCAV: Unmanned combat aerial vehicle.

UCLASS: Unmanned carrier-launched airborne surveillance and strike.

UHF: Ultra-high frequency.

unpentennium: A 7d transition metal with atomic number 159 predicted to exist in the second island of stability of the periodic table. Based on its molecular structure, metallic unpentennium would have a 45 percent higher density than iridium, its closest analog. Large-scale manufacturing of unpentennium is currently beyond the technological capability of planet Earth.

V28V: Third generation tilt-rotor military aircraft similar to the V-22 *Osprey*. It is smaller than the V-22 and capable of carrying fourteen troops. Entered service in 2037.

VASIMR: Variable specific impulse magnetoplasma rocket belongs to the family of MPD, or ion propulsion rockets. See MPD thruster.

VCNO: NAU vice-chief of naval operations.

***Virginia* class (improved) attack submarine:** The improved *Virginia* class SSN was developed from the Future Attack Submarine (SSN[X]). It incorporates significant refinements over the *Virginia* class, including the ability to operate and control multiple unmanned underwater vehicles (UUVs) and autonomous under water gliders (AUGs). The first improved *Virginia* class SSN entered service in 2044.

VLS: vertical launch system.

VRO: Vera Rubin Observatory. The telescope saw first light in 2023. It has a primary mirror that measures 8.4 metres with an angular resolution of 0.7 arcseconds. Able to detect objects as small as 250 metres in diameter.

VTOL: Vertical take-off and landing.

X-33GSS: A scaled-up version of the cancelled X-33 *VentureStar* SSTO spaceplane from the turn of the century. In the late 2030s, Griffin Space Systems resurrected the X-33 project and provided funding to Lockheed-Martin Skunk Works to complete its design. By 2045, a slightly enlarged final design was ready with five spaceplanes entering service to support GSS space operations, ferrying personnel to LEO, GEO, and their moon base.

X-87: Autonomous orbital vehicle and the successor to the X-37. Entered service in 2030.

X/UHF band: Radio frequency in the microwave radio region (eight to twelve GHz) used by advanced AESA radars. The shorter wavelength allows higher resolution for target acquisition including detection of stealth type targets. This frequency also exhibits a narrow beam, which minimizes propagation plus a wide-frequency bandwidth to aid in target discrimination.

Yaogan reconnaissance satellites: Chinese reconnaissance satellites similar to the NAU Topaz series. Like the Topaz, the Yaogan satellites employ both optical and advanced synthetic aperture radar (SAR) sensors.

YU-13 lightweight torpedo: A 324-mm diameter lightweight torpedo from the Chinese navy especially designed for the ATT role. The follow-on to the YU-7. Entered service in 2028.

Z-Luozi: The *Zhandou-Luozi* (*Combat Mule*) is a Chinese robotic combat support unit. It was developed from the *Da Gou* quadruped robotic mule first conceived in the early 2020s. The *Z-Luozi* is a multirole combat support unit that can be used to carry supplies or provide fire support. It is larger and heavier than comparable NAU and NATO-mechanized combat support units. Power is provided by Li-air high energy density batteries.

***Zumwalt-2* guided missile destroyer (DDG):** The *Zumwalt-2* was originally conceived under the Future Surface Combatant (FSC) program in 2014 to replace the *Arleigh Burke* class destroyers and address the design flaws and limitations of the original *Zumwalt* class destroyer. The *Zumwalt-2* features a clean, stealth superstructure similar to the *Zumwalt* class, a capacity of 90 VLS cells, and next-generation weapons including a 50-mm electromagnetic railgun that replaces the 155-mm Advanced Gun System. ABM capable using the SM-5 midcourse interceptor and the

SM-10 terminal intercept missiles. Compared to its predecessor, the *Zumwalt-2* is capable of performing fleet area defence using the RIM-188 medium-range SAM. A laser area defence system (LADS) replaces the RIM-116 rolling airframe missile (RAM) for point defence or SSDS. Displacement of 14,000 metric tons and length of 190 metres. Entered service in 2038.

GLOSSARY OF IBECCI WORDS AND TECHNOLOGY

-aku: Settlement or outpost in Ibecci or possibly Puquina. The earliest outpost from the Ibecci was established approximately twelve thousand years ago at Tiwan(aku) and at Pumap(aku), which the Incans later changed to Puma Punku.

aien: Affirmative used to acknowledge an order. Derived from the Latin word *aien*s. The modern equivalent is *aye*.

anni: An Ibecci year equal to approximately 250 Earth days.

arcubal: Name of a Ibecci paratrooper's personal weapon. Similar to an Earth assault rifle. The *arcubal* fires 9-mm caseless iridium-alloy projectiles dimensionally similar to a 338 Lapua, but at a high muzzle velocity of 1,500 m/s (~4,900 ft/s). The barrel is coated with a layer of nanocrystalline diamond (aggregated diamond nanorods, or ADNR). The higher density of iridium compared to lead (22.5 vs. 11.3 g/cm^3), plus the higher velocity, translates into a muzzle energy of 45,000 J (~33,000 ft.lbf) for their tungsten jacketed 40 g (~600 gr) iridium ammunition. This is twice the muzzle energy of typical .50 BMG (12.7x99-mm NATO) ammo and about equal to the muzzle energy of a 20-mm round.

Ardreker: The lowest element of the *Grisamir* cybernetic organisms. The *Ardreker* (excavator in Ibecci) is a six-legged cybernetic mining machine. It has a very tough exterior shell that allows the *Ardreker* to operate in harsh space environments including vacuums, and extreme temperatures, pressures, and radiation. They are slow moving. Able to withstand the concentrated heat from a CE for some time before its exterior shell fails. Impervious to cyberwarfare attacks as well as molecular disassemblers (nanotechnology attacks). Easier to destroy with high velocity projectile weapons.

balaco: Unit of weight. A *balaco* is slightly more than one pound.

Balistro: The equivalent of a heavy gunner. A *Balistro* is equipped with a caseless 25-mm four-barreled rotary autocannon attached to their battle suit and fed from a box magazine holding one thousand rounds. The box magazine is affixed to the opposite side of the battle suit.

Capac: The Ibecci equivalent rank of captain.

CE: Coherent electromagnetic directed-energy beam. Name given by the Ibecci to their directed-energy weapons (lasers). Their CE operate in the hard X-ray wavelength (3 EHz). Ibecci CEs combine two beams, consisting of coherent electromagnetic visible beam in the violet range, plus the energetic X-ray beam. The visible lower power beam serves as the "guide beam" that illuminates the target and helps avoid potential blooming that can occur because of the X-ray's high power density.

Centor: The Ibecci equivalent rank of commander.

crelon(e): Ibecci word for a sentient creature. This word would be the equivalent of human. *Crelon* denotes a male, while *crelone* denotes a female.

classis: Fleet in Ibecci.

Decanur: Highest rank, non-commissioned paratrooper

in the Ibecci Imperium Field Army (IIFA). The equivalent rank and responsibilities of a first sergeant, but also the lower ranked master sergeant.

DSA: Detection and surveillance arrays is the equivalent of an active electronically scanned array (AESA) phased array antenna.

Eder: The name of the Ibecci home planet. In the Iberian and the extinct proto Basque language, *Eder* means beautiful.

egunak: Ibecci day equal to twenty *jore*.

electromagnetic projectile batteries: Four-barrel electromagnetic rail gun. Fires 50-mm projectiles that pack 220 iridium-alloy darts plus a guidance module at an initial muzzle velocity of 3.8 passu/pu (5,600 m/s). The iridium-alloy darts are thin fin-stabilized rods with dimensions of 0.002x0.10 *passu* (3x150 mm). Designed to destroy *Irascilin* battle machines.

field propulsion engine: The Ibecci field propulsion engines are continuous boost engines. They use graviphoton field generators (GFG) to create a gravity-like propulsion force. Limited to 1.5 times the force of Earth's gravity (see GFG).

Frigun: Ibecci name for the cold brown dwarf star known as WISE 0855-0714 located in the constellation of Hydra. It is at a distance of slightly more than two light-years from *Perfal* (Barnard's Star) and 7.5 light-years from Earth.

GFG: Graviphoton field generator consists of a rotating ring above a large superconducting coil that creates an intense magnetic field 500,000 times stronger than Earth's magnetic field. The field gives rise to graviphotons, which interact with matter, creating a propulsive force with a strength up to 1.5 times Earth's gravity. A fusion plant provides the large electrical power needed by the GFG. Ibecci spaceships and smaller spacecraft are equipped with multiple GFGs for main propulsion and maneuvering.

Gradon: The Ibecci equivalent rank of major.

glosil: The Ibecci measure of time approximately equal to one minute.

Grisamirs: Cybernetic organisms and old foes of the Ibecci. Little is known despite the equivalent of four hundred Earth years of conflict, except for the purposely built mining organism known as an *Ardreker* and the *Irascilin* battle organism. It is assumed that there are higher-level organisms beyond these two, believed to reside in colonies near the cold brown dwarf star known as *Frigun* (WISE 0855-0714).

guberna: Helm in Ibecci.

gubernum: Helmsman in Ibecci.

Ibecci (*Ibeki*): The name of the Barnardian race.

IIC: Ibecci Imperium *classis* (fleet) is the prefix that identifies the Ibecci spaceships.

Iovian: The rank of an officer in the Ibecci military corps and political hierarchy. Higher than a *Centor*. An *Iovian* will perform the duties of overall commanders or engage in diplomacy on behalf of the Imperium.

Irascilin: Higher level *Grisamir* cybernetic organism purposely built as a battle machine. Cube-like with eight extremities. Four extremities face down for locomotion while the other four face up. It does not have a sense of up or down and can rotate on the vertical axis and use the upper extremities for locomotion if the lower extremities are damaged. Likewise, it can rotate by ninety degrees and move forward with any of its four faces. It is equipped with a powerful CE. Incorporates nanotechnology that aides in self-repair. Significant resistance to CEs due to its rapid self-healing capabilities. The *Irascilin* will only strike back to defend an *Ardreker* or itself.

jore: Ibecci measure of time equal to fifty *glosils*.

jugon: Unit of weight. A *jugon* is equal to 1,000 *balaco*, which is roughly equivalent to 0.6 metric tons.

Junct: The Ibecci equivalent rank of lieutenant.

liburnium: Ibecci term for their fleet escorts, similar to a frigate.

luce: Ibecci name for silica aerogel, a microporous, ultralight material that is 99 percent air and exhibits a high thermal resistance. It is also translucent.

mille passu: Ibecci unit of measurement similar to a kilometre. One mille passu is approximately 1.48 km.

mille passu/pu: Similar to km/s. 1 millepassu/pu is equal to 1.48 km/s.

lutee: Ibecci stringed instrument similar to a guitar. The Phoenician and Etruscan (later Roman) lute as well as the Mesopotamian oud are the direct descendant from the Ibecci *lutee*.

passu: Ibecci unit of measurement similar to a metre. One passu is approximately 1.48 metres. It is essentially the passus unit of measurement used by the Romans. Earth's historians state that the Romans' units of measurement were taken from the Hellenic system and from the Mesopotamian systems. The true origin of these is in fact Ibecci from the time when they established their second colony of Atlantis in the Iberian Peninsula in Andalucía.

Patros: The Ibecci equivalent rank of sergeant with similar responsibilities.

Perfal: The name of Barnard's Star in Ibecci.

punctum: Ibecci measure of time equal to one second.

reterit: A metal and synthetic composite material used by the Ibecci in the hulls of spaceships and spacecraft. The alloy primarily consists of *reterit* sandwiched together with sheets of multiwall carbon nanotubes (MWNT). *Reterit* is a superactinide element with atomic number 159 that does not occur naturally. It is manufactured by fusing lighter elements in a material's accelerator. *Reterit* is a noble metal that is chemically inert with a density 45 percent higher than iridium, its closest analog. Earth's equivalent is unpentennium, theorized to exist in the Periodic Table's second island of stability. *Reterit* is highly resistant to high temperature energy weapons. Its high density also provides shielding against gamma rays to ensure the health of occupants during extended presence in space. The MWNT layers offer very high tensile strength against kinetic projectiles.

THRAVES: Threat, Range, Vector, and Speed. Ibecci equivalent of Earth's radar.

Tiwan: The name of *Sol* (Earth's star) in Ibecci.

Tenz: Ibecci unit of power. The short form is *Tz*. One *Tz* is equal to 2.2 MW.

Viracoh: Ibecci equivalent rank of viceroy.

ABOUT THE AUTHOR

G. Todesco lives in Ottawa, Ontario, Canada. He graduated in Energy Systems Engineering Technology from Mohawk College in Hamilton, Ontario. For the last 40 years, he has worked in energy efficiency engineering in the private sector and as an energy efficiency specialist for post-secondary institutions. This is his debut novel.

www.ingramcontent.com/pod-product-compliance
Lightning Source LLC
Chambersburg PA
CBHW051435050726
7593CB00005B/1788